Cloudwalkers

Mark Wayne McGinnis

Published by:

Avenstar Productions

Paperback ISBN:

• **ISBN-10** : 1733514317

• **ISBN-13** : 978-1733514316

To join Mark's mailing list, jump to

http://eepurl.com/bs7M9r

Visit Mark Wayne McGinnis at

http://www.markwaynemcginnis.com

 Created with Vellum

Prologue

September 9th
In the Year of the Lord
2490

Dramarious MacLaren, already an old man, had just become *wretchedly* old come this midnight past, joining the ranks of five other centenarians currently living atop the cloudbank. Hunched and brittle, he felt the heavy weight of anguish press upon his tired shoulders, upon his very soul. Throngs of other Skylanders were gathered about, pressing and pushing against the rest of the crowd in their efforts to hear the CloudKing's words.

No better than a pack of hungry wolves, he mused, watching them.

MacLaren craned his neck to better observe the Cloudwalker and his accompanied approach. He was close enough now to see the shackled man's eyes, wide open and frantically darting about in a futile search for some way out of his dire situation. Clearly, the prisoner had not yet come to terms with what was already a forgone conclusion. Within mere moments, if that blowhard of a CloudKing would ever shut up—his useless explanation was already well known by everyone present—the man would be painfully prodded with a pointed rackstaff, forced to step forward and drop into the open abyss.

The old man wondered, Will the entirety of his life pass before his eyes? Can that happen, in the short span of time it takes to fall five hundred feet—down-down-down—to that unyielding hard surface below?

The frigid air continued to creep up the centenarian's bare legs. Gazing downward, past his worn kilt, he noticed how purple and knobby his knees had become. For as old as he was, and the years he'd lived, why should he have to endure witnessing a sadistic ritual like this Fall From Grace? MacLaren unconsciously winced, observing the young Cloudwalker's loosely bound feet approaching the dreadful patch of quickfall.

Despite his internal complaints, MacLaren knew the horrid verdict now being enforced was nothing new. It was the way of the Skylander realm. *Aye, and so it is for all those atop this cloudbank, whether right now, or during centuries long past.* This Fall From Grace, the public execution about to occur, was a keen reminder not to break the law, though this poor bastard's crime was not larceny or murder, but one more of indiscretion, an act of the heart. The young Cloudwalker was of good standing, of noble blood, but he'd fallen in love with someone not of this cloudbank realm and certainly not from among the nobility. No, but with one from the realm below: a Grounder. There was only one penalty for such an offense: death.

As he waited for the doomed Cloudwalker to take that final step, either of his own accord or prodded ahead by the grim-faced *Dorcha Poilea*, MacLaren made a mental note to enter this day's events into his worn journal. For nearly four hundred years life atop the cloudbank—and among the very tops of the magnificent, high-rise towers which pierced through it—had

been religiously chronicled by scribes, such as himself. He suspected he had enough time left in his life for only a handful more of such entries, but that fact didn't bother him.

The young man's time had come. The crowd's loud chatter had grown still; only their collective murmurs prevailed. Next to MacLaren, two men spoke in hushed voices.

"The laddie . . . will he scream?" asked one, his eyes intensely trained as he watched the final moments of the young Cloudwalker's life.

"Aye, I reckon. I surely would."

MacLaren closed his eyes in defiant refusal; he would not look at what was about to happen. The moments ticked by slowly. In a burst of combined exaltation, the crowd came alive —a strangely joyful ruckus considering the circumstances. MacLaren opened his eyes to see the young man was no longer standing at the precipice of the patch of quickfall. The crowd quieted in unison, heads tilted, and he too was listening.

There was no distant sound, no desperate scream.

Chapter 1

August 5th
In the Year of the Lord
2620

Standing atop the glistening cloudbank, a flock of pigeons flew overhead as the young man stretched, arching his back, which brought him up to his full six-foot-three stature. His build—narrow of hip, with broad muscular shoulders—was fairly typical of a Cloudwalker, but it was his blue eyes that usually attracted attention. Discerning and intelligent, yet also mischievous, his eyes held the power to intrigue, and just as easily unsettle, those who came into contact with him during the course of his *cicerones* duties.

Conn panned the distant skyscape for signs of quickfall, the dangerous cloudbank patches that all too often claimed the lives of both Skylanders and visiting Grounders. While most Skylanders could not spot the subtle differences in the cloudbank that betrayed a patch of quickfall—its appearance was slightly lighter, more ethereal—Conn was a Cloudwalker, in possession of the Sight, and to his well-trained eyes, quickfall stood out like a silhouette in a beam of light. The cloudbank could support hundreds of pounds of weight, but even after a lifetime of navigating it, Conn knew he was always just one wrong step from hurtling hundreds of feet to a grisly death below.

His breath suddenly caught at this latest invasion of dark thoughts. Death was often on his mind these days, and had been since the recent death of his friend and mentor, Professor Claremont Dob. If allowed to take hold, again, anguish would dominate his morning. Conn allowed himself a moment—one moment only—to mourn the brilliant old man, before shaking himself from his misery and returning his mind to his duties.

Conn Brataich, of the Brataich Clan, couldn't afford to be distracted. He was third in line to the throne behind his brother Michael and his sister Emma. But unlike his older siblings, succession held little interest for him. He'd seen firsthand what the pressure and responsibility of being the reigning Cloud-Master had done to his father, whose ailing health worsened by the day.

The ever-present winds buffeted his white, long-sleeved shirt. He swept wayward strands of black wavy hair out of his eyes and let out a patient breath as he waited for the winding, single file contingent of twelve Grounders to catch up. They lagged back, unsure of their footing—to them, clearly, this was a foreign, terrifying experience. He'd noticed the expressions on their pasty faces when they first started out, some two hours earlier. Expressions of equal parts awe and panic which, Conn noted, hadn't changed all that much since. Grounders weren't used to sunlight, he reminded himself yet again. They lived far below, where the cloudbank—and the continuous fall of acid rain which came from it—forced them to live underground in tunnels like rats, or in buildings protected by coatings of rubber and Ragoon sap. *What a miserable life,* Conn thought.

He smiled with the hope it would convey confidence, to let

them know there was little to worry about here, some five hundred feet above street level.

This was Conn's favorite time of day, the mere moments when the bonnie sun appeared suspended upon the cloudbank, a fiery globe of molten gold resting comfortably on soft tufts of cotton. He glanced to his left where the closest building spire rose high through the ever-present sea of white. A hundred shimmering golden suns on a hundred glass panels reflected back at him.

Twenty-six such skyscrapers, those few visible above the cloudbank, still remained after five centuries; no others had been erected since the Ruin. No, the ability to build more had been lost, along with so much else, and what remained was all there would ever be. When these finally fell, and fall they would one day, the era of the Cloudwalker would end. The thought saddened Conn. He loved this heavenly place—living within these Midtown Manhattan skylands—*his home.*

"A breathtaking sight, aye?"

Conn continued to stare off toward the distant horizon, then responded, "Aye, that it is, Toag." *Shhhick!* He heard the tip of his friend's rackstaff penetrate deep into the cloudbank. Glancing up, he found Toag casually resting his chin upon his staff's broad paw, made from the central wood of an elder Ragoon tree and worn smooth by a hundred years of palm sweat and constant friction.

Toag Munna stood as tall as Conn. His long black hair, which naturally clumped into rope-like locks, hung down to his shoulders. He pointed ahead. "Business must be picking up for Clan Baird . . ."

Conn had spotted them too, three men just now coming around the sharply angled rise of the ancient building their clan called home. The Baird tartans they wore were a solid royal blue from this distance, but Conn knew their kilts were actually a plaid of several shades of blue, with thin intersecting lines of yellow and orange. Their own contingent of eight, no nine, darkly dressed Grounders came into view shortly after, in a snakelike line behind their *cicerones*.

"... a good way to get someone killed. The stupid blowbag," Toag added with distaste, making a clucking noise with his tongue as he watched the approaching flock. Cupping his hands around his mouth, he yelled out across the divide, "You there ... Cloudwalker ... mind your order!"

Conn's nod was barely perceptible. The proper formation for a line like this had a *cicerones* at the lead, another within the pack's mid-section, and one at the very end, bringing up the rear. A flock needed to be closely watched. One wrong step—a lapse of attention by just one of the lemming-like Grounders— and they would disappear into the white bank. Five-point-six seconds. It was a number that had been drilled into Conn's head, and the head of any Cloudwalker, in school. 5.6 seconds was the amount of time it would take an unlucky Grounder—or Skylander—who fell through the cloudbank to fall five hundred feet before hitting the ground with a hard thud and splatter somewhere on one of a thousand dreary streets below.

The requisite training for a young Skylander to become a Cloudwalker was long and arduous. It took years, and only those individuals of noble blood, blessed with the Sight, would ever be accepted. To his knowledge and anyone else's, the Sight only manifested itself in those who had strong Celtic heritage. After the Ruin, the land called Scotland was uninhabitable due to rising ocean waters that had turned it into little more than a frozen marshland. People fled to all corners of the world, and Conn's own ancestors had joined thousands of others in immigrating to North America, where they found respite from the acid rains below the cloudbank by living in the high-rise skyscrapers that extended far above it. The fight to control those buildings was long and bloody, but when Clan Macbeth first took control of the Empire State Building, and their leader, Kenneth Macbeth, dared to be the first man to step out into the clouds, the world had changed yet again. Over the centuries, the Skylanders had worked hard to establish rules that would keep the Celtic bloodlines pure, but even still, those with enough Celtic blood to gain the Sight and become Cloudwalkers were scarce. Conn had always felt honored to be among the select few to represent the deep scarlet plaid of his own Brataich Clan.

At the sound of approaching footfalls, Conn refocused his attention on his Grounder contingent.

"I'll watch the median span," said Toag, looking back at the Grounders. "Step wisely, my friend."

"Step wisely, Toag." Conn counted the heads of his flock, a nearly unconscious action on his part. *Still twelve.* Their attire was dark, and as bleak as the pallor of their skin. They blankly stared back at him like zombies. Hanging around each neck was a long, chain-linked necklace, with an oblong medallion attached. Made from polished Ragoon wood, each was stamped with a clan imprint and gave the Grounders the right to pass through the skylands.

Conn gave a wave over his head and watched Toag and the other two *cicerones* give him a wave back. He then moved forward along the wide path, edged with the misty patches of quickfall that he could see quite clearly, knowing the lifeless souls that followed him could not. Without the Sight, they were literally walking blind atop the dense white cloud, one hundred percent reliant on their nearest Cloudwalker.

It took ten minutes for the two groups to converge within the open expanse. Conn recognized the leading Cloudwalker as Fib Baird. Barrel chested, Fib was somewhere in his mid-forties. The man rarely spoke, and had mistrustful, constantly darting eyes. When they were three paces apart, Conn did as tradition dictated. The path they were on was solid enough to support substantial weight, and about eight feet wide. Conn moved aside in a symbol of respect for the elder Cloudwalker, raising his own rackstaff horizontally in front of the line behind him. It was a gesture to his flock to move back and let the others pass. He watched Toag, Will, and Maggie—his fellow Cloudwalkers —follow suit with their own rackstaffs. The line of twelve uneasily took a step off to the side.

Fib gave an appreciative bow of his head and moved forward. Once parallel, the two Cloudwalkers gave quick taps on the paws of their rackstaffs.

"Step wisely," Fib said.

"Step wisely," Conn replied.

One by one, Conn watched the procession of Grounders move past. Then his breath caught in his chest as he recognized the Grounder in front of him. At nearly seven feet tall and completely bald, with a sharply hooked nose, Terrence Lasher's mere presence *demanded* attention. He walked with far more confidence than the other Grounders, and as he strode past Conn, Lasher's dark eyes locked onto his. He radiated power and something else, thought Conn, unsettled. Something dark. He was refuted to be the most powerful of the Midtown Grounders; a high deacon in the religious order of Purgeforth, which was followed by virtually every Grounder in mid-town Manhattan.

Grounders. Conn thought once again about the terrible plight of those who had survived the five centuries since the Ruin, living beneath the same cloudbank upon which he now stood. Life below the cloudbank was far different from the life that Conn knew. Acid rain fell continuously down onto Earth's surface, and it was the same way around the world, as far as he knew. The Ruin had served as a catalyst for a series of devastating effects on the Earth, but Grounders had the worst of it.

Forced to live underground, never to see the sun, most of them bitterly hated Skylanders for their privileged lives of relative luxury. Still, Skylanders and Grounders managed to share a relatively cordial co-existence, though resentment on both sides was natural and expected. But both societies depended on one another, so their symbiotic relationship had endured. Skylanders needed the food that the Grounders could grow in the depths below and the resources they scavenged from the dead world around them, and Grounders relied on the fresh water Skylanders collected from the high natural clouds within the upper atmosphere.

As the line continued to trudge past him, Conn kept his expression neutral. He held no malice toward any of them. Conn had been beneath the cloud a mere handful of times with old Dob, mostly for clandestine scientific experiments. Nothing, including the air, was safe down there. Bandits lurked everywhere. He thought about the families—surviving in subterranean caverns and ancient subway tunnels, sequestered away in their individual nooks and grottos. Some Grounders risked exposure, living in rotting buildings or exploring the city above them, hoping to find salvage to trade for extra provisions. He now watched as the tall bald man's figure grew small in the distance.

As the last of the line passed him, Conn resumed his own trek forward. In the far distance he could just make out the peaked building tops of Jersey City. Prior to the Ruin, the city had grown almost to the size of Manhattan, with many towering skyscrapers rising high there. Like Manhattan, Jersey City had been among the first in the world to react to the rising sea levels after the Ruin. Today, both cities were ringed by thick, tall rampart walls, made of a slippery, durable metal and generously coated in substances resistant to the acid rain. The huge walls were built along the banks of the now-swollen oceans, and there were smaller walls—still well over a hundred feet high—that were built within each city proper, sectioning them off into smaller, secluded quadrants. The walls had lasted five hundred years, but everyone knew the inner walls were a failsafe measure for the day—hopefully long into the future—when the outer walls finally were breached. The inner walls had originally provided for gated passageway, but the acid rains corroded the gateways until they became unusable. Grounders in both Manhattan and Jersey City became trapped in the inner cities where they lived, totally landlocked until Cloudwalkers in the skylands above agreed to guide them through paths in the cloudbank to other parts of the city. It wasn't a perfect system, but it worked for now, Conn reasoned.

These days, the Jersey City skylands were ruled by Cloud-Master Gordon Folais, of the Folais Clan. The threat of war hung heavily on the Skylanders of both cities; Clan Brataich clashed often with Clan Folais, and the delicate flower of peace they begrudgingly nurtured between them—Conn's own impending wedding to Lili Folais—was frail at best.

Conn shook his head; he'd known Lili since they were children, but physical distance and political tension between their families meant they had never been more than mere acquaintances. Conn thought ahead to the upcoming Skylander games; he would have a chance to get to know his fiancee then. He didn't know the girl at all, not really, but he knew that their betrothal was virtually all that stood between a tremulous peace and outright war.

Conn's status as a *cicerones* meant he was tasked with keeping people safe, he thought as he led his procession of Grounders onward through the clouds. If his marriage was the thing that kept his people safe from needless slaughter, then he would make the best of it.

Chapter 2

As they reached their destination across the city—a blockish and unremarkable building which rose a mere three floors above the cloudbank—Cloudwalkers up ahead ushered the last few Grounders inside, Conn felt himself dragging, tired after a long day and another sleepless night.

Three Dorcha Poileas stood guard at the entrance to the building. Only men were allowed within this tight-knit gendarme guard. None were of noble blood. Men of the Dorcha Poileas were selected from septs, the common folk among the skylands, and upon taking their oaths they swore allegiance to no clan, or any CloudMaster. The Dorcha Poileas served the law, and the law only. Their uniforms were bland and colorless —grey trousers and grey shirts, with a long, navy-blue cloak stretching from their shoulders to the heels of their boots. Their education and training started early—not so different from that of a young Cloudwalker—within the Onyx Building headquarters. Its obelisk was the only remaining high-rise structure in Manhattan south of the Empire State Building. None within the Dorcha Poileas possessed the Cloudwalker's special Sight—

found only in the pureblooded Celts of the noble class—and the necessity of having to rely upon a Cloudwalker before venturing onto an untrodden cloudbank had been a hot point of friction between them for centuries.

But Conn supposed the Dorcha Poileas were necessary. Probably more so in the distant past, but today they still had their usefulness. He recognized the tallest of the three standing guard—thin as a rail, Captain Bryant Peirce. Peirce's father served Clan Brataich, and Conn and Bryant had been friends as young boys until they entered their respective organizations at the age of thirteen. Once, they had conspired and laughed together as they helped Dob with his experiments and listened to him ramble about science. Now they detested one another.

"Hold up there, Brataich . . . I'm writing you up."

Conn closed his eyes for an extended beat. Any overreaction on his part would make Peirce's day. He watched as the rest of his flock disappeared into the building, signaling for Toag to go on without him.

Bryant looked smug, "This, I believe, will be your fourth dereliction tag, which means you'll be going up in front of the chancellor—"

"Oh come on. Don't be a boaby, Peirce. Everyone has a medallion. My Grounders are legit; no one's here who isn't supposed to be!" Conn stepped in closer. He'd never backed down to Peirce before and he never would. Now within a foot of the Dorcha Poileas Captain, they stared eye to eye. His once childhood friend fully embodied the look of his ilk. His hair was long and stringy, his eyes two inky pools of darkness. An ugly gash of a scar marred the left side of his face. Conn imagined he saw a trace of sorrow in the dark eyes of his former friend, and wondered if he, too, was missing Dob. Once upon a time, the three of them had been inseparable, and Peirce had loved Dob as much as Conn did. He resisted the urge to soften his gaze, and forced himself to remain stoic. It was far too late for empathy; Peirce's actions would not—*could* not—ever be forgiven.

"I found this here on the bank, mere feet from where you stand." Peirce's breath was stale as he lifted his hand up, holding onto a long chain, its wooden medallion swinging back and forth like a pendulum. "Clearly, one of your flock has moved about unregistered. And since it's your flock, it's your responsibility, and that will be in my report."

Conn knew exactly what Peirce had done. He'd elusively tugged the chain off one of the unsuspecting Grounders as they'd passed by, then hidden it in his pocket. Conn wanted to smack the smirk off his face, but instead he forced calm into his voice and said, "Do what you will, Captain. I have little time for your games. Now stand aside, so I can perform my duties."

Conn turned, then stepped around the three other Dorcha Poileas and proceeded into the building, where he found Toag waiting for him next to a concrete wall half their height. Toag shot a glance out the door toward the three guards, his expression quizzical.

"Don't ask," Conn said, joining him. He peered down at the descending line of Grounders as they made their way down the stairs. Circling around and around below, they followed behind Maggie O'Brian, who'd taken the lead. Already two levels down in the long winding stairwell, her bright red hair, worn short like a boy's, was hard to miss.

"You're looking a good bit peely-wally," said Toag, studying him. "Why don't you head on back? We've got this."

"You sure?" Conn knew he had his duties, but he was exhausted.

Toag nodded and asked, "Hypnos' drum keeping you awake at night?"

Conn shrugged, not wanting to get into it. He had begun to wonder if Hypnos, the Greek god of sleep, was personally targeting him. In fact, since the terrible accident that had caused Dob's death a few weeks prior, Conn hadn't had a single night of uninterrupted sleep. A few hours here and there—often in the middle of the day, like today—were all he could manage.

"Sleep well, laddie boy. Tomorrow we begin practice. The games are abreast, ye ken?"

"Aye, that they are," Conn said flatly. Normally, the prospect of competing with the best and most athletic Cloudwalkers of every clan in the Skylander games would excite him, but at the moment, the very prospect of the games—and the rigorous training he needed to compete in them—just made him feel more tired.

He watched as his friend fell in line behind the last of the Grounders. He felt guilty shirking his responsibilities even though the Grounders weren't in any kind of danger at this point. He would make it up to Toag and the others another time. He watched them descend lower for a while, as flames in high, wall-mounted lanterns danced in the drafty air. When he turned to leave through the still-open rooftop door, dusk was turning into night. A slight chill in the air foretold the approaching fall season.

"Conn! Conn!"

The voice was unmistakably that of young Brig, a boy of nine or ten who often served as a messenger for the Skylanders around him. Like most people living above the cloudbank, Brig was not of noble blood. He was a commoner, known as a sept. Some septs did possess drops of Celtic blood within their veins, but not enough to give them the Sight that allowed Cloudwalkers to traverse the cloudbank. Septs kept to the skyscrapers and the demarcated areas of cloudbank that were deemed safe by patrols of Cloudwalkers. Many of them were directly allied with certain clans, but most were simply skilled workers that supported the basic necessities of life above the cloudbank.

Most carpenters, cooks, masons, pigeon breeders, professors, glass-masters, healers, and mechanics were septs, as were the racksmiths, who would labor for a full year carving and assembling the intricate mechanics of a single three-way, collapsible rackstaff from the wood of the Ragoon tree. There were very few racksmiths alive who had the skill and knowledge to build a rackstaff, and those who excelled at their craft were as highly respected as any noble.

Conn first noticed the lantern flame as it approached in the distance, then the boy running along the same path he himself had traveled not ten minutes prior. Out of breath, Brig slowed, gasping in several deep lungfuls of air.

"What is it?" asked Conn. "And why in God's name are you traversing the bank without the aid of a Cloudwalker? It's nearly dark!"

"I can see where it's been trod. I may not have the Sight, Conn, but any *bowbag* can see a path well trodden." The exhausted boy's darkened hair, wet with sweat, was plastered down onto his scalp. "I've been looking everywhere for you!"

"Well, you found me. So what is it?"

"The CloudMaster . . ." Brig paused, drawing in another desperate breath.

Instantly on alert, Conn asked, "What is it? Has something happened to my father? Damn it, speak up, lad!"

"No," Brig said hurriedly. "He just needs to talk to you at the top of the hour. Those were his words: at the top of the hour. I suppose something has happened; it's all hush hush, though. No one will tell me anything."

Conn's racing heart slowly returned to its normal cadence. Robert Brataich, the reigning CloudMaster of Manhattan—actually more akin to a CloudKing, though the term has not been used in many a year—was sick. For three years now, he had been dying a slow death due to a congestion of the lungs that his healers had been unable to treat. Although his father went to great pains to hide his ever-weakening state, everyone knew he was very ill, especially the other clan CloudMasters within their own castle-like skyscrapers. For sure, those *dogs* were chafing at the bit for his early demise. Robert still maintained a firm grip of control over the seven other Manhattan Skylander clans, but once he was gone, the surrounding CloudMasters would jockey hard to take over and acquire the prized, more expansive Brataich Clan skylands for their own respective clan's usage. The next Brataich CloudMaster—probably Conn's older brother, Michael—would need to work hard to protect the skylands the Brataich Clan had maintained for decades.

"Hand me your lantern, boy," said Conn gruffly to Brig. "Follow close behind me. Keep up or get left behind."

Chapter 3

Six years earlier...

Conn and Bryant burst through the Empire State's front doors into a crisp early spring afternoon. Both boys, thirteen, had their bows slung over one shoulder, along with quivers packed with fowl-targeting arrows. A Saturday, the cloudbank was as crowded as Conn had ever seen it. Skylanders were out in force, enjoying the warmer weather, and the bright sunshine. Conn was unaware that today would see the end of his long boyhood friendship with Bryant Peirce.

"Hold on, where are you off to?"

Conn, not slowing down, turned to acknowledge his father, the reigning Brataich CloudMaster, walking alongside Bishop Hennessey.

"Lower West side, sir," Conn responded. "A whole flock of Band-Tails was spotted there."

"Well, good hunting, but slow down and use your damn rackstaff!"

"I will!"

"And be back by supper. Guests are coming tonight!"

"I won't be late," Conn yelled back, his mind already focused on today's adventure. Sightings were rare for Band-Tailed Pigeons. The birds were big and plump and lived in the wild, perhaps nesting in a copse of tall Ragoons many miles away, as opposed to everyday Feral pigeons, which were smaller in size and pretty much the prime food staple for most living above the cloudbank. Band-Tailed Pigeons were considered a culinary specialty, but all Conn knew was he loved hunting the big, stupid birds.

Out of breath, the boys slowed their pace down to a hurried walk. Since much of the cloudbank around them was untrodden, Conn used his rackstaff to stab the cloud every few paces. Possessing the Sight was relatively new to him. Sure, he could distinguish various hue differences, but if he was really honest with himself, he didn't fully understand which shades meant what. Since Bryant was not of noble blood—didn't inherit the genetic mutation that affected one's vision and allowed them the Sight—Conn would take the lead. They needed to progress a bit slower from this point on.

It was a four mile walk to the Lower West Side of the Manhattan cloudbank. Only once before had Conn and Bryant been allowed to venture this far on their own. At that time, Emma, Conn's older sister, had argued vehemently that Conn was neither old enough, nor smart enough, to venture so far out.

"What's your father talking to old Hennessey about?" Bryant asked.

"I don't know. Who cares?"

"Is he the one who's coming to supper?"

"I don't know. Why so interested?"

Bryant shrugged. Today, his long black hair was pulled back into a ponytail. Conn thought he resembled some kind of ancient warrior, especially now, with his bow and arrows. Bryant was a far better shot than Conn; something his friend took great pleasure in reminding him. To some, Bryant was something of a braggart. He sometimes could be insulting, or speak cruelly to people. But Bryant was usually nice enough to Conn, and he made him laugh.

Three miles from the Midtown towers, the far-reaching expanse of white was breathtaking.

"Strange, there's no buildings around here," Bryant said, looking around at the empty space.

"There used to be, like four hundred years ago. Looked like Midtown."

"You're shitting me!"

"All the buildings fell, one after another, due to the rising sea levels, and the acid waters. That's what got them to building the ramparts in Midtown."

"You ken a lot about a lot of things, Conn. Guess you're smarter than me."

"Nah, I just like school. And I spend a lot of time with the professor, that's all."

"Septs dinnae have the same opportunities. You blue bloods like to keep the rest of us in our place. Everyone kens that."

Conn had never heard Bryant talk like this before; he'd never played the *woe-is-me* card. Conn didn't know how to respond.

Bryant, hands on hips, gazed into the sky. "I think this is a bust. We haven't seen even one Band-Tailed Pigeon flapping around."

Conn could see Bryant was irritated, though not from the lack of Band-Tailed Pigeons.

"Hey, over there!" Bryant exclaimed, pointing a finger toward the east. He smiled, "You know what those are?"

Actually, Conn did. Most anyone who'd travelled south from the Midtown area knew about the Feral Farms—the hundreds upon hundreds of pigeon cages where birds were bred and kept. Made only of twigs and twine, the cages were ultra lightweight, which made them more resistant to falling through the cloudbank. Homing pigeons were bred there, also plain ol' Feral pigeons that ended up on everyone's dinner table.

"Must be a thousand birds in there," Bryant said, jutting his chin out toward them. "Let's take a quick look."

"Nah, we're not supposed to disturb the birds. Breeders will throw a fit." Conn peered at the lowering sun and figured they'd best be heading back soon anyway. It was rare his father asked anything of him, let alone acknowledge he was even alive. He sure didn't want to show up late.

They walked slowly as they approached the interconnected birdcages. Maybe a foot wide and a foot tall, Conn figured there had to be at least five hundred or so. He glanced about, checking to see if someone was overseeing their approach, but couldn't see anyone around. The birds certainly seemed happy enough. A soft chorus of cooing sounds filled the air, which he thought was nice, even relaxing.

Bryant, kneeling in front of an outside row of enclosures, poked his finger into the nearest cage.

"Hey, I dinnae think you should be doing that."

"Oh, so now what? You're an expert on birds, too? A professor of pigeons?" Bryant stood and looked about the bird farm. "I hate birds. They stink and never shut up." He used the toe of his shoe to tap on one of the cages. Startled, the pigeon inside began to flap its wings.

"Come on, don't do that," Conn scolded.

But Bryant was laughing now, captivated by the bird's frenzied response. "Stupid birds, look at them. Rats with wings." Raising his foot, he placed it atop the flimsy cage while staring at Conn. "These cages are no more than sticks. A big wind could do a lot of damage."

"Stop, Bryant! It's time now to head back," Conn said, just

as Bryant let the full weight of his foot pound down upon the cage. The pigeon stopped fluttering as it died.

Conn, sickened by his friend's act of cruelty, knew that challenging Bryant would only spur him on to do something worse. "I'm leaving. You dinnae want to be left alone without a Cloudwalker."

"Oh, so you think you're a full-fledged Cloudwalker now too? You want me to do what? Bow down and kiss your boots?"

"I'm going home. Bye, Bryant." Conn turned and strode off. Every so often he tested the cloudbank before him, giving it a few stabs.

Behind him came a torrent of high-pitched squawks. A thousand wings flapped wildly, desperately. It was the sound of countless terrified birds unable to escape from their pens. Conn turned around just in time to see Bryant, thirty yards out, running back and forth along the rows of cages. Stomping down on one cage after another, he was laughing hysterically. Conn wanted to scream back for him to stop, or to go face his friend. He could go back and bring about his lockwood to get him to stop. But instead, Conn dropped to his knees and threw up.

Chapter 4

Conn, with Brig in tow, passed by a group of four huddled Dorcha Poileas who seemed disinterested in them, and entered the Empire State Building at cloudbank level, the skyscraper's fortieth floor. Once inside, Conn expected Brig to head on home, but the boy stayed glued to his side. Together, they hurried to the stairwell access to begin the long ascent up Manhattan's tallest remaining building.

Robert, the Brataich CloudMaster, conducted all official clan business on the 86th floor. At times, he sat upon an actual throne there. But it wasn't unusual to find the clan leader outside, pacing the adjacent observation deck, which provided spectacular views of the Manhattan skylands and the few remaining Midtown high-rise spires. Conn and Brig entered the towering high-ceiling vestibule of the 86th floor. The view from here was amazing and he never tired of it. In the distance he saw the other clan castle-like structures, now looking more like giant candlesticks glowing in the night. The buildings of Manhattan had certainly aged in the centuries since the Ruin, in spite of the near constant care by Skylander craftsman and artisans. Each of the buildings here above the clouds was controlled by a different clan who called the towering structures their home.

Farthest off in the distance, where the Drummond Clan resided, was the 432 Park Avenue Building. Closer in, the Carmichael Clan's 30 Hudson Yards Building. The Baird Clansmen were over there in the W57th Street Tower, and the Fletcher Clan were within the 1 Vanderbilt Avenue Building. The Shaw Clan occupied the 53W53 building, and the Logan Clan abided within the former New York Times Building. The Buchanan Clan lived within the Spiral Building.

The only other rising tower, unclaimed by any one clan, was the beautiful 1,047-foot-tall Chrysler Building, which still looked much like it did in the pictures Conn had seen from before the Ruin. Below the cloudbank, Conn knew that it was coated in shingles made of rubber and painted with sap from the Ragoon trees to protect it from the constant fall of acid rain, just like every other building in Manhattan. But up here, the Chrysler Building still stood in all its historic glory. On top, where once brilliant electric lights had shone, the Skylanders now lit lamps and lanterns to shine as bright beacons that marked the tower as the pride and joy of the Manhattan skylands. When the seeping acid rains finally took the old New York Public Library some three hundred years back, The Chrysler Building became the new home for all the books that could be saved. Since then, the Chrysler had become a place of higher learning, which each the clans utilized. It was where young Celtic boys and girls began their training, not only to become Cloudwalkers, but also to become defenders of their respective clan's heritage, on-call *warriors* in their own right, though Conn had only known relative peace in his lifetime.

Conn stared across the dark void toward the glistening, ornate spire atop the Chrysler Building. Although the Empire State Building was certainly the power hub for all the Midtown clans, the Chrysler Building was the true educational and spiritual heart-center for all Cloudwalkers. Observing the flickering of candlelight in distant windows, his heart suddenly felt heavy as he thought of all the things that Dob had taught him there. *God, I miss him.* His thoughts drifted back in time.

Young nine-year-old Conn saw him, a contrasting dark shape on the distant white horizon: Professor Claremont Dob. Conn couldn't remember ever not knowing him.

No one else in his right mind would be out and about on a day like this. Rampage alarms had already started to chime, their loud Dings echoing even above the howling of the wind. The boy maintained his fast pace despite the winds pummeling him from all directions, all the while keeping a wary eye on the cloudbank. Although quite early for a Skylander boy, Conn had recently acquired the Sight, and he was confident in his ability to spot any shrouded quickfall patches along his route. He wasn't supposed to be out here, especially on his own, until his Sight strengthened to its full potential. Especially when God's Rampage was imminent. But he was with Bryant, and they wouldn't be on their own once they reached Dob, Conn reasoned.

Closer now, Conn watched the old man staring up at the clouds of inclement weather fast approaching, gesturing with his staff raised high into the air, and his other arm, the one missing the hand, waving wildly at the oncoming storm. He was yelling something passionately, though it was still unintelligible from such a distance. Conn wasn't sure if he was speaking to the largest of the cumulonimbus thunderheads overhead, or perhaps to God Himself.

Ding! Ding! Ding! Ding!

When the young Skylander finally reached the professor, he was heaving great big breaths and trying to pretend he wasn't scared. Conn noticed an old wooden crate lying next to Dob on the cloudbank, packed with an assortment of stoppered glass bottles. Some contained colorful liquids, while others were filled with granules of powder.

"There you are, my boy!" cried the professor, finally noticing his arrival. "Isn't this amazing? Can you feel the atmospheric ions all charged-up and clambering for our attention?"

Ding! Ding! Ding! Ding!

The professor's smile was contagious. "Aye, I think I can!" Conn yelled back into the howling wind. He wasn't exactly sure what an atmospheric ion was, but if the professor said they were about, then no doubt they were there.

The professor arched his back, his face now practically horizontal, then yelled, "Kalaminbusza!"

He did that sometimes. Made words up out of the blue to express something he was feeling or thinking. Conn was only nine, but this wasn't the first time he'd had the odd sensation that he was the most mature of the two. The Professor was strange, unanimously considered an oddball by the rest of Skylander society. But Conn figured a certain amount of leeway should be given to someone like him, considering how magnificently brilliant he was.

Word had it that as a young man, the professor had been a Cloudwalker. No one would tell him the story, no matter how much he asked, but Conn heard that it had something to do with the professor's missing hand. Conn couldn't recall seeing him ever wearing a kilt—only a seemingly endless collection of long, light-colored robes with a deep hood that he wore flung back over his shoulders. The look suited his wild and disheveled white hair, long white beard, and crooked nose, bulbous at its end. But despite his old age and wild idiosyncrasies, his piercing blue eyes were sharp and keen, a fact that often unsettled people.

Dob lived high up in the Chrysler Building in a modest, cozy suite of rooms, but he was seldom found there. More often, Dob spent his time in a classroom teaching, or tinkering in his clut-

tered laboratory, his spectacles precariously propped onto the tip of his big nose. Just as frequently he could be found outdoors, conducting some kind of strange experiment, For Conn, the professor's utter passion for the natural sciences had been catching. Conn's unbridled curiosity about such things was a tad annoying to just about everybody else—even his best friend Bryant—but not to Dob. Conn had no mother to watch over him, and his father was far too busy being a CloudMaster to spend much time with his children, and so Conn was left with Bryant and the professor, who had become both a father figure as well as his best friend.

Ding! Ding! Ding! Ding!

"What are you doing out here, Professor?" asked Conn now, looking up at the roiling sky. He had to yell to be heard above the wind. "Might there be a God's Rampage any second?"

Only a few decades after the Ruin, immense bolts of highly destructive lightning began striking outward from the cloudbank, both upward and down, as a result of the highly unstable electrical properties of the still-new cloudbank. At first, the strikes were thought to have been random, but it soon became apparent that the lightning was attracted to any source of external electrical energy.

Dob had explained it to Conn years ago. Everything—from energy emitted by the major power distribution lines that fed power to cities all across the globe, down to something as small and insignificant as the personal communication devices that people kept on them at the time—became targets. Even spark plugs, firing within a car's engine block, exuded enough energy to attract a devastating lightning bolt, and other vehicles were affected as well. Aircraft were knocked from the sky by lightning that flashed upward from the cloudbank, and transportation was crippled. During eruption periods, entire neighborhoods were sometimes targeted, with houses and building structures explod-

ing, one after another, in the blink of an eye. Even something so trivial as a spark created by static held the risk of attracting it.

The lightning was unlike anything the world had ever seen, because it wasn't of this world; like most of the world's problems in that era, it came from the Ruin. To preserve a population that was shrinking by the minute, the usage of all electrical devices became prohibited, and the world was quickly thrown into darkness and chaos. They had adapted since then, but in the centuries that followed, everyone—Skylander and Grounder alike—lived in fear of that lightning.

Everyone except Dob, it seemed. At the words 'God's Rampage' from Conn's lips, the professor actually smiled.

"Lightning is always possible, my young colleague, especially when such a large storm is brewing. But we have a bit of time. I'm conducting experiments on influences of charged isotopes on the cloudbank." The professor brought his lifted gaze back down to the boy's level, momentarily becoming the adult. "Hmm. It may not be such a good idea for you to join me on such a ferocious day . . ." But his own words were seemingly forgotten just an instant later, as the professor handed Conn his rackstaff then knelt down. Making a shovel with his straightened fingers, he dug deep into the surface of the cloudbank. Cupping his hand, he hefted up a heaping quantity of the white substance, which shimmered in his palm like both a solid and a gas, which it was. "Have I told you about the origins of the cloudbank, lad?"

Conn, back in the present, averted his eyes from the Chrysler Building. "You ken, Brig," he said thoughtfully. "Once, hundreds of years in the past, bright electric lights would have illuminated that building—this whole city." His eyes shifted to a building to his left where, partially obscured in the moonlight, he could make out the bite-shaped chunk taken from its side; a constant reminder how it all began.

The cluster of meteors that had caused the damage to that

skyscraper weren't supposed to be dangerous. Early scientists, from an organization called NASA, detected them with their powerful, long-distance telescopes, and assured Earth's populace that there was no imminent danger. The small objects, they said, would burn up in the Earth's atmosphere. Conn had read journal entries and newspaper stories from people who had watched the tiny asteroids streak across the high mesosphere of the Earth on the fateful evening of May 20, 2119; they had described the event as a brilliant, colorful meteor shower display, the likes of which no one on Earth had ever seen before. An exact count would have been close to impossible, but experts at the time estimated that there were close to eight hundred direct meteoric impacts across the globe, and no single continent was spared. The damage was considerable, but the aftermath was worse than anyone could have imagined. In the five centuries that followed, the event became known to Earth's survivors as the Ruin. Conn could remember the very words Dob had used to explain it to him: the end of one way of life and the beginning of another.

"Brig, you ken how this happened, aye?" he asked, gesturing to the silvery-looking cloudbank outside.

The boy looked up to him and nodded confidently. "I'm not stupid. I ken a lot of things. I listen. I watch."

"That's not what I meant," Conn amended. "I ken you've a keen mind, lad, but you don't have real schooling. Didn't get to attend classes in the Chrysler Building." And didn't have someone like Professor Dob, filling his head on a near daily basis with amazing and wonderful—and sometimes useless—knowledge, he thought to himself.

"Not everyone is born into aristocracy, Conn."

"Where'd you learn a word like that?" asked Conn, impressed.

Brig scoffed. "I ken lots of words. I like learning new stuff.

Maybe someday soon I'll learn to read." The boy said it casually, as though discussing whether he would go for a walk.

Conn glanced over toward a small clock atop a nearby side table. Ten minutes to eight; he still had a few minutes, though he knew better than to keep his father waiting. He looked down at the boy's curious upturned face. "We take a lot of things for granted, living up here so close to heaven. But it wasn't always like this, ye ken?"

The boy stared out the window then shrugged noncommittally. "We all used to be Grounders, right? Until the Ruin. Everyone kens that."

"Aye, and the Ruin changed everything, didn't it?"

"Aye," agreed Brig with a smile. "Before the Ruin, you couldn't walk on clouds!"

Conn rolled his eyes. "It took everyone awhile to figure that part out. The whole world fell apart first before anyone could start to put it back together."

"What do you mean?" Asked Brig, puzzled. "I thought after the Ruin, the Macbeth Clan—"

"You're getting ahead of yourself, lad," Conn interrupted with a laugh. "So many things changed after the asteroids struck. Almost immediately, and I'm still talking some five hundred years ago, a low-level haze formed about four to five hundred feet above ground. The haze appeared to be everywhere: above every continent and all the oceans. Within the year, it had thickened into something more like a cloud."

"The cloudbank," said Brig knowingly. Conn nodded in acknowledgement. He remembered learning about the Ruin with Dob, discussing the three otherworldly elements that had been introduced to the Earth from the meteorites that fell: Strongzine, Stadamine, and Starlox. All three of the new elements had an atomic mass so small it was determined by scientists to be actually negative, infinitesimally less than zero.

Each one was gaseous, and had been released when the frozen asteroids reached high temperatures upon hitting the Earth's atmosphere. As scientists soon discovered, Strongzine, Stradamine, and Starlox were all incredibly unstable, and none played well with some of the other, pre-existing Earth elements.

"Within three years after the Ruin, constant rainfall was an ongoing weather condition throughout the entire world. The frozen icecaps which once covered the Earth's poles, or what remained of them anyway, were quickly melting into the sea, and the landscape of the entire planet was dramatically being altered for the worse. Rising ocean levels completely destroyed coastal land areas, sometimes for miles. All over the world."

"But what about Manhattan?" asked Brig. "Isn't the city right next to the ocean? And Jersey City, too!"

"Right," answered Conn, pleased. The boy was quick; Conn was willing to bet he could have been a scholar if he'd had proper schooling. "But both Manhattan and Jersey City had looked ahead. They were some of the first worldwide to react to the rising sea levels. You've seen the rampart walls at the cities' borders, right?"

Conn had long suspected the boy had done his fair share of exploring beneath the cloudbank, and Brig nodded in sheepish confirmation.

"Our ancestors built those walls to hold back the sea."

"Why didnae all the cities build walls like ours? Then everyone would have been safe, right?"

"Maybe they would have, but as soon as the cloudbank began to form, it began to trap two substances—sulfur dioxide and nitrogen oxide—together, mixing them. They reacted with water, oxygen, and other elements to form the acid rain that still falls on the ground today. Before the Ruin, Brig, normal clouds rained only fresh water, like what we get from the clouds above the skylands, but this new cloudbase was completely different, being both solid and gas simultaneously, influenced by those negative mass properties of the Strongzine, Stradamine, and Starlox elements. In essence, the physical mass properties of the much-heavier-than-air cloudbase, to a notable degree, had the unprecedented ability to defy gravity. Understand?"

A deep crevice formed between Brig's brows, but the boy was too stubborn to admit he was getting lost. "What does all that have to do with the walls?" he asked.

"The acid rain began to destroy everything. People couldn't go outside without a heavy rain slicker, for fear of damage to their skin. Livestock—animals that people kept for food and such—were dying off at ridiculous rates, and those that remained needed to be kept sheltered at all times. A few organisms adapted, but most—both on land and in the sea—went extinct within just a few years. Pigeons survived, so did some rodents, and lots of bugs."

"Yeah," agreed Brig with a giggle. "There's no shortage of cockroaches around here!"

Conn shushed him. He was beginning to get into the story; thanks to Dob's teachings, he loved history and science, but rarely had such a willing outlet for his lectures.

"The rain destroyed physical structures as well. Homes and buildings began to disintegrate, cars—vehicles that people used to use to get around—rusted to oblivion. So you see, building new walls around every city would have been impossible."

"Why didnae they just coat the buildings like we do? People were stupid back then," said Brig disdainfully, with the sort of confidence that could only be possessed by a nine year old who knows everything.

"Who do you think first thought of the practice? No one could drive anywhere anymore because of the lightning, and everyone was encouraged to stay indoors where they were safe, so vehicle owners were quick to give up their rubber tires. The tires were used to create some of the first and most effective coatings for buildings. Most people cut them up into shingles, which they overlapped onto the tops and sides of structures to protect them from the rain, and melted down rubber in a huge vat to use as an adhesive."

"But they were still stupid," Brig insisted. "Because everyone kens the rain ruins rubber if you don't cover it with Ragoon sap."

Conn winked at the boy. "They figured that out too. But it took awhile, because Ragoon trees never existed before the Ruin. With Strongzine, Stradamine, and Starlox as new elements in the world, there came a number of *otherworldly* bio-matter elements. The most noticeable was the Ragoon tree, which grew exceptionally strong and tall, even thriving in the harshest of acid rain conditions."

"Everyone kens what a Ragoon tree is, Conn. They're all over the place down there."

Conn resisted the urge to laugh. It was time for him to meet with his father, but he couldn't leave the lad just yet.

"Well here's something you may not ken," said Conn, lowering his voice and leaning in toward Brig, a conspiratorial smile on his face. "The Ragoon trees aren't the only form of life to have appeared since the Ruin. Ye ken I told you most animals went extinct, aye?"

Brig nodded, intent.

Conn continued, "Most did, it's true. But some adapted. Some changed. And some say they're out there somewhere, fearsome creatures who live in the abandoned lands between civilized cities. They're told to be vicious, and hungry for human flesh."

"You're making this up," said Brig, but his voice uncertain.

"Nay, I'm not." Conn leaned in even closer, his voice barely above a whisper. "Some say they've even seen forms moving and living within the cloudbank itself, and what life form would have adapted like that? No, they cannae be adapted life forms from Earth, but maybe from somewhere else entirely. Something new, just biding its time until it wants us to ken it's there."

Brig's eyes were wide, his mouth open. Conn straightened, inwardly pleased at rendering the talkative boy speechless.

"But of course," Conn continued, in a normal speaking voice. "Such tales are likely nothing more than exaggerated nighttime fables, told to frighten young children into behaving."

He shot a pointed look at the boy. "Head home, laddie. Stay safe. Stay on well-trodden paths. See you don't let any alien life-forms eat you on your way home."

Conn winked and opened the door in front of them, disappearing into his father's study.

Chapter 5

Conn found his father, standing alone at another of the floor-to-ceiling windows. Before the Ruin, buildings of Manhattan were home to millions of people. Now, their number was closer to twelve thousand. Below the cloud, maybe twenty thousand people still survived, but Conn couldn't be sure.

His father was dressed not so differently from himself. Wearing a white blouse, and a knee-length kilt in the clan's red tartan plaid, the older Brataich wore the extended length of his kilt pulled up into an upper swatch of pleated fabric which angled down from one shoulder to his opposite hip. The upper half of the garment, Conn knew, could be used as a cloak if need be, but only CloudMasters wore it on a daily basis. Conn's own kilt was wrapped around his waist several more times to use the extraneous fabric. Gazing out the window, his father looked far too hunched over and frail for a man in his mid-forties, and he seemed deep in thought.

"Father?"

Robert Brataich, momentarily startled, turned to assess his

youngest son. "Ah, Conn. Aye . . . it is good you made haste." He coughed a wet rumble of phlegm into his clenched fist.

Conn felt guilty, idling away so much time chatting with Brig on the other side of the building. "Are you . . . not well, sir?" Conn asked, instantly regretting his words. It was considered rude to address the CloudMaster's ailments.

"I'm fine," said Robert brusquely, ignoring the slight. "Now listen to me closely. Someone fell through the bank this very night, and not more than an hour has passed."

"A Grounder? Not under my watch, Father . . . I assure you—"

"Shut up and listen!"

He could see the regret on his father's face for speaking so tersely. He seldom rose to anger this quickly.

"It is not a Grounder, though that would be a problem indeed. It is one of our own. A Cloudwalker."

Conn stared back at his father, wanting to dispute his words. Cloudwalkers simply didn't just fall through the cloudbank. "Not a Fall From Grace, sir?"

There were only four ways one could fall through the cloudbank: by accident, intentional suicide, murder, or punishment. The last one was referred to as a Fall From Grace. For Conn and his people, existence above the cloud was a life lived with honor, in accordance within the strict Cloudwalker code. Although there were more common, lesser punishments, a Fall From Grace was reserved for only the most severe misconduct.

"Of course not," his father said. "Hell, no one has done something that warrants such a condemnation in years. We honestly aren't sure who it is, Conn. Your brother Michael is the one who made the discovery."

"Discovery?"

"Several feet away from a lone rackstaff lying upon a path,

Michael spied the outline of a man's body through a void in the cloud."

"It must have been fresh, then," Conn mused. "The cloud-bank would have filled in before much time passed."

"Indeed. And lucky he happened by it so soon, or we might just have assumed some Cloudwalker dropped his rackstaff while passing through."

Conn, wanting to argue, instead held his tongue. The truth was, no Cloudwalker would ever leave their rackstaff unat-tended, they were simply too valuable. Cloudwalkers needed to be constantly vigilant regarding the weight supportable density of any given cloudbank route. A Cloudwalker utilized his long rackstaff to constantly poke at and test his next steps. But the Cloudwalker's rackstaff was more than just a hardwood walking stick, used for traversing along tops of the cloudbank. It was also a mechanical wonder, an ingenious, three-way, collapsible construct. In its most compact carrying position, a rackstaff measured at approximately one and a half feet in length, and most Cloudwalkers wore their rackstaffs securely hung from a lanyard attached to their belts, next to the small pouch called a sporran where they kept personal belongings. When ratcheted to its second position, the rackstaff could extend to three and a half feet in length. In this mid-way position, the staff was known as a lockwood, and could serve as a lethal weapon, like a sword. Sections of razor-sharp metal blades would unfurl, projecting outward from their hardwood sheathing and locking into place. This blade, when wielded with proper finesse, could easily remove an opponent's head from his shoulders.

The staff's third position would extend the rackstaff to a length of approximately six feet, with no blade but a sharp tip at the bottom. This long, full staff iteration was most often used by Cloudwalkers while traversing the cloudbank, as it could be used to test patches of cloud for solidity or quickfall. From very early on, Cloudwalkers learned to pull their rackstaffs quickly from their belts. Depending on the situation at hand, Conn could give a rapid, albeit casual-looking outward flick of his wrist to bring forth either a weapon or an extended walking staff.

Cloudwalkers were trained from the start to be careful, and Conn had a difficult time believing that one of his own had died by accident. A Cloudwalker, a Skylander of full Celtic blood, had died this night. He inwardly prayed it was not someone from his Brataich Clan.

"You will go to find the body," said Robert gravely. "Alone. Tonight."

Conn saw the worry in his father's eyes. A Cloudwalker's body, lying on the streets below the cloud, must be retrieved before street bandits got ahold of it. "I don't need to tell you what they do to our kind."

Conn shook his head. "I will go, Father. I will bring him home."

"Do not, I repeat, do not let yourself be seen below the cloud. We are not welcome there. Stay safe, son."

Chapter 6

Misty Casper fumed in silence as she listened. She stood not ten paces away, behind the corner of a wet and crumbling slumpstone wall out of view. She'd watched Deacon Terrence Lasher, a bald beanstalk of a man, enter their home without invitation. His two lackeys, both big and foreboding, stood quietly in the doorway, conveying a clear message with their very presence.

"You increased the quittance only last month," said Misty's father. "It was more than we could afford. We are simple farmers, we have nothing extra to spare, sir."

Misty peeked around the corner; her parents' backs were to her. Her mother was quietly sobbing into a dishrag while her father, head bowed, slowly shook his head in defeat. Misty's fingers tightened into fists. Her parents had insisted she stay hidden, but it took every ounce of her willpower not to storm into the next room and give that religious swindler a piece of her mind. Knowing that her outspoken nature had always demonstrated a higher proportion of fire than was prudent, she fought against her first inclination to go barging in.

"Look at me. Please, look at me! Who am I?" Lasher asked.

Misty wanted to tell him. She would have loved to tell him exactly who he was: a lying, manipulative, thieving swine.

"Astrid Casper, Halbert Casper," said Lasher, placing his hands on the shoulders of both her parents. Misty bristled. "I am none other than God's humble messenger. I am no more, and no less, than that. But we must all do our part. Suffering, as you surely are, shall one day bring us closer to piety. Are we not all interconnected? Do not your neighbors—the Drakes, the Perkins, the Franklins—all suffer too? Is it fair that they have made the same sacrifice this very day, whilst you have not?"

"Their farms are much larger," said Halbert quietly. His voice shook. "Their harvests are twice that of—"

"And whose fault is that?" Lasher yelled, his eyes filled with fury.

Misty gasped far too loudly, startled by the deacon's suddenly ignited rage. His eyes flicked over to where her partially hidden form was visible in the glow of torchlight. She glared at him defiantly, even as his eyes roved up and down her body. Lasher was a known lecher, a man with multiple wives whom he kept locked up in that great house of his. Misty suppressed the urge to shudder, feeling defiled by his gaze.

Both parents turned toward her, desperate foreboding in their stares. *Don't make a scene,* their eyes implored her. She knew the danger of speaking her mind in front of a man like this. Instead, she simply raised her chin and refused to divert her gaze. She would not cower before this horrible man.

"Casper daughter!" cried Lasher, his eyes still upon her. His lips curled into a predatory smile. "Misty, isn't it? Do you make a habit of eavesdropping on adult conversations?"

Misty pursed her lips but did not speak. She wouldn't open that door. The words she wanted to spout surely would achieve nothing good, and probably earn her a barebacked whipping by the Deacon.

Lasher looked at her for a moment longer before turning his attention back to her parents, specifically toward her mother. Placing a gentle hand on Astrid's lower back, he leaned in closer. Misty's own back straightened and her eyes narrowed. Her mother was still an attractive woman who looked young at the age of forty-one. Misty watched in terror as the dreadful deacon's eyes lingered far too long on Astrid's backside.

She could barely make out his whispered words to her. "I will show tolerance this day." The deacon then looked dramatically up at the family's low-hanging ceiling. Raising one palm up, his other still on Misty's mother, he let his eyes close. A full minute elapsed before he said, "I believe it is God's will for you to have a bit more time. I will allow you until the end of the week."

Misty watched his hand slide further down her mother's slender back, where it lingered. His eyes found Misty's across the room and he smiled. "I will return, and I advise you not to disappoint me. I may not be as amiable." He gave Astrid a few inappropriate pats on her backside, and then Deacon Terrence Lasher was off, hurrying out the door with his two goons close behind.

The *drip drip drip* of the leaky pipe that held their water, seeping down from above, echoed within the musky confines of their small dwelling, intermingled with her mother's continuous whimpering into a now-soggy dishtowel.

Misty felt sick to her stomach. Strangely, it was not so much by Lasher's foul actions—she expected nothing less from the cruel bastard—but from watching her parents humiliated by such a tyrant without showing any semblance of a backbone.

"I'm going out," she said finally, standing, and breaking their wordless silence.

"Misty," said her father, clearly exhausted. He was hunched over next to her mother, comforting her as she cried. "Please."

Misty ran a hand through her long, auburn hair, her fingers catching on the tangles that had formed from lack of care. Both of her parents had dark hair. She took after neither of them—both had brown eyes and slight features, while she had bright green eyes and full lips. She liked to think that her attitude was entirely her own as well, as neither of her parents seemed to possess a single ounce of defiance in their situation.

"You just sat there," Misty said, frustration seeping through every note in her voice. "You just sat there and let him take *everything* from us. How are we supposed to eat?"

Halbert looked abashed, but held her gaze. "What would you have me do? The Deacon has the power to . . ." He trailed off. "We had no choice."

"You *always* have a choice," said Misty, her eyes flashing. "You *chose* to let him walk all over us. Like you always do."

"He is the Deacon," cried Astrid, removing her face from her towel. "A leader of Purgeforth, and you would have us disobey him?"

"I would have us survive," Misty retorted. Misty's mother was staunchly religious, but her daughter did not share all of her views regarding respect for the church elders.

"You don't understand," said Halbert, shaking his head. "You are too young, too—"

"I am seventeen," interrupted Misty, indignant. "Soon I'll be eighteen. I'm not a child; I know the way the world works."

"You know *nothing!*" Halbert's voice was loud enough to make Misty jump. Her gentle father almost never raised his voice with her. He seemed surprised at his own tone, and lowered his voice. "Nothing, Misty,"

Next to him, her mother ceased crying long enough to embrace her husband, her face unreadable as she watched him discuss a past that clearly pained him. "We will not flout Purgeforth laws and openly defy Scripture. Fathers, mothers, *children*

---

have died for less here, leaving their families to struggle. Is that what you want? Would you allow your hotheadedness to destroy our family even further?"

Misty felt the heat of shame burn her cheeks, but she did not back down. "Defiance would not destroy our family," she said firmly. "But allowing ourselves to starve so that the Deacon can fill his larder? *That* will destroy us, Father."

"We will *not* starve," insisted Astrid, speaking up for the first time. Her eyes glared daggers at her daughter for even suggesting such a thing. "We will wake an hour earlier tomorrow morn to tend to the mushrooms and the pigs, and wash and hang last week's tangleweed. We *will* meet the Deacon's quittance by week's end, Misty. We must."

"I wish I had your optimism, Mother." Misty shook her head sadly. She knew that even if they were able to meet the quittance, the Deacon would not leave her family in peace. They were poor, and weak. Easy targets. Misty had once read a book about a creature that lived in the oceans hundreds of years ago, called a shark. The Deacon was like that creature, hungry and pitiless, and he could smell the Casper family's blood in the water from miles away.

Misty turned back into her small hovel of a room. Retrieving her long black slicker from where it lay crumpled in a ball on the floor, she reemerged. "Perhaps we can pull enough of a harvest to please the Deacon when he returns, with enough left over to feed ourselves." Her tone clearly intimated her disbelief at the possibility. "But if we can't, we're going to need to be able to trade for more food."

"It is getting late," Misty," Astrid said, but she sounded as if she had already conceded to her daughter's strong will. "At the very least, do not go into the chilly night above. Nothing but danger awaits there."

Misty had more experience scavenging at street-level than

either of her parents, and they knew it, but she held her tongue. It was rare that Astrid expressed open concern for her daughter's well-being, and inwardly, Misty savored the moment. She raised her brows then strode deliberately toward the still-open wood plank door.

"I will not be overly late," she said to her parents, who were both still hunched on the floor. "Don't worry. I'll take care of us."

She left the house, trying to block out the sound of her mother's sobs starting up again as she closed the door behind her.

Misty pulled her coat tightly around her and peered out from beneath its attached, oversized hood, merely a dark-shadowed form moving within the long, dimly lit tunnel. Once, people had ridden through these tunnels in the long, metal train cars that Misty saw sometimes used as small homes or shops, but now, the Grounders that moved through the maze-like system of underground subway tunnels and utility passageways, which stretched for hundreds of miles, went only by foot. Secured high overhead were planting beds made of thick Ragoon timber, a full eight feet wide and twelve feet long, one butted up after another. The planters ran the entire length of this tunnel and practically all other tunnels as well. It was here that the tall grain crops were grown. Rickety lean-to ladders provided access for watering and crop maintenance. The top ceiling of the tunnels were blocked from view, but Misty knew that they were outfitted with a myriad of reflective mirrors to direct daylight coming in through the reflection tubes, similar to the system used at her family's farm. The most privileged and profitable Grounder families owned various sections of these tunnel planters and took painstaking care of them as if their very lives depended on it. Considering these crops provided the grains necessary for Skylander whiskey, and the wheat for various baked breads, these many miles of planting beds were a crucial aspect of Grounder life and responsibility.

As Misty walked through the tunnel, she eyed the familiar, head-high stamped brick on her left inscribed *1912*. Today's date was August 5th, 2620; Misty considered the fact the passageway was now seven hundred-and-eight years older.

Living below ground, she gave little thought to the possibility of a criminal element in the tunnels. Purgeforth, the religious order that virtually every Grounder had blindly followed for the past four hundred years, was so deeply rooted within their consciousnesses that even ne'er-do-wells didn't dare risk the Order's wrath underground. God forbid anything should hinder the Grounders' crop yields, or their all important quittance percentages. But things were quite different above ground. There, all bets were off: bandits and hooligans were free to do as they pleased.

Turning left at the next T-juncture, Misty jogged to a metal rung ladder on her right. Ascending up ten feet, or so, she entered an identical-looking corridor to the one she'd just left behind. The Romano family's subterranean farm was probably three times the size of the one owned by her parents. She could already smell the fragrant aroma of various types of mushroom and black onion root, as well as the ever-present Ragoon sapling now taking root. She caught movement high above: her own cloaked, reaper-like form. Repeated a thousand times on tiny, ceiling-mounted mirrors, carefully angled this way and that, each mirror corresponded to another mirror positioned somewhere else. Polished reflection tubes, large enough to crawl through, if one was so inclined, provided muted daylight from above. They were interspersed along the ceiling, every twenty feet or so. Right then, since it was nighttime, they only looked like black holes.

The Romano family—two parents and their four kids—were

a raucous bunch, nothing like the fragile quiet of Misty's own home. Aurora Romano and Misty had been best friends for most of their lives. Aurora's father and her two brothers were boisterous, while her mother and her sister were all giggly and playful. No wonder Misty spent more time there than she did at her own home. Fun and adventuresome, with far more friends than Misty had, Aurora always managed to find humor in even the most serious of situations. For both Grounder girls, growing up beneath the desolate streets of Manhattan would have been much worse if not for their friendship. But this night all was quiet, the family subdued within the quadrant. A visit from the Deacon was no laughing matter: everyone paid, sometimes with something other than coin.

Misty found Aurora in the square, slump-stone room she shared with her younger sister, Amber. Amber, lying still atop her cot, looked to be asleep. Aurora was several inches taller than Misty, with no trace of the slender build of her best friend. Aurora's family could afford to eat, and it showed in her plump cheeks and more generous curves. She sat cross-legged on the floor playing *Golack*, a dice game that could be played either alone or with others. Aurora looked up as Misty entered. "What took you so long?"

"Had to wait for the Deacon to leave . . . wasn't a good situation."

Aurora glanced at her sleeping sister at Misty's words, her face full of concern. "Tell me about it! That drooling creep ogled Amber until she started to cry. We need to keep her well out of sight the next time he comes around."

"He gave us the rest of the week to come up with this month's quittance," said Misty quietly, and Aurora's gaze snapped right back to her.

"Do you want me to talk to my parents? I'm sure they would—"

"No," said Misty quickly. "We don't need handouts. I just need something good to trade for some more food, and we'll be fine."

"So I guess you need a trip to street level more than ever, huh?"

"I guess so." Misty bit her lip, trying to keep down her nerves. It was Aurora who usually encouraged their nightly excursions, and Misty felt odd being the one to push. "You still want to come?"

"Are you kidding?" A smile grew on Aurora's face for the first time that night. "Let me grab my coat."

Chapter 7

The two teenage girls climbed up the ancient, chipped, and rounded concrete stairs, past a weathered sign with the words *Herald Square* still barely visible beneath centuries of age and fading vandalism. As they approached street level, both girls double wrapped their scarves around their mouths and noses to minimize the amount of acrid air that made its way into their lungs.

Misty's eyes began watering halfway up the steps, but after similar late-night excursions to street level on numerous other occasions, she knew the caustic effects would dissipate in a few minutes. As they stepped up onto the sidewalk she took in the city's gloomy deserted landscape. Here, all buildings were outer-clad in matte black rubber. Reaching well into the cloudbank above, the rows upon rows of black rectangular tiles were all made from repurposed automobile tires. Covering the facades of buildings, where they were periodically recoated in Ragoon sap, the rubber tiles ensured that what still remained of the original concrete, marble, metal, or other material used in constructing the high-rise buildings would remain dry, unaffected by the constantly dripping acid rains. Standing there, Misty saw in the distance no fewer than ten empty lots, a cautionary example of what happened to buildings before the clever use of tiles was initiated. City engineers used the materials—bricks and whatnot—from a hundred fallen structures to build the intercity ramparts that kept the now-lifeless Atlantic Ocean at bay.

"Which way?" Aurora asked. Only her eyes were visible, but they expressed enough mischief to make Misty smile as she peered into the distant gloom. One good thing about the always-present cloudbank, hovering four hundred feet overhead, was the constant soft glow that gently illuminated the air beneath. Unlike below ground, here it was never pitch-black.

Two male Grounders, speaking excitedly to one another, hurried by on the opposite side of the street. They were arguing over something one of them held in their hands, a bundle of red and green fabric more vibrant than any Grounder clothes Misty had ever seen. Fortunately, neither of the men noticed the presence of the two young women close by.

Misty and Aurora waited until the men were out of earshot before they resumed their trek. "Let's head to Uptown, we can usually find some good—" Misty's words caught in her throat as she spotted a large shape on the sidewalk across the street. Both girls stared, transfixed, at what was clearly a man's body.

"We need to help him," said Misty, at the same time as Aurora exclaimed, "He's naked!" They met each other's eyes, unsure of what to do.

"Should we . . . um, see if he's really . . ."

"Dead?" Misty glanced up and down the street. They were all alone, as far as she could tell. Huddled together shoulder-to-shoulder, they crossed the road. Now close, they crept to the broken body. Dripping rainfall had washed away some of the mess, but he was still framed by a puddle of blood, dark against the pavement. The man lay motionless on the ground, obviously dead. He was indeed naked, with dark hair plastered to his face by rain, and open brown eyes that stared lifelessly into the distance. His head was turned to the side, and from behind it, an opaque grayish substance that was definitely not blood had congealed in a small puddle. Misty shuddered.

Aurora, raising a hand up to her mouth, said, "I think I might puke." She closed her eyes and breathed heavily in and out, but managed to keep the contents of her stomach.

Misty looked up at the cloudbank above them. "He must have have fallen," she said wonderingly, and tried to imagine those few seconds of freefall. It wasn't a pleasant thought.

Aurora pointed and said, "I've never seen one of those before. It's beyond disgusting."

Misty knew Aurora wasn't referring to the corpse itself, and let out a short huff, somewhere between surprise and laughter, as Aurora giggled beside her. Since he'd landed squarely on his back, the dead Skylander's manly bits were still fully in tact. It was Misty's first glimpse of a man's penis as well, but she couldn't bring herself to share in Aurora's amusement. She crouched down next to the body, her attention still on the dead man's face. She reached out with gentle fingers to close his eyes.

"Get the hell away from him!" The command came from behind them in an angry, authoritative voice.

The girls spun around. A tall man was running full speed toward them, wearing a hooded coat not quite long enough to hide his bare shins and ankles. Misty caught a quick flash of his red kilt. *A Skylander!*

"I said to move away!" Misty straightened from her crouch and stepped back, hoping without looking that the wet sound beneath her boots was rain and not blood. Out of breath on reaching them, the Skylander looked first at Aurora then at Misty. As he crouched down beside the dead body, he gently turned the deceased man's face toward him to better see. As Misty had suspected, the other side of the man's head was completely demolished, his blood, bone, hair, and viscera muddled together into a stomach-churning stew.

"Do you know him?" Misty asked, trying to keep her heart from dropping into her stomach, where it too might be vomited out onto the sidewalk.

"No." The Skylander's voice was strongly accented, and his tone was harsh and firm. It was a voice well used to being obeyed. "I dinnae ken if you're both deaf, or simply daft, but I told you to move off."

Misty bristled, her nausea forgotten. "No, you move off," she said, surprising even herself. "You don't know him. Who are you to tell us what to do?"

As the Cloudwalker glared up, she got a clear look at him for the first time. He had dark wavy hair that was long enough to be seen beneath his hood, and a small scar marring a proud chin. His deep blue eyes were narrowed as he frowned at her, but his face was smooth and unwrinkled, his strong jawline clean of facial hair. *He's barely a man,* thought Misty. Probably not much older than herself. *A mere boy.*

"I'm the one who was sent here to collect this poor sod," snapped the Skylander. "And I don't need a couple of wee Grounder bairns getting in my way."

Misty had never met a Skylander in person before, but Grounder children often made fun of their odd speech. She knew full well what he was saying, and for the second time that night, her fist clenched in anger. She had been unable to talk back to the Deacon for fear of what he'd do to her and her family, but this Skylander boy held no such power over her.

"You're no older than me, I'd wager," she retorted. The words—and the anger that came with them—felt good on her tongue. "So if I'm a child, then perhaps it's in your best interest to wonder why your people would send *you* to collect him? Or should I expect your mother to come calling for you any minute now, *ye wee bairn?*"

The Skylander gritted his teeth in silent fury at her mocking accent, while nearby Aurora's eyes were wide with amused surprise.

"This man was one of my people," said the Skylander finally, eyeing her carefully. "And his death is my people's business. Unless, perhaps *you* had something to do with his death?"

"Don't be ridiculous," she said with a scoff. "He fell. We found the body."

"And stole from him? Took his clothes? Thought you could get a few pennies for a good kilt and rackstaff on the Black Market, aye?"

"We did nothing of the sort," said Misty firmly. "He was naked when we found him. Here, on the ground. That makes it *our* business, not yours. I will yell for a parishioner to come deal with this situation, so you can leave now. Go back up into the clouds. This is our world, *boy*, not yours."

Frustrated, Conn placed his hands on his hips. He had to think, and this rambunctious *fud* was making that nearly impossible. Stepping off the curb, he glanced up and down the empty street and remembered his father's words. *Do not let yourself be seen below the clouds.* This had already turned into enough of a mess; the last thing he needed was some parishioner's involvement.

He turned to the outspoken Grounder girl, whose scarf had fallen aside, now draped loosely about her neck. For the first time, he could see her delicate features. A face illuminated in the cloudbank's glow. Her full lips were pursed in her thin, almost gaunt heart-shaped face, which was framed in tangled auburn curls. Her large green eyes stared back at him from beneath dark lashes. Noting the fire within them, he wasn't sure he wanted to stoke her anger more than he already had. He needed to keep a low profile here, after all, and he couldn't afford to blether away with a Grounder until someone took notice.

"Look, Miss," he said after a moment, fighting to keep his voice pleasant. "I dinnae want trouble. Let's start over, can we do that?"

Misty shrugged. "My name is Misty, not Miss." The other girl made no sound, but Conn had the odd sense that she was amused by the situation.

"Misty, I'm Conn. Conn Brataich." He smiled comfortingly at Misty, the way he did for the Grounders he led across the clouds, and spoke slowly, like he would to a spooked pigeon. "This man, another Cloudwalker like me, did indeed fall this night. I assure you, I would not be down here otherwise."

"But you said it yourself, that you do not recognize this man," Misty said. Her tone was sharp; she was obviously still ready to joust.

Conn stared down at the body. He had no idea who the poor bastard was. "You didnae see him fall, by any chance?"

"No, we didn't."

He sighed. "This really is a jobby."

The phrase made the other Grounder girl laugh out loud. She leaned in closer to Misty and whispered, "That's Celtic talk for a bag of shit, I think."

Conn noticed one corner of Misty's lips turn up for a split second.

"Aurora and I saw who took his clothes, if that helps any." she said. "Two bandits. They were running away from the body, all excited-like. One carried a bundle of clothes in his arms."

"That doesn't help much," Conn said with a disappointed

sigh. "I'm sure they're long gone by now. You didnae happen to notice the color—"

Misty cut him off. "Green and red squares. His kilt was green and red."

That news wasn't even remotely possible. The only Cloudwalker clan with a green and red kilt like she'd described was from Jersey City, nowhere near the spot in the cloudbank where the dead man had fallen. Green and red were the colors of the Folais Clan themselves, the family of Lili Folais, his fiancée and sole daughter to the reigning Jersey City CloudMaster Gordon Folais. This was a *boaby* situation, if there ever was one. The relationship between the Brataich Clan and the Folais Clan was precarious at best already. Conn's upcoming marriage to Lili had been arranged to mitigate any further unrest. But now a Folais Clan Cloudwalker had literally landed belly-up on the streets of Manhattan, which could very easily lead to war. *Maybe this bloke isn't that important,* thought Conn. One could only hope.

"Well?" Misty said.

"Well, what?"

"Are you going to just stand there, or should I call for a parishioner?"

The girl really was beyond annoying. "I'm taking him with me. Please don't call a parishioner. I'm asking you as a favor to me."

She crossed her arms in front of her chest, her noisy rubber slicker squeaking as she did. "Why on earth would I do a favor for you?"

Conn looked up at the dim glow of the cloudbank above. Of course she would make this difficult. "Tell you what. Someday, I'll do you a favor back. Anything you want. Big or small, ken?"

That made her laugh. "Oh, and I'm supposed to believe that? And why would I ever want help from a Cloudwalker anyway?" She turned to Aurora. "When was the last time I asked for a Skylander's help . . . can you place that?"

"Never," Aurora replied flatly. "You've never met a Skylander before."

Misty shot an annoyed glance at her friend, but held firm.

"Then I guess I'm at your mercy," said Conn. "But I'm telling you, the fella lying here should not be here. Not directly beneath a Brataich Clan cloudbank. It spells trouble. Lives could be at stake. *My* life could be at stake. Is that what you want?" Conn gave her his most earnest, trustworthy expression.

Misty returned his comment with a smile, one that said she knew his words were a crock of shit. "Fine. But I'm taking you for a man of your word, Conn Brataich. Anything I want, big or small."

"Yes. That's what I said. Now you better move off. What I have to do next won't be pretty. I assure you, the front of his body looks a whole lot better than his bottom side." Conn leaned over to pick up the dead body, hesitating until they'd both turned around and left. He could feel their eyes still on him from somewhere across the street, and suppressed a shudder. He knew his chances of running into Misty again for her to cash in on a favor were slim to none, but he had a sinking feeling she was the type of person to bend chance to her will.

Once the Grounders had gone, Conn removed his long coat, feeling exposed in his white shirt and bright red kilt. It wasn't raining outright, but he knew the ever-present mist would make his skin itchy and irritated before long, so he had to hurry. Spreading the jacket out next to the body, he rolled the corpse onto the coat's lining, doing his best to avoid any contact with the mess. The crushed bones of the Cloudwalker's body made a horrifying sound as he moved him, and Conn had to take deep breaths to stop himself from feeling a bit faint. With an effort not to pay attention to the man's mutilated face, Conn wrapped and tied the sleeves of his jacket together around the corpse's upper torso. Straightening the man's crooked and splayed legs, he next went ahead and tied the coat's long tails tightly around both ankles. It wasn't perfect, but it would have to do. Conn stood up and surveyed his work, brushing a small clump of bloody hair and skin off of his white sleeve with a frown. At the very least, the coat's wrapping should keep him from being covered in the dead man's blood and gore on the long trek back up.

Chapter 8

Both girls remained quiet as they crossed the wide deserted street and stepped up onto the sidewalk, but Misty's mind was still reeling. Misty repositioned her scarf, already felt the ill effects from her face's exposure to the caustic mist.

Aurora, the first to break the silence, said, "I still can't believe we spoke to a Skylander."

"He's just a person," said Misty irritably. "Not so different from you and me. No big deal."

"It's no big deal so long as we're not caught," Aurora corrected. "But if we had been—or still might be—how many of the sacred laws did we actually break tonight?"

"I don't know. But it doesn't matter. No one saw us. Look, see?" Misty gestured to the deserted streets. "Other than him, there's no one around here but the two of us."

"At least three sacred laws were broken, according to the Purgeforth doctrine," Aurora said. She recited them, the very picture of a devout Purgeforth schoolgirl, "One: Thou shalt not have direct dissertation with the sullied . . . which is pretty much anyone not of the Purgeforth sanctification. Two:

Underage girls shalt not converse with boys or men without an adult chaperone present. And three: Thou shalt not overly converse—or build relationships of any sort—with Skylander individuals. That last law comes with a pretty harsh punishment, though I can't remember what it is."

Misty was still watching Conn, the coated dead man awkwardly draped across his shoulders. His ridiculous bright red kilt stood out in sharp contrast with the bleak cityscape. She frowned at his exposed legs; the mist would quickly teach him why *that* was a bad idea. Skylanders acted so high and mighty, but they were stupid if they thought that would save them from the effects of the acid rain. He was just about out of sight. "Flogging, that's a punishment," Misty said, still watching his retreating form. "If a Grounder and a Skylander become involved, like, intimately, that's a death sentence."

"He was handsome," Aurora whispered, as though a Purgeforth official might be listening. "His eyes . . . I don't think I've ever seen that color of blue before—"

"I have no interest in men that wear skirts and talk with a funny accent," said Misty flatly. But she was indeed intrigued by the young Cloudwalker. She'd never encountered one before, let alone spoken to one. And Conn was handsome, she supposed, though perhaps good looks were much easier to come by in a place with real sunlight and adequate food. Grounders traded much of their food to the Skylander clans in exchange for the fresh water that fell from the high clouds far above the cloudbank, but Misty was willing to bet they had much better food up there than the mushrooms and tangleweed that Grounders relied upon for sustenance.

"You were so mean to him," said Aurora, her voice a mix of awe and accusation.

"He was rude, and cocky."

"Do you feel better now?"

"What do you mean?" Misty narrowed her eyes at her best friend, who only smiled in return.

"I mean you were as mad as a trapped rat after the Deacon's visit. You seem . . . better, now."

"It felt good to argue with someone," she admitted with a shrug, a smile cracking her own face. "Anyone would have been fine, but a *braw Skylander lad?*" Her voice slipped into an exaggerated imitation of Conn's accent, one she often used in private while cracking jokes with Aurora. "Aye, that was *right proper tidy.*"

Aurora giggled in delight. "That sounded just like he did!" she exclaimed. "Though I still have no idea where you learn all those words they use."

Misty's smile faded. The Purgeforth doctrine spoke little about those that lived above the clouds. She'd learned early on that ignorance was preferable to knowledge when it came to Skylanders, as it provided protection from becoming sullied. But Misty already knew far more about the enigmatic Skylanders than most Grounders did, and it was all thanks to her mother.

It had occurred about a year earlier, when she'd sleepily knocked on her parents' bedroom door, a door strictly kept locked. As she stood waiting for their response, she remembered the previous night, when Astrid had mentioned they would be leaving early that morning to collect their meager water allowance. Misty had no idea what time they'd left, so she couldn't be sure when they'd be back. *An hour? Less?* She tried the door latch anyway, and was surprised to find it unlocked.

Misty pushed away the inner nudge to enter—even took three full strides away—before turning back. She knew full well she was not allowed in their room, a rule that had been in place since she was a small child, but curiosity was quickly getting the best of her. She had often wondered what could possibly be of such great importance to justify such ridiculous secrecy, and over the years her speculations had run wild. Perhaps they were secretly rich, or had illegal provisions. Maybe her parents had a second child stowed away in there, or weapons, or dangerous electrical devices that could kill them all. Standing before the door again, she cautiously unlatched it and gave it a little shove. Made of heavy metal, the door swung open on noisy hinges, sorely in need of lubrication.

Inside, the small room still had its original electrical breaker panels, a whole wall filled with switches and levers that once had something to do with the trains but had now been repurposed as hooks for clothing and rain slickers. A lone torch burned high upon one wall. The one positive aspect from the continuous acid rain was mixing the horrid liquid with fermented alcohol. The mixture produced a clean flame that could burn for weeks, called ChemBurn. There wasn't much else in the room other than her parents' mattress, a small night table, some shelves, and the clothes hanging on their makeshift wall hooks. A lone metal chest sat on the floor. It looked old, like something from the world before the Ruin. *Well, I've already come this far . . .*

Misty sat down before the old chest, and noticed it wasn't locked. She opened the lid, letting it lean back against the wall, and peered inside. Within was a bundle of brightly colored fabric, in a pattern that made Misty gasp in recognition. The plaid design was woven into a distinctive tartan, primarily royal blue in color, with interspersing thin lines of yellow and green and orange. Misty had never seen its like before, as clothes made of such brightly colored material were not permitted on the ground under Purgeforth doctrine. Such bright colors were frivolous and disrespectful to God, she knew, but still, the plaid was gorgeous. Reaching in, Misty took ahold of the bundle only to realize there was something heavy folded within it. She turned it over on her lap to find the fabric loosely knotted closed. When she untied it, letting the heavy item fall free on her lap, she found an ancient leather-bound book, worn to the point that the binding seemed held together by mere threads. Grounders were taught to read at a young age, and encouraged to read Purge-forth Scripture, but nothing else. Misty found the dogmatic religious writings both boring and uninspiring, and sought out other books whenever she could. Hidden old books could still be found if one knew where to look—which Misty did—covering a wide variety of subjects, both non-fiction and fiction. She herself had found a stash of old books during one of her and Aurora's nighttime excursions, which she kept hidden under her mattress within her own room.

As she carefully opened the cover of the old book, Misty was surprised to find it was not like any of the others she'd read. For one thing, this one was penned by hand, in a beautiful cursive style of writing that took her a minute or two to decipher. *This isn't a book,* she thought. *It's a journal!* Each of the entries was dated, the first of which was from nearly twenty years ago.

Startled, she looked up toward the open door. Had she heard something? A creak, someone stepping onto a loosened floorboard, perhaps? She waited, listening intently, but no further sounds were heard. She inwardly chided herself for not being more vigilant. Being caught in her parents' room would surely land her in big trouble, and being caught reading the journal would likely land her a flogging under her mother's firm hand. Still, she read on.

The journal's owner, whoever it was, had written in the book like a long personal letter. Most of the entries were addressed to *My Dearest,* or *My Darling,* terms that made Misty think it was written for a lover. But the content itself was almost scholarly as though the writer had been conducting a study or trying to teach someone, and the book was broken into different sections that detailed many aspects of the world Misty had only heard of through hearsay. She skimmed through several of the journal's middle pages that spoke of rallying conjuring powers—undoubtedly, forbidden subject matter within the narrow confines of Purgeforth. But then, anything not pertaining directly to Scripture had been banned hundreds of years earlier. Growing up, she had so many unanswered questions about the history of the world, about why things now were as they were. This old leather-bound journal seemed to address some of them. Misty, capturing her bottom lip between her upper teeth, did her best to quell an inner excitement as she turned to a page that discussed her own people, the Grounders.

My dearest,

I wonder how much you know of the people who live beneath us, the Grounders who survive beneath the rain of acid that continuously drips onto Earth's surface. These poor souls live a rather dismal existence mostly underground, a life I am glad you will never experience.

Clearly, Misty mused, the author of this penned discourse was a Skylander, not from the lower realm. She read on,

They co-exist in relatively cordial conditions with those of us who live atop the cloudbank, though resentment is common. Most Grounders survive within subterranean caverns, the individual nooks and grottos, and within the subway tunnels of the pre-Ruin world, where theyAgrarian Grounders grow fungus, certain vegetables, grains, and other crops in the soil, not only for themselves but also for thewe Skylanders above, beneath redirected surface illumination. Some raise pigs, a strange four-legged creature and one of the few to survive the Ruin, for meat, leather, and other byproducts. Other Grounders tend to—and guard—the forest of Ragoon trees in Central Park, and harvest the trees for food, building materials, plant fibers, and sap. The

Grounders have no source of fresh drinkable water, untainted by acid rains, so they trade with Skylanders for this all-important resource.

Above the cloudbank, my sweet, we are privileged to enjoy relative freedom of our beliefs and religions. But Grounders are kept in dire poverty under the thumb of religious despots.

Misty thought of Deacon Terrence Lasher, and his band of deceitful bandits. She shuddered briefly, looking away from the journal and spotting three large brown cockroaches scurrying across the cement. One, changing its direction, headed directly for her. Using a finger as a placeholder, she closed the journal. With a well-practiced motion, she slipped off one shoe, smacking the sole down hard upon the vile, disgusting insect. As she scraped the remnants off her shoe back onto the floor, she glanced about the small room. The other two roaches, taking the not-so-subtle hint, disappeared into the darkness between the walls.

Misty reopened the journal and skimmed ahead to another section.

My Dearest,

We have not always been so lucky as we are today, to walk upon the very clouds themselves. Our abilities come from our Celtic (Scottish) heritage, which grants us the Sight and is what allows us today to be considered of noble blood. Let me tell you a story:

During the time of the Ruin Event, when the country known as Scotland sank beneath rising ocean waters and became mostly frozen marshlands, the ones who survived migrated. A select few fled to northeastern America. Kenneth Macbeth, whose documented Celtic heritage went back eight centuries, was the first person to take up permanent residency at the top of the Empire State Building, after three bloody years of fighting for it. Macbeth was a warrior, and the first to realize he possessed what later became known as the Sight. Only a select few men and women were able to see the slight variances of patterns atop the cloudbank. Macbeth, the first human to step outside while living in the high rise, dared to venture forth onto the very top of the bright-white cloudscape, then carefully trek across to a neighboring high-rise building. Soon others, those who also could see the subtle variations in color and light under Macbeth's prompting, made similar cloudwalking excursions. They each shared a similar heritage, the same Celtic origin. Apparently, some Scotsmen were genetically predisposed, or their genes had somehow been altered in the Ruin Event. Either way, non-Celtic men and women didn't seem to possess that same highly unique vision.

Misty reread the last few paragraphs again. *The Sight? Genetically predisposed? What did that even mean?*

It wasn't long before others of Celtic heritage came to settle above the clouds. Non-Celtics were forced out—killed, if necessary. Kenneth Macbeth, rising in prominence, was soon decreed to be the clan leader—the CloudKing—of the Macbeth Clan and all their followers. Living above the cloudbank became a way of life, and Skylanders were born.

In time, still-standing skyscrapers that rose high above the cloudbank were internally modified to possess large moisture reservoir tanks. Fresh rainfall from the higher clouds is captured then safely stored for drinking, bathing, and toilet use. Excess water is either bartered away or traded to the often-desperate Grounders below, who sometimes have to settle for what we call grey water—water drained and filtered from a Skylander's bath, sink, or occasionally toilet.

Misty looked toward the door, her brow furrowed. Their own water-supply cauldrons were periodically replenished via supplies from above the cloudbank. This was the first time she'd heard anything about grey water—*toilet water!*

Nowadays, each high-rise is home to specific Celtic clans. This is true for the skylands above Manhattan, as well as for the nearby Jersey City skylands, just across the Hudson River. There are rumors of other settlements, other skylands far from here, around the world. Someday, perhaps I can show you.

We no longer have CloudKings. Today, in the year of the Lord 2600, clan leaders are called CloudMasters.

That's just about the time I was born, Misty thought. She realized with a jolt that she'd been sitting still, reading here for far too long, and quickly skipped ahead. One particular entry spoke about the brave warriors who protected Skylander realms many years ago, during a time of mystical shamans and wise oracles that provided counseling to the reigning CloudKing, someone named Malik Macbeth. Perhaps it was just fiction— Misty wasn't sure—but she found it fantastic reading, none-theless. She wondered if life above the cloud was at all like what was written here. Were warrior Cloudwalkers still living above them, wielding razor-sharp rackstaffs and cutting the heads off enemies in some far-off place called Jersey City?

In the months since she had first discovered the book, Misty had found only a handful of other opportunities to steal a glance at it. It awakened in her a hunger for knowledge, one she could never satiate with the books and information that was available to her under Purgeforth. But even as she learned and read, Misty couldn't stop wondering who had written the book, and why her mother kept a journal like this in her possession. Had she considered what would happen to her should Deacon Terrence Lasher ever find out? The risk was great—perhaps even punishable by death. *Why, Mother . . . why risk so much to keep this book?*

It was a thought that had plagued her ever since.

"Misty? Are you even listening to me?" Aurora asked now, obviously annoyed.

Misty returned to the present moment, looked around. Already below ground, they were walking along the dark passageway. She'd been completely lost in thought, reliving the journal's world of warrior Cloudwalkers. Momentarily, she thought of the young Cloudwalker, the one called Conn, they'd met on the street. *Is he a warrior?* She wondered, *Is life above the cloud truly like the book describes?*

"Sorry," she answered Aurora finally. "I got lost in thought."

"More like love-struck, I'd say," Aurora said, teasing her. "You've been all starry-eyed since we met that Skylander."

"Don't even joke about that, Aurora," snapped Misty, her expression serious. "You don't know how dangerous something like that would be."

"And you do?" Aurora asked back, still grinning.

Misty nodded. "I might have read something about it . . ."

Chapter 9

Conn hurried toward the street-level entrance into the Drake Building, which was about half of a block down a dark and narrow alleyway ahead. The weight of the dead Cloudwalker's crumpled body upon his shoulders was not an issue, though he suspected grimly that it might become one during the long climb up the Drake's inside stairwell.

Certainly, the easiest solution to the problem ahead would be disposing of the corpse where it would never be found, like in the nearby East River. For five hundred years, all major bodies of water in the area—the East River, the Hudson, and the Atlantic Ocean—had served as the city's graveyard solution. With millions upon millions of rotting corpses that resulted from the Ruin, water burial was the only real solution. Erosive properties of organic material, like that composing the human body, supplemented by the continuous source of ever-falling acid rain, meant that the bodies didn't take long to disintegrate.

But Conn could not consider such a course of action. Not for a fellow Cloudwalker. Even though he did not know the man, he still was a brother, and one born of noble blood, albeit that of the Folais Clan. He thought of Lili Folais, his soon-to-be wife, and wondered if she knew the deceased he was carrying on his shoulders. Undoubtedly, she did. He wondered idly if his bravery in going to the ground to bring the body home would evoke her gratitude.

As he approached the entrance to the alleyway, Conn stopped to reposition the dead weight atop his shoulders. Glancing into the undefined murk above, he noticed how very different the cloudbank looked when viewed from underneath. Four hundred feet overhead, it was a mere one hundred feet thick. The cloud mass had been the cause of both bliss and misery.

Were things changing? Conn wondered, thinking back on the centuries of history that were fraught with war over those clouds. *Would life return to that chaos?*

Until this past year, the cloudbank had remained remark-ably stable—a whole century of stability. But historically, wars had been fought whenever the cloudbank shifted its position. Reigning CloudMasters watched their valued *skyscape,* their very existence, begin to move, and even sometimes—God forbid—dissipate entirely. Word was that the cloudbank over Jersey City could be shifting again, or even thinning. Those distant castles in the sky, not many miles away at all, could become nothing more than isolated islands, having nothing more than quickfall patches around it, and no direct access to the more dense cloudbank. *A horrid thought.* Skylanders dreaded nothing more than being forced to live beneath the cloud. There, they would be no better than Grounders, little more than furtive beasts fighting for their very survival.

Conn's thoughts returned to the two Grounder girls he'd met on the street earlier. The smaller one, the one with the challenging disposition and the fiery green eyes, was hardly a beast. He found her unlike any of the hundreds of lifeless souls he'd guided from one high-rise structure to another. Grounder or no, she was unlike *anyone* he'd ever met.

Turning the corner, he didn't expect to hear voices echo out of the darkness.

"Well, well. Lookie here," came the voice, deep and male. "It's a skirted freak from high atop the cloud."

Conn, staring into the darkness, saw movement; he could make out at least five shapes. *Grounder bandits.*

The same deep voice echoed out from the narrow-walled confines, "You know the rules, Cloudwalker. You keep to your realm, we keep to ours." Snickering came from several others. Conn stopped short when their footsteps came closer and louder. He could make them out now, a sorry band of disheveled thugs. Nary a one of them was without something clutched within a fist: a metal pipe, a length of rebar, and two of them even held long knives, a rare commodity.

"What do you carry upon your shoulders?" the leader of the gang asked. Neither the tallest nor the shortest man there, he was the broadest, the most muscular. A moment passed before he continued. "A body? Maybe some poor sod, eh, who stepped somewhere he shouldn't have?"

"Let me pass," said Conn firmly, though his heart beat hard inside his chest. "This does not concern you. I dinnae want any trouble."

"You know, I never liked the Scottish tongue. The strange way you people talk makes me a bit squirmy. What do you think, boys, does it make you squirmy, too?"

"Makes me want to cut that waggling tongue from his Skylander mouth," another of the bandits said.

Conn released his hold on the covered body draped over his shoulders and let it stay balanced up there by gravity alone. His right hand drifted down to just below his waist, where the paw of his rackstaff hung from its peccary leather thong. "Can I ask you a quick question," he asked, "before we take this any further?"

"Of course! We're as polite as a gaggle of old schoolmarms . . . until you make us angry."

Conn nodded. "Have you come up against one of us—a skirted freak, as you put it—before? Or maybe heard stories?"

A new voice entered the conversation. "Are we going to talk on like this all night?" The man sniffed and spat, then began tapping the end of his long metal pipe against the brick wall he was leaning on. A drumroll beat that only added to the mounting tension.

"Tell you what," the muscular leader said. "I'm feeling charitable this fine evening. Leave the carcass and we'll let you pass. His clothes—and whatever else he possesses—will be payment enough for free passage."

"Tempting as that is, I'm afraid I'll have to pass. Unfortunately, the poor man had no clothes on. It seems another band of merry men beat you to the punch."

Conn noticed the sixth man a moment too late, coming up behind him from the street's access to the alleyway. By the time Conn reacted, the bandit's metal pipe was already making its downward trajectory. All Conn had time to do was make the slightest pivot. The pipe barreled down, connecting with flesh and bone with incredible force and a sharp, distinctive *crack* which echoed through the alley. It was only by sheer luck that the flesh and bone being crushed belonged to the dead man atop Conn's shoulders.

Conn abruptly jerked upright then straightened his shoulders, catapulting the dead body off him. Conn's rackstaff, already firmly gripped within his right fist, was given a deliberate double-flick and a twist of his wrist. The staff's intricate inner mechanism instantly extended out to its full six-foot length. He spun the entire length of hardened Ragoon wood over his head with a whooshing sound that increased as the end of the staff picked up momentum. Tactical, close-quarter fighting was as familiar to Conn as putting on his sandals every morning. In the span of a split second, his eyes spotted the leader. *Clap!* The end of his rackstaff whacked into the man's cheekbone, spinning the bandit around a full 360 degrees, before he staggered and dropped to the blacktop, moaning in pain.

One down.

The Grounder who'd snuck up behind Conn only moments before was making a second attempt to crush his cranium, throwing a sideways blow from his metal pipe this time, but Conn blocked it with his rackstaff in time. Barely. The *clang* of the metal pipe striking his weapon echoed through the alley and into the city beyond. Conn felt the crack reverberate through his weapon all the way to his wrist; it had been a heavy strike even on the hardened Ragoon wood, and he knew the blow would have killed him if it had been allowed to hit home. He watched as the momentum from the bandit's over-extended strike forced him off balance. After a step backward, Conn's rackstaff came around in a low sweeping motion, smacking both of the man's calves simultaneously. As his legs flew up and out, his head moved in the opposite direction—plummeting down, and striking the street with a sickening crunch. The Grounder did not move.

Two down—four to go.

The remaining bandits, lined up in a perfect row, were eight feet away. The two in the middle, both carrying long knives, slowly stepped forward.

"What do you say we call this a draw, before someone really gets hurt?" Conn asked.

They came at him at the same time, their sharp twelve-inch blades slicing through the air from two different angles. Conn, stepping sideways, avoided one swipe, but he wasn't so lucky dodging the other. The tip of the knife raked midway across the width of his back, and he let out an involuntary roar at the white-hot sensation of sharp pain. Unsure how deep the slice was, he knew he'd have to worry about it later—if he lived that long. Clearly, these men intended to play for keeps. He blocked out the pain, as he'd been trained to do.

Conn brought the full length of his rackstaff up a bit higher, only this time he flicked his wrist upward. The staff's internal mechanism, complying with the physical movement, immediately withdrew part of its length. The rackstaff made an odd clicking noise Conn had never heard before, and worry spiked through him until he felt the rackstaff shift securely down into its lockwood function. He didn't need to look at it to know that a razor-sharp blade had unfurled during the rackstaff's mechanical process. Moving to avoid another attack, he found himself a tad clumsier as blood dripped down the backs of his thighs, soaking his kilt and threatening to ruin his footing. But the pain was still manageable, and he tried not to dwell on it. Bleeding out here was not an option. It was time to end this fight.

Conn waited for the next attack. It came from the bandit on the right, attempting to circle around him and force him to turn his back to the other man. Letting him think he had done just that, Conn spun around in time to confront the attacker coming up behind him. The counter-movement was purely instinctive. Conn next stepped off to the side, whipping his rackstaff sideways from right to left at the same time. The attacker's hand, along with the still-tightly clenched knife in his fist, dropped to the ground. Both Conn and the disabled bandit stared at the cleaved wrist. Blood spurted forth, rhythmically throbbing with the bandit's accelerating heart rate. The bandit let loose a stifled howl, a raw sob cut short by his own shock. He sunk to the ground, staring at the severed hand on the ground as though he couldn't believe it was there. He would be no more trouble for the moment. Conn turned to face the other knife-wielding bandit, prepared to do whatever was necessary to stay alive. But he was gone, as were the others.

Conn turned back to the one-handed bandit, now squatting on his knees, his bleeding arm stump drawn close to his body, as if to protect it from further harm. Conn looked about, but of course he wouldn't find what he needed here on the ground. He placed a firm hand atop one of the bandit's shirtsleeves and ripped it free of the shirt.

"Hold out your arm."

The bandit, tears in his eyes, shook his head.

"If you want to live to see tomorrow, you'll do as I say. Do it!"

The bandit tentatively did as told. Conn wrapped the torn-off sleeve around the man's arm, six inches above the bleeding stump, and pulled the ends of the fabric tighter until the spurting blood was reduced to a trickle. "I ken it hurts, but don't even think about loosening this tourniquet. You ken someone who can attend the wound? A healer?"

The bandit's eyes fluttered. He'd already lost a lot of blood, but then so had Conn. The Grounder thug slowly nodded and Conn helped him to stand. "Go now, get out of here!" Conn waited a full moment, making sure no other surprise attack would be coming. The two remaining bandits were still out cold.

Conn then moved toward the other inert form, groaning in pain. He was unsure how he was going to carry the dead Skylander's body up all those flights of stairs.

"You need help?"

Conn instantly recognized the boy's voice. "You shouldn't be down here, Brig."

"Aye, but down here I am. Do you want my help, or not?"

Conn sighed, his back throbbing where he'd been wounded. "Aye, that I do."

The boy showed himself, hurrying out from the shadows that enveloped him.

Chapter 10

Danu Macbeth was awake before the sun crested the eastern ridge line of the distant Adirondacks. Wearily, she tucked a strand of silver white hair behind her ear. A full night's sleep was more of an anomaly these days than the norm. She wasn't certain if it was simply the advance of old age, she was sixty-three, creeping up on her, or perhaps a growing inner unrest—knowledge that events, both above and below, would become far worse before they got better. She often thought her Celtic *knowingness* was as much a curse as it was a gift.

But all the same, Danu truly did love the early mornings above the ever-present cloud layer. She'd slept with her window wide open and now stood before it as the soft breeze floated in. A steaming mug of hot Tangine tea was held close to her breast, warming her and comforting her. She waited. Then, one by one, the distant mountain peaks caught hold of the sun's golden rays. She had observed this same spectacle a thousand mornings before—experienced the true wonder and majesty of a life spent within the high treetops. The last of the ascending peaks now turned a bright-yellow gold, creating a heavenly crown of light that seemed settled atop a fluffy white bed of cotton. She no longer allowed the contrasting knowledge of a life lived above the cloud, with those dreary, horrid lives below, to distract her from these stolen, blissful moments.

Now dressed in her clan's tartan plaid, a long draping material of royal blue with red, yellow, and orange pin striping, Danu moved sure-footedly across the two hundred foot expanse. The individual timber boards that comprised the tethered rope and hardwood plank suspension bridge shifted slightly under her bare feet as she made her way across to the other tree house-like structure, equal in size to the one she'd just left. Erected among thick branches, they were commonly referred to as roosts. She stopped midway to observe the thick supporting crop of Ragoons. Two to three times the height of even the tallest North America Sequoia, Ragoons were not native to this world, but they were a blessed addition just the same. They allowed folks like her to still live above the cloudbank. Not so different from those towering skyscrapers back home, so many miles away. *Or is this my home now?* Danu pondered. *Does it really matter?*

Danu was a Celtic high-priestess, as well as a clan Cloud-Master in her own right. The latter title was one she'd neither wanted nor asked for in years long past. She, among close to two hundred other Skylanders, lived high above the cloudbank— amongst the branches of the towering Ragoon trees—atop White Mountain. Today, she would be meeting with a group of Grounders. She didn't relish the thought. Grounders always possessed such dark souls. They openly coveted the life and freedoms of Skylanders and Cloudwalkers, but did little to enhance their own stead, their own lifestyle. Why was that? Today, they would be discussing water rights, yet again.

Danu glanced back at her roost, at the open window where she left the still-hot cup of tea. Raising her walking stick, a fully expended rackstaff, she made a subtle horizontal motion with it in the air. The little cup, still balanced atop its delicate saucer, moved silently across the open expanse. Slowing, it came to a gentle stop before lowering onto Danu's awaiting open palm.

Chapter 11

By the time they made it to the top of the stairwell, Conn had grown even more thankful for the boy's assistance. He watched Brig heft the trailing legs of the Folais Cloudwalker's body up over the landing and drop them there. Conn, weak, sat down before he could collapse.

"Cannae go another step," Brig said, his hair and face wet with perspiration. The boy, jutting his chin in Conn's direction, added, "You're bleeding worse than this bloke."

"I'm fine."

"So who's the stiff?"

"I've already answered that same question four times. Again, it is not your concern."

"Why were you sent down there alone?"

Conn stared blankly at the brash youngster. Of course Conn knew why. It was a test, one of a number of tests recently. The CloudMaster wanted each of his heirs to be self-reliant. He'd never coddled any of his three children. And as his father's illness steadily progressed, the ailing leader had only increased his trial-by-fire methodology.

Before Conn, again, could tell Brig to mind his own business, two tall shadows took shape upon the opposite wall of the entrance. His older brother Michael, followed by Toag, stepped into the cramped space.

Michael, the first to speak, said, "You're late."

"Aye, I stopped to admire the pretty view a few times." Conn stifled a groan as a fresh wave of pain swept over him. Both Cloudwalkers suddenly looked concerned.

"Who did this?" Toag asked, dropping to a knee and lifting the back of Conn's shirt.

"Six bandit *bowbags*," Brig said. "But they're in far worse shape."

Michael huffed disapprovingly. "The point was not to be seen, little brother. Did anyone else see you?"

Conn weighed telling him about the two Grounder girls then shook his head. "No." Almost imperceptibly, Brig's brows arched up.

So the boy did follow him below to where the body fell. He had been down there too, lurking somewhere in the dark, watching him.

"Fine. We'll tend to the corpse now. Go get that scratch tended to before it gets infected." Michael, pointing down to the dead man's feet, said, "Grab the legs, Toag."

Michael, while kneeling down, noticed Conn's rackstaff. "What's going on with that?"

Jobby! Conn closed his eyes, inwardly chiding himself for not hiding the staff. In parrying away one of the bandit's swinging metal pipes, he'd saved his noggin, but his rackstaff hadn't fared as well. Its intricate internal mechanism was damaged to the point where it no longer allowed for the multiuse staff to fully retract. Conn had used it as a walking stick on the way up the stairs, but there was no hiding the damage now. This was no small matter, either. Michael didn't need to remind Conn how disrespectful it was to the clan, not to mention the racksmith who'd meticulously labored near a year in crafting the thing. No one spoke for nearly a minute.

"I'll let you make your own explanations to Father."

Conn nodded, then watched as Michael and Toag left, carrying the dead Skylander's body away.

"You need help getting over to the Empire?"

"No, thank you. You go on, Brig. Head on home now."

Brig hesitated at first then scurried out the door. Conn, now alone, sat on the landing in the dim light of the flickering lamp on the wall. *Michael was right,* he thought, feeling like a numpty. *I've made a guddle of this whole situation.* The sun had not yet risen, but he needed to awaken Thannis McDuffie. The old, half-blind healer would dutifully stitch him up, hopefully without complaint. As for Conn, it looked as though he faced yet another night without a wink of sleep, no thanks to his insomnia this time.

Wincing, Conn rose to his feet.

A full day and another night had passed by the time Conn re-entered the vestibule on the Empire's 86th floor, his back still aching but now clean and bandaged. It would heal quickly so long as he did not push himself, McDuffie had told him, but he would likely bear a scar there for the rest of his days. In stark contrast to his visit the previous night, many a man and woman was present now. Although the red tartan plaid of the Brataich clan dominated, kilts of other clans were present too. Most, like Conn, were awaiting an audience with Robert.

"You move like a daft crony thrice your age, lad."

Conn turned to see Lidia O'Cain, a homely, middle-aged woman staring back at him. The CloudMaster was from One Penn Plaza, a relatively close neighbor among all the mid-town property towers. Her tartan garb was red and white, with opaque lines of yellow and thin, delicate lines of blue, and she watched him with calculating eyes from her place leaning against the wall.

"Aye, Ma'am," responded Conn with a smile. "I overdid a practice for the upcoming Skylander games. Still early days; just working out the kinks."

Her expression made it clear she didn't buy his excuse. Separating herself from the wall, she joined him at the tall window, placing an open palm atop her blouse just above her heart. Together, they stared out at the mid-morning view, at the bright-white cloudbank and the buildings that pierced through it. In the distance, a broad-faced building facade reflected back at them which was missing a gaping chunk from the lower portion of the building's flank. The area was ragged, as though a giant monster had taken a colossal bite out of the immense structure. Actually, it was a direct hit from a falling meteor that had destroyed the building, a visible reminder of the very start of the Ruin Event.

"You need not tell tall tales, Conn. I ken verra well of your nighttime exploit."

Conn kept silent, and waited for another reprimand.

"You came back with the poor sod," she said after a moment. "And from what I hear, you defended yourself with honor. I cannae excuse your clumsiness, though."

Conn's eyes fell to his belt, where the paw of his rackstaff should have been tethered.

"Conn!" He forced his eyes up to meet hers.

"Change is coming." Hesitating, she added, "Not just with your father, that is inevitable. The bank . . . it's . . . showing signs . . ."

She was referring to the shifting of the cloudbank. It had always moved to some degree—up an inch or two one year, and down a few inches the next. Some areas became less dense to the point they couldn't support a man's weight, while other areas strengthened. But Conn knew such fluctuations were not what she was addressing now. She was referring to the cloudbank above Jersey City. Last year, one of the skyscrapers there lost its connection with the cloudbank. The quickfall patches that formed all around it turned the very building into an island unto itself. A once powerful clan had been humiliated, forced to scramble for residence within another clan's tower domain.

"War is coming," continued Lidia. "It's coming as sure as the sun will rise in the morn. We cannae lose you to such foolishness. There are far too few who can lead."

"Both Michael and Emma are up to the task, CloudMaster. A good thing, because I assure you, I am no leader, ye ken."

The woman glanced over her shoulder, toward the rear wall where three ornate tapestries hung. The centermost, the most colorful, was his favorite amongst all the old hangings, and it was the one she gazed at now.

"It was once a way of life," she said quietly, studying the thirty-foot-long hanging tapestry. The woven face of a woman, red hair blazing around her, stared back at her, her eyes alight in the blood-pumping heat of some long ago battle. "It was a constant here, before it was outlawed."

She was speaking of the Cloudwalkers who made use of what later were deemed devilish occult powers. Conn had no opinion about that; all he knew was the price for demonstrating such powers would quickly result in the harshest of penalties. A Fall from Grace. His thoughts flashed back to last night, and the splattered body lying on the damp street below.

He asked, "Then it's true . . . they're returning to those dangerous ways, Ma'am?"

"Don't be so surprised, Conn. Survival is our most primal instinct. Do you hold some doubt that the Midtown clan leaders here wouldn't do the same if it were happening to our own cloudbank? Draw upon the ancient magic of those who can literally move the cloudbank with their minds?"

Conn stared again at the tapestry, now faded with age, then at the fierce-looking warrior priestess—Lana Macbeth. Her rackstaff was extended to its deadly lockwood position, poised high and ready to strike down the charging army of her enemy.

"With all due respect, CloudMaster, I think the day of Celtic high priestesses, Elysium Alchemists, and wizards is long past. The last of them are gone, along with the dishonored and disbanded Macbeth clan."

The woman didn't contradict him. Her only reaction was a bemused expression as she turned her gaze back to the view beyond.

"CloudMaster Robert will see you now, Ma'am," a young sept assistant said, bowing his head to her.

She waved him away with a dismissive gesture. "Come, young Cloudwalker, this concerns you as well. No need to wait the whole afternoon for your father to call on you. Best if you get this whole rackstaff ordeal out of the way first-off."

Chapter 12

Her hand basket was half-filled with black chanterelle mushrooms when she felt a presence behind her. Misty continued on with her harvesting chores, appearing to stop and closely examine an edible fungus sprout held between her thumb and forefinger. In reality, she was intensely listening. The Casper family had two pigs, which sometimes snuck up on her and tried to swipe mushrooms, but the presence she heard now was decidedly human. Not ten feet behind her, she heard the man's deep inhalations then smelled his rank exhalations. Without turning around, she asked, "Is there something you want . . . or are you simply here to ogle me?" Only then did she turn her head in his direction.

Misty recognized him, one of the High Deacon's bootlickers. He was wearing the same type uniform all Lasher's minions wore: a rumpled black suit, a dingy button-down shirt—it may have been white at one time—and a drooping ribbon bowtie. The garb was supposed to signify religious piety, and probably authority too.

"Did you not hear me? What are you doing here?" she asked

again. "The deacon gave us until week's end to meet the quittance."

His lack of response had her far more worried than any insult or lewd comment he could toss her way. She looked beyond him, toward the distant, out of sight cluster of small rooms she called home.

Rushing past him, she let the basket fall to the ground. As she crossed a dual set of subway tracks she clutched the folds of her dress, raising the hem to keep it from dragging or getting snagged on something sharp. In the near distance, seven or eight men could be seen standing in a semi-circle—three carrying torches. *What are they doing?*

She yelled out, her voice sounding as if it belonged to someone else, "Mother! Father!"

Heads turned her way, and several sets of black lifeless eyes watched her approach.

Misty barged through the small congregation, not caring that she'd nearly bowled over two men in the process. As she came to an abrupt stop, her mind tried to make sense of the horrific scene before her. Standing tall, his legs set apart in a wide stance, was the deacon, poised for another strike. In his raised hand was a cat-o'-nine-tails, the knots of cord dripping red. Below him on the ground was her father, his head buried in his hands. His shirt, sliced down the back and spread apart, exposed his torn back, where a hundred bloody slashes looked black and glistening, like wet stripes in the dim torchlight.

Misty's father turned his face up to her as blood trickled down his chin. He had bitten through his own lips in agony. "Oh God, no. Misty, turn away. Go on, I'll be fine. This is my own fault. It is what I deserve." His face turned back again into the shadows.

Misty slowly shook her head, unable to find her voice, unable to scream out all the things she so desperately wanted to convey. To let them know this poor whipped man had never, would never, hurt another living soul. What had her parents done to deserve—Misty's heart stopped as she realized only her father was present.

"Where is she?" Misty's furious eyes met Deacon Lasher's. "Where is my mother? What have you done with her?"

"Best you watch your tone, girl. My patience with this family has reached its limit."

Snap! Snap! Snap!

She flinched with each of the deacon's downward strikes upon her father's already ruined back. From the ground, Halbert's body shook with choking sobs as each blow struck its mark. Tears dripped from his eyes, mixing with his own blood on the ground beneath him. Sickened, she could no longer watch. Instead, she searched the faces of the other men standing there. "For God's sake, one of you has to possess a conscience!"

Snap! Snap!

She moved from one man to the next, and stared up into their stony, expressionless faces. "Tell me! Where is my mother?" Over and over again, she repeated the same question, moving from one man to another. She didn't care what the deacon would do to her, or how he would punish her for her insolence. Likely, he was planning on punishing her anyway, regardless of her actions.

Snap! Snap!

Misty caught a quick flicker in one of the men's eyes and hurried over to him. She got in close and glared up at him. "Where is my mother?"

High Deacon Terrence Lasher—his flogging punishment apparently complete—moved toward her. His blood-soaked instrument of torture hung down, dragging along the concrete.

"They will not speak to you. Do not waste your breath."

"Where is my mother?"

"Your mother is alive. That is all you need to know."

"Alive where? What does that mean?"

The others in the congregation began to move off in the direction of the obsolete tracks. Misty stared up into the soulless deacon's eyes before her. "Please, just tell me. I'll do anything you ask of me . . . just tell me . . ."

"It really is quite simple. A solution she herself agreed to."

Although she couldn't see him lying there, slumped on the ground behind the deacon, Misty could hear her father's dreadful sobs.

"It is only out of the kindness of my heart that I have agreed to assist this indolent family. Ones who clearly cannot meet their quittance obligations."

"We were trying!" Misty insisted. "You gave us until week's end!"

"I changed my mind," said Lasher blithely. "Luckily for you, your mother offered a different type of payment."

Misty's blood went cold. "What has my mother agreed to?"

"You read the Scripture, Casper girl?"

Misty nodded, holding back tears.

"Your mother will find grace in the eyes of our God . . . as my third wife."

"As your wife?!" Misty spluttered, disgusted.

"Your tone. Watch it!"

"My mother already has a husband. My father."

"That marriage will, of course, be annulled." Misty's glare did not abate, and the deacon smiled as he continued, "Look on the bright side. Your quittance obligations are now halved. One of your mother's conditions, as it were. But I warn you, cross me on this, and I can easily restore the amount due back to their previous levels. Then we'll see how you endure two hundred lashes of God's punishment." He started to turn away. Misty held in a sob. She would not cry in front of this man.

"Can I at least say goodbye to her?" she asked, forcing her voice to remain steady. "Tell her I love her?"

Without looking back, Lasher said, "No. She is not your mother anymore. She lives with me now. Forget her. Move on with your life."

Chapter 13

As he descended the Empire State's narrow inner stairwell, Conn mentally replayed back both conversations, first between CloudMaster O'Cain and his father, then the joint meeting afterword, once the three of them had moved off to a smaller unoccupied anteroom. They had spoken in low tones to avoid the possibility of being overheard. Conn had learned the dead man from the other night was none other than Janis Folais, nephew to CloudMaster Gordon Folais himself, and part of a contingent visiting from Jersey City to discuss the upcoming Skylander Games. Games in which Conn himself would be taking part. But it wasn't the annual competition between the two rival clans that the CloudMasters spoke so intensely about this morning, but of the dead man—Janis Folais —and the potentially dire consequences his early demise would have on the already-strained relationship between the two Skylander cities.

CloudMaster Robert Brataich glanced up at the old ornate wall clock, with its hanging weights and never-still swinging pendulum. "I am told they are making their way now across the three-quarters of a mile divide, between the Bank of America building over to our location, as we speak. They were overnight guests of Clan Baird."

"Your future wife is amongst them, young Conn," Cloud-Master O'Cain said. "It was meant to be a surprise."

"Lili? She's coming here?"

Robert stifled a cough then spoke with a raspy voice, "Aye. But the poor bastard, this Janis lad, is—was—her first cousin. They apparently were very close growing up, maybe too close. They wanted to marry, but eventually relented, listening instead to prevailing parental reason."

Both CloudMasters had focused their full attention on Conn. His father said, "Son, we think it best if you break the news to your fiancée."

"Me?" Conn was flabbergasted. "No way! I barely ken the girl, but I've seen her stormy temper firsthand . . . all on account of a poorly constructed sandwich. She'll skin me alive me for telling her about her cousin's death!"

Neither CloudMaster shifted their steady stares away, and finally Conn relented.

"Fine! I'll do it, but if all-out-war breaks out, don't blame me."

"Don't even jest about such a thing, boy."

As a series of gentle taps came from the door, Conn hurried over to it. The same sept assistant stood there. "Sorry to disturb you, but the Folais clan representatives—"

Conn turned away from the young man mid-sentence. "They're here, Father."

The two CloudMasters exchanged wary glances. "Let them in; best not keep them waiting."

Eight clan members entered, each wearing a kilt in the same tartan plaid of green and red squares. Lili Folais was the last one to enter. Her head was raised and her nose elevated, as if a pungent smell had entered her nostrils. *Typical Folais,* thought

Conn, and then forced himself to stop. This was his future wife; he needed to be kind. Lili's eyes lazily surveyed the entire room, moving past Conn. She yawned without covering her mouth and took up a position towards the back of the visiting group.

Conn, who'd relegated himself to be the official greeter, bowed his head to each one of them. "Welcome to House Brataich. I present to you CloudMaster Robert Brataich and CloudMaster Lidia O'Cain. I am Conn, son of Robert Brataich."

Conn addressed his welcoming greeting to the largest of the men, a robust fellow with red hair and a long red beard. He was identical to one of the men standing next to him. But it was the smallest one, a slight, pinch-faced man, who looked little older than Conn himself, who spoke first.

"I am Spinter Row Folais, third son of CloudKing Gordon Folais," he said, his voice flat and nasal. "You ken Lili, of course. These are my two brothers Dearth and Garret. Thank you for arranging such an impromptu audience."

Conn nodded to the two brothers but got nothing in return. The twins were of enormous proportions, as if born of an entirely different genetic pool than Spinter or Lili—perhaps vikings or gladiators. Their stony expressions conveyed nothing.

Conn turned his attention to the two CloudMasters' expressions for any overt sign of irritation, hearing the term CloudKing used in their presence. But neither man so much as blinked. It was not so subtle an insult, though, since all clans had voluntarily forgone the use of the outdated term and the actual title position nearly a century past. Jersey City, clearly, had reverted back—becoming a full-fledged aristocracy —into a monarchy with a lone, king-like ruler making decrees and axioms that could not be contested among the other clan leaders. That simple act by Gordon Folais, appointing himself the new CloudKing, unabashedly placed him above all Cloud-

Masters—those local to Jersey City, as well as those in Manhattan.

Spinter Folais continued, "My father has granted me complete autonomy to make the final arrangements for the upcoming Skylander Games. But there is one . . . provision, first . . . that we request at this time."

Robert cleared his throat, prior to speaking, but was instantly cut off.

"As you may, or may not have heard, Clan MacLeod has come upon dire circumstances. Their building has become isolated unto itself. Such a burden must be shared; residence must be made available—"

Robert's eyes flared, his sudden fury clearly evident. "Stop right there, Spinter. That is not going to happen. CloudMaster Folais will have to make do with whatever cloudbank real-estate is available on the other side of the Hudson."

Conn couldn't believe his ears; this was a blatant attempt by the Folais clan leader to get a strong footing into a prized-Manhattan skyscape building.

"But please, convey our sympathy and prayers to Clan MacLeod," Robert added.

Appearing indignant, the small man said nothing for several moments.

"Perhaps we should continue on with the subject at hand. Provisioning for the Skylander Games," Lidia O'Cain said.

Robert lifted a hand, "One moment, Lidia. There is terrible news that must be discussed first." He turned his gaze over toward Conn.

All eyes shifted at once to Conn. For the first time he saw Lili staring back at him. She was certainly striking, in her own way. Her long black hair was perfectly straight and incredibly shiny. Her thin lips almost looked as if they were painted onto her face, like a doll, or a mask. It was to her that he spoke now.

"I'm so sorry to have to tell you this. Janis Folais has been found dead. We discovered his body two nights ago beneath the cloud-bank . . . down on the street below."

It took several beats for his words to register. Then Lili's hands rose up, covering her mouth. "No . . . that can't possibly be true." She looked to Conn, her eyes pleading with him.

Obviously shocked, the others glanced to one another, first with confusion then in pain.

"How could you have let that happen?" Spinter asked, his eyes locked onto Robert, his fingers balled into fists.

"We were as shocked to hear of the incident as you are now. I was unaware the man was even here among us," Robert said. He hastily moved toward a sideboard table and retrieved a collapsed rackstaff. "This was found not far from here, lying upon the cloudbank. Beside the quickfall where the poor man had fallen through."

"Fallen?" Lili repeated, her loud voice echoing off the concrete walls. She barreled her way forward, to the front of the group. "Janis was the most skilled Cloudwalker alive. He couldn't have just fallen—stumbled—onto a quickfall patch. No! He had to have been pushed, which means he was outright assassinated!" Her eyes switched back and forth between the two CloudMasters then over to Conn. "*You* did this, you jealous claw baw!"

Conn almost laughed out loud. A *claw baw* was a compul-sive ball fondler, a wanker—something he definitely was not. Even more unbelievable was the fact she thought he was so smitten with her that he'd even consider doing such a terrible deed. Previous to today, he'd held no real feelings about her, one way or another, and he struggled now to keep his emotions from turning sour. *You still have to marry her,* he told himself. To her, he said, "I had nothing to do with his death, Lili, I promise you that. I was the one who went below to retrieve the body.

Grounders were already nearby, taking notice. I'm truly sorry for your loss." Lili continued to glare back at him, hatred burning through the tears in her eyes.

So, does this mean the wedding is off? Conn wanted to add, but he held his tongue.

Robert held out the dead man's rackstaff to her. "You should have this. It is a fine staff. Magnificent workmanship."

"You will deliver his remains to us, and we shall embark immediately for Jersey City," Spinter said. "Our attendance at the Skylander Games is a decision for the CloudKing to make. Our business here is terminated."

Conn's father nodded back, the proper amount of condolence on his face.

The robust man with the red hair said, "We will await any further contact at our accommodations in the Baird Building."

One by one they filed out. Conn watched with curiosity to see if Lili would glance back at him. *Jobby! After all, we are to be married.* But she neither looked back nor spoke out again before leaving the anteroom.

"That did not go well," Lidia said.

"It could have been worse," Robert added. "Lidia, do me a favor please, and do so with haste. Assemble the each of the Manhattan CloudMasters."

The rest of the meeting had been a rush. Lidia had practically flown from the room, and Robert had closed his eyes, clearly feeling the stress of the day. Conn had wanted to say something to him, something comforting, but he held his tongue.

Back in the present moment, Conn stepped out of the building and into the fall sunlight. Toag was there, waiting for him.

Chapter 14

Halbert Casper hadn't moved much, other than a slight back-and-forth rocking motion, from where he'd been mercilessly flogged by Deacon Terrence Lasher. Misty, despondent herself, didn't know what to do—how to help—so she continued to hold her father's hand, listening to his quiet sobbing for close to twenty minutes before the entire Romano family descended upon them in force, like an invading army.

Aurora's mother, aptly named Gladdy—short for Gladice—took charge of the situation and began barking off orders. None thought twice about following them as she knelt down beside Halbert and Misty. Placing a caring hand upon each of their shoulders, she said, "We're here and we're going to get you through this. I promise you that."

Misty threw her arms around her, burying her face into Gladdy's comforting warm bosom. "The crazy *animal* just took her," she cried. "Oh God, he took my mother." She gasped for air that wouldn't seem to reach her lungs as the truth struck her again.

"I know, dear. I know," said Gladdy softly, stroking her hair. "Just go ahead and cry, okay?"

Aurora's two younger brothers—Ben, thirteen, and Randy, fourteen—arrived, carrying oversized wicker baskets filled with an assortment of harvesting tools: Shovels, rakes, hoes, and various kinds of pruning clippers. "Boys, make haste attending to the hang-row planters," ordered Gladdy, gently separating herself from Misty, who was immediately taken under the wing of Aurora's sister Amber. "Then do a far better harvesting job than we've lately seen from the two of you back home."

Mr. Romano, typically happy, albeit somewhat browbeaten by his forceful wife, needed no such direction in getting down to the business at hand. Peering up, he was already assessing the myriad of small-angled mirrors that lined the concrete ceiling by the hundreds. "Not nearly enough light is being captured; no wonder the crop yields have been so low. But I'm on it!" Disappearing for a bit, he returned with a rickety old wooden stepladder. Climbing up, he called down from the top rung, "Ask Misty if they have adequate reserves of spores. We'll need to repopulate the hang-row planters once we fertilize them and till the soil."

"Now, let's have a look at you, Hal," said Gladdy kindly, helping him slowly to his feet and into the house, where she gently but firmly helped him lie down on the kitchen table. Aurora, without being told, had scurried off to the Casper's two water-holding tanks—one for personal use, the other for irrigation reserves. When she arrived back, she held a large white porcelain water basin. Steam rose into the air as she carefully set it down between her mother and Halbert Casper.

Gladdy was already assembling the medical supplies she'd be using in the next few minutes, a stack of clean towels set aside. She began tearing up long strips of fabric, which looked like bed sheets, then stopped to survey the wounds on Hilbert's exposed back. "Some of them will need to be stitched." Leaning closer down to his partially covered face, she said, "I'm so sorry, but this is going to be painful. First, I need to disinfect the wounds, and then suture them."

Misty watched Gladdy through brimming tears. "I should help. What can I do, Mrs. Romano?"

"You can leave me to this, sweetie. Why don't you go collect your things? Anything you or your father will need for the foreseeable future. You will both be staying with us, and that's not up for discussion. Go on! Aurora, go with her."

Aurora put her arm around Misty's shoulders, gently guided her in the direction of her room.

"Wait, I need to check on something else first." Misty veered them left toward her parents' room. Aurora kept her in a one-armed embrace as the two shuffled over to the metal door. Finding it slightly ajar, Misty shoved the door all the way open. The lamp mounted on the wall had been extinguished. The contents of the darkened room were in total disarray. The mattress, flipped up onto its side, leaned against the wall. Shelves, broken into mere splinters, lay upon the concrete floor. Clothes tossed into heaps were piled all around. Misty hurried inside and began searching.

"What is it? What are you looking for?"

Misty looked beneath the clothes, the broken shelves, and behind the mattress. Soon, she was throwing anything she got ahold of into the air, while frantically kicking the items on the floor. Turning, she screamed, hammering angry fists into the mattress. "It's gone!" she cried. "They took it . . . I can't believe they took it!"

"What . . . what did they take, Misty?" Aurora asked, still in the doorway, keeping a good distance away from her angry tirade.

Misty, hurrying past her friend, ran over to her own room.

That door too was ajar, just like her parents' door. She plowed into her room then stopped short. A single wall torch flickered light in the disturbed air. She took in the confined, orderly space, which was just as she'd left it. It was undisturbed. The weight of it all suddenly crashed down on her. Falling down onto the bed, she curled into a fetal position and cried into her pillow.

It could have been ten minutes, maybe even an hour that passed, Misty had lost all track of time. Aurora, sitting on a side of the bed, quietly stroked her hair.

"We fought so much," lamented Misty. "I don't even remember the last time I told her I love her."

Aurora sighed, a sympathetic sound. "She knows, Misty."

But did she? Astrid and Misty had always had such a strained relationship, but Misty had never loved her mother any less for it. Without her mother, who would help her sell salvage at the market? Halbert was a terrible negotiator, but Astrid always knew how to get the best prices. Who would comb the snarls out of the back of Misty's hair after a wash? For a moment, Misty thought she'd even miss the occasional whacks on the head with the hairbrush that she got for complaining.

But beyond sentimental reasons, she wasn't sure how her life could go on from here. Astrid had done all of the cooking and cleaning in the house, and she had been the one to handle the household finances, tasks that Misty supposed now fell onto her shoulders. She felt crushed under the weight of this realization. She would never be able to run the household, and moreover, it wasn't what she wanted for her life, she realized. Her mother had been gone for only a few hours, but Misty already felt trapped.

Briefly, Misty contemplated something she'd never thought about before. She could just end her own life. *But then,* she thought, *who would take care of Father?* She cast the dark thought from her mind. Perhaps she could find a way to get her mother back, make things right. There had to be some way.

Aurora stopped stroking her hair, preoccupied with something else. Misty, gulping in a deep breath of air, slowly let it out. *That's it. No more crying. No more feeling sorry for myself.*

"What is it you're doing?" she asked, once she had her emotions under lock. "What are you looking at, Aurora?"

Aurora, her back half-turned from Misty, glanced back over her shoulder. Her voice was full of awe as she said, "You're lucky they didn't find this. God, the colors . . . they're amazing! You'd be in real trouble if they knew."

Misty shot forward, practically shoving Aurora off the side of the bed. There, partially exposed beneath her mattress, was the distinctive tartan—royal blue plaid, interspersed with thin lines of yellow, green and orange. "Get up!"

Aurora quickly did as asked, startled.

Misty, jumping off the bed, hefted the corner of the mattress up as high as she could and stared down at what lay hidden beneath it: the rest of what surely was some part of a Skylander's frock, along with a weathered, hand-inscribed leather journal.

Chapter 15

The cloudbank held a bevy of Skylander men, women, and children—easily a hundred souls within a stone's throw of the Empire State Building. Another hundred, mostly Grounders, were being led, both this way and that, across the skyscape by a myriad of multi-clan Cloudwalkers. Farther off, a large contingent of able-bodied men positioned the lightweight, albeit remarkably strong, superstructures of staggered bleachers along the periphery of one of the playing fields. One particular cloudbank area had proved itself to be, over many decades, almost as dense as the ground far below it, and it was here that the Skylander Games would be held.

Toag asked, "Well?"

"Well, what?" Conn replied, walking along the well-worn cloudbank path alongside his best friend. Toag used his extended rackstaff periodically, driving its tip down into the bank with just the right amount of force to gauge the amount of resistance. A necessary precaution, and one that, after so many years, was completely second nature to him. Conn trusted Toag's abilities, but his hands itched to test the cloudbank with his own rackstaff; after three full days, it still hadn't been fixed, and he felt naked without it.

"Oh, come on! Everyone watched that Folais clan trudge across the bank. Such a stern-looking group! How was it seeing your betrothed again? Miss Lili?"

"I ken who my fiancée is, thank you."

Both turned, hearing the sound of running footfalls behind them. Young Brig darted between them and turned around, slightly out of breath and red-faced from the exertion. Walking backwards, he smiled up at them.

"What trouble are you getting yourself into this fine morning, Master Brig?" Toag asked fondly.

The boy became serious, his gaze settling on Conn. "So we're going to war?"

Concern grew on Toag's face, and he stared at his friend. "What's this?"

"Damn it, Brig! Creeping around behind walls and spying on the CloudMaster is a sure way to be locked up. If my father knew—"

"What's this about war?" Toag asked again.

"Gordon Folais is now calling himself a CloudKing," Brig said. "Also, the MacLeod Clan's building has become isolated, nothing but quickfall patches surrounding it. And the Cloud-King, he's—"

"He's not a CloudKing!" Conn corrected.

"He wants the MacLeods moved up here to Midtown."

"*Pfft,* like that's going to happen," Toag said.

Conn, reaching down, grabbed Brig by the shoulders and lifted him up to eye-level. "You really need to shut up. None of this can be spoken about any further. To anyone. Is that understood?"

Brig nodded, clearly unsure if Conn was really mad or only acting like he was.

Conn set the boy back down. "Make yourself scarce; I need to talk to Toag in private. And remember what I said. If one word of what you've heard gets out, I'll come looking for you myself." They left the boy where he stood.

Walking away in silence, after several minutes, Conn said, "When I ken something for sure, I'll tell you."

"Aye, you damn well better. I'm going this way. I take it you won't be practicing with us for the next few days, eh?"

Conn shook his head. "Healer says my stitches need some time to heal, but I'll give it a try next week."

"Where you off to now?" Toag asked, turning left at the fork in the path.

Conn shook his head as he continued going right.

"Oh, that's right, someone's jimmied up his rackstaff. Good luck with that."

Conn stood aside, letting a Baird clan Cloudwalker move past him, along with his small flock of four sullen-looking Grounders. "Step wisely," he said.

The older Cloudwalker raised his rackstaff to tap paws, but seeing Conn staff-less, he mumbled something undecipherable and moved off.

The glistening spire of the Chrysler building appeared just up ahead. Like near the Empire State building, throngs of people were out, taking in the splendid early fall day. As an elegantly dressed family of four approached him—parents with their two small children—Conn knelt down to his knee, knowing what was coming.

"Uncle Conn! Uncle Conn!" the twin six-year-olds yelled in unison. When close enough, their mother released their tiny hands to let them run into Conn's awaiting open arms. He winced as their forceful hugs jostled his stitches.

"We were watching the window-makers!" little Jeremy said, pointing up to the building.

"It was terribly hot. I hated it!" Tori, his twin sister added, scrunching up her face.

"Well, I'm with Jeremy on this one; I always like watching any artisans work," Conn said, mirroring back his niece's scrunched-up face.

Conn's older sister, Emma, smiling but looking a bit worn out, leaned over and kissed his cheek. He hadn't seen her Emma these past few weeks—not nearly as much as he'd seen Michael and his father. But there again, it was no secret she despised politics, anything to do with the clan's official matters. Her children were everything to her. His brother-in-law, who had been a healer prior to marrying his sister, gave Conn's upper arm an affectionate squeeze. "Good to see you, Conn. A proper tidy day, is it not?"

"Aye, Cleve, that it is." Conn let his gaze drift to the somewhat shorter man's nearly white head of hair. Cleve had begun to go prematurely gray at twenty-five, some ten years in the past.

"Where you off to, little brother?" Emma asked. Then, quickly covering her smile with her hand, she said, "Oops, sorry," as she looked down at his empty belt and the missing rackstaff.

"Does *everyone* know?" Conn groaned, embarrassed. Emma's expression was sympathetic.

"We passed by old Graham Gould," she admitted. "But I have to warn you, he didnae seem to be in a verra good mood."

Gould, easily ninety-years of age, was one of the few remaining racksmiths in Manhattan, and the old man was considered a true master of his trade. The last time Conn had been to Gould's quarters, he'd been with Dob. The two had been friends, but Conn didn't expect that friendship to extend to him. Not today, at least. Gould did not tolerate the misuse of a rackstaff well.

"I'll tread lightly. Thanks for the heads-up."

Leaving his sister, brother-in-law, niece, and nephew to continue with their walk to the Empire State building, Conn headed on toward the Chrysler building.

He passed through the town square, beneath the gold-topped bell tower which warned Skylanders of God's Rampage. The impressive cupola and dome had once topped another building in Manhattan, but sometime during the 23rd century, that building had started to succumb to time and the unforgiving acidity of the elements. A Herculean effort by all the Manhattan clans was made to save the beautiful tower and cupola. Piece by piece, the individual constructs were dismantled, lowered down to street level, transported uptown, and hauled up the side of the Leland-Brock building, which at 496 feet tall, barely crested the cloudbank. But with the addition of the bell tower and cupola, it became a stunning centerpiece for the Skylander Town Square outside the Chrysler Building, and a useful tool with which to warn Manhattan Skylanders of the approach of a God's Rampage lightning storm.

As Conn exited the town square and passed within the shadow of the Chrysler Building, he looked up to find no fewer than ten men and women, all sept craftsmen, attending to the never-ending job of keeping the building's façade looking as beautiful as the day it was completed.

Skylanders took great pride in the visible presentation of their buildings. Earlier, Conn had witnessed just as many septs working on the Empire's façade. A new window was now being positioned into place, some seventy-five-feet up. Over the past five centuries, every window had been replaced many times over. The building days of old, when manufacturing facilities existed, had been lost with the Ruin and the advent of God's Rampage. Today, a window's far less perfect panes, though perhaps more charming in appearance, were known as crown glass. Each replacement pane was hand-blown by clan artisans, accomplished glass blowers who routinely custom-made several big windows in a day. To create each pane, they blew molten glass into a large bubble using a long blowpipe. The bubble, maneuvered into position and then flattened, was next attached to the end of an iron rod, called a *punty,* and spun around as fast as possible by the artisan. This process allowed the flattened bubble of glass to fan out and form a circle, which the artisans then cut to size, into windowpanes.

Conn entered the art deco-style building through its south, cloudbank level entrance up. Taking the stairs to the 60th floor, he made his way to the central windowless suite of rooms belonging to Graham Gould. Most of the men and women who worked there were highly educated professors, masters in their respective fields. For Skylanders, getting a higher education was not an option. As a Cloudwalker of noble blood, even Conn was expected to continue his education at the Chrysler Building. Both of his older siblings, as well as his father, boasted multiple degrees in various fields.

Entering into Gould's dark and cluttered realm was like taking a walk back in time. The first thing to greet Conn was the rich aromatic scent of freshly cut Ragoon timber. There were other odors too: wood stains and varnishes, and smoky smells from the giant, black, iron hearth, filled now with scarlet and gray embers. All the walls were lined with hanging, vertical rackstaffs. Some appeared to be recently made and others polished worn and smooth by hundreds of years of use. While some were fully retracted, others were extended to their full seven-foot length or mid, sword-sized length. Rackstaffs filled all the walls and even hung from the ceiling.

Conn found the old man—hunched and skeletal-looking, with wispy white hair and a long white beard—leaning over his workbench. His spectacles were precariously perched near the tip of his nose. A partially disassembled rackstaff lay open before him, like a corpse being autopsied. The rack smith held the end of a long delicate tool, perhaps some kind of screwdriver, between both his thumb and forefinger; turning it with infinitely careful precision.

"You dare show yourself here?" he asked, not taking his eyes off his work.

Conn was well aware that the rackstaff that Gould was now attending to was none other than his own.

"I have no excuse."

"There was blood . . . dried and caked within the delicate workings."

Conn took a step closer and leaned in. He didn't understand the exact workings of a rackstaff, but from his perspective he couldn't see any sign of blood among the staff's shiny metal gears, ratchet spindles, actuating arms, locking turrets, or rotating bearings.

"You say you parried a pipe?"

"It was aimed at my head."

"Aye . . . well, a proper rackstaff would have survived that with no problem."

Conn wasn't sure he'd heard him right. His rackstaff was a good one, it had belonged to his grandfather. Easily one hundred-and-fifty years old.

Gould looked up. "This staff, it's a piece of shit."

Conn thought about that. A Cloudwalker's rackstaff had a close connection with the person who owned it and wielded it. Coming from anyone else, Gould's statement was the kind of insult that demanded physical confrontation. He momentarily imagined taking the old, frail racksmith to task, giving him a backhand to the face. Or maybe kicking him down the Chrysler building's inner stairwell. Of course, he'd never truly consider it. If Gould said something was wrong with his rackstaff, well, he was probably right.

"Is it even worth fixing, sir?"

"Aye, but not for you. Instead, this will be given to the school, for a young Cloudwalker in training."

Conn felt a stab of grief for the loss of his rackstaff, which had been with him for years, but he said nothing.

Gould let out a long breath and stared back at Conn. "Dark days are coming, young man. When you have lived nearly a century, as I have, you grow to ken such things. I can feel it in these creaky old bones."

Conn simply nodded, unsure if the old man really knew something.

"I have been waiting for the right person."

"The right person?"

Gould turned—staring up at the top row of rackstaffs hanging near the high ceiling—then used a crooked finger to help locate what he was looking for. "There it is."

Conn's eyes had already locked onto it before Gould pointed it out. The rackstaff was fully extended, the Ragoon wood darker than any he had ever seen before. Its paw looked to be somewhat larger than was typical, too.

"Reach up there and get it down for me."

"Aye, sir." Conn looked around for something to stand on. The staff's sharp tip was higher than he could reach.

"Don't be a *wallaper*, use my stool . . . go on, get up there, get it for me."

Conn did as told. Balanced on tiptoes atop the old man's stool, he reached up for the dark rackstaff. As his hand grasped the cool Ragoon wood, a powerful, painful jolt coursed up his wrist, then his arm and into his chest. He heard himself scream before everything went black.

Chapter 16

So many fierce Skylander wars had taken place throughout their history. Many thousands died, defending the honor of their clan. In the stability of the last two decades, such bloody business was easy to forget, but Gordon Folais had more reason than most to remember it now.

Stability and peace seemed to go hand in hand, Gordon figured, as he padded along the hallway of an upper floor in the 234-floor tower where the Folais clan—close to nine hundred men, women, and children—resided.

Through the soles of his bare feet, he could detect a chill through the hard Indiana limestone flooring. Rising up quickly under his ankle-length nightgown, the cold sent a shiver through his entire five-foot-two inch frame.

Gordon openly wept again, using his sleeve to wipe away a river of gooey snot from beneath his runny nose. The news of his Janis' death had hit him like a lightning bolt. Janis had been so bright, a force to be reckoned with, and now he was dead, splattered and cold on the damned ground.

Others, especially those narrow-minded Jersey City elders, had argued against his proposal. Well, if Janis' death could do some good, it was this: the day to act has arrived. He'd known for more than three years now, as he watched the cloudbank become more and more unstable over Jersey City. By the day, more and more of the cloudbank turned to quickfall, which would neither be walked nor stood upon.

Gordon transferred his grasp on the burning lantern from his right hand to his left as he reached his destination and unlatched the centuries-old wooden door. Pushing it open, its hinges complained audibly. No one was allowed in this section of the building, not even himself. The simple act of breaching this corridor was punishable, not so far as demanding a Fall From Grace, but it was a significant crime nevertheless. Gordon made a mental note to review such old decrees and have them updated. But he'd think about that tomorrow.

The air here was stifling. So much accumulated dust, and so many dark, lingering memories. An entire high-rise floor where those with extraordinary powers, often a hundred or more such individuals, once conducted their unique, often dark pursuits. Nearly twenty years ago, all of them had either been executed or banished. It was said the entire floor was still haunted by their dark spirits. Stopping mid-step, Gordon spun about. Had he heard the faintest of footfalls from behind? *No, of course not,* he thought, pushing away such ridiculous notions. He stole a glance toward nearby shadows that seemed to be moving and swaying in ominous and exaggerated ways. *Mind trickery,* he thought.

Gordon's lantern flared when he entered the suite of rooms once inhabited by the late High Priestess Lark Kincaid. He glanced at the heavy velvet draperies, covering the windows, and at the ornate tapestries adorning the walls, depicting various distant times in history, both collecting dust now. The Kincaid legacy was one filled with centuries of strange magic and sorcery. *Rubbish,* he thought. Nothing of the occult world took place back then. There was nothing that couldn't be explained by science.

Just as some humans were genetically more adept at perceiving the variety of shades and colors of the cloudbank, a few fortunate others could also subtly draw upon the unique elemental properties of Strongzine, Stradamine, and Starlox. It all came down to basic physics: How those strange and amazing otherworldly elements reacted. *No, not just reacted, but counteracted,* he thought, *to the presence of an electrical discharge.* That was why there was no technology about, why there never could be. But the human brain was a mass of electrical discharges—synapses firing millions upon millions of times daily.

Fortunately, the discharge was not nearly robust enough to call forth resulting lighting bolts from the cloudbank. Yet it was certainly adequate enough for select individuals to forge a sort of intimate relationship with it, an inter-playing of energetics where forces of gravity could be ever so subtly manipulated. Not magic, just science. But even knowing all of that didn't keep Gordon's lantern-wielding hand from starting to tremble uncontrollably. Last night, he had secretly commissioned the most abhorrent of all Skylander crimes. It would surely mean a death sentence for him, if discovered.

In retrospect, Gordon wondered if he had made a terrible mistake. *After all,* he thought, *it was put there for a reason.* Perhaps so, though he still deemed it was necessary at the time, the only way to ward-off the use of magic within the Skylander realms. The *Sùilean Uamhasach*—the terrible eye—had ensured for twenty years that any high priest or priestess would be powerless, unable to perform any kind of wizardry within the Skylander realms of Jersey City and Manhattan. It ensured peace—a balance of power between all the clans—and its placement set in motion the ousting of the Macbeth clan and their centuries of overbearing dominance. Heavily guarded by the

Dorcha Poileas, the beautiful, sapphire-glass meteorite dated back to the Ruin Event, and had been displayed upon a high pedestal within the Chrysler Building. Gordon's heavy influence over the Dorcha Poileas, plus the well-timed break that left the meteorite momentarily unguarded, were all that was needed for the hulking Grounder men to abscond away with the large stone. By now, they had carried it below cloud level, where it would be well hidden, its energetic influences now properly shielded.

Gordon, swiping at his dripping snotty nose with his hand, wiped the wet mucus residue onto his nightclothes. Standing upright, he again pondered the previous evening's burglary. Word had not yet spread of the theft. All too likely, the Manhattan clans were conspiring to keep it quiet. If they had it their way, they would never spread the news to the Jersey City clans, because as Gordon knew all too well, they looked upon him and his city as inferior. He stared down at the floor, as if he could see the well-hidden meteorite secured over a thousand feet below.

Gordon briefly wondered how long it would take before the aftereffects from the meteorites removal would take. It needed to happen soon. Jersey City's quickfall patches were spreading, and worsening conditions would soon make this entire realm uninhabitable. Attending to the twenty-year absence of High Priests or Priestesses was now more essential than ever. The very thought of the power that they would afford him made Gordon smile.

The self-appointed CloudKing moved farther into the complex of abandoned rooms, again struck by the level of luxury in which Lark Kincaid had lived. Each one of those supposed mystics had been both adored and feared in Skylander society, and allowed to live like royalty. But that same power they'd once yielded over CloudMasters and CloudKings alike eventually led to their demise. All too often, their powers became a liability, the worst of all prevailing evils.

Gordon soon found the one room in particular he'd set out to locate on this somber, sleepless night. He used the flame of his lantern to light up another, mounted high up on the wall. With the room now better illuminated, he noticed the library walls were paneled with dark Ragoon planks, and that the three outfacing, floor-to-ceiling windows had been replaced with beautifully intricate stained glass pictorials. Gordon raised his lantern to better make out the glass images. Some kind of battle seemed to be in progress. He confirmed as much seeing a beautiful warrior woman—her wild hair the color of a blazing setting sun—wielding a raised, fully-extended rackstaff. A lightning bolt was shooting out from its spear-like tip. In the distance, a ragged and smoldering hole was depicted with incredible detail in the glass cloudbank, with throngs of enemy combatants— kilted men and women—falling through to their imminent demise. The pictographs were a sobering reminder of just how dangerous a path that Gordon now walked. Was resurrecting such potential calamity upon them worth it? *But do I have a choice? Who else has the power to move the cloudbank—to save my city?*

As Gordon moved to the center of the room, he pondered whether Lark's very spirit still resided within the suite's four walls. Perhaps she was standing right next to him, waiting for him to do exactly what he'd come for. He swallowed hard and tried not to think about it, reminding himself he was a man of science and not mysticism.

Built-in shelves took up one entire wall, holding a countless number of books undoubtedly outlawed for their mystic themes eons ago. But it was a tall sideboard table against the back wall that captured his full attention. Made of Ragoon wood, with glass on its sides and top, it stood four feet tall and three feet deep, large enough to hold the stack of big leather-bound tomes that sat atop it. Decision made, Gordon quickly moved across to the sideboard then turned the top tome toward him so he could read the gold-embossed lettering. **Kincaid Lineage and Genealogy**

Putting that one aside, he read the letters on the next one. **Conjuring Disciplines**

Gordon raised a brow. That certainly sounded interesting, but it wasn't what he was looking for. He smiled when he read the embossed lettering on the third book. **Skylander Maps and Routes**

He hesitated before opening the leather-bound cover. *No— I've already come this far.* Turning it over, he took in the first colorful and intricate graphical map depiction of the Skylander world. Hand-drawn, pen and ink illustrations instantly provided a rare perspective of the Skylander realms beyond the borders of northeast America. Drawn from information gathered by pigeon messengers and travelers on foot, these maps were an extremely limited commodity, and many Grounders and Skylanders alike lived in complete ignorance to their existence. At first glance, Gordon noted there were easily fifty Skywalker realms around the world. Many were impossible to reach because of the dangerous, deadly oceans that stood between them, yet there were others much closer, such as the high-rise metropolises in Toronto and Detroit. On turning the page, this time both his brows arched upward. It was a geographical representation of North America's mountain ranges, which facilitated a number of other Skylander realms. Closest were the Adirondacks. Something illegible was written atop White Mountain, he noticed, and then later crossed out. *Not a good sign, being crossed out.* He dragged a forefinger across the page, coming to a stop at the highest peak in western

North Carolina, an area circled in red grease pencil. Perhaps Lark. Inscribed were the words *High Priest Dwaine Kincaid*. Gordon tapped his finger several times atop the name. He'd heard that name before, a relative of Lark's. Wasn't he one of the first ousted? Yes . . . maybe her brother, or perhaps an uncle. Definitely a dark soul, that one. Gordon remembered that much of past history.

Gordon was aware his heart rate had doubled, perhaps tripled. Had the Kincaid high priests and priestesses found solace among those mountain folk after their ejection from society? Did this distant location, so boldly circled in red, provide for a society much like theirs? If so, he would bring one or more of those so-called magicians back to Jersey City.

He turned back to the three stained glass windows, and the beautiful rackstaff-wielding warrior, who now seemed to be looking directly at him. Soon, Skylanders of both Jersey City and Manhattan would become one people, united under Gordon as CloudKing. But first, the issue of local cloudbank density needed to be addressed; there was so much quickfall. Moving the cloudbank back into position—perhaps even strengthening it further—would be their first order of business. Gordon wasn't quite sure how it worked, but hell, they could take some of it from Manhattan if that's what needed to be done. He didn't care, just as long they saved his city. Briefly, he wondered how much enticement Dwaine Kincaid and his ilk would need to get them here. As CloudKing of Jersey City and Manhattan combined, there was much he could offer.

Gordon Folais shrugged as he closed the book, placing it securely under one arm. First thing tomorrow, he'd assemble a team of skilled Cloudwalkers to start the long journey south across the cloudbank to the high peaks of North Carolina. Once there, they could later send back a carrier pigeon with news of their discovery. They would intuitively know not to return here should their mission be unsuccessful. His Cloudwalkers would throw themselves into a patch of quickfall before disappointing their CloudKing.

Quickfall. Gordon's thoughts returned to Janis, and tears began welling in his eyes again, impairing his vision, which was probably for the best. For as he departed the library of the late High Priestess Lark Kincaid, the wall-mounted lamp flame suddenly fluttered out. The remaining tomes, lying in disarray atop the sideboard table, slid back to their centermost position then restacked themselves—one on top of the other—in a far more orderly fashion than he'd left them.

Chapter 17

Misty sat quietly upon the floor, her legs drawn up, both arms wrapped around her knees. The Romano's grotto was surprisingly quiet, even for such an early hour. Typically, Aurora's father and two brothers would be bustling about, yelling this or that—making jokes and throwing insults—but not today. They'd already left, attending to what remained of her broken family's harvest. They would return home late in the day to start work tilling their own larger field of crops.

Misty tried not to think about the awful happenings of the previous day, but the mental image of her father being mercilessly flogged kept rising up and lingering, like steam above a boiling pot. Her negative feelings for Deacon Terrence Lasher went far beyond mere words. Hatred and loathing didn't come anywhere close to expressing what she was feeling. And then there was her mother's misfortune. Unlike her poor father, whose wounds would heal with time, Astrid would endure a different kind of torture, one that would last the rest of her life. *Where is she now? Has that repulsive, evil man already had his way with her?* Misty wondered.

She watched as Mrs. Romano attended to her father, now lying atop a mat on his stomach, his arms outstretched over his head. After she finished cleaning and disinfecting each of the wounds on his back, she said, "Let's get you sitting up, dear." She gently helped him, careful not to tear any of the previous day's sutures. She then proceeded to wrap his torso with several layers of clean bandages.

Apparently, Aurora was now awake too. Misty heard the clanging of pots and pans coming from the kitchen area. In her own home, the kitchen has in the same room as everything else besides the bedrooms, and Misty was still adjusting to all the extra space in the Romano family's house.

"That should do it for the time being," Mrs. Romano said, rising to her feet. She used her palms to wipe smooth the crease in the thick black fabric at the front of her dress. "Best I go see what Aurora is up to in the kitchen. Try as she might, everything she does leaves the skillet blackened to cinders. The poor girl is a terrible cook."

"Thank you, Mrs. Romano," said Misty, "for taking care of my father. For all you've done for us."

"Nonsense, it's what decent people do for one another, that's all."

"Can I ask you a question?"

"Of course, dear."

"Do you know where they took her? Where the deacon lives in the city?"

Mrs. Romano stared back, her expression more serious now. "Don't go there, Misty. Your mother is a survivor. She will make peace with her life as it is now, as the Purgeforth Scripture dictates. And you must do the same." She gestured toward Misty's father, now asleep on the thin mat. "Your father needs you. It will be a good week before he is strong enough to return home. Then the two of you will start over. Build a new life. You both will go on."

Just like that, the man gets away with what he's done? Misty slowly nodded her head, hoping that her true thoughts hadn't escaped onto her face. "I will try, I promise."

A minute or so later she heard Mrs. Romano having words with Aurora. The woman was right; Aurora was a terrible cook.

Misty knelt down next to her father and watched him sleep. His breathing was now steady and some color had returned to his cheeks. She placed a palm upon the wrapped bandages then leaned down next to him. "I love you, Father. I have to do this. I have to go find her. Get her away from him, so our family can be whole again. Please don't be mad, or ever think I've deserted you." She saw his eyes rapidly moving beneath his closed lids. Good—sleep was what he needed.

She rose to her feet and, like Mrs. Romano had done, used the palms of her hands to smooth away the creases in her own black dress.

The previous night, soon after Aurora had fallen asleep, Misty had packed a small satchel with some clean undergarments, enough food to last her two or three days if she was judicious, and her long coat and scarf. Also included were the tartan frock and the journal. Swinging the satchel over one shoulder, and moving as quietly as she could, she headed out of the Romano's grotto toward the same subway service-line corridor she and Aurora had traversed through just a few nights ago. How different her life had been before that night, she thought as she stepped into the dark tunnel.

Misty heard voices coming from up ahead. It was not uncommon for a young woman to be seen wandering around the subterranean tunnels alone this time of morning. But she was not just any young woman. Gossip concerning the Casper family would have spread like wildfire, all the juicy details of their predicament common knowledge amongst other Grounders in this part of the city. It would be best to stay out of sight.

Misty looked about for a place to hide, and spotted a darkened alcove some fifteen feet away on the right. She quickened her pace. As she ducked into the shadows, hoping she hadn't been spotted, Misty inched backward until her back was up against a metal door. Moments later, she watched a procession of identically dressed women wearing black, just like herself, but with black bonnets covering their heads, secured in place with ribbons tied into bows beneath their chins. With hands together, as if in prayer, one by one, the seven walked past, their profiles identical and their noses raised high in righteous superiority. These were no ordinary women, but Purgeforth Prioresses, religious devotees that served the Deacon. Misty listened to their murmured words, words she herself had been instructed to repeat thousands of times in her young lifetime.

". . . and thus contrite, we abhor the many desperate ways of sin. So while we are alive, while eating, drinking, sleeping, the vain delights elude us, cannot tempt us. Thus awareness comes, avoiding perpetual night. We dispatch such vain pleasures unto an eternal flight to hell, into the arms of the dark master."

Only then did Misty consider their presence, their being here. They were coming for her. It made perfect sense. She would be expected to become one of them, a Purgeforth Prioress whose life was dedicated to religious Scripture. It would be a life of piety and celibacy; she could never marry, or have a family of her own. For a brief moment, she thought about showing herself to them and offering herself freely. She had grown up with Purgeforth, she knew that the Prioresses were cared for and protected. She would no longer be poor, or hungry. And being a Prioress would offer her a much better chance of being able to see her mother again. She came to her senses and shook herself of the thought. *No! I would rather die than let the deacon—the man who has destroyed my life and so many others—win.*

Misty thought about her plan, which wasn't so much about planning as it was about hope. She hoped that she could make her way to the streets above without being accosted, and then find a building that provided access to that realm above the cloud. She hoped that she would be able to find Conn, the Skywalker who had made her a promise.

"What I need to do is stop thinking so much," she said aloud.

She stole a glance around the corner, the procession of women now off in the distance. Hurrying from the alcove, she double-timed it down the corridor. A different kind of procession was headed her way, but they weren't interested in her. There were no fewer than ten large rats in the line that scurried her way, single file. Rats were one of the few species, other than humans, that had survived these hundreds of years since the Ruin Event. Meat and protein hard to come by, except for them. Wild rats tended to be stringy and tough, but there were grotto farms that caged rats, bred them, and fattened them up for eventual slaughter, and Misty's mouth watered at the thought. As the rats scuttled past, Misty's stomach grumbled loudly, reminding her that she'd slipped out of the Romano's grotto before she had a chance to eat breakfast. *I should have brought a weapon*, she thought belatedly, watching them fade away into the darkness of the tunnel. Misty had never hunted for her meat before, but this would have been a good time to start.

Misty mounted the last steps, exiting the subway entrance and blinking in the increased light of street-level Manhattan.

There were far more people milling about the city now that it was morning. Although direct sunlight never made its way down through the cloudbank, there was still enough of a glow that she felt the sun's warmth just the same. Misty pulled her scarf out from the satchel and wrapped it around her nose and mouth to protect herself from the ever-present acid drizzle. She then pulled up her oversized hood, which obscured her face even more. Heading south down the sidewalk, she became just one more faceless dark figure amongst dozens of others.

Three nights ago, standing on this very street, she had watched the kilted Skylander carry the dead body away on his shoulders. He'd turned left into what she assumed was an alley-way. It made sense that he would take the most direct route upward. She suddenly felt lightheaded, wishing she'd eaten something before heading out. She passed by two large men. Their dark, hooded faces turned slightly, taking her in as they passed.

Misty crossed the street, and then slowed, fairly certain she'd come to the same alleyway. It was a narrow space, no more than twenty feet across, and all of the buildings were black with rubber shingle siding. She strained to find an entrance that would allow her some way of going up. The concrete under her feet was cracked and strewn with all sorts of junk: rusted pipes, a turned-over trash bin, and a rusted-out metal cube she assumed must have been some sort of technology before the Ruin. She spotted another small shape on the ground and nearly shrieked as she recognized a bloated, rotting human hand.

Misty stepped around the disembodied appendage, averting her eyes and trying to control her breathing, and hoped she wouldn't discover the rest of whoever the hand had belonged to. Street level was a dangerous place, and she felt sobered by the reminder. The deeper into the alleyway she went, the more junk she found strewn about. It seemed to have gotten darker too, and her imagination ran wild at the thought of what terrible things lurked in the nearby shadows. Stacks, then more stacks of rusted-metal items rose along both sides of the alleyway. She slowed as she spotted what lay ahead. A solid wall stood tall before her, and her heart sank, realizing she'd come—literally— to the end of the road. She looked left and then right for some kind of doorway entrance, but found none. Turning around, ready to head back the way she'd come, she hesitated. Something was just now registering. She spun back around to better examine the shingled wall. *There it is!* The thin, almost imperceptible seam that ran around the wall off to the right was almost impossible to see, but Misty had been looking for it. It could very possibly be the outline of a door, and as she approached it, she became more certain.

But how do I get in?

There didn't seem to be a handle or a knob of any sort. Looking down, she saw an arc-like scrape along the concrete. She smiled. At least she knew which way the door opened. At waist-level, she noticed that one of the rubber shingles protruded farther than the others. Tentatively, she reached out a hand and gave it a little tug. Secured at the top, it easily swung up—like a flap. Behind it was a doorknob. Grasping it tightly, Misty turned the knob. The door was heavy, and pulling it open required use of both arms. It was spring-mounted, and she was forced to prop the door open with one foot in order to be able to see into the blackness ahead. Within moments she noticed the dim outline of ascending steps on a stairway. She stepped forward, and the door slammed shut behind her.

Misty was more than a little accustomed to the dark, living a life a hundred feet below the streets of Manhattan. To gain her bearings as her vision adjusted; she extended both arms out sideways to feel for the nearest wall. But it was the sensation moving higher, away from the ground that was uncomfortable for her. *Going back is not an option,* she thought, *and even if it were, what would I be going back to?*

Her arms outstretched, Misty felt for the wall on the left. As her fingers grazed the rough surface, which was also a tad moist, fragments of cement came loose and tumbled to the floor. Imperfections in the rubber shingles combined with the mighty battering ram of time had allowed acid rain to infiltrate the building's defenses, weakening its very structure. She wondered how long it would be before this building suffered the same fate as so many others, crashing down from the cloudbank in a deadly heap of dust and rubble. She shuffled forward in the darkness until her right foot made contact with the riser on the first step. Up she went, first slowly then faster as she gained confidence. Soon, she was taking two steps at a time. At every thirty-third step—she'd been counting—the staircase leveled out onto a right-hand-side, ten-foot-long landing, before the staircase would rise again for another thirty-three steps. Up, up, and around she went. She liked the echoing sound her shoes made, bouncing off the walls. Somehow it made her feel less alone. Perspiration soon began to drip down the nape of her neck and the center of her back. Gasping for breath, she decided to take a short break. *How long have I been climbing? Ten minutes? Fifteen?* God, how did people do this centuries ago, and on a daily basis?

Glancing around the landing, she realized she could see everything in far more detail now. She didn't think it was some-thing as simple as her eyes having better adjusted to the dark. Looking directly above, the stairwell was indeed lighter. She now could make out the winding stairwell, and the flickering light of lanterns that hung on the walls of the upper landings. Misty figured the stairs went up another twenty flights. She wiped her brow with her sleeve. Stopping mid-motion, she noticed a door on the adjacent wall. *Of course.* Although she hadn't seen or noticed any before in the dark, each landing would have to have such a door. Misty stared at it, tempted to see where it led. *No, where I need to go now is straight up. Into the light.*

Chapter 18

Conn awoke to Graham Gould's concerned face, hovering right above him. Trapped between his full lips was the stem of a pipe. Aromatic tobacco smoke lazily rose from the glowing bowl up into the air.

"Oh good, you're awake. You took a nasty tumble. Been out cold for close to ten minutes now."

Confused, Conn looked about the smoky room, and realized he was flat on his back, on the floor. "I dinnae understand. What . . . what happened to me?" He rubbed at a substantial knot on the back of his aching head.

Gould offered Conn his hand. "Come on, let's get you up off that dusty floor."

Conn took the older man's hand and, with his help, managed to rise to his feet. Swaying, he reached out for the rack-smith's worktable to steady himself.

"Here, drink some of this."

Conn stared at the ancient-looking metal flask held out to him in the old man's hand. "Um . . . no, that's okay. I'm fine."

"Drink!"

Conn did as told and took a swig. The warm 26th century version of Scotch whiskey burned the back of his throat. Across the room, the old racksmith was using a long pole, a brass hook at its end, to secure an out-of-reach rackstaff. The same dark staff that Conn had attempted to grab earlier. "You ken," said Conn, rubbing his head again. "That pole would have been handy ten minutes ago."

"Aye, but I needed to see if the two of you had any chemistry," Gould replied. His eyes twinkled with excitement, in a way that reminded Conn painfully of Dob.

"Well, there certainly was something in that one. Maybe a different staff, aye? One that doesn't knock me on my arse would be better suited."

"Rubbish! You'll want a rackstaff that is more than mere mechanics or functionality." The old man swung the now-ensnared rackstaff around and lowered it enough to grab hold of it. "See? No reaction. Clearly, not meant for me." The racksmith smiled, revealing a mouthful of crooked, brown-tinged teeth. The pole swung around, the rackstaff still swinging from its lanyard. Gould, from the other end, waved it closer to Conn. "Let's try this again."

Conn took in the rackstaff's detail, now that he was close enough to reach out and grab it himself. It really was beautiful. A rich mahogany color, he could see the stained, swirling grain in the wood, and the intricately carved paw that had been worn smooth over time. He took another swig from the racksmith's flask before setting it down on the table. Clenching his teeth, he reached for the dangling rackstaff.

Conn went rigid, his eyes wide open and fixed. Though he managed to stay standing this time, the rackstaff sent an energized jolt coursing through his entire body. This rackstaff possessed something powerful. *Something magical*, thought Conn. And in an instant, he was transported somewhere else.

Another place.

Another time.

The sun was high in the sky with a strong wind coming up from the south. Conn stood upon the cloudbank, though some part of him knew he wasn't himself. The surrounding Manhattan skyscape appeared all-wrong. Almost twice as many high-rise buildings surrounded him. With a quick glance to either side he saw he was among many others. Perhaps two hundred of the Brataich clan, consisting of men mostly, and they wielded half-extended rackstaffs, the sharp blades of the lockwoods glinting in the sun. The very same deep-mahogany rackstaff with the intricately carved paw was grasped tightly in his own left hand. A distant, primal-sounding yell came from beyond.

The man closest to Conn, whoever he was, said, "Aye, and so it begins . . . for home and honor. Defeat is not an option!" The man, who was nearly a half-head taller than Conn, sneered toward those who were rapidly approaching from the north. Three single-file columns of men, an attacking force equal to if not greater than their own. Their kilts' distinctive tartan colors of royal blue, with narrow lines of yellow and green and orange, made it clear that they were under attack by none other than the Macbeth clan. A clan long gone in Conn's time.

"Come, Darryl. Today we become heroes!" The big man let loose his own primal scream, then strode away with his rackstaff held high over his head. Conn, or Darryl, as he was called here, followed close on his heels, running along a narrow cloudbank path he didn't recognize. Long lines of Brataich warriors, hollering various war cries, raced across the bank to meet the oncoming enemy. He could hear the beating of his own heart pounding in his ears. The large man, his friend, who he somehow knew was named Banyan, was the first to encounter the attacking enemy, although other enemy lines were now converging too. The sharp tip of an enemy's rackstaff suddenly appeared, thrusting out through Banyan's broad back. As crimson blood spurted from

the wound, Conn felt its wetness splatter onto his own face. As Banyan's body toppled over to the side, Conn—using a two-handed swiping motion, called a cruge strike—brought the blade of his weapon across the exposed neck of his friend's killer. The man's head slid from his shoulders with little resistance. The headless corpse toppled onto a quickfall patch, where the body disappeared into the mist below. In a flash, two more Macbeth warriors were upon him. He heard the whirling sound of lockwoods slicing through the air.

An instant later he was back within Racksmith Graham Gould's cluttered workspace. The old man, still standing on the far side of his workbench, wore an odd expression: a mixture of curiosity, and something else. Fear.

Chapter 19

I t seemed the higher Misty climbed, the less sure of herself she became. It seemed incredibly unlikely that she'd be able to find one Skylander in an unfamiliar realm, and much more likely that she'd be caught and punished the second she stepped foot into their world.

It's too late for second thoughts, she admonished herself as she came to a stop midway up the present flight of stairs. But that knowledge didn't stop her from having them. She glanced down into the darkness below. Before she could make a definitive decision to go up or back down, she heard multiple voices on the stairs above her, and the clomping of feet descending. She quickly slipped her shoes off and hurried back down, stepping lightly on her tiptoes. Reaching the landing, she stopped then glanced back up, and instantly regretted the decision to do so. Two men wearing flowing dark cloaks were quickly descending the flight of stairs right above her. They were close enough to easily catch her. She also realized if she could see them, they most certainly could see her too.

"You there . . . Halt!"

Instinctively she looked back up the stairs and made eye

contact with one of her pursuers, a young man with a scar that ran down the left side of his face.

She hurried down two flights of stairs as fast as she could. Quickly, she darted over to that floor's access door. Although it opened easily, its hinges made far more noise than she'd counted on. Surely, the two men had heard the loud screech, echoing off the walls.

Running, Misty found herself in a narrow hallway. The flanking walls were drab, with swatches of either peeling or missing paint. Wispy threads of some sort of fabric material lay on the floor, but it looked nothing like the woven mats they kept on the floors at home. The hallway changed direction, now heading off to the right. She quickly continued on before coming to an abrupt stop. Directly in front of her was an immense window that looked outward. All around its edges were the corrosive signs of acid mist intrusion. Why the window hadn't been shingled over, she had no idea. Perhaps an over-sight. Beyond the outer pane of glass was nothing but a bright-gray mist—the inside of the cloudbank—somewhere within the hundred-foot-span between the bottom of the cloudbank and its top layer. Considering the odd sight, she realized she had never stood before a building's window before. *How could I have? My entire life has been spent living beneath the ground.*

The door around the corner behind her, the very door she'd just entered through, squeaked open. Misty had heard stories of what Skylanders would do to Grounders if they were caught venturing into any one of the Midtown high-rise buildings. *What was I thinking, coming up here?*

She heard approaching murmurs of hushed voices. Unable to grasp their words, she quickened her pace and arbitrarily chose to go left.

She passed, one after another, what must have been indi-vidual living quarters. Surprised, she noticed that most of the homes were in squalor—not all that different from any number of Grounder grottos below ground. She saw a makeshift bed that was little more than a few spindly planks lying upon wooden crates. Pieces of a ChemBurn stove sat upon a burned and blackened floor. She passed the remnants of a tethered clothesline, hanging lifeless like a dead septent. She wondered how many had lived here? Dozens and dozens, she guessed. Was this how all Skylanders lived? Why had they abandoned this space?

Another door lay just ahead. As she reached for the knob, the door flew open. The voices behind her were growing even louder. "Check that way. I'll look down here," a deep male voice said.

Misty stared down at a small boy she figured must be about nine or ten. He had a mop of unkempt black hair, small pleasant features, and a scattering of freckles across his upper cheeks and nose. He wore dark green trousers, with red suspenders holding them up, and a tan-colored shirt that was stained in places. All of his clothes showed signs of much wear and tear, and small holes were visible along the neckline of his shirt.

Frozen in place, Misty continued to stare down at the boy. He must have seen the desperation in her eyes, because he put a finger to his lips. Opening the door wider, he signaled for her to hurry inside.

Misty gathered up the hem of her dress and scurried past the boy, who closed the door gently behind her. She watched him twist the lock on the knob. Again he gestured, a finger to his lips, whispering, "This way! Hurry!"

Together, they fled down another hallway. Much larger sectioned off rooms were off to the right—more modest living quarters. The same view of the gloomy cloudbank was visible beyond another large window that should have been covered by rubber shingles centuries ago. She felt a cool breeze on her cheeks and only then noticed the jagged gap off to the side that was open to the outside world. This old building was disintegrating.

The boy made a left through a gray metal door. The flame on the lone lantern flickered that hung from the wall flickered brightly for a moment then settled down. Gone were any scraps of carpet as they crossed a cement floor. Misty saw a series of electrical breaker panels on the walls. Farther on, large metal pipes traversed horizontally across the ceiling; some of them angled downward and ran vertically along the walls.

Misty could no longer hear her pursuers' voices, or their footfalls, and was starting to wonder just how far into the bowels of this building the kid was taking her. Making one last turn to the left, they entered into another small, albeit well-lit room, where two lanterns burned brightly. On the floor was a carefully made bed, comprised mostly of ragged blankets and filthy pillows. The walls were adorned with framed pictures, photographs, paintings, and other images, plus so many other various items that little of the wall could be seen. She noticed a broken wooden stick of some sort, and a round disk. She knew from her own explorations at street level that the latter was a car's hubcap. A window sign said *Coors*, and an antique flat-panel television—which of course hadn't seen use in centuries—was nestled up on the wall between a scattering of other items she didn't immediately recognize. The boy, it seemed, was a collector of anything and everything.

Turning her gaze back on the boy, she said, "Thank you. You probably saved my life. My name is—"

"I ken who you are."

Misty shook her head, thinking, *that's impossible.* Before she could speak, he said, "I was there. You and that other girl . . . and a dead naked bloke, splattered there on the sidewalk." Offering up a crooked smile, he said, "My name is Brig. Aye, and I already ken your name is Misty."

That threw her. She tried to recall if she'd seen anyone else that night. No, she was sure she hadn't. "Okay . . . Brig," she said slowly. "Why did you help me just now? Not that I'm ungrateful, but—"

He shrugged and ignored her question. "Tell me, why you up here anyway?" Shooting a glance over to the door, he added, "It's not safe for a Grounder girl to be wandering around up here. What were you thinking, doing such a stupid thing?"

Misty contemplated on that for a moment. *Can I trust this kid?* "You live here? Like, all alone, you live in this room? Where are your parents?"

"I don't have any," said Brig casually. "Not that I know of, anyway. I'm what's called an orphan."

"I know what an orphan is."

Brig shrugged. "Sorry. Cannae be too sure. Everyone kens Grounders are pretty stupid."

Misty pursed her lips, but ignored the slight. "You still haven't answered my question. Why did you help me?"

"I'm not sure I will help you. Why should I? What's in it for me?"

"I'm looking for that young man," Misty said, taking a page out of Brig's book and ignoring his question in favor of another. "The tall Cloudwalker I was speaking with on the street. Conn. Do you know where I can find him?"

Brig narrowed his eyes. "He wouldn't be interested in speaking with you. He's important. The son of a CloudMaster, he is . . . "

"I don't care about that. He made me a promise, and if you were there, lurking around in the dark, you would have heard him make that promise." Misty raised her brows. "Then again, he may be a scoundrel. A liar who does not keep his word."

"Take that back! Conn is the most honorable person in all the world!"

"Oh, all the world, huh? That's quite a statement."

"Aye, but he won't have anything to do with the likes of you. A Grounder girl who has no business being above the cloudbank."

"I can give you three pennies if you bring me to him."

"I already told you, he wouldn't be interested in a simple Grounder girl."

"I don't need him to be interested in me, I need him to fulfill his promise."

"What do you want from him?"

"That's my business. Will you help me or not? I'm sure there are others willing to take my coin for such a simple task."

"Make it four pennies and I might consider it."

Misty, expecting him to negotiate up to five, pursed her lips as if weighing the increase. "Fine. But you'll keep me safe up there. Don't abandon me. Is that the deal?"

"Aye, that's the deal. But I want to see the coins first."

Misty, nodding, separated the coins in her pocket and withdrew four pennies, the minted words and images worn smooth with time, then showed them to him on her open palm. Truth was, it was a hefty portion of Misty's life savings, and she felt sick at the thought of spending so much at once. "I keep my promises," she said warningly to Brig. "You'd best do the same."

"Or what? Maybe you should be careful making threats," Brig said, with a smirk. He looked her over. "Ken, you can't just go walking around up there looking like that. Not without a passage medallion." Turning, he knelt down to an ancient looking two-drawer cabinet. He held up several long chain necklaces, inspecting the wooden medallions on each. "This one will do." He stood and held it out to her. "I'll be wanting it back; you're only borrowing it, ye ken?"

"Sure. Just borrowing it." Suddenly she found herself out of breath, feeling the excitement of the moment brewing within. *Is this really happening?*

"Well, don't just stand there, put it on."

Misty couldn't help but smile at the kid's cheekiness. She pulled the chain over her head and then straightened the medallion. "Like this?"

"Aye, how else would you wear it?" He moved to the door. "Look, stay behind me, but don't be treading too close on my heels. And if I signal you to stay back or hide, do so quickly."

Misty nodded rapidly, too excited and nervous to speak.

Brig opened the door and peered out. Without looking back, he motioned for her to follow. "Close the door behind you. I have a lot of important things I don't want pinched."

He dashed away, and within minutes they were back within the stairwell. Brig waited for her to catch up to him on the landing. "Look, Grounders are not supposed to be anywhere without an accompanying Cloudwalker."

"You're not one of those?" Misty asked. "I thought all Skylanders could walk on the cloudbank."

"Me? I'm just a sept. You really dinnae ken anything, do ye?"

She shook her head. She thought she'd learned all she needed to know from the journal in her parents' room, but she was quickly realizing how many gaps there were in her knowledge, and didn't mind letting Brig know it.

"We'll need a story, a reason why you are up here alone. Let's just say you got separated from your flock."

Misty had no idea what a *flock* meant, but she nodded anyway.

"Just let me do the talking. The less you say the better."

"Got it."

"We're just about at the top of the building. Hang back here and let me see if anyone's out there."

"You know where he is? Where we'll find this Conn boy?"

"I usually can find him without too much problem. Predictable, he is. Stay here."

Misty watched the boy hurry up the last flight of stairs and disappear around the bend. When a door opened, an incredibly bright swath of light was cast onto the wall of an adjacent stairwell. Instinctively, she raised a hand to shield her eyes.

Brig, impatient, called down to her, "Get on up here, quick!"

Misty nervously gulped in one last steadying breath. Up the flight of stairs she went, her mind reeling, not knowing what to expect. Stepping onto the last floor landing, she made a right-hand turn and faced the open doorway. There was so much light there, she could barely make out Brig's waiting silhouette.

"Are you coming, or are you just going to stand there like a blithering *bowbag*?"

"I'm coming!" Misty hurried over to the open doorway then stopped and looked out. As a gasp came from her parted lips, she unconsciously brought both hands to her mouth. "Oh my God . . ." Tears filled her eyes.

Once, Misty had seen an open patch of quickfall from below. A thin beam of sunlight had streamed through it, a beacon that dropped a thin tunnel of light down to some far away part of the city. A small group of Grounders had gathered to see it, pushing at one another in their vain efforts to get just a little bit closer. The group had remained for almost an hour, watching and waiting until the cloudbank repaired itself and the light faded. It was the brightest and most beautiful light Misty had ever seen, but it didn't hold a candle to the sight she looked upon now. Feeling weak in the knees, she reached out to Brig for balance. When she spoke, her words were little more than a whisper. "So this is what heaven looks like? This is what the sun looks like?"

Looking all around her, her cheeks wet with tears, Misty admired the cloudbank, so pristine and white. It was like something out of a fairytale, like in the ancient books she'd hidden in her room. She marveled at the buildings, at how they shimmered in the sunlight, so different from the black rubber-tiled structures beneath the cloudbank. Even at street level in the city, her view was always blocked by the hulking, dark forms of buildings, but here above the clouds, she could see for miles. "Oh Brig," she breathed, "look at that sky. It's so blue. Everything is so bright."

People in vivid-colored outfits moved all about the cloudbank. Women in long, elegant dresses, and men dressed in well-fitting trousers. Some of the men and women were wearing knee-length kilts, in varying bright tartan plaids. Their long-sleeved white shirts blazed bright in the sunshine. She noticed their long staffs. These were Cloudwalkers. All in all, it was a dazzling spectacle, far beyond anything she could ever imagine.

As her eyes adjusted to more light than she'd ever seen, Misty continued to stare out at the realm in front of her, face uplifted to receive the sunbeams that warmed her cheeks. Beside her, Brig tugged on her sleeve. "You ken, Misty, in the light, you dinnae really look much like a Grounder. At least, not like any Grounder I've ever seen."

Chapter 20

Conn left the racksmith's workspace frustrated with himself. The old coot hadn't allowed him to negotiate the price down so much as a dime. Subsequently, Conn's purse was substantially lighter than it was when he'd entered. He was quite sure few others had ever paid anywhere near so much for a rackstaff. He was sorely tempted to turn right around and get the coins back. He could find another staff from one of the other racksmiths in Manhattan, but he knew deep down he'd never find a rackstaff more suited to him than this one.

As he strode down the corridor, the fully collapsed rackstaff hanging from its tether gently bumped against his hip. The wound on his back ached, as did the bump on his head from his fall in Gould's quarters. He tried to make sense of that incredibly real vision he'd experienced. *Was that only my wild imagination at work, or did it really happen?* Had there really been a Cloudwalker warrior named Darryl, who once possessed this very same rackstaff? Conn was tempted to make a detour over to the library's Hall of Records. Lineage of a rackstaff was fairly straightforward and well documented. Inscribed into the

Ragoon wood, along the side of each paw, was a distinctive signature. With every new owner, often a direct descendant of the previous owner, records would be updated. The racksmith had suggested the library be his next stop, saying, "Get to know exactly who wielded this staff before you, son. I assure you, it will change your perspective."

But that would have to wait for another time. Right now, Conn was already running late. He wanted to catch the Folais clan contingent before they headed back across the cloudbank to Jersey City. He needed to speak with Lili, to try and ease her anger. Secretly, he wanted to find out if their marriage-to-be was still on, and after the events of their previous meeting, more than a small part of him hoped that perhaps the wedding could be canceled. As far as his father was concerned, their betrothal continued, but he needed to speak to her one on one. He'd seen hatred flare in those dark eyes of hers this morning; she clearly didn't want this any more than he did. Yes, he'd talk to her, and get the lay of the land, so to speak.

Two doors down from the old racksmith's enterprise, Conn approached another door. He read the polished brass nameplate: **Professor Claremont Dob**

Apparently, no one had yet had the heart to clean out his rooms. Conn wondered if anyone had dared enter the professor's sanctum since his accident? Conn pictured his old friend and mentor now standing next to him, but the image he conjured was ethereal and faint, nothing like the powerful and purposeful presence that Dob had exuded in real life.

Conn had been in these rooms hundreds of times; he was the closest thing Dob had to an apprentice and had always been welcome here. The door was unlocked, but of course Dob had every intention of returning that day.

Conn swung the door open and stepped inside, closing it behind him as he took in the large, familiar space that was both cluttered yet strangely organized. Dob's sanctuary reflected the mental state of its chief occupant: compartmentalized and complex. The space was physically organized by classification of the science being conducted there. Three twenty-foot-long, waist-high benches segmented the room, while multiple end-to-end benches ran along the periphery. Cabinets were mounted onto the walls above the benches. To the left of the door was Dob's chemistry section; where he had performed experiments and taken notes on the properties of matter, and how substances interacted with energy. Of course, much of Dob's interest had to do with the elements of Strongzine, Stradamine, and Starlox, and their influences within the atmosphere and on existing matter. Lying atop the benches were heating plates, scale balances, various glassware, and various pieces of distillation and evaporation equipment. As a young boy, Conn remembered sitting at these benches, sometimes alone sometimes with other students, listening to Dob explain the often highly-complex experiments. He encouraged interaction and debate.

Conn remembered one particular morning, years past, when he must have been around nine years old. He was helping the professor work with compounds that were lighter than air; ones that had Starlox anti-gravitational properties. Suddenly, one of the lidded glass flasks began to rise off the workbench, and then another, and another. Soon, no fewer than twenty different colored flasks were rising and floating all around them. And then Dob, himself, was also elevating up-up-up off his stool. Within moments, he was six feet off the floor. Conn dropped the flask he had been holding, staring in awe, and it too floated up, leaking colorful liquids that stained the ceiling.

"Oh my, oh my!" Dob cried, his face serious for once. "Do something, laddie boy! Help me! Hurry!"

The boys leapt into action.

"What should we do?" Conn asked, now panicking and

becoming more frantic and dismayed with each passing moment. He reached for the professor, jumping to grab hold of Dob's hanging robes. The professor started to laugh so hard that tears streaked down his cheeks.

Only then did Conn realize it was all one big spectacular joke. One that probably had taken Dob's a number of hours to conjure up the previous night.

That was just one of a thousand scientific lessons Conn was sure not to forget. Now, gazing upward, he found there were still multi-colored chemical stains on the ceiling.

ChemBurn heating elements were still burning at various workbench stations. They gave Conn the feeling that Dob had simply stepped out—that he would return at any moment. He wished that were true.

Conn meandered along the row of Dob's botany experiments—mostly mushrooms that had been coaxed to grow bigger and plumper. They easily were five times their typical growth size. Next came the entomology section. An upside-down dead cockroach lay beneath the multiple lenses of Dob's most prized microscope. A nearby ChemBurn burner—its directed firelight magnified down to a pinpoint—was focused on the bug's abdomen. Conn leaned over the heavy brass microscope, with all its knobs and gears, and peered into the viewing lens. *Ah, that's right,* he recalled. *We were studying the effects of Starlox on the digestive system of blattodea genre insects.* He blinked, thinking he saw movement. There was movement—a kind of vibration of tissue—the cells impacted via molecular agitation. Excited, Conn looked up and said, "Dob! Come look at this . . ." But of course, Dob wasn't there. He felt like there was a rock stuck in his throat, and knew that it was time to go. Maybe someday it wouldn't hurt so much for Conn to be there. Upon leaving, he locked the door. He had his own key.

Taking a shortcut to the other side of the Chrysler building, he passed through one of several open sparring areas. From a variety of clans, fifty young boys and girls, each about fourteen or fifteen years of age, were assembled in ten neat rows. They were swinging their lockwoods in fast, downward arcs, and then defending.

"Step! Step! And Parry!" the instructor yelled. Hands on hips, he looked disgusted with his students' lackluster performance. The bearded, gray-haired man caught Conn's eye as he hurried along the far wall. "I've warned you, this isn't a shortcut, Mr. Brataich!"

"Sorry, sir!"

"Best you come back later, ye ken. We can work together with that new rackstaff of yours."

Is nothing I do kept private anymore? "Yes, Master Donahue. I promise." Conn noticed the students were watching him, all interest in posture and footwork procedures temporarily disrupted. Conn was famous among all the clans. As last year's overall champion of the Skylander Games, he was expected to lead the Brataich Clan team to victory again this year. But Conn had serious doubts he'd be ready in time. That deep slice he'd taken across his back from that bandit's knife was only days old. Rarely was there a time during the day when he wasn't aware of just how much it hurt to even move.

By the time Conn exited the Chrysler Building, the sun's position told him it was pushing on one o'clock. In spite of the burning pain across his back, he doubled his pace along the narrow path leading north. He'd spent too much time moping in Dob's rooms; he needed to catch the Folais Clan before they left.

"Conn!"

Brig, off in the distance, raised his hand, waving at him. Conn returned the wave then continued on his way.

"Conn! Come over here!"

"I cannae now, Brig. I'm in a hurry!"

"Conn, please! Come here!"

Conn knew the kid looked up to him, and he certainly appreciated that. But sometimes it was just too much. Annoyed, he slowed, glancing over to see what was so damn important. Standing close to the Drake building, the boy stood in the shadows next to a woman in shapeless dark clothing, clearly a Grounder. *Crap!* She'd obviously gotten separated from her flock. *What is so difficult about following behind the person right in front of you?* Irritation flooded through him. *The stupid numpty.*

Conn stared toward the distant horizon, but couldn't see the Folais contingent anywhere. With any luck, they hadn't left the Midtown area yet. Reluctantly, he changed course and hurried toward Brig and the Grounder. He slowed his pace the last few yards and, after catching his breath, took in her black dress, made of worn thick fabric. Their eyes met. He knew this girl, but up here in the sunlight, she looked nothing like the pasty Grounder he'd met days earlier on the dark wet streets below the cloudbank.

"Hello again. Um, do you remember me?" Misty asked.

Unable to find his voice, Conn nodded. Now, seeing her in the light of day, her lustrous auburn hair looked windswept instead of wild, her green eyes clear and inquisitive rather than scared. She was absolutely radiant.

"Aye, I remember you. What are you doing up here? What do you want?"

Noticing some of the light dim from her eyes, he regretted being such an ass. "You just look like you've stepped onto another planet?" he said, backtracking. "All wide-eyed and bewildered looking."

"Bewildered? So, you're saying what, I'm a simpleton?

Ingrate Grounder girl can't cope with being out in the sun. Little more than a troll, huh?"

"I didnae say that. But now that you bring it up . . ."

"Uh huh, well you're just as cocky and obnoxious as you were before."

He saw her glance, irritated, over to Brig, who seemed to be enjoying the exchange.

"If you're any example of how women are treated above the cloudbank, I've clearly made a mistake coming here." She stewed for a moment, then pointed off to the distance where a lone figure was slowly ambling across the cloudbank. "Brig, is that another Cloudwalker there, yonder? He looks like someone who would offer help to a person in need a bit of assistance." She leaned forward and squinted. "I have to say, he's a handsome one at that. "

Conn snickered. "Aye, he's a real charmer, too. That's Billy O'Clark. He has all but five teeth remaining in his mouth, and breath that could topple a building. He's also pushing seventy-five. But hey, let me call him over for you. Just a heads up, he's also partially deaf." Conn raised an arm high in the air and waved his hand back and forth in the direction of Billy O'Clark. He yelled, "Billy! Over here . . . Billy!"

"Put your arm down!"

Conn continued to wave at the elderly man who still hadn't noticed he was being hailed.

Misty stepped in closer to Conn and physically yanked his arm back down to his side. "You're beyond aggravating!"

"Just being of assistance. Isn't that what you said you—"

"Are you going to help me or not?"

He realized he was enjoying this, whatever *this* was. He looked down at her, into those probing green eyes of hers. Judging by the close-mouthed smile on her face and the color in her cheeks, she too looked to be enjoying *this*.

"She wants to ask you something," Brig said, clearly fed up with their banter.

Misty's smile faltered, looking for just the right words.

"Just spit it out, I won't bite."

"You said," she began, uncertain. "Your exact words down below were, 'Someday, I'll do you a favor back. Anything you want. Big or small.' Do you remember saying that?"

Unfortunately, he did. Conn nodded back.

"So the real question now is . . . are you a man of your word?"

"He is! Conn always keeps his word," Brig interjected, ever Conn's most staunch defender. "To say differently, it's an insult to both him and his clan."

"Relax, Brig, take a breath. She meant no insult, I'm sure," he responded as Misty continued to stare up with him with her captivating green eyes.

"I'm at your service, Ma'am."

Misty's eyes narrowed.

"I'm sorry, I mean, Misty. What exactly is it you want me to do?"

Nervously looking over at Brig, she said, "Maybe he shouldn't hear this."

"You can trust the kid," Conn said, even though he wasn't all that sure about that. "Speak freely."

"I want you to help me save my mother. She's been taken."

"Taken by whom."

"There's a man. He is well known on the ground, and above the law. He *is* the law. But he's bad—evil—though no one else would ever dare to say so. He damn near killed my father, whipped him to the bone. Then he took my mother against her will to make her his third wife."

"That's horrible," said Conn. "What is his name?"

"He is a high deacon. His name is—"

"Deacon Terrence Lasher." Conn blurted out. "Say no more, I ken this man. His reputation is well kent here above the cloudbank. And you are right, he is a dark soul. I saw him no more than three or four days past, very near where we are standing now."

"Then you'll help me?" Misty asked, her voice pleading. "Help me save my mother?"

"How? What do you expect me to do? Swoop down like some kind of caped superhero?"

"I don't know. I don't know anyone else who can help."

He saw the pain and desperation on her face as tears formed in her eyes. "Look, I didnae say I wouldn't help you. I will, I just dinnae ken how yet."

She stared up at him, as if studying his features—deciding if he was telling the truth. And then she smiled. A smile so true and honest it carried up into her eyes. *God, she's beautiful.* If Conn hadn't already agreed to help the girl, he would have now.

"I don't know where the deacon lives. I've asked around, but no one does," she said.

"I think I can find out. From what I remember, he lives above the ground in a building."

"Up here?" she asked.

"No, below the cloudbank. But rescuing your mother isn't the only issue. What will you do after?"

"I don't know. We can't go home and act like nothing happened. He'd come for her again. And for me, and for my father, too, this time."

Conn nodded. "You'd have to escape to one of the other quadrants beyond the local rampart. Are you prepared to do that?"

Misty shrugged, resigned. "What other choice do we have?"

"None that I can think of. Look, I'm going to have to think about this. Plan things out."

"I can't go back, Conn. By now, they're already looking for me. The deacon knows everything. People are willing to talk just to stay in his good graces."

"She can stay with me," Brig offered. "There's room in my place for her to hide."

Chapter 21

Ten years earlier...

He awoke with a start. Nine-year-old Conn Brataich continued to lie in bed for a long while, just listening. He knew what had awakened him were the far-off rumblings of another building dying. Tomorrow, another tower would be absent from view. The thought saddened him, and also scared him. Pulling aside his bedcovers, he swung his legs over the side of the bed.

Fifteen minutes later, Conn descended into the Empire State's elegant lobby, festooned with granite and marble adornments. As with all Midtown towers in the past hundreds of years, their original street-level lobbies, along with the adjoining establishments, had painstakingly been dismantled, then reconstructed—down to the smallest detail—up above. Even their street level entrance doors, often elaborate and massive, were nearly identical to the ones originally built below.

Conn kept a low profile as he wound and wove his way through the throngs of mostly boisterous men. One particular Skylander, staggering about, was only saved from toppling over by his nearby mates, now bellied up to the bar. Ginny's Trap smelled of strong Scottish whiskey, sour body odor, and flatulence.

The boy found his mentor sitting in an overstuffed chair by the circular stacked-stone fireplace. A raging ChemBurn flame danced beneath a black ironworks hood that seemed to do little to exhume the pub's ever-present thick layer of smoke.

Although Conn found Professor Dob seated where he was most evenings—granted, usually inebriated—Conn didn't expect to find him in the midst of entertaining a *friend*. Sitting upon his lap, her ample bosom seemed to be captivating his full attention. She tugged on his long beard, while whispering into his ear and giggling.

Conn stood nearby and silently waited. Arms crossed, he coughed, then coughed again louder. The woman eyed Conn disapprovingly with a cold sideways glance. A full minute passed before she finally sat up, wiggling and tugging the fabric of her bodice. She then dismounted from his lap, which appeared to Conn to be a well-practiced motion. After giving the old professor an affectionate pat on the cheek, she turned away, disappearing into smoke and drunken laughter.

"I suspect it is well past your bedtime, my young apprentice. Although I have little fathom of the actual time." His words were slow and slurred as he reached for his pipe, lying upon the stacked stone seat that encircled the fire.

"Dob?" Conn asked after a moment.

"Yes, what is it my boy?" Dob asked, leaning somewhat in to light his pipe with a burning twig.

"Why do the Midtown buildings fall?"

"That is an excellent question. Short answer, erosion . . . from those nasty acid rains below the cloudbank."

"I already kent that. Everybody kens that."

"The detailed explanation is far more complex. I suspect my

alcohol-saturated brain would hardly be up to the task. Tomorrow . . . let's discuss tomorrow."

"But I'm here now. Can I hear it, anyway?"

Dob blinked at the boy through a wispy-gray funnel of rising smoke. "Well, I told you about Strongzine, right?"

"Sure, one of the three elements that arrived on Earth at the start of the Ruin Event."

"Aye, the meteor shower: Strongzine, Stradamine, and Starlox. Well, Strongzine formed what's called coordination complexes with the primary molecules of Earth's air . . . nitrogen (N_2) and oxygen (O_2). In addition, Strongzine absorbed the UV light from the Sun. Are you following?"

"Pretty much." Conn sat down on the rock-topped ledge and let the fire warm his back.

"So this absorbed energy was transferred to those newly coordinated molecules; made them far more reactive. As a result, nitrogen and oxygen underwent what we call an intramolecular reaction. This formed a new chemical entity . . . nitrogen oxide. Strongzine functioned as a kind of catalyst for this transformation. Nitrogen oxide quickly reacted with the oxygen and water vapor in the air and formed nitric acid. Nitric acid is extremely corrosive. It dissolves, well . . . just about everything, including most metals and, of course, organic materials."

"Organic materials, like people?"

"Yes . . . people, plants, animals. It's why our Grounder friends live below ground."

"But not Ragoon trees? Nitric acid doesn't dissolve Ragoon trees?"

"Oddly, no . . ." Professor Dob said, taking a long drag on his pipe.

Chapter 22

I t was another sleepless night filled with restless dreams of Dob, and well into the following evening before Conn could slip away from his Brataich Clan obligations, as well his scheduled *cicerones* duties. Now, walking beside Brig, he discovered there was another, potentially big problem. For the last two days, the Dorcha Poileas had posted additional guards at the top entrance to the Drake Building. According to Brig, five guards were there last night, while this afternoon it looked like six. Getting past them had not been easy.

"How did you get out of there unnoticed?" Conn asked.

"I had to listen inside the door for close to an hour, waiting for the guard to change. Even then, I was almost spotted dashing out of there."

"So what is Misty doing now?"

"Doing?"

"With you here now, talking to me, is she—I don't know—keeping busy?"

Brig shrugged, an exasperated expression on his face. "I have no idea. Who cares what she's doing?"

"Well, I certainly don't," Conn said back, laying on his indifference a little too much.

Brig appeared not to notice, and said, "We may have to go down the top south access entrance of the MetLife Building, then proceed all the way down to street level. From there, we can cross onto East 43rd, then head up 5th Avenue and catch East 37th to get to the Drake."

"Jeez, how much time do you spend down there, boy?"

"I dinnae ken. I guess quite a bit."

"How do you manage it? If the bandits and scalawags down there aren't bad enough, the air . . . it's unbreathable," Conn said.

"Who are you? My momma now?"

"Doing all that, using another building, would take us an extra hour, maybe more. And I'm a bit worn out," Conn volunteered. He figured Brig already knew about his ongoing lack of sleep. Approaching the Drake, he tried to make out who was on sentry duty. Fortunately, Captain Bryant Peirce did not seem to be among them. "I ken several of those guys, let me try to talk us past."

Two of the Dorcha Poileas had disappeared around the other side of the building, while the other four lingered just ahead. At their approach, the guards stood up a bit straighter, several puffing out their chests in an attempt to look more authoritarian. Conn remembered one of the men's names, the one now clearly in charge: Sergeant Brock Dresden. Getting on in years, he was maybe in his mid-seventies. Conn wondered why he hadn't hung up his Poileas cloak yet.

"Hey, Sergeant!"

"Hold up," she silver-haired guard said. "Building's off-limits for the rest of the week."

"Aye, I heard as much. It's good you're here. Damn Grounders are sneaking up right and left these days."

"That they are," the older man said, giving Conn a sideways glance. "So what is your business here?"

Conn, looking left then right, leaned in closer, his voice just above a whisper. "You'll have heard about the fall the other night."

"We hear certain things."

"Well, I'm on a special mission. Here to retrieve certain articles of clothing that were absconded with."

"Heard the poor bloke was buck-naked," Sergeant Dresden offered back, in an equally quiet and conspiratorial voice.

"Here's the thing," Conn said. "We can't have a Grounder putting on a dead man's duds, then sneaking up here disguised as a Cloudwalker."

The old man, raising his two bushy eyebrows, said, "I guess I see your point."

"The boy here kens who has the dead man's kilt and blouse. We'll have to pay for them, probably, but it'll be worth it, keeping out the riffraff, aye?"

"I don't know. My orders were pretty explicit."

Conn slowly nodded. "No worries. Let's have one of the younger lads make that tough decision. I'm willing to take a risk and go out on a limb for a friend." Conn signaled to one of the other Dorcha Poileas.

"Hold on! I can make my own decisions. These youngsters don't know their arses from a smoking chimneystack. You just be back here before my shift ends at ten. Arrive after that, and you'll have a bit of explaining to do."

"I'll be back long before then, Sergeant. Oh, and um, best we keep this secret mission just between ourselves, okay?" Conn tried to move toward the door, but the sergeant put out an arm to stop him.

"Now hold on a bit. I can't exactly allow you to pass, but if we were to be looking the other way . . ."

"Understood," Conn said.

After a brief huddle, the sentries, sending a parting glance their way, began wandering off in multi directions. "Go!" Conn said. Heading for the door, Brig was close on his heels.

Close to two hours had passed since Brig left Misty alone in his cluttered room. Prior to leaving, the boy showed her where all the facilities were. She was astounded and delighted by the concepts of flushing a toilet and having hot water with just a quick twist of a faucet. The Skylanders heated it in great vats and tanks at the top of each building, Brig explained with child-like glee, and with a little help from gravity, piped it down through the walls for heating and hot water. There was nothing so elaborate below ground, not by any measure. They heated water on a ChemBurn pad when they needed to, and the scarcity of water meant that washing up was limited to special occasions. Anything more would be a waste of a precious commodity. As for toilet functions . . .

Suddenly mortified, Misty thought of Conn. *God, he must think I'm some kind of primitive beast.* When you come from a place that actually has running water and flushing toilets, instead of chamber pots and grey water storage cauldrons, the difference must seem horrific. She felt her face flush with embarrassment then became angry with herself for even caring. *Just who was he to her, anyway? Judgmental ass, that's who he was!*

Wandering around the boy's room, picking up this and that while examining the strange things mounted on the walls, she heard a muffled noise. *That has to be Brig,* she figured, standing quietly and listening. When she heard multiple footsteps approaching, she suddenly wasn't all that sure. Dashing across the room, she stood right behind the door, so when it opened she would be well hidden behind it. *Damn, why didn't I think to lock it!*

The door suddenly swung open. Whoever was there was being quiet as a mouse. *If it's Brig, surely he would have said something by now, right?* Obviously, it was someone else, perhaps some of the men dressed in black who'd been looking for her yesterday. She stared at the door, knowing another person was mere inches away on the other side. *Oh no, can they hear me breathing?* She covered her mouth with one hand to stifle the noise.

"Well, Brig, I guess she went down on her own, so I might as well go back upstairs. Make sure she kens I kept my promise . . ."

Misty recognized Conn's voice. *Ha ha, very funny,* she thought. Using both hands, she shoved the door hard and heard it *thump* against something—*his big head, no doubt.*

"Hey! Ouch!"

She moved out from behind the door and found both of them standing there. Brig, in the hallway, was smiling back at her, while Conn, leaning over, rubbed a red spot on his forehead.

"Why'd you have to do that?" Conn asked, seeing no humor in the situation.

"Poor sensitive Skylander baby," Misty teased, but she was grinning. "Are we going now, or what? I'm worried about my father. And I don't even want to think about what might be happening to my mother. I thought you were coming here last night."

"I couldn't break away. Sorry, but I am here now. Grab your coat. We should go."

Misty rolled her eyes. "Ready when you are, Cloudwalker."

Descending the stairs was certainly a lot faster than going up. As they reached the final flight of stairs, she glanced back over her shoulder at him. "You know, you don't exactly blend in, wearing that bright-red skirt. Couldn't you find something less conspicuous to wear while you're down there?"

"It's a kilt."

"I know it's a kilt, Cloudwalker. Everyone knows what a kilt is."

"It's *my* kilt. It's who I am."

"Whatever." She'd forgotten what an ass he could be. But truth be told, it wasn't like she'd be sticking around down there. So what if the Skylander was seen? She and her father, along with her mother—once they'd rescued her—would be leaving that quadrant immediately.

Down they went, descending one flight of stairs after another in relative silence. Stepping off the stairwell's last step, she waited for Conn and Brig to make the final bend then head down too. In spite of her exhaustion, she realized she'd raced ahead in an attempt to prove to Conn that she wasn't the weakling Grounder he clearly thought she was. She was gratified, noting he and Brig were both huffing and puffing.

Once they all stood together on the cement landing, she remembered how dark it was behind the door. She wondered if she'd ever be content beneath the cloudbank again, now that she'd seen the sky. "Before we go," she said, suddenly feeling shy. "I just wanted to thank you again for helping me and my family." She looked up but couldn't really make out Conn's face; his eyes were shadowed and unreadable.

"Don't mention it," he responded. "I haven't really done anything yet."

"Can we get out of the dark now? It's stuffy in here," Brig pleaded.

As they cracked open the door, an outer shaft of dim light entered the confined space. Brig poked his head out.

Misty and Conn exchanged a quick glance. She still wanted

to hate him and that crooked smile of his, but the Skylander was proving to be nothing like the haughty, arrogant man she expected. She gave him an annoyed expression and looked away.

"I'll go look farther down the alleyway," Brig said, disappearing outside.

"Do you hear that?" Conn asked.

"Hear what? It's an old building. It creaks and moans—"

"Och, do you ever stop blethering? Just listen. There, hear that rumbling sound?"

Misty, listening hard, heard it too. As the noise grew louder, she looked up to see Conn place a hand on the wall.

"It's trembling," he said quietly. A small avalanche of loose cement and tiny rocks spilled onto the floor.

"We've got to get out of here," said Misty urgently. She grabbed his hand and tugged. His skin was warm.

He glanced down at their entwined hands and then looked up to meet her eyes. "Aye," he agreed. "And I think we'd better hurry!"

Chapter 23

Sprinting from the building, they made it halfway through the alleyway before the ground started shaking violently beneath their feet. Ahead, Brig stumbled and fell to the ground. Conn thought, *Is this it? Is this building going to come down right on top of us?* Great plumes of dust swirled and rained down on them from high above. Conn let go of Misty's hand and almost lost his balance as he bent down to swoop the boy up in one arm. What had sounded like mere rumblings only moments before had now become so incredibly loud that Misty, ahead of him, needed to cover her ears with her hands while she ran, herky-jerky, toward the street. Conn watched in abject horror as an immense slab of concrete struck the rubber-shingled wall to their right, erupting into countless tiny fragments.

"Let me down!" Brig yelled, trying to twist free of Conn's grip.

Conn ignored him until they were well out of the alley with Misty, standing on the sidewalk on the opposite side of the street. The horrific rumbling sound suddenly ceased. Setting the squirming boy down, Conn spun back around to see if the Drake building was still standing.

Barely visible behind the settling cloud of dust, the building was, in fact, still standing, though dramatically off-kilter and leaning against the shorter building just south of it. He then knew for certain why the Dorcha Poileas had added extra sentries above. Others must have heard the same sounds of rumbling, coming from the Drake, and known them for what they were: the sounds of the building's superstructure faltering. "It's just a matter of time before she crumbles down all the way. Could be days, could be a year. No way of knowing," Conn said.

He stared at the partially collapsed building, and suddenly let out a defeated breath. Quietly, he said, "Every time a building falls, it's just another reminder of how fleeting the Skylander way of life could be. Soon, they will all fall, and it will be over for us."

"I'm sorry," Misty said, her voice genuine for once.

"Me too! I live in that building, ye ken," Brig said, not pleased. "All my stuff is in there!"

Conn forced himself to look away from the fallen Drake building. "We should go. You both okay?" he asked, looking from Brig to Misty to see if either had been hit with pieces of falling rubble.

"You're the one who's bleeding," Misty said, reaching her hand up and wiping at his cheek with her thumb. She held her hand up so he could see the blood.

"I think I'll live."

Misty pulled her hood up over her head, casting her face in shadow, and said, "Follow me. It's not far."

Conn noticed other people starting to emerge onto the side-walk. Hesitant, they stared up at the now-leaning Drake build-ing, which distracted them enough not to notice how he was dressed. Again, he became aware that it was never wise for a Skylander to roam the streets of Manhattan—especially at night. He felt exposed in his kilt, and suddenly missed his long jacket, ruined by the blood and gore of carrying Janis' body up from the ground.

At the 34th Street subway entrance, they descended the stairs together. Not a moment too soon, either, to be inside and away from that caustic mist. Conn's arms were protected by his long sleeves, but his bare legs, exposed by his kilt, were starting to badly itch. He watched Brig frantically scratching one of his elbows.

Misty slowed and then turned around to face them. "Listen to me," she said gravely. "Neither one of you—nor me for that matter—can be discovered by any of the deacon's parishioners. They're his strong-arm brutes, and they're always milling about. I have little doubt that the deacon has issued new standing orders to have me apprehended on sight. I'm guessing the punishment for those helping me would be extreme. Skylander laws and noble titles won't protect you down here."

"I can take care of myself," Conn said, a bit too loudly.

"What did I just tell you? Be quiet, and keep your eyes open. Be ready to hide. You both got that?"

Brig nodded, saying nothing.

Conn held a hand out, gesturing for her to lead them on. She headed away and, picking up her pace, entered into a long narrow service corridor.

"Are we going to your family's place?" Conn asked. He had to admit, he was curious to see the environment that had bred such a strange young woman.

"No. No one lives there anymore."

Although the tunnel was dimly lit by the occasional torch on the wall, Conn still felt disoriented by the deep level of darkness beneath the city. He wondered how people did it, how they survived without the light and warmth of the sun in their lives. They passed a number of small, shanty-like dwellings, tucked away into the shadows. An old man, standing within a corrugated steel shack, was methodically stirring the contents of a large black pot. The escaping aroma made his nostrils flare.

"What's that smell?" Brig asked, over-dramatically pinching his nose.

"Rodentia stew," Misty said in a quiet voice. Brig glanced up at Conn with his brows raised questioningly.

Over her shoulder, Misty explained, "Various kinds of mushrooms and vegetables, herbs and spices, and rat meat. It's somewhat of a delicacy down here. Not everyone can afford rat meat." Her voice was cold and defensive; Brig's reaction had obviously offended her, though she was trying not to show it. Shooting an embarrassed glance back at Conn, she added, "Welcome to life among us sullied Grounders."

Conn looked down at Brig with a stern expression and then shook his head. Insulting someone's home was not nice, and he reminded himself to tell Brig just that later, when Misty was out of earshot.

"This way," Misty said. "Best you keep to the right, stay in the shadows."

To Conn, everything around them was pretty much in the shadows, but he did as he was told. They entered a grotto farm where the air was thick with the musky scent of soil and fresh-cut mushrooms. Brig tugged on his arm and pointed to something overhead. Hundreds and hundreds of reflective pieces of metal shimmered high up on the ceiling. *Grounder version of starlight,* Conn supposed, and thought of the brilliant, star-filled skies above the cloudbank. Perhaps he could show that starry sky to Misty someday. He knew it would make her smile. Catching himself, he inwardly chided himself for that dangerous thought.

As they approached a better-lit area, Conn sensed, more than saw, a few people nearby. Misty, who'd removed her long coat somewhere along the way, was turning her head from side to side, as if looking for someone.

Two teenage boys, both holding long wooden hoe handles, stepped into the light just off to the left as two women exited the main structure. Conn recognized one of them—the girl who was about Misty's age—from up on the street.

"Aurora! Mrs. Romano! I'm so glad you're home!" Misty exclaimed, sounding profoundly relieved to see them both. The three quickly moved into a tight embrace.

Conn noticed it even if Misty hadn't: their nervous expressions and forced smiles. *Aye, there is something most definitely amiss here.*

Mrs. Romano, taking a step back, held Misty at arms length and stared at her, her expression solemn.

"What . . . what is it?" Misty asked, turning to Aurora. Confused and frightened, she said, "Tell me, is it my mother? Has the deacon—"

Aurora said, "No, not your mother. It's your father. He was improving. Was able to move about, some. He had started to eat. But he then began asking questions about your whereabouts . . . and about your mother."

"Where is he? What's happened? Just tell me!" Misty cried out, her face twisted in frustration, then in anger. "Tell me!"

"He's gone, dear." Mrs. Romano said softly. "I'm so, so sorry. He hanged himself not more than two hours ago."

Chapter 24

"I want to see him. Take me to him," Misty said, a surprising lack of emotion in her voice.

Aurora's arms, holding her in a tight embrace, said, "I'm so sorry, Misty. We thought he was, you know, dealing with everything. We thought he was at least somewhat okay."

"I want to see my father's body," Misty repeated in that same emotionless voice. She felt an empty buzzing in her head.

"You can't, that's not possible," Aurora responded.

Misty pulled away from her. Stone faced, she turned from her friend to Mrs. Romano. "Let me see him!" Her now-raised voice echoed around them.

Behind her, Conn and Brig remained silent, both clearly concerned and uncomfortable with the situation.

"Dear girl, Mr. Romano has already taken your father's remains—"

"He took him where? Disposed of him with the rest of yesterday's rubbish?"

"Come on, it won't be like that, Misty," Aurora pleaded. "You know us. Dad will pay him the proper respect. He said he knew an appropriate Scripture; he'll send your father off—"

"Send him off? To the river? He can't!" Her cheeks were still dry, but her voice shook with the effort of not crying. "Tell him to come back. Tell him to bring my father's body back."

"Misty," said Aurora softly, reaching out a hand to her friend. Misty flinched away.

"Which way did he go? I'll go find him myself. You can't put him in the Hudson—that foul river. You can't!" Misty knew she was being unreasonable. The dead were laid to rest in the river, it had been the Grounders' way for eons. She knew that. But she didn't want to be reasonable—didn't want to be nice—she only wanted her father back.

"Actually, I think it's the East River," Aurora said, apologetically.

Misty just stared at her. *Is she trying to be funny . . . at a time like this?* No, she just hadn't known what to say. Didn't know how to console someone who'd just lost everything in the brief span of two days. All at once, something inside Misty crumpled.

"I didn't get to say goodbye," she said quietly, and the tears finally began to fall. She wiped them from her cheeks with her hand, then inhaled a deep steadying breath and held it. She slowly exhaled, and said, "Thank you, Aurora, Mrs. Romano, for being here for him."

"Misty, listen to me carefully," Mrs. Romano said sounding grave. "You can't stay here, not for very long. Twice now, the deacon's men have come looking for you, his parishioners, too. We'd have you stay with us forever, but—"

"No, I'd be putting you all in danger. And there's nothing left for me here, anyway." Belatedly, she remembered Conn's presence. She glanced over at him, and the sadness in his blue eyes almost made her lose control again. She looked away and added, "I'm going to find my mother. Conn's going to help me get us out of Midtown. Far away from the deacon's clutches."

Mrs. Romano and Aurora exchanged a nervous glance.

"Dear, the deacon's reach goes well beyond Midtown, as it has for years now. Simply moving past the ramparts will not keep you safe."

"Then I'll take her to Jersey City," Conn said.

Mrs. Romano looked at him as if for the first time. Her gaze was appraising, and a little suspicious. "You'd do that? For a Grounder girl you hardly know?"

Misty watched the young man turn his gaze back on her. That crooked smile of his reappeared again. She felt none of the annoyance she'd felt when he grinned at her earlier, only reassurance. He shrugged. "Aye. Brig, here, and I will find a way. Get her and her mum to someplace safe. You can count on that."

"Well, you'll stay here tonight," insisted Mrs. Romano. "We'll get you fed and into a proper change of clothes. Get you on your way first thing in the morning, before dawn prayers." Mrs. Romano looked at Conn and then at Brig. "I may have some more appropriate clothes for you, from when Ben or Randy were your size. As for you, Conn, well, Mr. Romano is a good bit shorter, but—"

"Thank you, sincerely, Ma'am. But no, I must wear my kilt and blouse."

"You do know, you stand out like a beacon in the dark," Aurora told him. "All those bright colors, you'll be spotted from a mile away."

"I've already tried," said Misty. "He won't budge on the kilt. I think they live by some sort of honor code. The way Cloudwalkers dress is a part of all that." Both Mrs. Romano and Aurora looked at her questioningly. She knew what they were thinking: *How does a young Grounder girl know so much about the ways of Skylanders and Cloudwalkers?*

Chapter 25

They didn't spend the night at the Romano's grotto. Conn knew they would need the cover of night if they were to have any chance of getting past the deacon's men and finding Misty's mother.

Brig was wearing a T-shirt that once belonged to Ben, and trousers that once belonged to Randy. Both were of a dark, heavy material, but they fit the boy far better than the rags he had been wearing. Conn figured this was the first time, probably, that Brig wasn't wearing high-water trousers, or a shirt not totally vented with holes, and then briefly considered the fact that he'd never thought to offer the boy any of his own hand-me-downs. Conn did relent to wearing a long coat that had once belonged to Mr. Romano. Although it didn't completely cover his bare legs it almost did. It would have to do.

"How sure are you that you know where we're going?" Conn asked Brig as they exited the now-familiar stairwell at street-level on 34th Street.

"Very sure. I've already told you that."

"Is it far?" Misty asked, clutching a drawstring satchel to her chest. It was filled with her clothing items, and the food Mrs. Romano had kindly given them to eat.

"Nah," said Brig confidently. "Thirty minutes, if we don't dawdle."

They kept to the shadows as much as possible, with Brig leading the way. Sometimes jogging along, and sometimes walking fast, they often needed to stop to catch their breath. They changed their direction a number of times, first heading down some smaller street or alleyway, then heading a different way again. Conn was totally lost. He didn't recognize any of the black, rubber-clad buildings beneath the cloudbank. He soon gave up on attempting to navigate and instead kept an occasional eye on Misty, trying not to be too obvious about it. Her jaw was set, a look of quiet determination on her face. She held that tote of hers so tightly to her chest, he wondered if it brought her a certain kind of comfort? Was she still desperately attempting to hold onto a life irrevocably stripped away from her?

"You can stop doing that, " she exclaimed, between heavy breaths.

"Stop what?"

"Checking on me every few seconds. It's making me self-conscious. Just mind your own self. Let me be."

Conn did as asked, and the three hurried on in silence. It was more like an hour before they reached their intended destination. Conn had never been this close to any of the Midtown ramparts before. An ugly puke-green in color, the ramparts' outer wall shone glossy with the coating of Ragoon sap that was used to protect it from acid rain. Conn looked up to see vertical ragged swaths of rust that looked like long streaks of dried blood. The wall loomed over them, some two-hundred-feet into the air. It seemed like a great foreboding dam, holding back an ominous angry sea. Beyond the enormous rampart, he mentally pictured grotesque, monstrous sea creatures lurking there, just waiting to feed. He knew, of course, that the sea was dead, and such envisioning wasn't the case, but the freaky mental image stayed with him, anyway.

Brig nudged him. "That's it. That's the deacon's compound. And yes, for the hundredth time, I'm sure of it."

Conn tore his eyes away from the rampart wall and turned his gaze to the building standing in front of it. Stubby-looking, it was no more than five or six stories high. The rubber-shingle-clad structure was just as nondescript as most of the other Midtown buildings they'd passed. One defining aspect was that it stood isolated, alone on a city block. All the buildings bordering it had long since fallen to the ground. Above the cloudbank, an isolated building spelled despair and devastation for its occupants, but here, the deacon's secluded lair looked foreboding, clearly meant to display power. It looked strangely out of place, as if it were purposely set apart, deliberately isolated. But the lots surrounding it were anything but bare. Multiple clusters of thickly trunked Ragoon trees rose up high into the air. Several even pierced the bottom of the cloudbank.

"I don't see any easy way in," Misty started to say, but then four men emerged, exiting through a shingled door located on the building's forward-facing facade. Each one wore a dark suit, a black ribbon bowtie, and a flat-brimmed hat. "Never mind," she corrected.

They quickly stepped back into the building's recessed portico, where deep shadows partially hid their presence. Still in view, the deacon's men crossed the street coming their way, holding up once they were on the sidewalk. Now a mere eight feet away, Conn's right hand slowly found the paw of his rackstaff. Misty's eyes, momentarily drawn to his quick movement, caught his eye and shook her head. She silently mouthed the words, *"Don't do it!"*

More men, five this time, exited the same building across the street. Fortunately, they didn't cross the street, but instead headed east, going in the opposite direction. Conn kept his attention on the first four, standing near the corner. So close, it was easy to hear bits and pieces of what they were sharing. Of beatings, subsequently followed by the rapes of two young Grounder girls—sisters, no less. Apparently acting on their own initiative, they didn't get permission to take things to such an extreme level. The three men, speaking just above a whisper, couldn't afford the deacon to find out about their impulsive actions—but actions they were having no problem reminiscing, even bragging, about. Conn listened as they came to an easy decision. Both girls, along with their parents, had to be silenced—permanently. Conn could feel Misty's eyes boring into him. Killing these sub-human Neanderthals would be the right thing to do. It was about honor—what the Cloudwalker's code called him to do. But this was not his realm. *Hell, he could spend an entire lifetime down here, attempting to right the many wrongs inflicted by such an uncivilized populace.* He felt Misty's firm handgrip on his arm—holding him steadfastly in place. Brig, Conn was sure, was far more cognizant of the seedy side of life down here than any ten-year-old boy should have to be. The boy watched and listened in silence.

Once the deacon's men progressed far enough away and were out of earshot, Conn said. "That way in is like a revolving door. No way we'd make it very far inside.

"There's a much better way," said Brig. "Where we won't be seen by any of the deacon's goons. It's below street-level. Come on!" Brig quickly headed back the same way they'd just come, with Conn and Misty following closely behind. Moments later, Brig suddenly stopped and looked back, his expression confused.

"What are you doing?" Conn hissed. "This is not the time to go all *numpty* on us, boy! The goons are all over around here."

"Hey, I've only been there once. There's a narrow alleyway around here somewhere."

The three moved up and down the block, searching for the kind of landmark similar to what the boy described.

"Are you talking about that . . . over there?" Misty asked, pointing a finger toward a mere crevice between two buildings across the street.

Brig took two steps back. A thick Ragoon tree, growing in the middle of the multi-lane street, had blocked his view. Squinting his eyes, he assessed what was on the opposite side of the street. "Aye, I think that could be it."

Running together across the road, they slowed once they reached the sidewalk.

"That's no alleyway," Conn said, peering through the narrow crevice between the two towering buildings. Rubber shingles were not affixed to either walled surface, so he could see the rotting, worn brick facades on both buildings. "I don't know if I can squeeze through there."

"Sure, you can," Brig said. "Turn sideways, and sidestep. Watch me." The boy, clearly enjoying himself, made no attempt to hide his amusement. Being small and thin, he only needed to turn partially sideways before disappearing into the darkness. Within moments, only the sounds of his shuffling feet gave an indication where he was.

"After you," Conn said to Misty.

She hesitated. "I don't like this, not one bit." She held her tote bag closer to her side as she slowly began sidestepping into the crevice.

Conn gave her a few seconds head start before following after her. He quickly realized both buildings were so close together that he was unable to turn his head forward. Something dropped onto the top of his head. When it started to move, he knew it was probably a cockroach. He felt its little legs tickling the top of his scalp as it moved about, and tried not to panic. There were very few insects above the cloudbank, and they'd always creeped him out a little. Combing the fingers of his right hand through his hair, he flipped the bug away, but soon felt another one drop onto his shoulder. The roach, quickly scurrying inside his the back of his coat, scrambled between the collar of his shirt and the nape of his neck. Unable to easily get to it, the cockroach scurried around a while before settling between his shoulder blades. Conn stopped, unable to think of anything beyond the free-riding insect. Now, pressing his back flat, and firmly, up against the brick wall, he felt the crushing, squashing, of the cockroach. Shaking his shoulders, the roach's carcass dropped freely from beneath the hem of his blouse. Continuing on, he heard nearly imperceptible sounds of Misty quiet sobbing. There were shuddered inhalations—followed by several quick sniffs. He'd forgotten what the poor girl was going through.

It took another ten minutes before Conn stepped free of the oppressively tight space. Both Brig and Misty were waiting for him, standing within some sort of open courtyard. Rubber shingles, which had fallen off the rear of the buildings, lay strewn around the ground. In the middle of this courtyard space there was a raised patio, made from worn, rounded bricks. Heavily rusted and a bit off-kilter was an arched, wrought-iron arbor that curved overhead, below, the metal framework of two benches. Their wooden slats had disintegrated centuries ago.

Misty said, "I can almost see it . . . once upon a time, people found respite here, away from bustling city life. It was like a mini hidden Shangri-La." Standing quietly for a moment beneath the constantly falling rain, her face was now partially lit from the glow of the cloudbank above. She looked nostalgic for a past time she'd never known, but clearly wished she had.

Three of the courtyard's inward-facing buildings had steps leading down to a doorway just below ground level.

"Okay, this next part is easier," Brig said, though his eyes roved from one doorway to another, clearly indecisive.

"Seriously?" Conn asked, feeling the skin on his face really starting to burn. He adjusted the hood of his jacket, trying to protect himself from the mist.

"It's this one." Brig hurried over to the only door that still had most of its shingles, and down the steps he went. A second later he called up. "Aye, it's this one. "Come on down!"

Conn heard the squealing of an opening door's rusted hinges as they followed after him. Brig was waiting, holding the door partially open. "Hold up there, Brig." Conn came halfway down the steps, stopped, and turned. He looked up to Misty, "Give us a quick second."

Conn descended the rest of the steps. "We're going the rest of the way on our own."

"No way!" Brig said. "Like you'd ken where to go, anyway. You need me to—"

"What we need is help. You're fast . . . a hell of a lot faster than I am. Go back and find Maggie and Toag . . . let them know what we're doing and bring them back here. Can you do that for me?"

Brig still looked ready to protest, but instead nodded his head.

"Go now then." Before Brig could turn to go, Conn placed a hand on the boy's shoulder. "Hey, thank you."

The boy fled up the stairs and a moment later had disappeared into the night.

Misty joined him at the door and led the way inside. They entered into a dark and musty-smelling dwelling. It may have been someone's home or office—not visible enough inside to make the distinction. How Brig had known his way around a place like this was a mystery to Conn. *He must spend nearly all of his free time exploring.* The farther into the space they went, the darker and creepier it got. Conn was momentarily startled when he felt Misty's hand reaching back and grabbing for his own. After two right turns, they descended steep stairs, its wooden treads wobbling and creaking beneath their feet. Firelight was coming from somewhere below—no doubt the flickering illumination of a torch. Apparently no longer frightened, Misty released Conn's hand.

They were obviously in a basement. Its surrounding gray slump-stone walls were cracked, gaping chunks of stone missing here and there. A massive space, spanning beneath multiple buildings perhaps, maybe even a whole city block

Finally, they came to what had to be the farthest back section of the basement. Here, a lone torch flickered next to a hole in the slump-stone wall—a hole large enough for a person to pass through. A big sledgehammer lay propped against a nearby supporting beam. Mounds of rubble were piled on the floor.

"I figure this hole leads right into the deacon's compound," Conn said.. "Into the adjoining building's basement."

Conn peered in; it was pitch black. Turning to Misty, he said, "Grab me that torch, okay?"

Misty struggled a bit to free the torch from the post it was attached to then handed it over to him. Together, this time with Conn in the lead, they stepped across what remained of the broken section of wall, and entered the basement of Deacon Terrence Lasher's compound.

Chapter 26

Lili Folais found her father on the 63rd floor balcony, attending to his flock of caged pigeons in his bathrobe and slippers. Stacked four high in a U-shaped configuration, the rickety metal cages shook and rattled from the constant movement within them. While the adult pigeons relentlessly cooed, the babies endlessly snapped their wretched little beaks, hissing their demand for more and more dried Ragoon seeds.

As far as Lili was concerned, the birds were little more than flying rodents. She detested the lot of them, though she had to admit a properly roasted squab, served with a nice chestnut-colored gravy wine sauce, was one of her favorite culinary delights.

"Father?"

The self-appointed CloudKing continued to pet the head of an exceedingly large carrier pigeon clutched tight to his abdomen. Gordon Folais made little kissing sounds as he stroked the plumed head.

"Father, I'm not going anywhere. So you can stop pretending I'm not here, standing right in front of you."

The little man's eyes looked up and found hers. "What is it now, daughter? Are you in need of a new gown? Or have the jewels that adorn your neck and wrists become tediously heavy?"

Lili, giving him a snarky look back, said, "Janis' funeral is today. Or have you forgotten?" She watched his eyes appraise her head-to-toe black apparel, including the delicate dark veil now resting atop the crown of her head. She'd pull it back down when covering her face would be more appropriate. She watched his expression change, his sadness return, and almost felt guilty for being the one to remind him of the loss of one of their own. But she grieved too, and why should he be able to forget so soon?

She did not want to think about Janis right now.

"What are you doing up here, anyway?" she asked her father.

Gordon gave the pigeon several more affectionate pats before placing it back into its cage. He turned to face Lili, plunging a hand deep into a side pocket. Extracting a curled-up piece of paper, he held it up for her. "See this? This little insubstantial scrap of paper?"

"You know I do," she said, feigning boredom.

"It changes everything." He held it out at arm's length so he could better read what was written on it, and continued, "They're coming. As we speak, they are trudging across distant cloudbanks, coming home to us. And then Manhattan will tremble before our power."

"What madness now, Father, are you speaking of?" Lili rolled her eyes. "Never mind. You need to bathe; you reek after fondling those ridiculous birds. And then get dressed. The funeral service commences in less than two hours."

Gordon nodded, letting his arm drop to his side. Sadness returned to his face before it quickly brightened again. "There's another kind of service you need to concern yourself with, child."

Lili allowed a bemused smile. She thought of Conn Brataich, the handsome broad-shouldered Cloudwalker with those alluring blue eyes. As far as arranged marriages went, it could be a lot worse. She held no illusions about falling in love with him, but she had fantasized about their wedding night. Lili was not inexperienced when it came to sex, and the thought of being with Conn excited her.

"Tell me nothing will get in the way of our marriage, Father," she said, raising an eyebrow in warning. "Your constant talk of war scares me. It scares everyone. Once Conn is my husband, there will be no need for war. Our two skyscapes will be united, and he will help us save our people, once they are his people as well."

Her father ignored her hopeful statement, and moved over to the decorative ironwork banister, which rose to nearly chest high on the height-challenged ruler. "Someday you will rule all of this, Lili. And your offspring, after you."

Lili, joining him there, gazed out across the cloudbank. In the far distance, the tall towers that made up the Manhattan skyline sparkled and glimmered in the morning sunlight.

"If there's anything left to rule, Father," said Lili quietly. That very morning, Clan Haig had discovered a growing patch of quickfall near the entrance of their building. They still had cloudbank access for now, but no one knew for how long. Evacuations had already begun.

"I have taken steps to ensure there will be, daughter." Gordon met her gaze evenly, and continued, "The approaching Skylander Games festivities . . . I have decided we will attend the opening evening ball after all. We must put the terrible fate of our young Janis behind us. While there, you will announce the date of your wedding day."

"I haven't discussed that yet with my betrothed, Father," Lili said. "Truth be told, our time together has rarely been cordial. The news of Janis' death, it surprised me so, and I acted so—"

Lili felt like crying again at the thought of Janis, and Gordon lifted a hand to his daughter's cheek. "I know," he said, raw grief in his voice as well.

"Conn and I," Lili continued. "We just need to spend some time together. We barely ken one another, and he barely seems to give a whit about me."

Gordon shook his head. "The cloudbank here is weakening by the day, Lili. We have to move up the date. A year's span is far too long; who knows what Jersey City will look like by then. Use the Skylander Games, and the Gala, to get to know your betrothed. Do what you must to get him to agree to having your wedding nuptials in . . . say . . . one month?"

"A month?" Lili was flabbergasted.

"Aye. You must be married soon, so our families are irrevocably united. Robert Brataich has no taste for war. What balls once filled his scrotum have all but withered to naught from that sickness of his."

Lili raised her nose at her father's crude language. "And the foreigners that travel this way across the cloudbank," she wanted to know. "Those wizards and witches you spoke of from days past, yes? Tell me, was there not good reason they were shunned and repelled? Were they not a dangerous breed overstepping their place? Aren't these same concerns still relevant now?"

The CloudKing shrugged. "Perhaps," he admitted. "But without their adept conjuring, I fear our cloudbank will not survive the year. We're well beyond hiding the fact that quickfall worsens by the day here in Jersey City. And what then, my daughter? Grounders will invade upward. It has happened before, and could happen again. We would become no better than them. Can you resign our people to that fate? Could you see yourself living in the darkened depths below? Roaming beneath deserted city streets, just one more Grounder girl on the brink of survival?"

The mere thought of such a thing happening did more than frighten Lili. She'd just as soon fall from the cloudbank as Janis had done. "Aye," she conceded after a moment's thought, determined now. "We must welcome our new guests with open arms, Father. For my part, I will ensure that Conn Brataich foretastes our wedding night with unbridled anticipation."

Chapter 27

Conn led the way into the basement of the deacon's compound. The murky dank space smelled of rot and mold, but something else too: the unmistakable stench of decomposing flesh. *It's just a very large dead rat,* Conn told himself firmly. He almost believed it.

They moved single file, winding their way through the dim space where barely recognizable shapes could be seen, such as tables, chairs, and couches, along with innumerable high-stacked boxes, precarious towers that could easily be toppled over with the slightest nudge of an arm or a misplaced foot.

Conn's torch, held out before him, suddenly began to flicker. Its bright flames, now diminished somewhat, were nearly blown sideways. He felt a strong, cool, steady breeze against his left cheek. It was slow going, and the two of them progressed no further than fifty steps into the cellar. Misty moved within inches of where Conn stood waiting. He heard one of them was breathing hard, more like frightened panting. Between the bad smell and oppressive darkness, he had a bad feeling about this place.

Ancient floor joists, directly overhead, suddenly began to

creak under the weight of footsteps. Carefully, Conn turned his body clockwise, attempting to at least partially block the strong air currents from further tampering with the torch's flame. The torch flickered brightly again, its warm amber glow fanning out around them. Conn glanced back to see Misty, he was surprised to see she looked neither scared nor daunted by their current endeavor.

"What are you waiting for? Maybe you should just give me the torch," she said impatiently.

Like that's going to happen, Conn thought. He continued on, now more cognizant of the strange cross-breezes around them. "You haven't been this far into the compound before?" he asked Brig in a hushed voice over his shoulder.

"Uh-uh."

"So you don't ken the layout of the rooms up above?"

"He just said he hasn't been here before," Misty said. "You should give me the torch. At this rate we'll be too old to climb the stairs if we ever find them."

As if on cue, the still-agitated fluctuating torchlight allowed barely enough illumination to catch the outline of a rickety staircase just ahead.

"That smell . . . it's getting worse," Brig said, a little too loudly.

"Shhh, keep your voice down!" Conn scolded.

"What's that?" Misty asked, pointing a raised finger.

Conn was wondering the same thing. He repositioned the torch to illuminate the odd shape they'd spotted below the staircase. Stepping closer in, he lowered the torch. The supporting vertical studs on the staircase cast dark shadows onto what clearly was a female body. The woman was lying face down, her head turned away from them.

Misty gasped. "Oh no. Oh God."

Conn handed the torch to Brig, fighting back a reflexive gag.

The smell of death was overpowering. Burying his nose and mouth into the crook of his sleeved elbow, he turned again to the human remains on the floor. In a muffled voice he said, "Misty, maybe you should turn away."

"Turn her over," said Misty, her voice steady again. "I need to know."

Conn nodded. He'd never met Misty's mother, so she needed to make the identification. Slowly kneeling down, he reached for the dead woman's shoulder when suddenly a blurry black shape suddenly scurried out from the shadows, startling them all.

Misty covered her mouth, quickly quieting her shriek of surprise, but not before the sound echoed through the room. Conn reached for his rackstaff as the large rat squealed then darted back into the darkness.

Both Conn and Brig glared at Misty, then up to the top of the stairs, expecting to see a door suddenly fly open. But the deacon's men did not come rushing down the stairs brandishing knives and pipes. Conn gave Misty a wary glance before reaching out again for the dead woman's shoulder. Stiff with rigor mortis, the body flipped over like a plank of wood. Conn recoiled as a waft of putridness rose into the air. He could tell the woman was attractive once, before she was savagely struck with something hard on her right temple; a force hard enough to crush a portion of her skull. Blood, now dried, had seeped out from both nostrils and the left corner of her open, gaping mouth. Her half-lidded eyes were cloudy white. Conn looked back to Misty for confirmation.

She stared for several beats before shaking her head. "It's not her. It's not my mother."

Conn stood all the way up. Each let out collective breaths, sighs of relief.

"Give me that," Misty said, taking the torch from Conn's

hand. Moving towards the stairs, she lifted the hem of her dress up with one hand as she began climbing. The fourth step creaked so loudly Conn grimaced. Again, he shot a glance toward the door at the top of the stairs.

Misty, letting go of her dress, waved her free hand at Conn and Brig to follow. Carefully stepping over the fourth step, they met at the top of the stairs. A flickering light could be seen beneath the door. When Conn pointed to an empty torch bracket high on the wall, Misty let him take the torch from her hand. Carefully, he secured the torch handle into place.

Misty, taking a firm hold on the brass doorknob, ever so slowly turned it. Cracking the door open an inch, she peered through the gap then swung the door open wider, until there was sufficient room to poke her head through. Conn watched her as she peered about. Apparently satisfied that the coast was clear, she opened the door wide enough to pass through. Brig followed her next, then Conn.

Entering into some kind of foyer, there was a large door off to the left. Conn was fairly sure it was the same front door they'd spotted earlier from the street. The walls here were clad in worn, wood paneling. Two windows flanked the front door, blackened from the rubber tiles on the other side. Overhead, a swaying chain with interwoven wires hung down minus an attached chandelier, which had undoubtedly been removed many long years past. There was a large fabric scroll hanging six feet, nailed high on the wall opposite the front door. It had ten numbered lines of text; Conn figured they had something to do with the Purgeforth Scriptures.

Misty, walking on her tiptoes, hurried forward into an adjoining hallway. "Wait!" Conn ordered in an angry whisper, but she was already gone. Following after her, Conn noticed the hallway, paneled in the same drab wood, was easily twenty-feet long. Several open doors flanked both side walls. From up ahead came the sound of multiple men and women conversing, and the clattering of dishes and metal flatware being put away. Misty, glancing back over her shoulder, mouthed the word, "Kitchen."

Hugging the wall, she slowed and checked each of the open doorways before proceeding. Conn and Brig were close behind. Reaching the end of the hallway, Misty peered around the corner. Bringing his face close to her level, he took a looksee for himself. Sure enough, it was a large kitchen. In the distance beyond was a dining area with a wooden table that could easily seat twenty people. There were six men seated together at the far end. Mere feet away, three women, scurrying about inside, were identically outfitted in long, wine-colored dresses, aprons tied about their waists, and white bowed bonnets secured atop their heads. One dutifully was washing dishes in a large copper tub, while another was drying then stacking the dishes. The third woman had suddenly stopped what she was doing to stand in the middle of the kitchen, statue-like. She stared back at them. Clearly caught off guard, she wore a confused expression on her face, like she couldn't believe her own eyes.

"Mom?" Misty asked in a voice barely above a whisper.

Clack!

Conn instinctively knew that was the sound of the front door latch sliding clear behind them. He heard the door swing open on rusty hinges, followed by sounds of multiple heavy boots striding into the foyer. Both Conn and Brig spun around to see Deacon Terrence Lasher turn the corner into the hallway. He took three long strides before looking up and seeing them standing there. Four other men came into view behind the skeletally thin, towering deacon. His men didn't hesitate. Pulling their long coats aside, they exposed their standard issue weapons of choice: Blackjacks. Their wooden handles were connected to a short section of rope that, in turn, was connected to a wrapped canvas ball. Balls that were probably filled with sand, or even something heavier, like lead. Swung with sufficient force, the ball weapon could crack bones—even fracture a person's skull. Conn thought of the poor woman, lying dead beneath the staircase. He took hold of the paw of his rackstaff. The deacon moved with surprising speed, not to attack, but to escape. He fled into one of the hallway's side doors. His men were already twirling the balled ends of their lethal blackjacks.

Conn knew, in addition to these four thugs, there were six more waiting in the dining area. *Plus, how many others are in the building?* he wondered. It was too late for that sort of thought now, he thought, preparing himself as they approached.

Chapter 28

Misty took a tentative step forward into the kitchen. It felt as if time had suddenly come to a screeching halt. No longer was she concerned about Conn, who was somewhere behind her, or the group of men getting up from their chairs in the dining area.

"Come with us, Mom," Misty said, reaching out her hand. "We're here to take you away from all this," Her hand hovered extended in the air, a lifeline—a means of escape—to a new life, one far removed from the deacon and the tyrannical rules and physical assaults he made in the name of Purgeforth.

Astrid Casper, the only mother she had ever known, was still beautiful, though the clothing she wore now made her look like an actor playing an alternate character in a play. She stared back at Misty, her eyes filled not with nurturing love, but with contempt.

"What have you done, child?"

"What do you mean? I've come for you . . ."

Her mother's lips parted, ready to speak, but then he was there, rushing to her side. The deacon pulled Astrid toward him, looming over her. With an arm clutched possessively around her, his long knobby fingers grasped hold of her shoulder like the spindly legs of a grotesque tarantula.

"I will never leave here, Misty. This is my home now. Where I am loved . . . where I am needed," Astrid said, gazing up to meet the deacon's cold black eyes. "I am home."

Misty's knees went weak and she found it hard to breathe. *This isn't happening! This couldn't happen!* Her mother loved her. *Didn't she?*

"Mom?"

Astrid's face twisted into an angry snarl. "Don't call me that! Don't ever call me that . . . I'm not your mother. You're one of them, and I've done my part. It's over!" She turned away, burying her face into the deacon's chest.

Only then did Misty notice the hulking men lurking behind their towering leader. Each one grasped something in his hand, a club of some sort. She heard Conn yell in the background, "Misty! Run!"

The deacon glanced over to the hallway. "Take my wife and the girl upstairs to my quarters. Kill the Skylander." With that, Deacon Terrance Lasher hurried out of the kitchen.

Conn assessed the small army of men advancing forward with slow, steady deliberation. Close quarter fighting had been an important part of his Cloudwalker training—with scenarios not so different from these now. With a flick and a twist of his wrist, he felt the rackstaff's finely tuned internal mechanism come to life. In the blink of an eye, the rackstaff ratcheted out to its half-extended, sword-like lockwood position. Ten feet separated him from his nearest opponent. Tightly grasping the paw of his weapon, he felt a familiar jolt of stinging electricity. *Oh no, not again!* In that brief instant, Conn was no longer standing within the confines of the deacon's seedy, wood-paneled hallway.

The sun was incredibly bright, and the reflection coming off the dazzling white cloudbank was bright to the point that he found it difficult to see his opponent's fast-as-lightning movements.

In the absence of sight, a distinct whipping sound was the only indication of Glen Garry's rackstaff slicing through the air— missing his head by mere fractions of an inch. Conn, who was no longer Conn but once again the one called Darryl, inwardly yelled, "Parry, you damn fool!" then sidestepped and lunged. The razor sharp tip of his rackstaff made a glancing slice, penetrating his opponent's upper arm. A crimson flow spread first across then down Glen Garry's torn sleeve. Undeterred, Glen Garry spun away and ducked just as Darryl furthered his driving attack. Thrust . . . miss . . . slice across . . . miss, Glen Garry moved with grace and fluidity, anticipating Darryl's attacking barrage. The two men separated and circled each other. Leaning over, both out of breath, their chests heaved in and out. Conn—Darryl—noticed there were far more high-rise buildings encircling this vista than in his own time. His tartan was that of the Macbeth Clan. He knew his opponent was none other than Glen Garry, the very same man whose portrait hung up high in the Chrysler Building's refectory chamber.

A smile found its way on to Glen Garry's lips. "You've been practicing, Darryl, aye? Not sure it'll be near enough, though, lad."

And then, suddenly, Conn was back, standing within the dimly lit hallway. Two of the deacon's men lay moaning on the floor amidst an expanding pool of blood. Conn had no memory of cutting them down, but evidently he'd performed well enough. But two still-standing brutish men were poised before him, ready to make an attack. Chancing a quick glance behind him, Conn watched as six men entered the hall from the kitchen, no sign of Misty or her mother. He knew going up against this many combatants would be a losing battle. And the truth was, it wasn't even his battle—it was that *infuriating* girl's.

Facing forward again, Conn raised his rackstaff high over-head, then—letting out a war cry, of sorts—charged toward the deacon's men in what looked akin to a wild and crazed attack. Surprised, his opponents flinched and staggered backwards, several tripping and falling over their comrades in the process. Conn quickly sidestepped away, exiting into the same open doorway the deacon had slipped through earlier. He silently prayed he wouldn't find himself trapped wherever he ended up.

He needed to find Misty and get the hell away from here before they were both clubbed to death.

Chapter 29

High Priestess Danu Macbeth stepped down from her elevated tree house perch and onto the cloudbank, which glimmered like quicksilver under a particularly bright September moon. Easterly breezes, cool and irregular, tugged on her flowing white robe as she mindlessly probed the misty surface before her with her rackstaff. In the distance, a lone mountain peak crested above the cloudbank, appearing dark and foreboding without the sun's bright illumination.

Danu had been dreading tonight's up and coming meeting, but then again she neither liked nor trusted Grounders, and rarely felt pleasure being amongst their kind. At a brisk pace, she walked the two miles along a solidly packed route, one she knew quite well by now. For sure, there was the occasional quickfall patch but her Sight allowed her to distinguish them as easily as she could the twinkling stars above from the darkened night sky. She came to a stop long enough to turn around and face back the way she had come. In the distance, she could make out the tree house village, built atop the high-reaching branches of nearly one hundred Ragoon trees. Freish Kinloch. Windows, glowing with the soft amber light of the lanterns within, provided just enough light outside to illuminate the many inter-connecting swing-bridges. Two hundred-and-fifty-five Skylander souls called the surreal treetop village their home. What still remained of the once-powerful Macbeth Clan now lived peaceful, simple lives up there. She thought of home—her first real home—among the steel and concrete Manhattan high-rise buildings, where war more often than not was the norm. Where, for five centuries, the shortsighted clan CloudMasters and arrogant CloudKings—always so greedy and envious of each other—constantly resorted to murderous conflict and warring rather than establishing a society that was lasting and good. Danu mused, *So why do I miss living there so much? Why have I been counting the days when I can return again?* Her thoughts turned again, as they so often did of late, to her final days in Manhattan, and the wickedly difficult pregnancy she had endured nearly twenty years in the past. She had been in her forties at the time, and knew that there was more than a small possibility she would die in childbirth. She knew there was a good chance she would never meet her child, but she never imagined she would be the one to survive the ordeal. She closed her eyes, remembering how her long-awaited child had finally arrived into this physical world but was so ominously quiet. Hemorrhaging in the darkened confines of her high-rise bedroom, and in and out of consciousness, Danu remembered hearing those two words that would alter the course of her life forever: *She's stillborn.* She recalled seeing the tiny, lifeless infant whisked away by one of the midwives. She had lost consciousness shortly afterward, from grief or blood loss or both, and by the time her condition had stabilized, her daughter's tiny corpse had been removed. Danu had never gotten the chance to say goodbye, or kiss her baby's cheek even once, and it was a fact that saddened her to this day.

At the time, there had been little opportunity to mourn her

child's death, because the coup against her family had soon followed. She was still in bed recovering, only a day or two after her daughter's birth, and she could still recall the clattering of Dorcha Poileas boots storming up the Empire State Building's inner stairwell. They were coming for her and there was nothing she could do about it. She didn't understand it at the time. How such an event could inexplicably happen just like that. How the Manhattan and Jersey City high priests and priestesses had been suddenly stripped of their conjuring powers, their magical abilities derived from the elements in the cloudbank suddenly ceased, like someone had suddenly turned the handle of a tap to stem the flow.

Danu remembered finding out about the *Sùilean Uamhasach*—the terrible eye—a Ruin-era meteorite that had lain lodged perhaps a hundred feet below ground, burrowed deep within another building's subterranean foundation. It eventually became loosened by the constant flow of acid rain runoff and the subsequent erosion of everything around it. Some twenty years ago it finally became dislodged, and had literally rolled out onto the tracks of a Grounder tunnel. The Grounders who discovered it saw that the meteorite glowed with a pulsing, throbbing light, as if it were some kind of living thing. It was spectacularly beautiful, a near-perfect sphere of sapphire glass, and it didn't take long before word of the discovery spread all the way up to the Skylander realm. Scientists within the Chrysler building couldn't wait to examine this amazing, glowing artifact. Purchased for a nominal fee, it took four heavyset Grounders several days to carry the meteorite up the Chrysler's winding narrow stairwell.

It was soon discovered that the meteorite's presence there within the Chrysler Building, and in such close proximity with the cloudbank, had the power to completely diminish the abilities of every high priest and priestess within their respective high-rise clans. The changes that ensued were swift. No longer did the once all-powerful Macbeth Clan hold the same level of influence that it had for five centuries. CloudKing Loch Macbeth's dominance over the other clan CloudMasters was in serious jeopardy. The attacks that came from the other clans were sudden, and the Macbeth Clan was swiftly defeated, purged from their home within the towering Empire State Building. The *Sùilean Uamhasach* remained atop the cloudbank, ensuring there would be no unnatural sorcerers around to disrupt their new balance of power.

Within days, all high priests and priestesses, as well as any survivors who had been associated with the Macbeth Clan, quickly fled for their lives. Danu was among them. Having just lost her child, she was still weak and heartbroken. These clan survivors escaped to the north. Once they were a sufficient distance away from the *Sùilean Uamhasach*, Danu and others like her found that their conjuring powers were once again restored.

Danu's thoughts returned to the present as she reached the mountain's summit, cresting above the cloudbank like a massive stone surrounded by a sterling lake. She saw movement on the banks ahead. *Grounders*. A few who'd dared to enter her realm if only to view it from the security of the rock and soil beneath their feet.

Chapter 30

Four men, each bearded and unkempt—their hair tousled and their clothes dark and soiled—converged as Danu approached the point where the cloudbank met the rise of the mountain peak.

"A good evening to you, Brian, and to you, Sam and Leon." She then focused her gaze on the fourth man, someone she did not recognize or ever remember meeting. "Hello to you, good sir. I am Danu."

"I know who you are. This is not a social visit. How about we cease pretending we like each other's company and get right down to business?"

Danu let the man's rude behavior pass. Instead, she offered a polite nod back and a facial expression without malice. "You still haven't told me your name, young man. Do I assume you are speaking for the others here?"

"I'm Howard and yes, I'll be the person renegotiating any further dealings here."

There seemed to be a perpetual crease between the man's close-set eyes. A head taller, and a half-body's width wider than the other three men, he suddenly began pacing, his hands on hips, his chest puffed out, and his chin raised. A strutting peacock, clearly this man used his bulk and nasty temperament to intimidate others. Danu wondered if he had recently been elevated to a position of power? Maybe he was a mayor, or a governor below the cloudbank? While the Grounders she had come to know in Manhattan lived mostly below the ground, these Grounders resided within timber dwellings, which were heavily coated on an annual basis with a rubber-like sap extracted from mature Ragoon trees. This allowed them to live at surface level, but also meant that they lacked any of the deference and respect that Manhattan Grounders showed to Skylanders.

Danu's level gaze moved from Brian to Sam, then over to Leon. Not one of them looked her in the eye. They either looked away or peered downward toward their feet. Whether it was from embarrassment or from shame, she wasn't sure, but she knew she would have to tread carefully tonight. "Fine. Well, you requested this clandestine, late-night meeting, so please tell me what is so important we could not meet during the daytime, as we've always done."

"Well, that's just the thing, isn't it?" Howard said, taking a step closer and invading her personal space. He towered over her. "Always you setting the rules, huh? I'd heard that you were a real ball-buster, uppity and superior. That you think you're better than the rest of us mere Grounder folks down below."

With his too-close proximity, sour body odor infiltrated Danu's nostrils. The skin on his upper cheeks and forehead looked dried and scaly: fallen flakes of dead skin clung precariously to his beard and mustache, ready to be dislodged at any moment. It was a stark reminder of the effects of constant acid rains and acid mists Grounders had to endure day in and day out, and one that allowed Danu to hold her irritation in check.

Her voice calm, Danu said, "We've maintained a solid

symbiotic relationship for decades now. Have things changed so much? Is it that you need more fresh water? Perhaps our holding tanks have become fouled. Shall we give them a good scrubbing?" Danu knew fresh water was everything to those living below. Even the water runoff that flowed down the mountainside into streams and rivers quickly became contaminated by the overhead acid rains. The pure rainwater collected by the Skylanders at Freish Kinloch was essential to their very survival, just as the food supplies from covered Grounder crops below were essential to the Skylanders above.

At first, Danu surmised Howard's hulking proximity was solely meant to intimidate her, but there was another reason behind it. His intention was to block her view of the mountain terrain behind him, she realized. Just over his right shoulder, on the rising mountain peak, she saw the subtle movement of dark shapes hurrying along the crest line. No less than ten figures, taking up position there.

"You don't want to do this," Danu said, again trying to catch the eyes of the three other men. She had never actually become friends with them, yet she'd always found a balance of mutual respect whenever they'd met.

Danu realized there were far more than ten men in the distance as they descended together toward the place where mountain met cloudbank, a kind of shoreline. It was an impressive show of force. She would have a hard time confronting so many men, all of whom wielded makeshift weapons like spades, rakes, hoes and other repurposed equipment. *An army of Grounder men,* she thought, and wondered how long this forthcoming attack had been in the works. A sudden sadness crept up on her in that moment—she hadn't expected any of this.

For the first time, Brian, the smallest of the four men there, made eye contact with her. "I'm sorry, Danu. I don't necessarily agree with the others here. You've been straightforward and honest enough, at least with our dealings over the years. But not everyone feels the same. I guess they feel you and your kind—"

Howard cut him off, "Shut up, Brian." The big man gestured toward the distant tree house village. "Stop apologizing. You're like a whimpering child." The muscles in Howard's jaw flexed. He raised a forefinger and repeatedly pointed it at Danu's chest, like a spike being driven into her heart. "It's time you people share the wealth. Time for us Grounders to live up here, beneath blue skies. It's our turn to feel the sun on our faces."

"No one's ever stopped you," Danu said, though she was as aware as they were that all previous attempts by Grounders to venture up onto the cloudbank eventually led to missteps into quickfall patches.

"You think we are simpletons? That we cannot learn? Cannot adapt?" Howard asked. Without turning his eyes from her, he said, "Show her, Kyle."

Twenty feet away, a man took a step forward, separating himself from the long line of Grounders. Grasping a tall pole in one hand, Kyle tentatively stepped out onto the cloudbank. Danu gave the poor sod points for bravery. He continued on, poking and prodding the bank as he went. Three strides in front of him, Danu spotted a quickfall patch, one that would not hold the weight of such a big man. About to warn him, Howard raised a hand to stifle her.

"Let him proceed," he said.

The man slowed then came to a stop; his head now tilted to one side, as if changing his visual perspective would make some kind of difference. But apparently it did, because he then moved to his right, completely avoiding the dangerous patch along his route. As he continued going forward, three more times he was able to discern what no other Grounder had, at least one she had ever come into contact with. He clearly had the Sight. It took another five minutes before he'd navigated his way across to where Danu, and the other four men were standing.

With a smug expression that included a taunting smirk, Kyle said, "I'll have no problem guiding us over to the village."

"And what then, Howard?" Danu asked, appearing unfazed. "Are you prepared to jeopardize the status quo? Risk the lives of your people, all on the abilities—shaky at best—of this one man?"

"I've traversed the cloudbank a hundred times. In the dark of night, I have moved about your village as easily as you do. There's nothing to it," Kyle said.

"Good. Impressive. You have found yourself a guide. What we call a CloudWalker, where I come from. Although the training to become one takes years and much dedication." Danu's outer demeanor remained unfazed, though she knew, full well, this was a pivotal moment for the Grounders as well as the Skylanders living within the village. The hundreds of Skylanders, mostly asleep in their beds just yonder, would be no match for this hoard of Grounders that may soon infiltrate their serene treetop village of Freish Kinloch.

"Seems to me Kyle will be quite busy, one person to guide so many. You must hope he doesn't have a misstep, or fall ill. Then what?" Danu queried.

"Kyle's eldest son. He too has the ability. And we'll find others."

Danu suspected the man was right. Without a doubt, there was Celtic blood running through this man's veins. Undoubtedly, his spawn also was blessed with the Sight. "And what of my people?" Danu asked. "Is it your intent to cross the cloudbank this very night with your crude weapons and kill men, women, and children in their beds? Are you ready to shoulder that burden? Such an ill deed will lie heavily on one's conscious for a lifetime. Perhaps for generations to come."

"War is never pretty," Howard said. "And it's not like we haven't considered all the pros and cons prior to tonight. But your time here atop the cloud, well, it's over." He made an almost imperceptible gesture, the slightest raising of his chin, to Sam and Leon. They both moved fast, rushing forward to grab ahold of Danu's arms. Simultaneously, Brian wrenched the rackstaff free from her grasp and held it away from her.

She did not resist. "So why have I been spared this cowardly attack?" Danu asked, and for the first time the tenor of her voice revealed her unsettled emotions. "I too could be sound asleep in my bed when you attack."

Howard's eyes glistened in the moonlight. With an unsettling, child-like grin, he said, "We are not completely barbaric, Danu. There is no need for the children to be harmed. A good-faith gesture I am willing to consider."

"How kind of you."

"But there is one condition."

"Which is?"

"That you and the children—as they mature—become our . . . what did you call them? Our CloudWalkers. As you rightly pointed out, how could our poor Kyle here possibly be a guide a to so many of us?" Howard said, raising his brows.

Fifty-three children below the age of twelve lived within the village. Howard was proposing they become life-long indentured servants after enduring the horrendous pain of watching their parents be murdered this night.

"You leave me little choice," she said, sounding defeated. "You promise the children will go unharmed?"

"That's what I said, isn't it? Keep in mind, though, I am still prepared to end all of your lives if necessary. Yours, and the children . . ."

"Aye. I can see that you are." Danu said looking into the large man's eyes. She gazed past him, toward that sweet village atop the cloudbank—her home for nearly two decades. Perhaps a few Skylanders would be caught off-guard in their beds sleeping, but these Grounders were unaware of the kind of conjuring power of which that populace was capable. What magical forces they would find themselves up against. But still, some Skylanders would die tonight. Some children might die tonight.

"As I said, what choice do I have?" Danu asked, now looking resigned to the gruff Grounder's demands.

Howard chuckled, then over glanced to Brian. "Didn't I tell you this is our time to show strength? To take what is rightfully ours?" With that, Howard raised an arm over his head. His army of hundreds of Grounder men standing side-by-side became still, then each of them, in turn, raised his shovel, hoe, or other tool up high in the air.

"Lead on, Kyle. Lead us across the cloudbank," Howard said, moving quickly to join the newly anointed Grounder-CloudWalker, taking position right behind him. Kyle proceeded forward, using his pole. Slow and sure, he strode toward Freish Kinloch, a single file line of Grounder men falling in behind. They trudged forward in total silence.

She watched in silence. This invading army clearly had practiced tonight's invasion a number of times; they had come to terms with the fact they would be killing hundreds of Danu's fellow Skylanders. She felt sickened by a human race void of any real humanity.

By now, about half the procession of Grounders had made their way onto the cloudbank. Nary a one looked particularly sure-footed. In fact, they looked somewhat vulnerable, but each had made their choice, either collectively or individually, to be here and to do this awful thing. Kyle and Howard, now a hundred yards away, were little more than slow-moving dark shapes, and behind them was a long, snaking line of Grounder men. Men fully intent on killing so many others this very night.

Brian, Sam, and Leon gave no indication they would be joining their brethren. They simply watched, like Danu, with apparent sadness in their eyes.

"You didnae want this," she asked. "You argued against this, didnae you?"

Brian, the only one to nod, said, "There were other ways to handle things." He looked to Sam and Leon. "Three against an army. We chose the lesser of evils: to keep watch over you. To stay behind."

"I suppose I should thank you. At least for that."

Brian shrugged, while Sam and Leon said nothing.

"And for that, I will let you live," Danu said. "This will be a hard lesson . . . a very hard lesson learned this night. I am sorry."

Now alerted, three sets of eyes flashed wide onto Danu. But it was already too late. She thrust out a hand, grasping her rackstaff and jerking it back into her own possession before any of them could make a move. Swinging it horizontally into a two-handed grip, she abruptly thrust the staff outward. An invisible energy force, coming from the staff, hurled the three men off their feet and high into the air. They fell hard, landing on their backs some thirty feet away. She kept her gaze upon them just long enough to ensure they were still alive but unconscious. Danu turned back toward the cloudbank. The last of the Grounder men had joined the end of the line. She crossed the short distance of dirt and rock, and stepped onto the far more familiar cloudbank surface. Raising and pointing the tip of her rackstaff toward the distant head of the snakelike file, she let the tip of her staff hover there for several moments. High Priestess Danu Macbeth closed her eyes then whispered the words, "Oh God . . . please forgive what I must do this terrible night." When she opened them again, no longer were they full of remorse or pain.

Inwardly, she began drawing upon that which was ancient

and eternal, the unbridled energy that waited there, deep within the cloudbank. The energy was dangerous beyond comprehension, for all too easily she knew wild bolts of lighting could ignite, then engulf, the entire surrounding cloudbank. With even the slightest conjuring misjudgment on her part, all would be lost—including herself. Faint at first, flashes of blue light began to strobe on-and-off deep within the misty sea of silvery white before her. As Danu zeroed onto a specific distant point on the horizon, her concentration intensifying, the flashes of blue light became even stronger and brighter. Suddenly, a jolt of energy shot up through her feet, legs, torso, arms and hands, coursing out through the tip of her leveled rackstaff. The increasing force—this very essence of the cloudbank—became so intense she nearly released her hold on the rackstaff. The tip wavered and became unwieldy in her grip. Danu was frustrated by her own lack of deliberation; perhaps after far too many years without adequately practicing this kind of conjuring, she'd become weak and lackadaisical in spirit, no longer the warrior she'd once been all those years past. Now angered, she doubled her efforts, concentrating to the point her head and eyes began to hurt. *The pain is good.* She remembered pain was a part of it; it was necessary. Tears filled her eyes as searing heat began to singe her hands where they grasped the rackstaff. Finally, in the distance, she watched as the cloudbank changed color. Colors, she knew, only those gifted with the Sight would be able to see. As the shade of the cloudbank changed from blue to green and then to red, Danu knew that though moments before, it had been almost as solid as the ground far below, the cloudbank was now becoming soft and vaporous. *Quickfall.* Guilt infiltrated her thoughts. It was never acceptable, this action of hers. How many years would it take for the atoms and molecules to reassemble into something substantial enough to support a person's weight? Purposeful destruction of the cloudbank was a sinful act. An unforgivable, sinful act. She could use her abilities —her connection with the cloudbank—to rebuild its integrity, but it would not last.

Off in the distance, Danu watched as first Kyle, then Howard, suddenly disappeared from view, as if a hidden trap door had sprung open beneath their feet. Both were gone in an instant. Then, slowly panning the point of her rackstaff to the left toward the Grounders next in line—now clearly horrified at the sudden loss of their leaders—she watched as they spun around and began to run before they too found the new patches of quickfall and fell below to their deaths. Soon, all those farther down the line were also clumsily running back toward the safety of firm ground, their desperate cries and shouts carrying across the cloudbank. But Danu's resolve did not falter. A continuous wide swath of quickfall besieged their desperate exodus. A few lucky souls were able to make their way back, and as the last of the surviving Grounders headed back toward safety, she heard their fading yells and screams as they scrambled down the mountainside below the cloudbank, where the ground was, no doubt, littered with the battered corpses of their fallen brethren.

Sometime later, as Danu approached Freish Kinloch, her decision to venture back to Manhattan, so many miles away, had already been made. The pull to return to her true home could no longer be denied. The timing was right. In the past, the threat of a Grounder attack was always a possibility and reason for concern. As the elder High Priestess, the one making the often-hard decisions, she had been obligated to stay exiled from Manhattan. But after tonight, no further threats would come from those that lurked below the cloudbank. A hard lesson learned on this night, and one that would ensure continued proper deference from those below. Freish Kinloch, and those that chose to stay behind, would be safe.

As her resolve hardened in her mind, Danu contemplated on the simple fact that her conjuring powers would not be accessible to her once back in Manhattan. Not as long as that meteorite was kept enthroned within the Chrysler Building. Nevertheless, she still felt compelled to return.

Chapter 31

Misty was bookended between two of the deacon's men, attempting to walk but mostly being dragged along as they made their way through Lasher's lair. With their vise-like grips clamped tightly around her upper arms, she tried in vain to squirm free. She had already been manhandled up two flights of stairs, and now she was being escorted along a hallway. She'd lost sight of her mother, who was ushered away earlier to whereabouts unknown.

Over and over, as if on a continual loop, she reheard her mother's cold and final words to her. *I'm not your mother.* How could she say such a cruel thing? And she didn't even ask about her father's condition. *Would she even care if I told her that he's dead?* With her vision blurred by tears, Misty momentarily caught sight through an open doorway of no less than five women, sitting on straight-back chairs arranged in a circle. With books open on their laps, one of the women was reading aloud from Purgeforth Scripture.

"Where are you taking me?" she asked.

"Be silent," said the man to her left.

"I need to talk to my mother. Just let me see her for—"

But in that moment she was wrenched sideways through another open doorway. Both men released their hold on her at the same time. Forward momentum, combined with her sudden loss of balance, caused her to fall hard onto the hardwood floor. She then heard the door close and the sound of a lock being engaged. Lying prone in the muted silence, she was aware that a lone candle flickered *somewhere* in the dimly lit room. As her head rested upon her forearm, uncontrollable sobs racked her body. Was this to be her existence? Living here among all the Purgeforth zealots? Was she to become one of those stern and emotionless Purgeforth Prioresses or—worse—one of the deacon's wives? The thought sickened her. *NO! I'd rather be dead. Someway, somehow, I'll kill myself first.*

She thought of Conn. She'd gotten him into this mess. Undoubtedly, he'd been captured by now, since there were too many of the deacon's men for anyone to fight alone, even a Skylander warrior like the ones she'd read about in her book. So this was all on her. She was responsible for what they would now do to him. She mentally replayed back the beating, the awful whipping her father endured at the hand of the deacon. *I've been so selfish, forcing him to come with me. It's my fault if he's in a dungeon somewhere, beaten and bloody,* she thought, miserable. Her mind flashed to the dead woman they had discovered in the basement, and she felt sick and horrified all over again. *Oh God, what if they've killed him?*

Conn flicked his wrist upward, causing his rackstaff to spring back into its compacted form. He quickly sidestepped into the same doorway the deacon had escaped through to evade the growing number of blackjack-wielding, brutish men back in the hallway. The room—even the ceiling—was painted a dirty, drab orange color. From a demarcation line halfway up the walls, blackish mold hung like a dingy curtain. He sprinted past the room's sparse furnishings to another open door he spotted at the room's opposite end. Some moments earlier, while making his brief stand against the deacon's men, he'd heard the religious leader's menacing voice coming from the kitchen. So clearly there was a way to circle back around and get to Misty. And then get the hell out of here.

Suddenly, Conn found himself standing in another hallway. *God, it's a freaking maze in here!* Hurrying through a doorway on the left, he found himself trapped in a small bathroom. Backing out, he heard his pursuers storming through the orange room next door. Back again in the hallway, he turned left, then quickly made another left and entered into a large dining hall. With its long wooden tables, he recognized it as the same dining room he'd spotted earlier, only from the perspective of the kitchen, now off in the distance. And also standing there, just ten feet before him, was a smirking Deacon Terrence Lasher. A small army of identically dressed men stood at his rear. Conn didn't need to look behind him to know his pursuers from the hallway were also assembling to block off his retreat. *There will be no escaping them this time.* He tightened his grip upon the paw of his rackstaff, contemplating on the last two times he'd racked it out into its lockwood form. *Had he lost his mind earlier, or had he somehow been magically transported back in time?* He could ill afford to be dispatched in such a way right now.

"This is not a rightful place for a young Skylander such as yourself, " the deacon said. A thin crease formed between his eyes. "I know you, boy. Were you not my own Cloudwalker, no more than . . . what, two . . . three days past?"

"Aye, that was me."

"Your name?"

"Conn Brataich, of the clan with the same name."

The deacon's chin rose slightly at the mention of the ruling CloudMaster's surname. "What are your dealings here with my wives? I warn you, speak only the truth to me."

"Misty is not your wife. Best you just let her go."

The deacon smiled. "Go with you? A Grounder girl leaving here with a Skylander boy?" The deacon glanced at his men and exchanged a wry smile. "No, I think I will keep her here, for myself. Besides, if I recall correctly, there are harsh punishments for a noble clansmen interacting with a Grounder of the opposite sex. Does not the Dorcha Poileas enforce clan dictums, preside over the Fall From Grace ritual?"

"It's not like that. I dinnae really ken her. What I do ken is she doesnae want to be here. Certainly, she does not want to marry someone the likes of you, an old man."

Suddenly gone was the deacon's bemused smile. "You are clearly ignorant of Purgeforth Scripture. But that does not excuse your lack of respect to one's elders. Add to that, you have injured two of my parishioners."

"Aye," responded Conn, his body tensing. "I was defending myself from your bowbags!"

The deacon continued, "Given who you are, and who your father is, I was prepared to let you leave here with a stern warning never to return. But your loose tongue cannot be ignored, nor your rudeness. Not in here, in this virtuous house of Providence."

The deacon gestured to the men standing behind Conn. As strong hands took ahold of him, his rackstaff was ripped from his grasp. Next, they pulled Mr. Romano's borrowed coat away from his shoulders. Conn, forced down onto his knees, struggled but there were too many men around him. He made no attempt to speak out, all the while keeping his eyes locked onto the deacon's skeletal face. Startled, he felt his shirt torn open, exposing his bare back.

Conn swallowed hard and forced calm into his voice as he said, "Do you really want to start a war with a Skylander clan, Deacon? The Brataich Clan, no less? It will not end well for you, old man. I promise you that." One of Lasher's lackeys handed him a cat-o'-nine-tails, which the deacon held grasped in one hand. *Terrific*, he thought. Things were going from bad to worse. All for a Grounder girl he didn't really know.

"You will take your punishment like a man. And, if you are fortunate, no mention will be made of your presence here, or of your relationship with the Grounder girl."

What relationship? Conn thought. Immediately, he was forced further down, his forehead pressed hard onto the floor. He saw the deacon's rail thin legs approaching, the cat-o'-nine-tails, like tendrils of an otherworldly creature, dragging loosely behind him along the hardwood floor.

"Hold him tight," the deacon ordered, as Conn watched him lift the cat-o'-nine-tails up off the floor.

Crack!

Conn's mind registered the sound a mere nanosecond before the whip struck, sending such intense pain through him he nearly fainted.

Chapter 32

Conn had never experienced such white-hot hatred—such rancor. Not for anyone, never before in his life. But he truly did hate this pretend, counterfeit man of God. As he gasped and panted through the pain, he promised himself of a reckoning to come for Deacon Terrence Lasher.

Crack!

He didn't think a second strike could hurt him as much as the first, but he was wrong. The pain engulfed his mind to the extent he felt dizzy. He felt the blow land on his still-healing stitches from the wound he'd received just a few nights before, enveloping him in a fresh wave of agony. But the pain wasn't the worst of it; it was the utter humiliation. Another strike with the whip and he surely would piss himself. Probably cry. Or even worse, beg for mercy.

"Eight more, boy, and then we are done," the deacon said.

With a sudden burst of adrenaline, Conn started to buck and thrash about. His surge of crazed power was strong enough to tear him free of those grasping his arms. He bared his teeth, like something primal, a rabid animal, and a sound emanated from a place deep within him, part growl, part scream. It was a summoning cry, a battlefield hail to *Charge!* Now onto his feet, his hands balled into fists, Conn delivered a devastating right cross to the jaw of the man on his left, staggering him. Without pause, he kicked out hard behind him, and both heard and felt the gratifying crunch of a man's kneecap being fractured. Something solid dropped to the floor and rolled. The deacon's men had taken a step back, giving him a wider berth. The circle of men stared, their eyes leery.

How long can I keep up this act? Conn wondered. *I'm already tiring.* Something nagged at his subconscious. Something was out of place. The deacon's men shuffled their feet, poised to close in on him from all sides. There it was again: a fast moving blur of red beyond the circle of men, a haircut worn like a boy's. Conn continued to spin about, first one way then the next with his fists raised, ready to engage any or all of them. The corners of his mouth turned up as he realized help had indeed arrived. *Bring it on!*

Snap Click, Snap Click, Snap Click . . .

Conn knew those sounds well, sounds which could only mean one thing: the sound of three rackstaffs being extended after forceful flicks by three Cloudwalkers' wrists.

Then another unmistakable sound rang out, the painful cry of a man who had either been stabbed or sliced by razorsharp steel. A second man also cried out, and then a third. Total mayhem ensued. Angry Grounders yelled out orders in their rough voices, but Conn also heard whoops and commands in the distinct Gallic overtones of his own people. He recognized the female voice of brash, red-haired Maggie O'Brian, and caught sight of her wielding her rackstaff against two of the parishioner's thugs. His friend Toag, smiling, momentarily caught his eye as he joined into the fray. Even more surprising, though, was seeing his brother Michael entered the kitchen, his weapon already slicing through the air. Conn stepped back fast, his elbow catching the man behind him in the face. The Grounder men continued to wield their blackjacks, but with this surprise attack, they were in disarray. Even with their superior numbers, the hulking thugs were used to intimidating and beating defenseless Grounders, and were no match for these young, well-trained Cloudwalker warriors.

Conn spun around, his eyes sweeping the floor. *There it is!* His rackstaff lay between the feet of none other than the deacon himself. Still grasping his cat-o'- nine-tails and looking enraged, the deacon charged for him while lashing out with his bloodied implement of torment. Sidestepping, Conn dove to the floor. Reaching for his rackstaff, he felt the tips of his fingers make contact with the staff's paw, only for it to spin farther away into the tangle of staggering Grounder men.

The toe of a boot connected hard with Conn's right cheek just as another vicious kick painfully struck his right ear. Stars swam in his vision, and he nearly blacked out. Sensing motion above him, he spotted a raised boot heel poised to drive downward, ready to eviscerate his face. He spun his prone body sideways, and in doing so, barreled into more legs. Down came two bodies, landing atop him with grunts and curses. Trapped on the floor, lying amongst both grime and floating dust bunnies, Conn spotted it just inches away—his rackstaff. Energized again, he reached out and tightened his fingers tight around the staff. As he struggled to regain his footing, amongst the flailing legs and arms that surrounded him, he felt a strong grasp on his arm. Looking up, he saw his brother Michael. He hefted him up onto his feet.

"We need to get out of here, like right now!" Michael yelled. With an arm around his waist, helping to support Conn's weight, his brother began to push through the crowd. The floor was slick with blood. They stepped over an immobile body—

Conn was relieved to see it wasn't a Cloudwalker. Michael raised his rackstaff, a warning: open a path or else.

Conn said, "Wait!"

"No time. We need to clear out of here."

"Misty. I'm not leaving here without her."

"Who?" Michael asked over the deafening noise.

"The Grounder girl."

"She's not our concern. You should never have come down here in the first place!"

Maggie called out to them from the far door, the one leading out of the kitchen. "We have to go!"

Toag yelled back, "We're coming!" He shot Conn a quizzical glance—*what's the holdup*—as another hand began tugging hard on Conn's left arm. Looking down, he saw Brig staring up at him.

"I found her!" Brig said, his eyes wide with excitement or fear. "But the door is locked."

A blackjack came out of nowhere, smacking Michael on the side of the head. He staggered and blinked several times in quick succession, then raised his rackstaff to parry the next blow coming his way. One thing Conn knew for certain was that his brother could take care of himself in a fight.

"Take me to her . . . hurry!" Running fast on Brig's heels, they wound their way through the continual brawl. Brig dodged several kicks and a flying fist, while Conn took more of a battering—a hard hit to his head followed by another hit to his already ravaged back. He tripped but still managed to keep his footing as he ran, the tattered scraps of his ruined shirt fluttering behind him like wings. Clear of the dining room and once again in the hallway, Brig led the way to a staircase that Conn hadn't noticed earlier. He immediately clambered up without looking back. The first flight wound around to a second set of stairs that led up to the left. Brig took off, and Conn followed, running down a narrow hallway with doors located left and right. Wide-eyed women parishioners with their heavy black dresses and black bonnets watched them with wide, terrified eyes as they stood in the doorways or pressed their backs flat against the wall in an effort to stay out of their way.

Brig stopped in front of the last door on the right, "It's the only door locked. I think I heard her in there . . ."

Out of breath, Conn tried turning the doorknob.

"I just told you, it's locked!"

"Fine, stand back. Move!" Conn took a step back then leapt forward, driving his right foot into the door just left of the knob. The doorjamb splintered into kindling. As the door swung inward, it smacked hard into the opposite inside wall. Both Conn and Brigg stared into the room's murky darkness.

A moment later, Misty—puffy-eyed from crying—stepped hesitantly into view. "Conn?"

Chapter 33

Misty ran to Conn, throwing her arms around him with enough force to cause him to stagger backwards. "Oh God," she said, her cheek pressed hard into his chest. "I thought you were dead."

"I'm all right, but we need to go."

With her arms still wrapped around him, she looked up into his eyes. "I'll never forget this—what you've done for me, Conn. Never."

"Aye, okay. But we really need to get going. Or none of us will be

leaving here alive." Extricating himself from her embrace, he kept hold of her hand.

Misty let him pull her toward the door. She felt, then noticed the sticky, warm blood on his hand. When she saw the crimson slashes across his bare back, she didn't need to ask him what had happened. She *knew*. She forced self-condemnation from her thoughts—there'd be time for all that later. The boy, Brig, smiling at her, stood waiting in the open doorway.

"Thank you, Brig," she said to the boy.

"Not to worry, Misty. It's all good."

Still pulling her along, like a locomotive dragging a dependent caboose, they hurried down the hallway. Misty searched for her mother's face among the onlookers but only found strangers staring back. She slowed, beginning to resist Conn's quick and steady pace. This moment might be the sole opportunity she'd ever have to see her again, to speak with her. Misty needed to look into her mother's eyes and see that she really did love her, that she had only been playing a part for the deacon's benefit.

"What are you doing?" Conn asked. "Hurry up, we have to keep moving!"

"Just hold on!" Misty brought their run down to a fast walk, her head pivoting left then right. *Where is she?*

Then Brig joined her side. Raising an arm, he pointed a finger and said, "That door. The one that's closed."

Misty stared down at him, wondering how he could possibly know these things. The door suddenly swung open and there before them was her mother. Conn, relenting, stopped pulling. Misty stared. Eyes wide, she suddenly felt unable to find the right words to say.

"Take this, Misty," her mother said, pressing something into Misty's chest. "It will help you find the answers you seek."

Looking down, Misty saw it was her own satchel. Her mother must have retrieved it from downstairs when they first were taken.

"Listen to me," said Astrid intently. "Listen to me carefully. You are never to come back here again. Not ever. I am not worth your tears, girl. I am not who you think I am."

"But of course you are! You're my mother!"

"Hush! Go." Her mother's voice was firm. "Stay above the cloud. You don't belong here," she said, positioning the satchel's long strap over Misty's shoulder.

"Neither do you," said Misty. "You don't belong in this horrible house. Come with us!"

A loud racket ensued; multiple people were ascending the stairs. "We have to go!" Conn said, tugging on her arm again.

Astrid nodded, her mouth set in a thin line. "Go. Now. Forget me."

"Mom, please come with us. I'm scared," Misty pleaded.

Her mother, looking frustrated, then did something unexpected. She smiled. "I will be fine. For the first time in a long time, I feel free. And so are you, Misty." Gazing up to the ceiling, she continued, "Go! I will pray for you, child." Her smile suddenly vanished just as quick as it had come. "Never return here." Leaning close, she placed a kiss on Misty's cheek, then spun around and hurried back inside her room. The door closed firmly, the lock engaged with a definitive *click!*

Misty continued to stare at the closed door as Conn began pulling her back along the hallway. Tears filled her eyes and her chest ached to the point she wondered, *Is it possible for my heart to actually break apart in my chest?*

"Oh, please don't cry, Misty."

She felt the boy's fingers clasp her free hand. Brig looked up at her, deep concern in his eyes. In that moment she knew this young boy was the closest thing she'd have to a family moving forward.

Two young men crested the stairway up ahead. Both wore Cloudwalker kilts, and each brandished a rackstaff sword in their hands.

"Where's Maggie?" Conn yelled to them, releasing his firm grip on Misty's hand.

"Keeping guard," Michael said.

"She's got a few of those Grounder *bowbags* backed into a corner," Toag said. Noticing Misty for the first time, his eyes gave her a head to toe once-over. Tall like Conn, there seemed to be a wildness about him, perhaps due to his long dreadlocks. Or maybe it was the animalistic way he looked at her. She wasn't sure she liked him much.

"Maggie's by herself, against all of them?" Conn asked, sounding alarmed.

"Nah, most of them left," Toag said. A group of five now, they descended the stairs together.

"The deacon? Did he leave, too?" Misty asked to no one in particular.

Toag shrugged. "I dinnae ken. Which one was he?"

"The tall, bald guy. Sunken eyes. The one telling everyone else what to do," Conn said.

Michael said, "Aye, he left along with the others. Got a feeling they're just regrouping. A good many of them will need stitches."

Misty watched as Conn, the first to reach the bottom of the stairs, sprinted toward the kitchen. "Maggie? You okay?"

He sure is concerned about her, whoever this Maggie person is, Misty thought.

Toag, now at her side, said, "They're all lucky they left with their heads still attached." He glanced at her to see her response.

Several moments later, they entered the kitchen. Like a battlefield, blood appeared to be splashed everywhere—on walls, cabinets, and even the ceiling. Misty was fairly certain errant body parts could be found, scattered about the floor, if she dared look that hard.

Three of the deacon's men remained, huddled close together. Each was wounded. A slice to an upper arm on one, what looked like a stab wound on the thigh on another, and a cradled bloodied hand, missing several digits, on the third. They looked frightened as a short, red-haired Skylander girl pointed her rackstaff at them, waving it back and forth in front of their faces. Glancing back over her shoulder, a crease formed between her brows on noticing Misty.

"What do you want me to do with them, Michael?"

Pretty, Misty thought, staring at her. In a tomboyish sort of way.

Conn placed a hand on Maggie's shoulder. "You did well. Thank you for coming to our rescue."

Maggie's eyes brightened. "Don't get mushy. I had nothing much else going on." *Flirting with him?* Misty wondered if she and Conn were smitten.

"Leave them," Michael said. "Brig, can you find us a way out of here? Back to civilization without being spotted?"

"Aye. You know I can."

"She's coming too?" Maggie asked, studying Misty and looking like she'd just tasted something sour.

"Of course she is. She's no longer one of them," Conn said.

"Well, she's not one of us either," Maggie replied, heading out of the kitchen.

Chapter 34

Conn, holding a lantern high in one hand, was surprised when the route they'd chosen upward put them back inside the Drake Building. Was it going to start shaking, then tumble into a pile of rubble down onto 34th Street any moment now? No, probably not. But this old building, so beyond repair, was destined to fall sooner rather than later. Three-quarters of the way up, the damage inside became even more noticeable. Wide black cracks, spider-like, crossed the stairwell's concrete walls. Thick dust permeated the air, plus there was an obvious twenty-to-thirty degree-tilt to everything, which made climbing the stairs immensely difficult.

Maggie and Brig, several steps further up ahead, spoke in low tones, their indecipherable murmurings echoing back within the eerie space. Maggie shot a quick glance back over her shoulder, catching Conn's eye. Her gaze moved farther back to where Michael, Toag, and Misty, now hugging her satchel close to her chest, were bringing up the rear. With a note of open surprise, Maggie asked, "Is that a Macbeth kilt in your bag? Where on earth did you get that?"

Conn looked at Misty and noticed a section of blue tartan

fabric hanging out of satchel's top; it did indeed look like the Clan Macbeth pattern that had been forbidden so long ago. Misty hurriedly stuffed the kilt back inside and re-closed the flap. She opened her mouth to say something but simply shook her head instead.

Maggie rolled her eyes, "Whatever . . . any thoughts on where she's going to stay?" she asked, not looking back this time.

Nobody spoke for a full minute.

"She can stay with me in my room. I haven't checked it since earlier, when the building started to . . . ye ken . . . but I think it's still okay," Brig offered.

"You're no longer staying in this building, boy," Michael said from behind them. "We shouldn't even be in here now. You'll need to find another home, one suitable for squatters such as yourself."

Conn watched as growing consternation appeared on Brig's face.

They reached the upper landing, before climbing the final top section of steps. Maggie and Brig turned around and stepped back, allowing enough room for the others to huddle into an impromptu gathering. In the dim light, it was evident that each of them, except for Misty, had received a pummeling at the deacon's house. Each had incurred a variety of injuries from the men and their blackjacks: bruises, scrapes and lacerations, split lips, and sore limbs. Maggie's left nostril was caked with dried blood, and even Brig was sporting a nasty bruise on his cheek.

"Look, we all can't just come pouring out of that door up there. We need some kind of plan," Maggie said.

Conn assumed Maggie was referring to the ever-present Dorcha Poileas. "Come on, you really think they've posted someone up there to guard the upper entrance into a building that's partially collapsed? Who'd be crazy enough to go near such a building?" he asked to his friends, a group of people crazy enough to go near such a building.

Maggie, with a snarky expression, asked, "You want to take that chance, Conn? What if it's your old friend Bryant Peirce standing guard? Sure, maybe we could talk our way out of this, but not with her tagging along. Look at her! She's dressed like she's been shoveling danka-roots all day. Smells like it, too."

Conn's stony stare was enough to convey his disapproving thoughts to Maggie.

"Sorry. I didnae mean that the way it came out," Maggie said, though she avoided looking at Misty directly.

"She's right," Misty agreed. "Maybe it's best if I . . . I don't know, do this on my own. Maybe cross over the east rampart, make a start in another quad."

"Deacon's parishioners are all over the east quad. Seen 'em first hand," Brig said. "Besides, remember what your friend's mom said? The deacon's power goes a lot further than just your quad."

"Forget it. She's not going back underground," Conn said.

Michael rolled his eyes, "Oh really? And what, you've made this decision on your own? I guess nobody told me you're in charge here."

Toag, often the mediator between both brothers, said, "She doesnae look much like a Grounder lassie to me. Not with those freckles. Skin's not flaking off either, and her hair's not so bad."

Misty glanced over to Toag with a somewhat pained expression, "Thank you, I think?"

"Can we at least agree she's not going back down there? Where she'll either be killed or become another one of the deacon's wives?" Conn asked.

"Aye, right along with her mother," Toag said, and then grimaced, regretting his comment.

"Fine," Michael said.

"Fine," Maggie said.

"Fine," Brig said.

"You're not part of this discussion, squatter boy," Michael said to Brig.

Conn, gesturing with his chin toward Maggie, asked, "You have relatives within the Drummond Clan, aye?"

Maggie shrugged. "So?"

"Who are they?"

She seemed annoyed with the question. "Gunther Drummond, the CloudMaster, is a cousin on my mother's side, I think. Maybe more like second cousins. We don't see them much. Not even on holidays."

"Anyone about your age? A girl?" Conn asked.

"Think so. Aye, there's Adaira. She's seventeen." Maggie looked directly at Misty. A corner of her mouth edged up. "She kinda even looks like her."

"Adaira Drummond . . . that's her name? And she keeps away from these parts?" Conn asked.

Maggie shrugged, then nodded. "Aye. She's got mental problems. A close-in. Won't venture outside."

Everyone looked at Misty.

"You want me to pretend to be her? This Adaira Drummond? Why not just make up a new name for me . . . a brand new person?"

"Nah, that's a stupid idea. Won't work," Michael said.

Conn shot Michael another stony expression, then realized at some point the Grounder girl would need to fend for herself.

"Dorcha Poileas are always on the lookout for brazen Grounders, those parading around as one of us—real Skylanders. Plus, try entering into any of the clan's high-rises and you'll be noticed," Michael said, his tone now at least somewhat cordial and more amiable.

"Back to Adaira Drummond," Conn said to Maggie.

"Would it be conceivable that your cousin would come and stay with you?"

"You mean to live? Just show up one day and say, 'hey, I'm your long lost distant cousin, and I'm going to live with you'?"

Nods all around.

Exasperated, Maggie looked away, shaking her head, her eyes vacant for a moment. "I dinnae know. Maybe . . ." She gave Misty a fast once-over glance. "I'm not sure how many people ken about her mental issues. My parents would be a problem. I'd need to come up with a believable story. With that said, I'm independent, it wouldn't be uncommon for me to bring a friend over to stay. "

"Aye, you are an independent one," Toag said with a grin.

With a furrowed brow, Maggie pointed to Misty. "But still, it isn't going to work. She talks like a dullard . . . an uneducated Grounder. Sorry, but it's true."

This time Conn didn't come to the girl's rescue. He looked to Misty to respond—or not—on her own behalf.

But when Misty finally spoke it was with the similar high-brow-elocution of Maggie. "Aye, I am but a young Skylander lassie of seventeen. My name is Adaira Drummond. Perhaps you ken my father, Gunther Drummond, CloudMaster of the Drummond Clan. I dinnae get out much, but I'm here to stay with my bonnie cousin Maggie for a time."

All eyes were transfixed on Misty, as silence filled the confined space.

"I think I'm in love," Toag said, looking like he meant it, too.

Conn had to admit, he hadn't expected to hear a Skylander-accented voice escape through Misty's lips. He considered the strange tangle of emotions—surprise and pride and something else—that rushed through him as she spoke.

Michael said, "That may have been a little over the top, but I guess we can work with that."

"You think?" Maggie asked sarcastically, as Misty still beamed from Toag's off-handed praise.

"So then we're really going to go forward with this?" Conn asked, looking to each of them. No one contradicted his statement.

"For a while, anyway. I mean, we can't forget there really is an Adaira Drummond out there. Right?" Maggie said. "But I think we can pull this off short term." She stepped forward and took hold of the abundant black fabric draped around Misty. Gathering the material up with both hands, she pulled it tighter around Misty's waist. "Girl's actually got a body hidden under there somewhere." As a wide smile appeared on Maggie's face, her eyes sparkled with mischief. "I've got an idea!"

"Oh God, what?" Michael asked.

"The Skylander Games Gala! She'll make her social debut there," Maggie said.

Conn thought about that. By far, it was the biggest inter-clan event of the year, and the largest culmination of Skylanders anywhere, as far as he knew. The Skylander Games were all that anyone talked about these past few weeks. It was where athletes, both young and old, were given the opportunity to proudly represent their respective clans. There, they would demonstrate their collective, but also their individual physical prowess over others within the realm. Beyond the mere bragging rights, competitors strove to win the coveted, heavy, sterling silver award Chalices. Conn had been awarded one for Junior Dueling Lockwood Excellence during the previous year's Skylander Games. His older brother, Michael, had received the prized Dueling Lockwood Excellence Chalice for adults. No award was more coveted than these atop the cloudbank.

"Conn, I asked you a question." Michael said.

"Um . . . say again?"

"I thought you'd be happy. You've just been invited to be her date."

Conn, clearing his thoughts, was suddenly nervous and a bit excited. "Date?" He glanced over to Misty.

"Not her—Maggie!" Toag said, putting his own elbow out for Misty to take. "Miss Adaira Drummond, would you do me the honor of accompanying me to the Skylander Games Gala?"

Misty shot a quick glance toward Conn before offering a shy smile back to Toag. "Aye, my good sir, I would be verra honored and pleased to do so," she said in her best Skylander accent. Her radiant smile seemed to brighten the stairwell, as if the sun had suddenly risen within its very walls.

Conn forced himself to look away, placing his full attention back on Maggie, whom he knew was watching his face. He smiled and offered her his elbow and then withdrew it just as quickly. "I'm . . . betrothed," he said quietly. "Remember? To Lili Folais. Not sure how things are with the Folais Clan, or if they're even coming to the games this year. But it's probably best you find another date, Maggie. Sorry."

She took his arm anyway and smiled. "Save me a dance?"

"Sure, be happy to."

Brig said, "Who is going to be my date?"

Maggie patted him on the head, "You're a bit young for me. Plus, you're not my type."

The others laughed as they headed up the last flight of stairs.

Michael asked, "You all do know the penalty for harboring a Grounder, aye?"

No one spoke.

He then said, "And Toag, a relationship with a Grounder girl? That's a Fall From Grace punishment. Ye best be careful, laddie."

Toag's happy smile froze on his lips as full comprehension of Michael's words took ahold.

Conn, stealing a glance back, momentarily locked eyes with Misty, who was the first one to look away when the building began to shake. Somewhere far below, hidden by darkness and an abundance of billowing dust, came the echoing sounds of walls crumbling and the clanging of falling steel girders. The entire stairwell suddenly dropped.

Chapter 35

Jarring tremors, along with violent back and forth swaying, not only continued, but worsened. Conn, thrown off-balance within the tomb-like murk, dropped his lantern. The group's lone source of light fell away, cartwheeling end-over-end down the stairs, and disappearing into the dust cloud below. The cloud billowed upward, like a convulsive last gasp from deep within the doomed building.

"Run! Up! Up!" Michael yelled, still a half-flight of stairs below Conn.

But Conn didn't run. Holding tight to the metal banister with one hand, he blindly reached back for Misty with his other hand. Although Toag was his best friend, Conn wasn't entirely sure he wouldn't just leave the poor girl behind in order to save himself. A moment later, he thought he heard the rustling of Misty's heavy dress on the step below him. His hand, grasping out, found her—clasping onto her right breast.

"Aahh!" she screamed.

Conn, finding her arm and taking a firm hold, said, "I've got you. Keep climbing up; don't stop!"

"Then let go of me!" Misty cried, swatting his hand away. "Get the hell out of the way!"

He did as told but then heard something thud down onto the stairs and continue to roll down the steps into the darkened stairwell below. "Oh God . . . no, no, no! My satchel, I have to go back!" Misty looked desperate in the dim murk. She attempted to turn around. Both Michael from above and Conn, occupying her same step, took hold of her arms.

"There's no going back, Misty! " Conn yelled above the near deafening rumble.

"He's right," Michael yelled. "The building's falling and whatever's in the bag isn't worth your life."

Conn saw the despair on her face. Abruptly she turned back around and hurried upward.

A faint swath of light suddenly illuminated the top of the stairs. Conn saw Maggie, propping open the door and holding it against the violent tremors of the doomed building. Frantically waving them upward, she shouted, "Come on! Hurry! Hurry! Hurry!"

Misty collided with Conn hard from behind, causing him to slip and then trip. As she and Michael bowled on past him, strong hands clasped onto Conn's left arm and half-dragged him, half-pulled him upward. Reaching the top of the stairs, he saw that it was Toag, who'd stayed behind to help him. He felt a quick stab of guilt for thinking Toag would leave everyone behind earlier, but there was no time to dwell on it. Together, with arms around each other's shoulders, they staggered upward to the open door.

Staring out into the night, it all seemed wrong. *Where were the cloudbank's white, moonlit dunes? Where were all the Midtown towers?* All Conn could discern was a solid wall of gray. The Drake building shook and groaned, coming apart all around them as large sections of concrete fell from the ceiling and walls. Conn and Toag, the last of the group still within the crumbling confines, looked at each other. *Was it too late?* If they stepped out now inside the cloudbank instead of on top of it, they risked quickfall, acid burns, or being trapped. Toag's expression was grim; he was clearly resigned. Conn's heart sank.

But then an arm reached down through the mist. "Take my hand!" He recognized his brother's voice. Conn did as told, and in turn, using his free hand, grasped onto Toag's hand.

Just as Conn leaned outward through the threshold, the Drake building fell away beneath them. Michael's handhold was their only lifeline to the realm above.

He was disoriented inside the cloudbank, and found it difficult to discern which way was up or down, or even sideways, for that matter. Conn forced himself to calm down. He took several deep breaths. He knew he and Toag were both suspended within the upper layer of the cloudbank. Fortuitously, it was not a quickfall patch. The strange visionless composition that now surrounded them was like being underwater, though he remained dry except for the mist that had begun to sting his exposed skin. Michael's grasp on his hand held fast, and he felt himself being elevated. A moment later the top of his head broke free—up above the cloudbank—and he could see the familiar Skylander realm around him.

As Michael, now using both hands, hoisted him upward then free from the cloud's thick depths, Conn tightened his own grip on Toag's hand. The injuries on his back protested painfully as he pulled his best friend up to safety, but within moments, they were both standing on their own atop the cloudbank. He turned around and saw the now open void the Drake Building once filled. He could see the dark Grounder realm far below, a strange and eerie sight. Distant streets, moist with mist and rain, glimmered beneath a now-penetrating shaft of moonlight.

"Will it always stay like this? Be an open void in the cloud?"

Conn turned to see Misty, standing by his side, staring down at the world where she'd lived her entire life. A life now consigned to memories. "No, this section of the bank was pretty thick. It'll take some time, but it will fill back in. At least, I hope so."

Michael, Maggie, Toag, and Brig, joined them at the void's precipice. A full minute past before anyone spoke.

"I didnae hear it crash. Did any of you hear it?" Maggie asked.

"No," Michael said, "it didn't. Not completely, anyway." He walked carefully around the outer perimeter of the void below, prodding the cloudbank with his rackstaff to be sure the building's fall didn't compromise its integrity. Once on the far side of the hole, he nodded. "It only fell about one hundred feet farther down," he called from across the void. "It's still leaning against another building."

"Wonder if my room's still in one piece down there?" Brig asked.

Misty, suddenly snapping out of her funk said, "My satchel. My journal. It's still in there, too. Perhaps—"

Collectively, they all threw her a threatening glance. "Nobody's ever going back inside that deathtrap. Neither you nor Brig," Michael ordered.

Brig nodded. But Conn doubted there was anyone alive who could keep the lad from doing exactly what he wanted to do. He'd lived too long on his own to start changing his ways now. He caught Misty and Brig exchanging a conspiratorial look.

Distant voices and yells, proclaiming the Drake's sudden demise, carried toward them from afar.

"Best we make ourselves scarce," Michael said. "It won't be

Mark Wayne McGinnis

long before the Dorcha Poileas show up." All eyes turned to Misty.

"She'll come with me, like we talked about," Maggie said. "My parents will be asleep. God, it must be after two or three. Good thing it's dark out; hopefully no one will notice what she's wearing. I'll get her some proper clothes and burn those." She smiled at the clearly nervous Grounder girl. "We have the rest of the night to come up with a sound justification for why she's suddenly here visiting me."

Conn, Maggie, and Toag extended their respective rack-staffs out to their full length. In unison, the group turned and headed toward the distant, towering Empire State Building. Moments later, Conn glanced back, finding Brig still standing where they'd just left him. The boy stared down at the empty hole where his home had once been, clearly at a loss.

"Hey!" he called. "Come on, Brig, we'll think of something to do with you too, lad."

232

Chapter 36

L agging several strides behind, Misty's knees suddenly felt weak. She forced herself to concentrate, deliberately setting one foot down in front of the other. Eyes wide, her breathing harsh and ragged, her hands trembled at her sides. *It's all too much*, Misty thought. Her father was dead, and her mother as good as dead. Added to that fact, she'd almost died twice herself—back within the deacon's building, and then later, trapped within the falling Drake building. The past few days were starting to catch up with her. *It's all been too too much. I can't—*

"Come along," Maggie urged. "You need to keep up, girl. And pay attention. One misstep and you'll tumble into a quickfall patch."

Misty looked around, suddenly aware she had no clue where she was, or where the others in the group had scurried off to. Maggie's shadowy shape stood stationary up ahead, waiting for her. "Where are we going? Do you live in the Empire State, like Conn and Toag?"

"No," Maggie replied, "but it's not far. The Pavicon tower is maybe a quarter-mile farther along this trail. It's nothing like the Empire, but it's home. And hey, it's still standing."

What trail? Misty mused. All she could discern in the bleak darkness were varying shades of gray. Thank God for all the distant lanterns and torchlights; hundreds of flickering flames surrounded the area. They seemed to hover, magically tethered high in the nighttime sky itself. It struck Misty again that she was in a completely foreign place, and not even close to being out of danger.

Maggie, took hold of Misty's arm and wrapped it with her own. "Oh my, you're shaking. Take deep, slow breaths. That's right, just like that, in and out. See that cluster of lights yonder?" Maggie gestured ahead, off to the right. "That's where we're going. It's a mere six stories above the bank. Sometimes the building goes totally unnoticed during daytime hours compared to all the other far more magnificent towers around here. But it's old and charming, and just as magnificent in its own way. You'll see."

They walked the rest of the way in relative silence. Maggie kept her close by her side, occasionally slowing to poke her rackstaff here and there into the cloudbank. When they reached Maggie's building they walked around it, approaching from the opposite side. Even in the relative darkness, the outside looked far more ornate, exhibiting stylized stonework and stamped concrete patterns. Angular geometric swirls were visible within the stacked square blocks.

"This building was erected way, way, way back, during the early 1930's: a period, or era, called Art Deco in architecture." Maggie gestured with the point of her rackstaff toward a set of prominent hardwood double doors. She spoke as though reciting from a book, which Misty suspected she might be. "This secondary, cloudbank-level entrance was added about a hundred years after the Ruin Event. Skylander craftsmen and master artisans matched the form and function of the original entrance that's down at street level. Of course, the fine doors down there are hidden now behind thick rubber shingles and layer upon layer of Ragoon sap sealant."

Misty's eyes followed the upward contours of the stout, six-story building that stood atop so many unseen stories below the cloudbank. It was hard to believe that the ugly, rubber-coated buildings she'd grown up seeing at ground level had ever looked so beautiful as this. She appreciated Maggie talking to her in this way: a normal, soft conversation that helped to settle her frayed nerves. It was a nice respite from all the havoc of having her world so recently flipped upside down. But the aftermath, experiencing one adrenaline rush after another, was now crashing down on her, and sheer exhaustion was settling in. Misty tried to appear truly interested in what the Skylander girl was saying. "It all looks so unblemished. Like it's a new building. Nothing like what's below the bank."

Maggie's expression turned wistful. "Aye, as a people, we take much pride in these few remaining towers. They're constantly being attended to. Cracks quickly filled, windows replaced, lightning strikes repaired immediately . . . we strive to keep things looking as they were before. Perhaps it's all in vain. We ken everything's on borrowed time. It's ours to experience for mere moments only, within God's greater timeline."

Maggie abruptly sniffed and blinked away what Misty surmised were bittersweet tears. Musings, perhaps, about another era, when buildings didn't just suddenly fall apart and the sky didn't occasionally erupt into furious, thunderous, dangerous bolts of lighting. Where each tomorrow was expected to be a day just like today—where normal *was normal*.

Maggie smiled and held out a free hand. "Come on," she said, all traces of sadness gone from her voice. "Let me show you how Skylander lassies live."

Together, they pushed through the building's double doors, entering into *heaven*. Misty took in the grand circular vestibule, lit by a chandelier hanging high overhead. A dozen individual ChemBurn lanterns illuminated the warm and welcoming space around them. Framed portraits of men and women, wearing scarlet kilts, hung high on the walls. Hanging tapestries stretched long across the walls, chronicling various epic events from the past. They stopped mid-center in the expansive foyer. Misty gazed up and then all around, her eyes taking in the opulence, the grandeur. She noticed the reflective surface beneath her feet, and recognized it as marble. She'd read about it. Textual descriptions didn't nearly do it justice. "Oh Maggie, this is *dazzling*! So much more than I ever could have imagined." She quickly brushed new tears from her cheeks. "And those smells! Oh, the smell in here."

"Smell? There's a smell?"

"Oh yes, it's wonderful! Scents of lingering perfumes and soap and brewed coffee," she glanced upward again, taking in the aromas from cooked meals, made with strange and exotic spices. Closing her eyes, she inhaled another deep breath. "I could just stand here and fill my senses forever."

Maggie laughed. "Well, there'll be more than enough time for you to do that in the days to come. For now, do come along; it's late and I'm ready to drop."

The stairwell was nothing like the one they'd climbed in the decrepit Drake. Here it was well lit, the walls donning more artwork. When they reached the third floor landing, Maggie was quick to inform Misty they were actually on the Pavicon's sixty-second floor. Off to the side stood a wide, deep mahogany-stained door, decorated with six metal inlaid squares. Made in the art deco style, eyes on contoured relief faces stared back at them as they approached. The door was amazing, but also a little creepy.

Maggie put a finger to her lips and whispered, "Let's tread quietly, we dinnae want to wake everyone up, aye?"

Misty nodded, wondering, *How many is everyone?* They entered into a miniature version of the foyer below: a half-circular space, with a smaller chandelier that hung down from overhead. Maggie hung her retracted rackstaff onto an available peg on the wall, where six or seven other rackstaffs hung in a row. More artwork donned the walls: broad-shouldered Cloud-walkers, wearing kilts, held extended rackstaffs proudly upright in their hands, and all wore the Brataich Clan tartan colors. There were men with muttonchops and men with full beards. A little girl, no older than five or six, whose yellow-coiled curls flowed out beneath a red plaid cap, was all dressed up as a little Cloudwalker. The largest of all the portraits took up one entire wall: a majestic woman wearing a long, sky-blue gown. Poised upon one substantial hip was a balled fist. *Clearly,* thought Misty, *She's not a lady you would want to mess with.*

"That's my Great Great Aunt Gilda O'Brian," Maggie whispered.

Misty smiled appreciably. At a closer glance, the woman didn't look angry as much as she did sad, as if her thoughts had been far, far away when she posed for this portrait.

"Supposedly she was like me," said Maggie casually. "She also had a proclivity towards girls."

Misty nodded, ensuring her face remained expressionless. Below the cloudbank, females of any age discovered to be lesbians were flogged as often as it took to get any such notions out of their heads. It was considered a serious sin under Purge-forth Scripture. Misty had always thought it strange that males with same-sex proclivities were also discouraged, but endured a much milder form of punishment, the worst being a forced three-day fast.

Maggie took Misty's hand and pulled her into the adjoining

room. Misty's line of sight extended through the expansive space to one of the building's outer walls. Three large windows provided breathtaking views of the moonlit skylands outside. A small lit lantern hung in each open window—the reason all the high-rise buildings looked so beautiful at night, she realized. In the far distance, other tiny glowing lights gave evidence of other Midtown high-rises. Tearing her gaze from the windows, Misty took in the huge room: easily larger than the entire grotto where she'd grown up, and probably larger than Aurora's as well. A central, communal space held two facing overstuffed couches with a long, low table placed between them. Some sort of game board lay atop it, multicolored pieces strewn about. The room was dimly lit; some of the wall-mounted ChemBurn lamps and lanterns had been extinguished. To her left, Misty could see a kitchen area, and a room adjacent to it which held a long timber table, with no less than a dozen chairs pushed beneath it.

She watched as Maggie crossed the room on her tiptoes and entered the kitchen. She searched the countertops and opened up a few cabinets, clearly looking for something. When she returned, her arms carefully cradled several food items: a small loaf of golden-colored bread, a tall bottle of some kind of liquid, and several round foodstuffs Misty did not recognize.

"Best we make do with this," Maggie said, giving Misty a conspiratorial grin. "This way, come on!"

Misty followed the copper-headed girl down a long hallway that showed three closed doors on flanking walls. She stopped in front of a lone door at the far end of the hall. Gesturing with her chin, she asked, "Can you get that?"

Misty reached passed her and turned the knob, which she noticed was made of either cut glass or crystal. As Maggie hurried in, she quickly followed behind her.

"Close the door."

Obviously Maggie's bedroom, Misty didn't know what she

had expected to see, but this wasn't it. Decorated nothing like the other parts of the building, this space—with its two windows and a large bed pushed against one wall—had none of that formality. No hanging portraits or tapestries were anywhere to be seen. The walls were bare, painted a pleasant light tan shade. The room held a small white couch and Misty wondered if it was something she'd read about. Was it a love seat? She'd thought it a silly name for a piece of furniture, but seeing one now, she thought it did look quite cozy. A furry blanket lay casually draped over one end.

"I'm more into a minimalist decor," said Maggie, watching her reaction.

"It's nice! I like it!" In fact, Misty really did like it. Strangely, it reminded her more of home. Nondescript concrete walls and floors were all she had ever known. As Maggie placed the food items down onto a table in the corner, Misty's mouth began to water just staring at the loaf of bread. She was starving. *When was the last time I ate?* she wondered.

Maggie disappeared behind another door. Misty could hear her talking to herself. A moment later she reemerged, holding out some clothes—a pair of leggings and a matching shirt. The soft cloth was nothing like the densely woven fabric of her dress, and the colors—a deep green—were more vibrant than anything she'd ever seen on the ground. "Nightclothes for you," said Maggie, by way of explanation.

Misty nodded, as if she understood. *What in God's name are nightclothes?* She'd always slept in her undergarments. That's what everyone did down below.

Then Maggie disappeared behind another door. A moment later, Misty heard the sound of water running.

"Get in here!"

Misty entered the bathroom and took in the floor-to-ceiling gleaming white tiles. A row of small pink candles flickered just above the sink's basin. Maggie, sitting on the rim of the tub, had her hand immersed in the water that flowed from the tap.

"I'm making it a little hotter than you'll probably be comfortable with." Maggie shot a glance back at her and said, "I have to be honest, Misty, you're beyond ripe. Stinky, stinky. Come on, get out of those *maukit* clothes. Say good-bye to them, because they're going into the incinerator first thing."

Misty nervously chewed the inside of her lip. *Does she expect me to undress right here in front of her?* Her mind flashed back to the image of Great Great Aunt Gilda who, to Misty's surprise, smiled and winked at her in her mind's eye. Minutes passed as Maggie hummed a melody she wasn't familiar with.

"You needn't worry your self. You're not my type," Maggie volunteered.

Misty nodded, as if she already knew that. She then wondered who Maggie's type was.

"And besides, it's quite evident there's another Cloudwalker who's got you all a-flutter, anyway." Maggie smiled up at her and waggled her eyebrows up and down.

Misty swallowed hard. Grounder girls talking in such a lurid way would have evoked swift punishment. Purgeforth Scripture dedicated entire passages to proper conduct by one and all, and everyone, particularly young women, were expected to avoid any talk dealing with sexuality.

"Toag is single, ye ken," continued Maggie. "He's a verra striking male, I guess, if you're so inclined." But she must have picked up on something from Misty's expression, because her expression turned quizzical. "Huh. So it's not Toag."

"I'm not the slightest bit interested in anyone. I already have enough on my mind, thank you very much."

Maggie continued to stare up at the Grounder girl, her facial expression becoming more serious. "You do know that

Conn is already betrothed to Lili Folais, daughter of a Jersey City CloudMaster."

She didn't know, and she didn't like the way that information made her feel. "I told you," she said, trying to keep her face neutral. "I'm not looking for romance. I'm thankful for his help. He's been wonderful in that regard, but like a brother. Ick! I'm not sure why you would think—"

"Oh please. Just stop it! I may like girls, ye ken, but I'm not completely daft when it comes to the workings of boy-girl romances. But Misty, if it's anything more than mere idle fantasies, these . . . thoughts of yours . . . well, they could be verra dangerous. For one thing, you are a Grounder. Not of noble blood. Aye, we can keep that a secret for as long as this whole Adaira Drummond scheme continues to work. But we shouldn't lose track of the fact you're a Grounder girl."

Misty wasn't completely sure why, but hearing those words angered her. She heard her mother's words in her head again: *You don't belong here.* Misty took a deep breath, wondering where, if anywhere, she did belong. "And the second thing?" she asked, doing her best to sound disinterested.

"Two, Conn is the most sought after single man above the cloudbank. His forthcoming nuptials have been a forgone conclusion for, I don't know, years!" Maggie looked away, turning one knob first then the other, until the water ceased flowing. She stood, "I'll leave you to it. There's soap and shampoo on the shelf there. Use liberal amounts of both. And dinnae hurry . . . just soak a good while, aye?"

Misty felt her cheeks redden, growing hot with embarrassment. *Do I really reek?*

"Towels are there on the rack. I'll wait outside while you throw your, um, dress and undergarments out into the hall." Maggie let out a long breath, then nodded to her. Before she stepped out the door, Misty reached out a hand, her fingertips touching Maggie's arm.

"Thank you," she said. "And I'm sorry."

"Why sorry?"

"I must seem like some kind of wild beast to you. A dirty, mangy troll, and so stupid, too." Misty's eyes welled with tears.

Maggie shrugged, but didn't deny Misty's words. "Aye, well, one step at a time. Hot water and soap will go a long way helping you conquer the first part. Now, get out of those rags."

Chapter 37

High Priestess Danu Macbeth maintained a relatively steady pace in spite of the fact that every muscle in her body was rebelling. She felt time's passage—the past twenty years—with each stride she took, and each forward jab of her rackstaff into the unblemished cloudbank. She estimated they had traveled a good two hundred miles thus far, with one hundred and fifty miles still to go.

There were fourteen travelers in all. Like her, eight were the elders. They were the very same ones who had been forced to travel this endless white bank once before, when, not by choice, they had traversed northward in the opposite direction, fleeing for their lives. The other six travelers were young, those born amongst the treetop roosts of Freish Kinloch. Between the ages of eleven and fifteen, their request to join the elders on this excursion back to Manhattan was unexpected. Novices, the entire lot of them, they were still learning the ways of the High Order. With rackstaffs in limited supply, each carried a long length of polished Ragoon hardwood—a makeshift rackstaff—instead. Their conjuring abilities were rough and inconsistent, although they probably made up for that with their enthusiastic gumption. Danu marveled at their willingness to experience life to its absolute fullest. Not just the thrill-seeking adventure on this southbound trek, though that was a big part of it, but their willingness to engage in the broad spectrum of human emotion. For two hundred miles Danu quietly observed the constantly changing dynamics within this clique of youngsters. The not-so-hidden crush one boy, Jeremy, had on a spirited girl named Julie, who in turn had a crush on a different boy, Greg. And then there was Hansen, fifteen and a loner. He was their leader, which had not come about through conscious selection, at least not from what Danu observed, but something more natural. He would be a force to reckon with someday, Danu was sure of it.

High Priest Oliver Macbeth, Danu's first cousin and her closest friend, had taken up the lead for the past ten miles. A powerful and big man—six-and-a-half feet tall—his broad shoulders supported the weight of two fully-laden backpacks. His own, as well as Julie's, after she had grown too tired to carry it herself. When he glanced back at her, Danu noticed ice crystals had formed on his mustache hairs and around his mouth. His long black beard glistened frostily in the late afternoon sunlight. Three paces ahead of her, his exhalations, billowing white puffs in the chilly air, rose before quickly dissipating into a swirling mist above his abnormally large head.

Oliver slowed and pointed the tip of his rackstaff toward *something* up ahead. "More, over there," was all he said.

Danu knew he was referring to the same thing he'd pointed out two hours earlier. A swath of deep tracks ran perpendicular to their own trail upon the cloudbank. To say it was merely an anomaly, encountering such tracks, was an immense understatement. Here, upon these high white plains, no life existed other than human Skylanders. Sure, there were pigeons, and other rare species of birds spotted lately, that would land up here—perhaps to catch their breath during long migrations. But for actual animals to live on the cloudbank was impossible. *What would they eat?* Yet, these were not the tracks of humans, but more likely a four-legged breed. Apparently, there were a good many of them, too; perhaps ten or more, something akin to a pack.

Oliver waited for Danu and the others upon reaching the disturbed bank area. He knelt down and ran his fingertips over the churned-up surface, the young novices circled around him.

"I know what these tracks are from," Julie said, feigning boredom. She really was a pretentious know-it-all. No one asked her to expound more, but she did so anyway. "They're Smite tracks."

"Ha ha," Jeremy said. "Like the creepy lullaby?"

Julie nodded. Eyes widening, and her hands raised up, her fingers apart, she sang:

"So still the Smite, so very still—upon the tree the Smite shall wait.

So dark the night, so very dark—upon the branch the Smite shall watch.

So late the hour, so very late—upon the sniff, the Smite shall smell.

So starved the Smite, so very starved—upon the prey the Smite shall eat."

"That lullaby's totally meaningless, just meant to scare little children. Doesn't mean anything," said Dillard Stallworth, an elder high priest with bad teeth. He dismissed Julie's impromptu performance with a wave of a hand. "More likely," he continued, "They were caused by heady winds blowing a tumbling Ragoon branch across the bank."

Oliver stood, not bothering to acknowledge Stallworth. Turning to Danu, he said, "This was no tumbling branch."

Danu pointed the tip of her own rackstaff south, toward a

dark cluster she could see along the horizon. "They were not here two decades ago."

All heads turned, looking southward. "What is that?" Hansen asked.

"The tops of branches. A forest of Ragoon trees breaching the cloudbank."

Julie sang the verse again. ". . . Upon the tree the Smite shall wait . . ."

"Shut up, Julie. You're just trying to creep us out," said Mandy, one of the other novice girls. She stared off to the distance. Like giving a salute, she held a hand over her eyes to block out the sun's glare.

Danu and Oliver exchanged a glance. She said, "We should keep moving. Set up camp for the night when we get well past that area."

"I'm too tired," Julie said, looking pouty. "We've already walked lots longer today than usual. I say we put it to a vote: Who wants to camp here for the night?" She raised a hand, the first and only voter.

"Says the one who's not even carrying her own pack," Mandy scorned.

"This isn't a democracy. You keep walking until we say it's time to stop," Danu said, striding across the strange tracks of unknown origin.

They continued on for another three hours, hoping to pass beyond the breaching Ragoons. But that was not to be. In fact, even more tree top outcroppings became evident the farther south they went. Danu imagined great Ragoon forests hidden below the bank.

Noticing the younger travelers falling behind, she said, "Oliver, we'll set up camp here for the night."

He stopped and surveyed their surroundings. Treetops were everywhere. Noting that he was about to protest, Danu said,

"We'll keep torches and lanterns burning all around us. Elders will take turns keeping watch. There's little other choice. Look at them, the kids are about ready to drop."

"Aye. I can take first watch, after we make camp," Oliver said. He let the packs he was carrying slide down from his shoulders.

Typically, they slept under heavy blankets beneath the stars. But Danu didn't feel comfortable doing that this night. She wished they had brought the tents with them, but they'd lain in disuse for so long that most had been completely useless. They'd left Freish Kinloch in too much of a hurry to try and mend them.

Darkness came fast that night. Oliver made a ChemBurn campfire that was twice the size of any they'd had on previous nights. In a circle, they brought their bedding close to the fire, even when it became uncomfortably warm.

"Better hot than being *Smite* bait," Greg said, turning a long gaze toward the dark silhouette of treetops off in the distance.

Danu heard Oliver's slow rhythmic steps, moving around the camp's perimeter. Glancing over her shoulder, she could see his flickering torchlight. He stopped every so often to raise the torch higher into the air and gaze intently at the cloudbank around them.

Danu gazed at the young faces, lit brightly by the amber firelight. The youngsters always chose to stay close together.

"High Priestess?"

Danu found Mandy's eyes. "What is it, lass?"

"What's it like there?"

Danu knew she was referring to Manhattan. It was a question she'd heard a thousand times before. "It's like living in a storybook. Great castles in the sky, where clan CloudKings and CloudMasters rule the spires, and thousands of people—"

A sudden scream, more like a screech, interrupted the still

night. Everyone sat up and warily looked about in the surrounding darkness. Danu, rising to her feet, spun about and walked slowly toward Oliver's distant torchlight.

She called out, "Oliver . . ." then called again, even louder. "Oliver!"

"I'm scared," Julie said, back at the camp behind her.

"Damn it, Oliver, answer me!" Only then did she note Oliver's torch was not clutched within the man's hand, but lying upon the cloudbank. Oliver was nowhere to be seen. Off in the distance, she heard a rustling clamor. Then came screeches from multiple creatures. She saw their silhouettes as they charged ever closer. Only then did Danu realize she'd left her rackstaff back at the campsite, safe beside her bedding.

Chapter 38

Conn awoke far too early the next morning. Groaning, he placed his pillow over his head and tried to drown out Brig's incessant snoring, to no avail. Giving up, he rose up onto his elbows and scanned his darkened bedroom. The boy, asleep in the far corner, was curled into a ball. Asleep, he looked so young and innocent, his mask of brashness and bravado temporarily staved off.

Conn flung the bedcovers aside and swung his legs over the edge of the bed. There was a lot to do today, starting with some much-needed practice for tomorrow's Skylander Games. Standing, he first twisted left then right. The welts across his back from the deacon's lashing stung like hell, and the knife injury to his back was still sore, but the stitches no longer felt as if they were going to tear apart with the slightest movement. He'd be fine to compete so long as he was careful. Still, he should take it somewhat easy today. He smiled at the thought. *Yeah, like Michael and Toag would allow for that to happen.*

Conn threw his pillow across the room where it flopped down on Brig's head. The lad didn't move an inch. "I ken you're awake under there, boy. You need to rouse and then make yourself scarce. This isn't an inn and my family won't take kindly to finding a vagrant lying about the floor." Brig still didn't respond. Turning his attention to the world outside the window, Conn saw a flurry of activity atop the cloudbank.

Twenty minutes later, showered and dressed in a clean shirt and kilt—his rackstaff tethered to his belt next to his sporran— Conn descended the Empire State's inner stairwell, taking the steps three at a time. Hardly winded, he bounded out the main entrance into a glorious, sunny day. There was excitement in the air, as dozens of septs prepared for the Open-Air Fair Jamboree that coincided with the opening of the Skylander Games Gala, later in the day. In the distance, he could see even bigger crowds of people near the Skylander Town Square Bell Tower, where they were setting up stalls and spaces for the main fair. For the next three days, all *cicerones'* duties were suspended; Midtown life atop the cloudbank would be completely devoid of Grounders.

Well, thought Conn, thinking of Misty. *All except for one.*

Conn jumped out of the way as a bright-red slipskid sled, pushed by two brawny septs, whisked past him, nearly flattening him. Wheels of any sort were useless on the cloudbank. Sleds, with their runners, moved much more smoothly, and didn't cause the deep, long lasting ruts that wheels left along the cloudbank's surface. He watched as the slipskid came to an abrupt stop ahead, its two sept drivers hurrying to unload its cargo. Piece by piece, the high-stacked lengths of Ragoon timber would soon take shape into one of many concession stands or market booths.

Easily spotted in the crowds were the Cloudwalker Tamachins. A special function for retired, mostly-elderly Cloudwalkers, many of them were hunched over and slow moving. On their heads, they wore special clan-tartan berets, each embellished with a large, brightly colored, pigeon feather.

The Cloudwalker Tamachins, with their trusty rackstaffs, typically roamed about during all such festivities where septs might mistakenly wander into unsafe quickfall areas. They marked out safe spaces of cloudbank before crowds arrived, and kept watch to make sure everyone stayed safe. The Tamachins took great pride in their role, but Conn knew, from first-hand experience, they could sometimes be mean, bossy old farts when patrolling their routes or manning their posts.

Conn strode north, farther into the hustle and bustle, where a good number of booths had already been set up. Open crates, full of brightly colored fruits, vegetables, and an assortment of plump mushrooms were being positioned onto display tables. *Whoof! Whoof! Whoof!* Bright yellow flames suddenly shot high into the air on his right. A series of ChemBurn burners had been ignited, one after another. Conn eyed a nearby cage, full of squawking pigeons. "Sorry guys," he said to the caged birds. "Things aren't looking too good for you."

Music began to fill the air. Nearby was a seated group of musicians, mostly playing string instruments such as violins and cellos, though Conn spotted a flute or two, and several clarinets in the mix. By the sound of things, the group would need every minute of practice time before things really got started later in the afternoon.

Conn waved and nodded, seeing one familiar smiling face after another. Pastry chefs and grocers, candlestick makers and fabric weavers, merchant guildsmen and bookkeepers, cobblers and brewers—regular folks he'd known his whole life, many since childhood. He'd sustained friendships with them, even after sept interactions were frowned upon by the upper class clan gentry. He couldn't care less about such snooty nonsense. Up ahead in the near distance a large red and white tent was being raised; twenty men held ropes, positioned around the perimeter, and pulled and hoisted in unison. Their loud grunts carried across the white dunes. The outdoor fields, one hundred yards beyond, were correctly marked and delineated with long, tapered flags on posts that snapped and whipped high overhead, as brisk, briny-smelling winds blew in from the Atlantic.

Conn, no longer walking, first began to jog, then ran full-out toward the distant fields. Competing clan athletes were there early, practicing for their featured events. It occurred to him he should have awakened a good hour earlier. Maybe even two. He passed by huddled groups of both male and female competitors. Their multi-colored tartan kilts blazed notably against the white cloudbank and the vivid blue sky. *Shit!* His own clan team members were already here.

Conn's brother, Michael—one of their team captains—stood upon a wooden crate, addressing the rapt, attentive Brataich competitors. A good many of his fellow Cloudwalkers, who also were Skylander athletes, stood around him. With very few exceptions, the assembled men and women were the biggest, strongest, and most badass Skylanders atop the bank. They had to be in order to duel with rackstaffs, or toss a nineteen-and-a-half foot long, one hundred and seventy-five pound caber across the field. In old time Scotland, during the original Highlander Games before the Ruin, the caber was typically made from a Larch tree. These days, a Ragoon tree, stripped of its branches, was used instead.

Conn caught Toag's eye. Halfway around the now huddled group on the other side, his brow noticeably furrowed, and he shot Conn a disapproving glance. Several other players cast similar glares his way.

"Now that my brother has finally graced us with his presence, we can review a few last minute changes to the roster," Michael said. "McCaslin, you'll be second in the caber toss event tomorrow . . ."

Conn only half-listened to his brother's ramblings. Truth was, he was only competing in one event: a solo Dueling Lockwood's Match. There was little expectation he would win, or even place amongst the top two or three competitors. Last year's win, he knew full well, was a complete stroke of luck on his part. The problem was not that he wasn't proficient; at rackstaff swordplay, he was far better than proficient. He could best the lot of them, if judging was based purely on various attacking and parrying points. The problem with Conn's swordplay methodology was the amount of fouls he managed to accumulate during a match. No matter how hard he tried, Conn found it difficult to stay within the 14 by 2 meter combat arena known as the Strip. In other words, Conn was a beast of a rackstaff swordsman, but paid little attention to the finer elements of the sport.

Conn's eyes scanned his teammates' faces. Jordy Gillian was there, and Calvin Branniff, both pretty good friends of his. He caught a flash of red at the back of the crowd and saw Maggie O'Brian. She was listening intently to his brother's monotone voice. *Where is Misty?* His eyes drifted toward the distant horizon, where the top of the Pavicon Tower could barely be seen peeking above the bank. He tried to remember which of the windows belonged to the O'Brians. *Were they up on the second floor, or the third?* He pictured Misty, still lying in bed. *Did Grounder girls sleep in the nude?*

"Hey *claw baw*! You think you might want to join us for a minute?"

Conn's attention returned to Michael, who was staring at him. Everyone was staring at him. "What? I heard everything you said. You said Donaldson's got a plantar wart on his left foot. Shot Put's a no-go tomorrow for the poor lad, but Gallagher's taking his place."

"And?"

"And what?" Conn asked back, already chiding himself for daydreaming.

Michael looked away, clearly disgusted with him. "Look, not only do we need to know our own positions, but those of our teammates, as well. I guarantee, Donaldson's plantar wart won't be the worst thing to happen to a player during the competition. With a few exceptions—" Conn felt the glances of his teammates upon him. "—you've all been good about making it to practice these last few weeks. Today, we're switching things up a little. Whatever your event—tossing the Caber, Hammer Throw, Shot Put, Tug O'War, or Dueling Lockwoods—today, you'll be trading off with a teammate. One who's not competing in your own sport." Michael gave Conn a sideways glance. "Let's start with you, little brother. You'll swap with Calvin Branniff."

"Seriously? That's the Caber Toss!" Conn, indignant, thought of the wounds on his back, and the yet to be removed row of stitches.

Michael, ignoring Conn's outburst, continued, "Maggie, no swordplay for you today. How about you trade with Jordy, try your hand at Tug O'War?"

Everyone laughed with good humor. There wasn't a single Tug O'War competitor weighing less than two hundred-and-fifty pounds. Maggie couldn't top one-ten on a scale, soaking wet.

"Hey, I may be small but dinnae underestimate the raw power in these guns," Maggie said, raising up her lean arms like a muscleman flexing his biceps.

Even Conn couldn't help but laugh. Five minutes later, when Michael completed the day's roster changes, Conn headed in the direction of the Caber Toss field. In the distance, several of the event coaches, each one a mountain of a man, waited with their arms crossed over their broad chests. He eyed the stack of long Ragoon cabers and inwardly groaned. Off to the west, a band of men were assembling bleachers for tomorrow's spectators. *Was it only last year that he and Dob had sat over there together?* He remembered being annoyed at the old professor, who'd gabbed pretty much non-stop, talking incessantly throughout the entire event. He'd felt he had to explain all the root sciences, the underlying physics of things to Conn. How the caber's mass, along with its quick upward speed and momentum, and the pulling effects of gravity during the timber's inevitable return to the cloudbank, were constants. The real immeasurable variable was the athlete's strength, a strength that more or less depended on all kinds of things—what he'd eaten for breakfast that day, who was seated in the stands, and the level of applause or cheers he received. It was odd how strength could depend on something as trivial as how inspirational his coach had been, just moments before the big man on the field launched the Ragoon timber into the air.

"Don't you see?" Dob had asked excitedly. "One's consciousness impacts the very properties of physical matter, my boy!"

Conn stared up at the sky. "I really miss you, Dob."

Chapter 39

Conn, in a foul mood, moved as any man would who'd recently undergone a re-suturing of an open, eight-inch knife wound. He stepped slowly and deliberately with no extraneous swinging of his arms. It took them close to ten minutes to descend three flights of stairs, and that was with his sister, Emma, by his side, offering needed support. The healer had been clearly surprised to see the additional welts and cuts on Conn's back, but had said nothing as he tended to him. Conn had requested the healer to administer three extra bandage wrappings around his torso. Bleeding through his shirt was not an option tonight.

"Sweetie, I'm so sorry, but I'm going to have to leave you here. Need to run down to the Gala." Emma blew at a wayward strand of hair. Flustered, she secured it into an ornate hair clip worn at the back of her head. "I didnae ask for this, but certain duties come from being the lady of the house."

Conn resisted the urge to roll his eyes. Emma would never allow anyone to takeover the reins of hostess for the Skylander Games Gala. She shot a quick glance up the stairs. "Cleve, hurry on down here and take Conn's arm. You ken how I hate being late!"

"Sorry that I'm holding you up, sis," said Conn. "Go on, both of you. I've got this. Just moving a bit slower tonight."

But Emma was already clomping down the flight of stairs, holding the hem of her long gown above her ankles. The shiny green fabric made *swishing* sounds as she hurriedly descended each downward step.

Cleve joined Conn's side and clasped a hand onto his forearm. "What were you thinking? The Caber Toss . . . good God! I could have told you that was a bad idea."

Conn, not wanting to get into it, didn't bother to answer. His brother-in-law, a former healer, took care in helping him down the stairs.

"Well, you must be excited to see your pretty young lady again."

Conn had to think about that, before remembering Lili Folais was, in fact, his date for the night. The pain in his back suddenly intensified just thinking about it.

"Aye. I hope she's not wanting me to spend a lot of time on the dance floor."

"Who else amongst the Folais Clan is attending?" Cleve asked, as they slowly descended several more steps.

"The Folais Clan appeared well-represented out on the field today," Conn said. "Their tartan colors were present for each event. I saw both of Lili's twin brothers—God, they're big. There may have been a few cousins, too, and an uncle or two. They all were wearing black bands around their arms."

Cleve pursed his lips, looking somewhat mystified at that. Then his brows shot up. "Ah, I forgot. Yes, Janis Folais and his, um, untimely accident."

"Well, according to the death glares they were shooting my

way throughout the day, I don't think they've viewed it as any kind of accident. More like murder, due to us in the Brataich Clan."

"That's crazy! Why would we do harm to that Folais lad?"

Again, Conn didn't have the energy to respond. His brother-in-law was family, one of the nicest people he knew, and just perfect for Emma. He allowed her to be the more dominant one between the two. Conn seriously doubted there was a malicious or envious bone in Cleve's body. But he was clueless when it came to discussing clan or family politics. Conn couldn't remember ever seeing him attend any of the CloudMaster's weekly briefings, not even once. Although he lacked interest himself in that regard, he tried to always show up because it meant so much to his father that both his sons attend.

A rousting burst of music echoed upward into the stairwell. Conn heard his sister's voice resonating out: "From Clan Carmichael, a warm welcome for CloudMaster Jonah Carmichael and his wife, Miriam." The sound of applause followed.

Conn could sense Cleve's attempts to hurry them down the stairs. "Sounds like the Skylander Games Gala has officially commenced," he said, with far too much enthusiasm.

Another rousing burst of music echoed up into the stairwell, followed again by his sister's voice. "Of Clan Baird, a warm welcome goes to CloudMaster Toric Baird, and his lovely bride, Carissa."

"I really should be down there, standing beside Emma," Cleve said, sounding apologetic.

"Go. I'm fine, I promise. In fact, I'm feeling much better. Scoot on down there, Cleve."

By the time he reached the Empire's 81st floor landing, Conn was more than ready to find a place to sit down. Instead, he took in a deep breath and opened the door to the floor known as Storm View. Under his sister's direction, he was sure, the expansive room had been expertly decorated. Hanging down on ribbons from high above, mirror-like bedazzlements glimmered, gently spun about by invisible currents of air. Higher up, each evenly spaced around the room's perimeter, brightly colored flags hung down one after another, representing each clan participating in the Skylander Games, their individual colors and coat of arms on full display. Warm, indirect amber light flickered within art deco sconces, their ChemBurn flames burning within. Conn eyed no less than ten Dorcha Poileas strategically placed around the room and standing at attention. Each was wearing their dress uniform. They were not here to participate, as they were not of noble blood. He wondered if Bryant Peirce was somewhere about; undoubtedly he would be.

The music, loud and far too upbeat for his current mood, was the first thing to accost his senses. Second was the bustling crowd of Skylander nobility in attendance. They were already present in force, and waiting to be introduced as they entered the Gala; Conn was certain there was nary a one who wasn't talking, yelling, or laughing. He looked longingly over his shoulder, back toward the closed stairwell door.

"Conn!" It was Emma, her hand held high in the air, waving him over. "Come on, you need to be formally introduced before you head on in."

Terrific. He smiled and unenthusiastically waved back at her. He spotted Cleve, standing a few steps away from Emma, half-hidden behind an ornate pillar. His chin, bobbing up and down, kept beat with the overloud music.

Straight-backed, and with measured steps, Conn slowly ambled forward in their direction, only to be cut off by two Baird Clan Cloudwalkers. Drinks in hand, they gave him a once over then chuckled. He heard Smitty Baird, the taller of the two, mumble, "*Fud*," Scottish slang for a daft cunt.

Conn moved past the line of waiting guests, ignoring their incensed stares. By the time he reached Emma, she had her back turned and was speaking to an older woman he didn't recognize. He patiently waited, not in any particular hurry to join the Gala. Catching sight of himself in one of the reflective hanging decorations, he thought, *Pathetic*. Formal attire for a Cloudwalker, like him, required a neatly pressed black shirt and a dress kilt, in his clan's unique tartan plaid. Added to the latter was the formal element of a gold fringe that always seemed to tickle his kneecaps. An elaborately designed sporran hung from his belt, the peccary leather stiff from disuse as it was only brought out for special occasions. Brass buckles on black shoes that were polished until they gleamed, and black and gold striped stockings completed the look. Berets were optional, and as a general rule, the younger nobles wouldn't be caught dead wearing them. God forbid they look even remotely like one of the ancient Cloudwalker Tamachins.

Across the room's expanse he could see the band playing on an elevated platform. Soon hundreds of people dressed in their best garb would be mingling, dancing, or standing along the periphery, where finger-food appetizers filled trays on linen-covered long tables. Conn took in the amazing room, where the most architecturally structural alterations had taken place since the Empire State Building was first built, back in 1931. It was midway into the twenty-third century when Storm View was constructed, the name first coined by CloudMaster Doreen Macbeth. Apparently wealthy, and never one to personally miss a Gala event, she desired there should be a midtown Manhattan ballroom the likes of none other. Although the Empire State's overall number of floors remained the same, three of its floors—

the 81st, 82nd, and 83rd—were renovated, eventually becoming this magnificent, highly vaulted ballroom.

"Oh, there you are, dear," Emma said to Conn, disengaging herself from her conversation with the older lady. She looked past Conn, as if searching for someone. "Where's your date?"

"My date?"

"Lili, for goodness sakes. Would you have her enter the Gala alone without her betrothed? Sometimes I marvel that you ken how to put your shoes on in the morning. You'll have to wait. Stand aside and let this other couple pass. Oh, and Father wants to speak with you. He said it's important."

"Well, where is he?" Conn asked, glancing around.

Not so gently, Emma began nudging him over to the side. "I have no idea. He's probably back in the Callanish. Conn, please step aside, let your friend and his pretty young lady be properly introduced."

Conn did as told, feeling more than a little exasperated. Emma referred to the Callanish Standing Stones Room, a private dining hall with its own bar. There were other side rooms, ones used for smaller occasions, that were named after Scotland's numerous, ancient standing stone monuments, like the Brodgar Room, for the Ring of Brodgar monument, and the Stenness Room, for the Standing Stones of Stenness.

"So, are you lost, stupid, or just plain daft?"

Conn spun around, more than ready to unleash his own volley of insults at whoever was spouting off. Surprised, he found his best friend, Toag, smiling back at him. His skin the color of dark caramel, with uncharacteristically hazel eyes for a man of color, Toag looked relaxed and happy. Shaking his head just enough to make his dreadlocks dance upon his shoulders, he clearly was showing off for someone. And that's when Conn noticed her, a half-step behind Toag.

She had clearly taken a bath since he saw her last, and in her soft pink gown—which fit far better than the rags she had been wearing—and her auburn hair gleaming in the soft light, she was the most beautiful creature he had ever seen. Conn couldn't take his eyes off her. *Misty.*

Chapter 40

Misty froze, not expecting to suddenly see Conn standing so close. She jerked her hand free from Toag's grasp, then instantly regretted doing so. She hadn't done anything wrong; she certainly didn't *belong* to anyone. *So why then do I feel so guilty for holding Toag's hand?*

"Mist—"

Toag quickly interrupted Conn. "Hey, this is *Adaira Drummond.* I'm not sure if you two have met. She doesnae get out all that much."

Conn closed his eyes for an extended beat, then shook his head in a gesture of self-deprecation. "Yes, of course. Hello Adaira. You look, um, verra nice tonight."

"Thank you, Conn, and you look like you'd rather be anywhere but here," she replied, hoping her Scottish accent sounded both real and natural.

Conn laughed, which in turn made Toag laugh. Misty wasn't sure if it was because she'd totally fobbed her Skylander dialect, or because she'd nailed it so perfectly. She realized Conn was still staring at her so intensely she was beginning to feel self-conscious. Suddenly, she was conscious of her low neckline, and her exposed cleavage. In her entire life she had never before revealed so much skin in public. Most definitely this would be a flogging offense beneath the cloudbank. The ornate pink gown she wore was on loan from Maggie's mother. A sweet, good-humored lady, she had assured Misty the day had long passed when she'd be able to squeeze into such a tight garment again. Even so, with both Maggie and Mrs. O'Brian's help, the dress needed to be taken in at the waist with a needle and thread, but let out some at the bust. For the first time in her life, Misty's long auburn hair had been trimmed properly, and by someone other than her father, who'd never spent more than five minutes at the task.

That afternoon, leaning in close enough to feel her breath on her face, Maggie had instructed Misty on how to apply makeup to her eyes, cheeks, and lips—another punishable Grounder no-no. Misty, watching Maggie and her mother's 'mother-daughter' interactions, couldn't help but compare them to her own relationship with her mother. A mother, she reminded herself, who had disowned her in favor of a tyrant. But Mrs. O'Brian, an easy person to be around, was friendly; her relationship with Maggie seemed almost sisterly. Accepting of Maggie's views and opinions, she laughed easily at her lack of understanding things important to a younger generation. They spoke openly of Maggie's sexuality, and of other personal things that brought color to Misty's cheeks. As if instinctively knowing not to pry, Maggie's mother hadn't asked her about her own upbringing, or her purported life among the Drummond Clan. Perhaps she suspected something of the truth, or perhaps she believed that Adaira had run away from home, but she'd accepted, without giving it a second thought, that she too would be part of their little conspiracy. Clearly, she loved and trusted her daughter that much. They primped and fussed over Misty for three arduous hours. Once done, they marched her in front of a full-length mirror, Maggie holding her left arm and Mrs. O'Brian holding her right. Both beamed at her. Misty simply stared back in the mirror at the beautiful young woman dressed in a lovely pink gown.

"Oh no," Maggie scolded. "Don't even think about crying."

Misty blinked away tears that weren't from sadness but gratitude. She honestly didn't recognize the person in the mirror. She had never felt like one of those stooped, sallow-skinned Grounders merely surviving deep below the Earth's surface. She certainly didn't look like one of them anymore.

And now, as she blushed under Conn's appreciative gaze, she never wanted to go back to looking like that ever again.

She stood silent, waiting for him to say something, until a voice interrupted them. "Is that my tall, dark, and handsome fiancé?"

Misty was taken aback by the sudden approach of a strikingly beautiful woman. Wearing a fitted, ivory-colored gown, the woman didn't seem to walk so much as *glide* across the floor. Her hair flowed down her exposed back like black ink. And those eyelashes! When she blinked they fluttered like two perfect winged butterflies, and within them were two orbs of dark intensity. Everything about this woman seemed measured and calculated. Immediately, Misty knew exactly who she was: Lili Folais. And she hated the woman, without knowing or caring why.

Toag leaned in close and whispered, "That's Conn's future wife there, in case you hadn't figured that out."

Emma's voice rose above the hum of the crowd. "From Clan Brataich, please welcome Cloudwalker Conn Brataich, along with his betrothed, Ms. Lili Folais, of Clan Folais."

Misty tore her eyes away from Conn and Lili, feigning indifference. She retook Toag's hand in hers, offering him her warmest, and hopefully her most alluring smile, but the smile was gone quickly. *This was a mistake. A terrible mistake!* It was clear that everyone knew everyone here. The mere notion that she could get away with this deception was ludicrous. She pulled Toag close, her eyes boring into his.

In a hushed and desperate voice, she said, "This isn't going to work. There is a *real* Adaira Drummond."

Toag didn't seem to share her concern. "You haven't met any of the Drummonds—and neither have most of the Skylanders in Manhattan. They're weird and unsociable, like hermits, the whole lot of them. Sure, there's a real Adaira Drummond, but no one's ever even seen her. Just stick to the plan, it'll be fine."

Together they stepped up to Emma's side. Emma put a hand affectionately on Toag's shoulder, but when her eyes leveled onto Misty next to him, she looked perplexed.

"This is Adaira Drummond, Emma," said Toag casually. "This is her first Gala."

Emma stared at Misty for a long moment and then smiled. "And here I thought I kent every man, woman, and child atop the cloudbank. Welcome, my dear. I'm Emma; Toag is my brother's best friend. So, will your parents also be attending this year?"

Without thinking, Misty shot a questioning look over to Toag, and instantly regretted doing so. *Why would he know more about my supposed family than I do?* Almost imperceptibly, Toag shook his head. Misty replied, "No, they're . . . not much for participating in this sort of thing these days."

Starting to feel desperate, Misty glanced around at the crowd accumulating behind them. She scanned their faces, looking for Maggie and her date—a Skylander girl Misty had not yet met. She saw no sign of them.

"Well, you two have a splendid night. Now let me introduce you," Emma said, taking Misty's hand in hers. She signaled the distant bandleader and another rousing interval of music filled the ballroom.

"From Clan Brataich, please welcome Cloudwalker Toag Munna, and Ms. Adaira Drummond, of Clan Drummond."

Toag and Misty stepped forward. He raised their clasped hands in the air in appreciation of the applause. All eyes were on them, no—on *her*, the never before seen hermit Drummond daughter. *This is a sorry mistake,* Misty thought, *and they are going to find out.* She pictured herself being chased outside by an angry mob of Skylanders, where the only escape would be to jump into the void left by the Drake when it collapsed.

Toag and Misty moved over to where the side tables were positioned, in front of the outer wall's surrounding row of windows. Other guests mingled there, picking at finger-food offerings. A couple who both looked to be in their fifties moved toward them; the woman wore a satin dress that shimmered as she walked. The man, no doubt her husband, was wearing his dress kilt but also a drape of plaid fabric angled down across his torso, where several rows of glistening gold medals were displayed.

"General Craig Howkland and his wife Grafton Howk-land," Toag said in a voice just above a whisper. "He pretty much leads all of the combined Midtown forces of our military."

"And that cheerless man over there?" Misty asked, gesturing toward another man who was easily seventy-five with a shock of silver-white hair. She recognized the long cape and the dark colors worn by the Dorcha Poileas. He too wore a good number of medals, although his were shiny silver, clasped to the left breast of his formal jacket.

"Commander Gains Bask. He's in charge of the Poileas, at least on an interim basis. His boss, Colonel Milligan, died last year."

"He doesn't look too pleased to be here," Misty commented, noticing Bask's dour expression.

"I don't know much about him. He transferred here from Jersey City. Rumor has it, he may have mixed loyalties. Probably nothing but idle gossip; the Poileas aren't exactly well-liked."

Misty heard distant bells start to ring. Soon multiple ringing sounds were coming from multiple buildings.

"Now? Really?" said Toag with a groan. "That'll be the Bell Tower." He noted Misty's confusion, and added, "Rampage alarm. It's a warning for an imminent God's Rampage. It's for everyone to hurry and get under cover."

Sure enough, dark and angry-looking clouds had swept in outside, high above the Skylander realm. As she was about to ask Toag more about God's Rampage, the entire sky suddenly blazed bright. Misty flinched and grabbed Toag's arm. As far as the eye could see, great bolts of electricity were stabbing and branching out, both upward and downward. Deafening thunderclaps assaulted Misty's ears, to the point where she was tempted to crawl beneath the nearest table. But she was held spellbound with the atmospheric event. It was as if a war had commenced between two godlike creatures, fighting each other from above and below, each delivering one momentous counterstrike after another. The sky was on fire. Misty was certain this had to be the end of the world; the end of everything.

It lasted four or five minutes before ceasing almost as quickly as it had begun. Misty continued to stare out the window, slowly realizing she was still clinging desperately to Toag's left arm. Others who'd stood at the windows near them had casually refocused their attention back on the Gala festivities inside. She heard Emma's voice; another Cloudwalker and his date were being introduced.

"Storm View," Toag said at her side. "Room's appropriately named, wouldn't you say?"

Misty nodded. "How often does this happen?"

"Every few months in the summer? In the winter, once or twice a month," Toag said.

"Being out there, during a God's Rampage . . . is it dangerous?"

"Aye! You don't want to be out there when that happens. You head for the closest building and pray you dinnae get struck."

Misty nodded, finding it hard to pull her attention away from the window, even minutes after the last lightening bolt had flared so brightly and the warning bell had stopped ringing.

"Come on, let's dance," Toag said, leading her toward the dance floor farther inside the room.

Misty pulled back on his arm. "I don't know how," she said nervously. "Dancing is not permitted for a Grounder girl. Do you know anything at all about the Purgeforth Scriptures?"

"You'll be fine," said Toag dismissively. "I'll walk you through it."

He steered her gently toward the dance floor, where no less than ten couples were now slow-dancing to a pretty song sung by a young man on the stage.

"It's called, 'The Bonnie Banks o' Loch Lomond'," Toag said. He placed a hand over his heart. "It would be a crime not to dance to such a stirring melody, aye?"

Misty spotted Conn and Lili dancing, their bodies close, with her waif-thin arms raised and clasped behind his neck. They were looking deeply into each other's eyes as they rocked back and forth to the beat of the music. The soloist sang along to the old, hauntingly beautiful melody:" But me and my true love will never meet again, On the bonnie, bonnie banks o' Loch Lomond."

Misty felt a sudden physical pain in her chest she couldn't describe as Toag maneuvered them farther onto the dance floor.

He took her hands in his, placed them around his neck, and drew her in close. They moved and swayed to the music as the others did around them. *So this is dancing!* Misty smiled up at him. *Dancing is nice.*

Toag, staring at her, scrutinized her expression. "They will be married soon," he said, glancing at Conn and Lili. "Misty, you are so beautiful . . . beyond words. It would be a shame to squander your love on a lad so unavailable."

She wanted to assure Toag he had it all wrong. That he was misreading the situation—misreading her. But with one look into his wounded hazel eyes, she knew any such justification would be a wasted effort. She opted for silence instead, and placed her cheek upon his chest, letting the bittersweet music console her heavy heart.

Chapter 41

This was not the Lili that Conn had come to know, though admittedly, he really didn't know her all that well. Gone was the spoiled daddy's girl who, on the few occasions they'd been together, had seemed resentful of their predestined espousal. Now, peering up at him, her lips turned up into a demure, coy expression, she fluttered her eyelashes at him then glanced over at Toag and Misty slow dancing.

"So, my handsome Brataich Cloudwalker," she said in a silky voice. "You have caught the eyes of more than a few pretty lassies this fine night. And to think, we will be married in what, a month? I do hope you are ready and still find me a suitable mate?"

"Lili, so much has happened. Talk of such things—"

In a flash, her expression turned menacing. "Our parents have worked tirelessly for years to bring this union about. It's bigger than us. Or do you not care about anything but yourself?"

"Of course I care, Lili. Can we talk about this some other time?" *Like never,* he thought.

"It's for your own good," she added not attempting to hide

the not so subtle threat. Her expression held none of the sweet coyness from just seconds before; her eyes filled with anger, and her mouth slipped into a sneer as she momentarily shifted back into the real Lili he knew. But just as quickly, her anger disappeared as she changed the subject. "So you know that Drummond girl over there?"

Conn shrugged, treading carefully. "Not really."

"Toag seems entranced. Isn't she a little, I don't know, awkward? Unrefined? Like the poor girl's been locked away in the Drummond's basement all these years?"

Conn continued to show indifference to her questioning. Although, there was some truth to what Lili said: Misty had indeed lived her entire life in a Grounder basement of sorts. "She's a nice kid. Not a pretentious bone in her body." Conn regretted the words just as soon as he said them, noting the true jealousy that sprung in Lili's cold, almond-shaped eyes.

"Oh, I see," she said, her voice soft. "So that's what I am to you? Pretentious? Good to know what my future husband thinks of me."

"I didnae mean it like that, Lili. It wasn't a comparison. You're both verra different; nothing alike."

"Fine! Maybe you should be dancing with her?"

She pulled him close, and allowed her hips to subtly grind and rub against his groin in cadence to the music. Then she took both his hands and pushed him away. Now leading, she raised his arm and twirled beneath it, then pulled in close to him again. The quick dance movement hurt Conn's back, but he covered the grimace with a smile. He realized she had maneuvered them over to Toag and Misty.

"Come on, let's switch things up a little, my love," Lili said, loud enough to be heard above the music. She let go of Conn and effortlessly spun away, only to position herself, *somehow*, between Toag and Misty. Forced apart, Lili laughed. She took hold of Toag's still-raised hand, and placed his other hand onto the small of her back. As they spun away, Toag shot Misty an apologetic expression.

Conn, now standing alone and feeling stupid, raised his brows at Misty, who looked both disconcerted and embarrassed at being left alone on the dance floor. She nodded back and took a hesitant step forward. He pulled her in close, his hand firmly on her back, as she took his raised hand in her own.

He said, "Is this too weird for you? You want to stop—"

"No! I mean, please, it's fine," she responded a bit too abruptly. She smiled, not looking up at him, as color rose in her cheeks. "I don't think I could bear to be abandoned twice on the dance floor in so short a time."

"Nah, I won't abandon you, Misty. I promise. " He pulled her even closer, breathing in the scent of jasmine perfume. "How you holding up? You've had a lot of changes in the past few days. I know you're not used to any of this."

When she finally looked up to him, he thought, *God, I could get lost in those emerald eyes—if I let myself.* Her smile was warm, with a hint of shyness. Now, so close to her, Conn noticed the ever so faint freckles that dappled the bridge of her nose, a detail he hadn't observed before.

Conn was faintly aware of the music changing, the musicians flowing seamlessly from song to song as he and Misty remained on the dance floor. He knew he should stop, that he should go and find Lili, but with Misty in his arms, he didn't care.

"Conn!" Michael was at his side, looking perturbed. Conn, distracted, hadn't even sensed his approach. "Are you deaf? Your presence has been requested by Father."

"What? What are you talking about?" But even as he spoke, Conn remembered his sister's words as he entered the Gala. *Father wants to speak with you. He said it's important.*

Michael glanced at Misty and seemed surprised.

Conn lowered his voice, "Yes, it's Misty. But remember, she's going by Adaira."

"I know who it is. Hi. You look . . ."

Conn cut him off. "Where's Father?"

Michael, still staring at Misty, said, "The Callanish; there's a dinner for all the CloudMasters and immediate family members. Lili's there. Alone. She said you abandoned her."

Conn glanced about the dance floor and sure enough, she and Toag were nowhere to be seen. He turned his attention back to Misty, still held closely in his arms. "Sorry, I have to go."

"That's okay, I see Maggie over by the side tables." Waving, she smiled at her across the room. When she released Conn's hand and moved away, he could still smell the scent of jasmine in her wake.

Conn followed Michael through a rear door, down a winding flight of stairs, then through another door leading into the Callanish Room. Upon entering, he immediately knew *something* was wrong. There was conversation, even some subdued laughter around the massive, raw timber-planked table that seated forty comfortably. But at the head of the table, seated at the far end, was none other than Gordon Folais. Conn's father, Robert Brataich, the only real Skylander leader in Manhattan for as long as Conn could remember, was seated to Gordon's left. Robert coughed and struggled to clear his throat of accumulated phlegm. Hunched over, he looked as sick as Conn had ever seen him.

Then realization hit him. There was but one CloudKing. The Midtown clans hadn't rallied together yet to promote Robert Brataich. Only now did Conn see beyond the smiles and joviality; as he met the eyes of individual Manhattan Cloud-Masters, he saw through the pretense to the forced smiles and uneasy chatter. CloudMaster Lidia O'Cain showed fear in her now-downturned gaze.

Standing behind Gordon Folais, one at each shoulder, were his two sons Dearth and Garret. Seeming larger than life, both big and muscular—like identical cast statues—they appraised the new arrivals. Their eyes were cold and unblinking in their sunken sockets. Conn could feel their hatred bore into him. Spinter Row Folais, the third son, sat quietly to the CloudKing's right. But it was Gordon Folais' demeanor that was most unsettling. He looked both calm and confident, as if he'd just heard a bit of good news. Perhaps a healer's proclamation, telling him he'd been cured of a terminal illness. Without a word, Conn and Michael crossed the room to stand by their father.

A loud thunderclap outside the windows, followed by a flash of lighting, brought silence into the room. Conn still didn't know what was going on—what sort of discussion he'd just walked into. One thing was for damn sure, there was tension in the room. He could both feel it and smell it.

Gordon Folais suddenly stood, his chair pulled back and set aside by Dearth.

"Very good; we are all present. And good that the entire Brataich family is in attendance." Gordon paused a moment to survey the faces around the table. "This is a momentous occasion. Soon, each one of you will have a choice: either to embrace change or attempt to fight it. We are but one people—a proud people—each of us a derivative of Celtic heritage. God has bestowed upon us a unique blessing. Our genetic mutation, which allows us to live upon the cloudbank, is a blessing which makes us superior to all others alive on this good earth."

Conn caught sight of Lili, leaning against the far wall by one of the windows. Her bemused expression irritated him almost as much as her father's talk of genetic superiority.

"It is time we come together and unite as one people, living in one city."

Cross-talk murmurs rose from those seated at the table.

"Silence!" Gordon barked, his face momentarily contorted in anger. He pulled his rackstaff from his belt and, with the flick of a wrist, extended it out into its lockwood prolongation. The unfurled blade glimmered, reflecting the room's ambient light. Gordon raised the weapon, pointing its tip toward the window. Every eye in the room was upon him; it was a serious sign of disrespect to unsheathe a weapon in polite company, but no one spoke. "Out there—not far to the east—are thousands of souls in dire need. Our Jersey City cloudbank is succumbing to quick-fall. Conditions are worsening by the day. My people must migrate, and soon."

Conn's father finally looked up. His eyes were furious, wild with rage. He tried to stand, but needed the assistance of Cloud-Master Baird to help him rise to his feet. "I have told you time and time again that we cannot accommodate your people. There is simply no room. I am sorry, Gordon." Robert glanced toward the window and shook his head, releasing a sigh of resignation. "Perhaps there is minimal Midtown vacancy on select floors . . . those deep within the cloudbank. I can check. "

Gordon slowly nodded, offering a condescending smile. "So that is it. The very crux of the matter. Your unwillingness to bend. You refuse to assist a friend in need, and deign to offer your Jersey City brethren only those floors hidden deep within the cloudbank? The dredge of Skylander real estate, where my people would live only a notch above the lowly Grounders?"

"It's a start, Gordon! And one hell of a lot better than the alternative, which is staying where you are now."

Conn and Michael, still standing at their father's side, exchanged wary glances.

"You have conveniently forgotten, Robert, old friend, that

there is but one reigning CloudKing. The matter is not for you to decide."

"That's quite easy to correct," Lidia O'Cain said, also rising to her feet. "All ye in favor of reinstating Robert Brataich, of Clan Brataich, as CloudKing, say Aye. Say Aye now!"

"Aye!"

"Aye!"

"Aye!"

"Aye!"

Before the fifth CloudMaster could rise to his feet, be the next to say 'Aye,' a man suddenly stepped forward. Conn had never laid eyes on him before. He strode forward from his hidden place in the shadowy corner of the room, and gasps of shocked recognition rose from those around the table. Apparently he was not a stranger to everyone. He appeared to be in his fifties or early sixties; his hair, obsidian black, had a single white streak running from his forehead to his crown. He wore a long robe, not too dissimilar to the kind Dob once wore, although this man's robe was black.

Gordon said, "Please, allow me to introduce you to—"

"We know exactly who he is," Lidia O'Cain said with disgust in her voice. "High Priest Dwaine Kincaid, purveyor of dark conjuring, instigator of war and misery. How dare you, Gordon! For two decades we have had peace and prosperity atop the cloudbank; we've quelled disputes between clans that had lasted for centuries. All thanks due to our vanquishing the likes of him to far away places. Why? Why have you brought this abomination back to our realm?"

Robert, frail and needing the support of Baird's shoulder, turned around to face the robed man. He spoke just above a whisper, but his voice was commanding. "You will leave here. Leave and never return. "

High Priest Dwaine Kincaid gazed placidly at the ailing

CloudMaster. "Or what? You'll cough on me? Or maybe you'll wet yourself?" The High Priest smirked as he raised the point of his fully extended rackstaff. Robert Brataich's eyes suddenly went wide, and he looked down, horrified. Urine, now freely flowing beneath his kilt, was visibly running down his legs. "No, *CloudMaster*, my people have suffered under your exile long enough."

Both Conn and Michael watched their father's humiliation in horror. Without a word spoken, both sons charged, Conn around the left side of the table and Michael to the right. But then Robert Brataich was lifted suddenly into the air, first vertically, then abruptly spun around horizontally and onto his back. Conn slowed. He had no idea what was happening, or how, but he was desperate to assist his father. Now everyone was up on their feet, yelling for the priest to stop, to put the poor man down, as Robert was slowly lifted higher and transported through the air. Even Lili, still at the edge of the room, looked shocked. Hands reached up, attempting to grab an arm or a leg, but Robert's struggling form rose ever higher out of reach.

Gordon, who had moved back into an unused portion of the room, stood perfectly still, only his eyes tracking the elevated approach of the Manhattan CloudMaster. Then, in a blur of motion—with an overhead two-handed strike—Gordon Folais severed the head of Robert Brataich. It fell to the floor with a wet-sounding *thunk,* and rolled until it came to an abrupt stop at the feet of Robert's youngest son, Conn Brataich.

Chapter 42

I n the breadth of the two seconds he stood there, Conn initially experienced a state of confused mental paralysis, one that then transcended into some kind of foggy disbelief. Inner trepidation came next, and the faint understanding that something *so, so, so* terrible had just occurred. Then he realized that the odd-looking bloody object lying at his feet actually was his father's decapitated head. *My father is dead.*

Reaching for the paw of his rackstaff, nestled by his hip, was as unconscious an act as blinking his eyes, or taking a breath. His gaze leveled onto the man wearing the long dark robes, and Conn moved without thought or calculation. A flick of his wrist brought his rackstaff into lockwood position. He stormed forward, crossing half the space between them while bringing up his blade into position. High Priest Dwaine Kincaid's eyes caught the movement of his charge. Conn came at him with a *Fleche* move, an all-out attack that provided Kincaid no recovery to guard against. Conn leapt into the air toward his opponent, bringing his rear foot forward for the landing. Even before his foot touched the floor, Conn's thrusting strike came at Kincaid's heart as fast as an in-flight arrow. Conn expected Kincaid to attempt a *Counter-Riposte*—a defensive parry with his own extended rackstaff—but none came. Somehow Kincaid had maneuvered out of the way. Conn's thrust—one that was certain to end the man's life in an instant—missed its mark. The high priest, still alive, was now in a far superior position. As Conn attempted to regain his off-balance footing, he realized Kincaid had not moved even an inch. His forward thrust had somehow been diverted. And had he not, in fact, felt a subtle, invisible push against his outstretched arm? Conn, still off-balance, stumbled forward onto the floor.

In that instant, Conn was suddenly aware of the others in the room. The clamor of turned-over chairs, the snapping sounds of rackstaffs being engaged, and loud voices shouting as orders were issued. No less than eight CloudMasters charged toward the robed man.

But High Priest Dwaine Kincaid looked as calm as a man taking an afternoon stroll. Raising the end of his rackstaff, he made a gentle sweep of the room from left to right. As if struck by the force of an invisible, oceanic wave, one by one the priest's attackers were lifted up and thrown backward. Some landed on the long dining table, while others crashed hard into the wall behind it.

Rising to his feet, Conn took in the surrounding chaos. Michael, somehow, had managed to get to his feet before anyone else. With ease, he jumped onto the table top and leapt, not toward Kincaid but toward Gordon Folais. *Of course!* He was the orchestrator of this barbaric, ungodly act. But the high priest, also quick to act, targeted his rackstaff's tip toward Michael's inflight location. Conn's brother's trajectory came to an immediate halt in midair. Immobile as a sculpture, Michael ceased to blink—his chest no longer expanding and contracting with his breath. The room became quiet, and everyone stilled. Only faint sounds of music, and of happy partygoers, spilled down from the ballroom above.

Lili, along with her three brothers, Dearth, Garret and Spinter Row, and their father, Gordon, weathered the commotion without so much as a scratch. The twins remained captivated by the sight of Michael Brataich's motionless form, hovering high above the dining table. Lili was breathing hard, her eyes wide as her gaze darted around the chaotic room, but her expression remained stony. Together, they all stood at the back of the room in a dimly lit area. Conn spotted a pretty, wide-eyed steward, probably no older than Misty, standing motionless and terrified behind the bar.

Gordon said, "Things dinnae have to progress this way, with all this unnecessary upheaval and violence. Are we not one people? All I ask here is for a little accommodation for your brethren in need, that's all." Gordon didn't seem to notice, or care, that his so-called *brethren* were shooting cold glares of hatred his way. "Now, there can be no mistaking who the master of the realm is. After all, there can be but one CloudKing. Make no mistake about that."

Gordon's focus shifted to the floor, to the headless body of the late Robert Brataich. Bemused, he tilted his head. It looked as if he were contemplating something—something only he could fully appreciate. When he spoke, his voice was calm, almost jovial. "Each of you is thinking this is war. That you will defend your Midtown realm to the death, if that is what's mandated, aye?" Gordon surveyed the stern faces glaring back at him. "High Priest Kincaid, if you would be so kind?"

Kincaid, bowing his head in deference to the CloudKing, walked over to the far right window, which exploded in a flash of light. Some of the glass shards fell outward while others cascaded onto the floor inside. Cold winds buffeted the Callanish Room. The High Priest stood aside, providing them an open view to the darkness outside. He raised his chin and held up his rackstaff with the gauche posturing of a stage magician. His extended rackstaff, all six feet in length, pointed outward through the open window. In the far distance they could see the ignition of a tiny spark. A moment later, a burst of brilliant lighting erupted, emanating from both above and below. The Midtown realm was momentarily illuminated, the blackness of nighttime now turned into the stark brightness of day. And in that brightly lit moment an army could be seen off in the distance. A thousand armed men and a hundred Cloud-Walkers marched toward Manhattan, interspersed together upon the cloudbank.

Lidia O'Cain, a bloody gash marking her cheek, was the first to speak. "You have no idea what kind of hell storm you've unleashed here this night, Folais."

"Careful, Lidia," said Gordon. "This is not the time to be making idle threats. Or shall I have your head cleaved from your shoulders as I did your dear friend Robert?" Gordon eyed his family, and gestured toward the closest door. "Come children, I believe we've outstayed our welcome. The rest of you, you have one week to prepare proper accommodations for my Jersey City populace. All floors now occupied above the cloudbank must be vacated. Once my people have found accommodation, perhaps some of you may move back above the cloudbank, if you prove loyal to your CloudKing." His eyes found Conn's. "Any remaining members of Clan Brataich will have to find somewhere else to live, perhaps in Jersey City? It's up to you. But the Empire State is now mine, and you are no longer welcome in Manhattan."

Together, the Folais family moved toward the lower-level exit. Lili looked straight ahead, not meeting Conn's eyes. The high priest fell in behind them. One by one they filed out until only Kincaid remained in the room. He turned back, standing within the door's open threshold, and pointed his rackstaff above everyone's heads. Michael Brataich, his arms and legs suddenly beginning to flail, dropped with a loud crash onto the large Ragoon timber dining table.

Chapter 43

Two days later...

The Jersey City army was gone. Only the trampled surface of the distant cloudbank provided any evidence that they indeed had been there. The news came from the band of Brataich Clan scouts, who'd returned the day before from the southwest.

Appropriately, the morning was bitter cold and the encroaching fog had enveloped the surrounding building tops like a blanket. Translucent white puffs glided wistfully across the bank like angel effigies, like a half-forgotten dream coming to life.

Eight bagpipers played a sorrowful, mournful melody. The pipe major, striding a few steps ahead, led the funeral procession heading now for the cloudbank above the Hudson River. More than two hundred Cloudwalkers—some very young and some very old—stood watch for quickfall along the winding route. Of all the *cicerones'* duties, this one was the most dreaded. Nary a Cloudwalker's cheek was dry on this frigid fall morning.

Behind the bagpipers came the six pallbearers. Upon their strong, rigid shoulders, they supported Ragoon poles, which in turn supported a polished brass bed upon which was the body of deceased CloudMaster Robert Brataich. Conn and Michael had taken the forward left and right carrying positions, while the late leader's closest friends took up positions right behind them. These two were CloudMaster Morg Baird, and his son, Fib Baird, on his right. The other two pole-carrying positions went to Hansen Brataich, a cousin of Robert's, and to Cloud-Master Lidia O'Cain.

Behind the pallbearers carrying the bedded CloudMaster's remains were all those Midtown Skylanders who wished to pay their final respects, and offer a fond farewell to a leader they would wholeheartedly miss. Tightly bundled within their long dark coats, the precession of thousands—men, women, and children of both the nobility and the sept class—snaked along the funeral route that stretched two-and-a-half miles in its entirety.

In the distance beyond the procession, large tents stood empty, void of the cheerful markets and vendors that should have filled them with noise and music and laughter. The barren, unoccupied bleachers and the unused fields of the canceled Skylander Games held vigil over the funeral procession like solemn monuments to a forgotten future.

It took close to an hour to reach the chosen spot. A vast open space of white, it was a place void of city towers or the meandering paths of other Skylander pedestrians. Here, twenty stout brass columns—ignited ChemBurn flames atop each—encircled the quickfall patch. In between them, tall poles reached high overhead where Brataich Clan-crested flags snapped smartly in the high, onshore winds. Directly below was the midway point across the Hudson River.

Conn could see Bishop Longstep patiently waiting for them ahead. He stood on the opposite side of the quickfall patch, which measured approximately twenty by twenty-foot. The bishop, pushing eighty, still maintained the erect posture of a much younger man. He had a full head of long white hair, which he wore down to his shoulders. As part of his liturgical dress, he wore the traditional *biretta* upon his head—a scarlet-colored, puffed-up hat that had four raised, stiffened corners. His long, cream-colored satin gown shimmered in the torchlight. Upon his shoulders lay a scarlet draping that matched his biretta. In his hands he held a small black booklet—verses of the Kirk's teachings—that Conn assumed were read for just such an occasion. The bishop had a surprisingly unlined face, and a just-scrubbed appearance, with pink cheeks, nose, and chin. His bright and alert blue eyes watched Robert Brataich's bed as it was lowered by the six pallbearers onto the cloudbank.

Conn's eyes took in the cluster of seven other clergy members, huddling behind the bishop, and found he was getting somewhat annoyed. Not so much because they had all gathered here for his father—for the late CloudMaster was far more like a CloudKing—but that nary a one of them had paid an equal deference to Professor Dob. Conn loved his father, but in a more abstract way than he had loved Dob. The professor had been far more paternal than the deceased man, dressed in his Brataich tartan-colored wraps, resting before him now upon an ornate brass bed.

Now they needed to wait while the winds blew, and for the long line of mourners to shuffle past them. They would encircle them, keeping a good distance back from the quickfall, as the bagpipers continued piping their mournful ballads.

Emma appeared at Conn's side, a silk handkerchief held beneath her reddened nose. Sniffing, she took ahold of his upper arm and leaned her head against his shoulder. On her other side, Michael placed a comforting hand on her back, stroking it with brotherly condolence. His eyes glistened. Both he and Emma had always been closer to their father than Conn.

Now standing taller, letting out a slow, shuddered breath, Emma said in a hushed voice, "I still can't believe it. That he's been taken from us."

Conn nodded his head.

She glanced toward her father's body, then leaned in closer to Conn. "How did they, um, secure his head back on to his body?"

Conn stared at her, dumbfounded. "Does that really matter, Emma?"

"No, no. Of course not," she replied, as the bagpipes played on. "It's just that . . . I couldn't sleep last night, so I got to wondering. It wouldn't be right for it to . . ." She let her words trail off.

"What? Right for it to what?" Conn asked irritably.

Michael, scowling, shushed them both.

"You know, to separate again during the fall." She gestured with a hand wave to the left, then waved the other hand right.

Conn closed his eyes in righteous indignation. He also hadn't slept much last night. But then again, he rarely did. And, if he was being honest with himself, he too had wondered what means the mortician used to affix his father's cleaved head back onto his body. Perhaps a strong wrapping of some sort, or sutures, though he didn't think either would be sufficient to withstand the jostling from a long processional walk, or multiple lifting ups and setting downs. Best would be some kind of sturdy metal spike, driven sufficiently down into the neck area then up into the head.

Conn glanced over to his right and saw Michael shaking. His bottom lip captured between upper and lower teeth. Only then did Conn realize his brother wasn't caught in the throes of despair, but of controlled laughter. Thinking back, that was how it usually started when they were children. It only took one kid, forcing down a smirk, or a smile, or—God forbid—stifling a giggle. Then like a virus, it would spread to them all, and choking back the ensuing laughter was almost impossible. And, of course, it always happened at the most inappropriate time. *Times like now.* Conn forced himself not to look at either sibling, concentrating instead on the music, on the blowing wind, on his shoes atop the cloudbank. He looked up and saw the mourners, taking up positions directly across from him, lined up on the other side of the flaming, stout brass pillars and the swaying, narrow, clan flagpoles. The sadness reflecting off their faces instantly sobered him.

Conn saw a boy of no more than nine or ten, weeping openly into his palms. He realized it was young Brig. Brig, who never had a real father, spent much of his youth scurrying and scampering about within the Empire State's superstructure. Lurking in shadows and behind walls, he had watched and spied on Robert, and also on Conn, Emma, and Michael. The Brataich family was, in a true sense, his family too, though he was more like a ghost figure, unable to connect physically or emotionally.

Conn, letting his eyes drift farther back into the shuffling crowd, caught sight Maggie's red hair. She stared back at him with a blank expression. He then looked to her right and, on seeing Misty, his heart skipped a beat. She mouthed the words, *I'm so sorry Conn.*

Misty stared across the white cloudbank at the tall, dark-haired Cloudwalker. She found herself scrutinizing Conn's every expression, trying to dissect his emotional state, moment by moment—like a healer would an ailing patient. She wondered if Conn had deliberately chosen not to wear a coat on such a chilly day. Other CloudWalkers wore theirs, as did his own brother, Michael. She watched the collar of his dress shirt being buffeted by the winds.

The bagpipers had stopped playing and the bishop began to read aloud from his little black book. He paced the outer perimeter of the empty space encircled flagpoles and torches. A span of white, the space looked, at least to her, like any other area of cloudbank surface. She briefly wondered what the significance of this place was, so far away from Midtown Manhattan. She meant to ask Maggie about it, but hadn't felt comfortable talking about such unimportant things on a somber occasion like this. One thing had been made perfectly clear. Everything was different now. Nothing would be the same. How that affected her personally, she didn't know. Again, it didn't seem appropriate to speak selfishly when the whole world had flipped upside down for so many here.

Other well-dressed religious men joined the one wearing the red hat, and together they stroke forward single file, one after the other. They were all muttering words in unison; what sounded like some kind of Scripture. Maggie hadn't told her much about the Kirk—Skylander religion—but it seemed very different from Purgeforth. Misty's mind flashed back to beneath the cloudbank, to the streets far below, where Grounder parishioners and solemn women, their heads always covered, wore dark frumpy dresses and kept their eyes downcast as they lived their desolate lives.

Movement caught Misty's eye and brought her back to the present. Conn and the others were moving around the bedded remains of the deceased. Music was playing again, a woman singing a mournful and moving Celtic song. Although she had never met Conn's father, Misty found she was hurting just the same. Not for herself, but for him. The pallbearers, moving in unison between the brass torches, set the funeral bed down. Then the others departed and only Conn and Michael remained, until Emma rejoined her brothers. In unison they knelt, each placing a hand upon their father's wrapped chest. Emma spoke softly, perhaps a prayer. Or well wishes to her father, on his next journey. The three stood, and Emma took a step back. Conn and Michael, taking hold of the two poles at the head of the funeral bed, together lifted it waist-high. The body of CloudMaster Robert Brataich slid down the bed's other end and fell away, disappearing down into the white void, where, undoubtedly, in moments, it would splash into river far below. A tear escaped from Misty's eye, blazing a shining, wet trail down her cheek as she remembered her own father, consigned to the same fate only a few days earlier, though it felt like much longer.

The onlookers began to applaud, a subdued clapping at first, then more excitedly. Smiles had replaced their sorrowful frowns. Soon, thousands were cheering and yelling, whooping and hollering, pumping fists into the air. The music too had come alive, and a happy ballad now filled the air. Misty watched as Conn and Emma embraced, them Conn and Michael. *What strange people these Skylanders are,* she thought. The large crowd began to move away, starting their long trek back to the city. Misty hoped Maggie would want to wait and talk to Conn first. She was fairly certain she would.

Off in the distance, well beyond the Brataich cluster of family and friends, past the mourning line of Skylanders, she spotted six individuals standing apart. But these people were not joyful and rejoicing, Not Skylanders, by any means, they were easily recognizable by a Grounder girl like herself. Tall and awkward in appearance, the contours of High Deacon Terrance Lasher's bald head was most familiar as he loomed; his mere presence there felt somehow sacrilegious. Three darkly clad women stood by him—two on one side, and one on the other. All had their heads lowered. And then her mother raised her head.

Chapter 44

Now, making eye contact with Astrid, they stared over at one another for several long moments. *Is that an expression of concern?* Misty wondered. Her mother tentatively brought a hand up—as if reaching out to her—but then seemed to think better of it. People continued to mill past them. Momentarily, a group of five or six completely blocked her view. When Misty looked again, both she and the deacon, along with his other wives, were gone. Misty stepped left then right, up on her tiptoes, trying to get a glimpse of them, but they'd suddenly disappeared. *Why had they come here, anyway? Was it a show of condolence, of support, from those below the cloudbank?* she wondered.

"Oh no," Maggie said, taking Misty's arm. "We need to get moving."

"Why, what's happened?"

"It's because of what's about to happen. Damn. I should have been paying more attention. Someone's been watching you."

"I know that."

"Really? You know that Captain Bryant Peirce, of the

Dorcha Poileas, has been glowering at you from afar?" Maggie asked her, confused.

"Who?

"Don't look. It's best we just merge into the crowd, and try to blend in. Don't act suspicious."

"And how do I do that?" Misty asked, trying to act casually, like she was just one of the many Skylanders now trudging along. She tried to keep her head and eyes lowered, but the temptation to look around was just too great. She stole a quick peek. The sweep of her glance missed him the first time, then her eyes shot back to him, a reflex reaction. The uniformed man stood twenty feet away and he was indeed glowering. She recognized him—the man who chased her in the stairwell. She took in his long cape, and the scar that ran down the left side of his face.

"Crap!"

"You're acting suspicious!" Maggie murmured without moving her lips. "We're going to have to walk past him. No way around that."

"But he's seen me before, escaping down the steps of the Drake. He knows I'm a Grounder."

"Smile like I just said something funny," Maggie said casually, waving toward someone off in the crowd.

"What will they do to me?" Misty asked with a forced smile on her face.

"You dinnae want to think about that right now, Misty."

"Tell me!"

"Best case? They'll imprison you within the Onyx Building's headquarters for an indefinite period of time. I'm betting they dinnae take kindly to Grounders pretending to be Skylanders, especially ones of noble blood."

They slowly moved to within ten feet of the still-staring Dorcha Poileas captain.

"And worst case?"

Maggie shook her head. "Shush! Keep your voice down."

"Tell me?"

"Execution. But hopefully it won't come to that."

"Isn't that extreme?" Misty said, her voice rising several octaves.

"Aye. But they like to make an example of certain offenders. Keeps other Grounders from getting any ideas about sneaking up and living above the cloudbank."

"You mean like me? Shouldn't we have talked more about this earlier?"

Maggie shrugged. "You didnae have much choice at the time."

Misty nodded. "I know, I know. I'm just scared."

Maggie abruptly glanced up and smiled. "A chilly good morning to you, Bryant."

Now a mere two paces away, Pierce pulled his gaze away from Misty just long enough to peer down at Maggie. "I suppose. If you can call a CloudMaster's funeral a good morning."

"Oh, aye. I suppose you're right about that."

"And who is this with you, Maggie?"

"Oh come on! You know my cousin, Adaira of the Drummond Clan. She's staying with us for a few days. The rest of her family is sick."

Pierce refocused his attention fully on Misty, staring down his nose, scrutinizing her.

Misty nodded. "Barfing and shitting non-stop, the whole lot of them. Couldnae wait to get out of there. Maggie's my true savior," she added in her best Skylander accent.

Pierce chuckled at the bathroom humor. "Aye," he said slowly, but his expression was marginally less suspicious. "I think I've seen you around. Drummonds dinnae get out much; keep to yourselves mostly, aye? Surprised your parents—"

"Oh, I've been pushing back on all that."

He slowly nodded, though he continued to stare at her through narrowed eyes.

"Well, looks like we're holding up the line," Maggie said, grabbing Misty's elbow and ushering her forward.

"Um . . . bye," Misty said, as they hurried to catch up with those ahead of them.

"At some point he's going to remember who I am. I just know it." Her heart was pounding in her chest.

"Maybe not," Maggie said.

"I remember him, why wouldn't he remember me?"

"You dinnae look anything like that Grounder girl creeping around those stairs. It was dark, right? So relax. I think you're in the clear. And besides, you're with me. What would a Cloudwalker be doing with a Grounder girl?"

Bells began to ring, different from the ones Misty heard prior to the God's Rampage electrical storm at the Gala. These bells were far quieter; they sounded more like chimes. Misty gazed quizzically at Maggie.

"The draft is being called into action. Septs between the ages of sixteen and sixty need to check in with the Dorcha Poileas, over at the Onyx Building's headquarters."

"Is that something I should do, too?"

"Oh please! Adaira Drummond is not a *sept*. The draft does not apply to people like her. Like us."

Misty continued walking, quietly thinking.

"I didnae mean it like that." Maggie put her arm around Misty's shoulders. "I'm sorry, I can be a real bitch sometimes. I wasn't thinking."

"Maggie, I am a Grounder. How many rungs on the ladder is that below a lowly sept?"

"I'm an arse. Forgive me?"

"Never!" The two girls laughed, then a crease formed between Maggie's brows.

"What is it?" Misty asked.

Maggie frowned. "Cloudwalkers are warriors, the most trained Skylanders for combat. During times of war, when draft personnel are called in to report for duty, it's the Cloudwalkers who are their leaders. We're officers in the Midtown army."

"That makes sense," Misty said, still not following.

"Adaira Drummond. I went through Cloudwalker training with her. It's kind of required. Most Cloudwalkers stay to become full *cicerones*, but she stopped attending after the three year minimum."

"Uh huh . . ."

"You're not getting my point. Adaira Drummond will be called up for duty, like the rest of us. War with Jersey City is imminent. Don't you see? The real Adaira Drummond will be called up for duty!"

Misty's eyes went wide. "And when the real Adaira is forced from her self-imposed reclusion, what happens to me?"

"I might have an idea," Maggie offered. "We'll need Conn's help. And maybe Brig's, too."

Chapter 45

Darryl, arms and legs trembling from fatigue, took a moment to catch his breath. It was a brief lull in which the two exhausted opponents could take stock before reengaging in mortal combat. Events seemed to be happening in slow motion as his eyes were drawn to a clash of other warriors nearby. He watched the arc of a severed arm as it flew through the air—arterial spray spewing about. Darryl was ill prepared for the sudden, reverse, full-body spinning motion and the subsequent incoming strike from his opponent's lockwood. So here he was, totally caught off guard. He was left with just one thing: A moment in time, and profound clear awareness. Just a second before that blade would strike the right side of his neck, undoubtedly cleaving his head from his shoulders, there was just enough time to realize that this lifetime might very well be over. But instinct took over—action without conscious thought—and he jerked backwards. The tip of his adversary's blade painfully nicked the bottom of his chin. He had survived the lethal strike, and he knew without a doubt he would also survive the day. He would vanquish this warrior. But with that hopeful realization came another stark truth: that he had so miserably failed in life, *not only for himself, but for her, too. Perhaps there was time left in this lifetime to do better, to make amends. He spun and swung, not seeing him, but knowing where the strike would land. Then he felt it, the cold hard steel of his lockwood slicing into its intended mark.*

With a start, Conn jerked awake, screaming into the darkness of his bedroom. His arms were raised defensively to fend off the incoming strike. One moment passed, and then another. His chest heaving, he tried to catch his breath. Conn figured the mortal battle had occurred centuries prior. Another vision, but this one felt all too real. Conn was beginning to have trouble defining the lines between himself and the ancient warrior, Darryl.

"You scared the *shite* out of me, Conn," came a small voice from a darkened corner of the bedroom.

"Sorry. Go back to sleep, okay? There's still a good many hours before dawn." Brig didn't answer. Several minutes passed before Conn heard the boy's slow steady breathing. He envied the boy's capacity to fall asleep at will, and to sleep so soundly, too.

Jumbled segments of the prior day's events invaded Conn's thoughts, especially the funeral march ending above the Hudson River: his sister's concealed giggles turning into grief-stricken tears of anguish, Michael's face as they'd dropped their father's body through the clouds. He thought of Misty, her eyes locked onto his—*I'm so sorry, Conn.* He had wanted to go to her, had felt the pull of her like gravity.

Soon after the funeral, he, Michael, and Emma had been individually tracked down by sept assistants. There was to be a reading of Robert Brataich's Last Will & Testament. Their presence was needed immediately on the Empire State's 86th floor.

Barrister Thomas Argive, ancient and emaciated-looking with his tufts of wispy white hair protruding from ears and nostrils, was waiting for them within their father's personal office. Standing up on shaky legs as they entered the room, Conn could see the prepared documents laid out on the table in three separate stacks. Conn, third in line to his father's title, hadn't had many dealings with the Brataich Clan business. Emma and Michael, both older, were far more involved in such matters, while Conn was content pursuing his work as a *cicerones* and his love of the natural sciences. It occurred to him that no one here would have his best interests at heart. He thought of Dob. He wondered what counsel he would have given him to deal with this situation. *Break each problem down into its most elementary parts. That, sometimes, works best. Then you can approach the problem from multiple angles!*

Argive cleared his throat and glanced at the three through watery eyes. "I am beyond sorry for your loss. Robert was a dear friend to me for many years. I had hoped he would long outlive me. But since that was not to be, I am here with you now." Motioning for them to sit, he waited before reseating himself.

Emma and Michael nervously exchanged a quick glance. Conn simply watched the proceedings with interest.

"Your father's holdings were substantial. I suspect far more than you may have surmised."

"Yes, the Empire State. Father already told us he owned it outright. No liens, no debts," Emma said, a little impatiently. She obviously wanted him to get on to the reading of the will.

"Well, he had other holdings too, Emma. Other Midtown real estate," Argive said, rising back onto his feet. Conn could almost hear his dry old bones creaking as he unrolled a four-foot-long sheet of paper. A blueprint-style diagram, it showed all the Skylander towers locations within Midtown. The page was nearly covered with handwritten comments; corresponding arrows pointed to this or that. A circle encompassed the Empire State building. Circles in different colors were drawn around other high-rise buildings. Conn noticed a key diagram, located at the bottom right-side corner of the page. It revealed the particular color of a circle denoted other owners. He recognized several names, mostly other CloudMasters, such as Cloud-Master Baird, and CloudMaster O'Cain.

"As you can see, there are significantly more red circles than circles in other colors."

"Looks like six more, to be exact," Emma said, leaning closer to inspect the page.

One after another, the old man tapped a crooked finger at each red circle. "It was not common knowledge that Robert Brataich was both owner and landlord of these other buildings. That he was collecting, from both nobles and septs alike, significant rental income."

Now Michael and Conn exchanged a glance.

"What is to be done with them?" Emma asked.

"Your father and I had a number of conversations on this same matter. More so recently, with his illness."

"Just tell us," Emma urged.

"We should go through the will, at this point. There is much detail, and much explanation we'll need to wade through."

"Yes, yes," said Emma. "We will do all of that, I assure you, sir, but first just give us the bullet points."

"There's far more here than financial holdings. There is also the matter of his position as CloudMaster," Argive glanced from Emma to Michael. "Are you not interested to learn which one of you was bequeathed your father's title?" he asked, a bit flabbergasted.

"Of course we are," Emma said, a bright flush rising high on her cheeks. *She's always been like this*, Conn thought. Preoccupied with money and material things—and being magisterial. Not superior, so much, for she was kind and self-effacing, too, but behind all that she loved being the daughter of the ruling

CloudMaster. It gave her an elevated place within society; queen-like within Midtown's clan aristocracy. Conn didn't mind. None of it affected him. He suspected little would change now; her holdings would only increase. His brother would become the clan's next CloudMaster. And that was how it should be. Michael was ready for it; he had been groomed for it since childhood.

Argive looked from Emma to Michael. "Okay then. The six Midtown tower holdings, as well as their earnings, are to be split evenly amongst you two. Three buildings apiece. I assure you, their values are equitable."

Emma turned to Conn, sympathy in her eyes. He'd apparently been left out of the will. He shrugged. It mattered little to him. What would he do with a Midtown building or two?

Argive continued, "Michael will indeed take the title of Brataich CloudMaster." Michael let out an anxious breath and smiled.

Apparently, Michael wasn't as certain of things as Conn assumed he'd be. He gave his older brother's shoulder a squeeze. "You'll do our father proud, Michael."

"There'll be a meeting of CloudMasters this evening," continued Argive. "It is imperative you attend, Michael. A vote will be taken. The Midtown CloudKing will be elected." Argive shook his head. "That will not be you, son. You are much too young and untested. It is presumed that CloudMaster Lidia O'Cain will be selected."

"That's all well and good, sir, but can we get back to learning the details of the will?" Emma asked impatiently. "What about the Empire State?"

Only then did Barrister Thomas Argive turn to Conn. "It is his and his alone."

"What? No!" Emma said defiantly. "There must be a mistake." Reaching out for one stack of paper, she began rifling through them. Brows set in a V, she huffed as she whipped through one page after another. "Show me! Show me where it says my home belongs to . . . show me the page, you stupid old relic!"

Brig's snoring brought Conn back to the present moment. He lay in bed, trying not to think about his sister's indignation. The way she'd glared at him—as if he had conspired to take the building away from her. He hadn't. He would never do that. But he'd never seen that side of his sister before, and it made him nervous. He understood her fears, he supposed, but he tried to assure her that she and her family would have a home in the Empire State for as long as they wished. She hadn't seemed so sure, and despite Conn's claims that he didn't care if he was left out of the will, when the exact moment came for him to volunteer handing the building over to her—signing all applicable papers or deeds—he hadn't done so. Conn thought about it now. *Why didn't I?* It occurred to him—he *wanted* this old building. He loved the Empire State, and he had inherited something that was so important to his father. He felt deeply honored being bequeathed something so precious from the man he barely knew.

Chapter 46

The second day after his father's funeral, the young crier boy's wailing call came echoing across the cloud-bank: "Hurry, hurry, report for duty! Septs and Cloudwalkers, defend our home!"

Conn and Toag ran together toward the distant, chrome-topped tower. The town square, with its gold-topped bell tower and cupola, was teeming with activity. All around them, nervous excitement permeated the air. War was abreast.

"You're handling your loss better than I would be," Toag said.

"We all deal with things differently."

"Still, he was your—"

Conn stopped and stared at Toag. "Look, I ken perfectly well who my father was. I was right there, remember? Just feet away from him. I saw his head cleaved from his neck. It landed at my feet, Toag. I'm going to kill Gordon Folais, and that damnable priest too, if it's the last thing I ever do. I'm going to kill them both, then spit on their cold, dead corpses. I think of little else, Toag. So now can we go and get checked in?"

Looking sheepish, Toag nodded. "Aye. I'm sorry, I'm such an obtuse arse."

The entrance to the Chrysler Building, even more so that day than usual, was bustling with people. Conn and Toag were forced to dodge around three hurried sept boys as they entered the building. Each had a strung bow and a quiver of arrows upon his back. Clearly, they did not want to be late checking in to verify their assigned clan postings. In most cases, the Midtown high-rise in which they were domiciled, would, by default, be the same clan to which they would be assigned. But not all of the buildings which above the cloudbank had such clear-cut clan ties. There were close to one hundred buildings that rose a mere one or two stories above the bank, and other buildings which pierced up through the bottom of the cloudbank, but did not crest out through the top of it. Clan nobility rarely visited, let alone lived within such meager quarters. But all structures that rose up, even partially into the cloudbank, were considered part of the Skylander realm. Subsequently, they came under the purview of one of the Manhattan clans. Territory was often disputed, and the rightful purveyor of the real estate as well as the sept populace within them came down to historical records. More often than not, back-and-forth wrangling between the clan CloudMasters ensued.

The Midtown Skylander realm—close to twelve thousand souls—had sustained a relative peace for twenty years now. Two decades had passed since the eviction of the High Priests and Priestesses of the Elysian Alchemy practice, so conflicts were rare, and violence almost unheard of. The need for individual, full-time clan armies had become too expensive to maintain, and were considered unnecessary.

But so much had changed during the last few days. Conjuring was possible again. Conn's thoughts flashed back to High Priest Dwaine Kincaid's powerful wizardry the night of his father's death. Shortly after his father's murder, it had been discovered that the *Sùilean Uamhasach*, the alien meteorite counted upon to curtail such dark psychic activities, was now gone. It had been stolen, if Midtown gossip could be believed. In any event, it no longer pulsed out any dampening affect on those able to evoke the ancient, mystical art of conjuring.

Conn and Toag, entering the Chrysler building's packed lobby area, headed past the banks of closed, long-inoperable elevators toward the wide marble staircase in the back.

Toag had to yell to be heard above other loud voices, "Brataich Clan duty officers are set up on the 60th floor."

"Lead on, I'm right behind you," Conn yelled back, weaving through the throngs of hundreds. Most of the people there, both sept and Cloudwalker alike, had brought along their own Ragoon bows and arrows. Hunting pigeons was a necessity of life atop the cloudbank, and if the septs weren't actively trained in war, at least they could be expected to know how to shoot. *It's good that they brought their own weapons,* Conn thought as he watched them. Going to war with an unfamiliar bow, or rack-staff for that matter, was never a good idea.

When they reached the 60th floor, they joined the end of one of the numerous Brataich Clan lines, where there were easily two hundred Skylanders rushing about and clamoring for attention. Tables had been set up, arranged all around the room's perimeter. Hand-penned overhead signs gave some directional insight to lost and confused clan members. Conn scanned the myriad of faces, and found he was pretty much familiar with most everyone there. Several young *cicerones*, caught roughhousing in line, were quickly chastised by older men who showed little patience for any kind of rowdiness.

"Hey, have you seen Maggie around here?" Conn asked.

"No. But check-in continues until late tomorrow. She still has some time," Toag said.

When they reached the front of the line close to a half hour later, they each were put in charge of their own company of one hundred-and-thirty septs. The novice warriors, those assigned specifically to be under their command, were now their responsibility. A gruff older Cloudwalker told them to move along, and directed them to another line. Another half hour later, they were given instructions of where to meet with their assigned companies to commence training exercises. Yet again, they were directed to another line where new Cloudwalker uniforms would be issued.

With a sigh, Conn once again surveyed the faces around him. Everyone looked just as tired and hassled as he felt. Feeling a tug on his sleeve, he looked down. "Brig, you're not supposed to be in here."

The boy rolled his eyes and motioned for Conn to lean down. "We need to talk."

Toag laughed, "Top secret, huh?"

"Don't be a fud, Toag," Brig replied.

"Language, young Brig," responded Toag with a laugh. "You're speaking to an officer, ye ken."

Brig ignored him, his expression serious. Conn leaned down, his ear close to the boy, who said, "We have a problem."

"What is it?" Conn asked.

"The Drummond girl completed her three years when she was younger."

"So? Brig, I have no idea what you're talking about."

The boy glanced around, making sure no one else was listening. "I'm talking about Adaira Drummond. The *real* Adaira Drummond. She's expected to report. She'll be required to serve, just like any other Cloudwalker."

Conn stood back up and looked at Toag. "You hear what he said?"

Toag nodded. "Could be a problem, actually a big problem

for Misty. Maybe for us, too. More than a few people saw her at the Gala."

Brig waggled two fingers for Conn to bend down again. "Maggie has a plan. But we need your help. Tonight."

"Where and when?" Conn asked. Thinking of Misty, he felt his heart rate accelerate.

"Midnight. Meet us outside the Empire State. We'll go over to 432 Park, where the Drummond's live, together."

Conn pursed his lips. Ten o'clock curfew was now in place, so Dorcha Poileas would be out in force. "Fine, I'll be there." He looked over to Toag. "I may need your help, if you're up for a little troublemaking?"

"Sure. Why not? A week from now I might be killed at the hands of some Jersey City bowbag. So, whatever you need."

Just before midnight, Misty saw Conn's tall form emerge from the Empire State's front entrance. Wearing a long dark coat, she spotted his exposed ankles below the hemline and held in a smile, remembering how ridiculous his bare legs looked that day on the ground when she'd first met him. She and Maggie had made it over from the Pavicon building without being spotted. The Dorcha Poileas, making their rounds in groupings of three and four, were easy to both spot and hear since they made no attempt to be stealthy.

Conn, spotting the girls in the darkness, hurried over. "Hey."

"Hey," Maggie said. Misty noticed his hair was wet, like he'd just stepped out of the shower. He smelled of soap.

Conn looked at Misty. "How you doing?"

She shrugged. "I'm nervous. All day I figured the real

Adaira Drummond would come out of hiding. Maggie says she's supposed to report for duty."

Conn shrugged. "I didnae see her. Not that I'd ken her even if I tripped over her."

Maggie said, "We should go."

Conn looked about. "And Brig?"

"He told us not to wait up. I expect he'll meet us there."

Maggie led the way, heading north. They jogged, sometimes walked, keeping a good distance away from the illumination of lanterns in the windows of the high-rises.

"You there! Stop!"

Misty spun to see a group of five men, wearing long dark capes, emerge out of the darkness to the west, some fifty yards away. The Dorcha Poileas. Two looked to be clutching black-jacks in meaty fists, and the other three were unslinging long-bows from broad shoulders.

"Run!" Maggie said.

"No . . . wait," Conn said.

Chapter 47

Misty watched as Conn put two fingers into his mouth then whistled so loud she was tempted to cover her ears.

"What are you doing?" Maggie said to him accusingly. "You want every Dorcha asshole atop the bank to come running?"

"We need to go!" Misty said.

"Just wait a second," Conn said, staring up at the Empire State Building.

"Look!" Misty said, as two more groups of Dorcha Poileas emerged from the darkness. She searched Conn's face, wondering at his bemused expression. Whatever he was up to, he seemed to be enjoying himself. Although part of her was beyond scared, another part was a little intrigued. "Just what is it you're up to, Conn?"

"Wait for it . . ."

The closest of the Dorcha Poileas began notching arrows onto their bowstrings. "Halt!" one called out.

Maggie, desperately yanking on Conn's sleeve, urged him to move. "Come on!"

Suddenly loud pops and cracking sounds came from the

south. Bright shooting lights flared out through all lower windows of the Empire State building. Within seconds, additional showers of bright light could be seen shooting upward, moving vertically higher and higher up the tower as they exploded out one window after another.

Conn cupped his hands around his mouth, and shouted, "Fire! Don't you see it? Fire!" Dramatically, he pointed toward what seemed to be a fully-ablaze Empire State Building.

More groupings of patrolling Dorcha Poileas were now visible on the illuminated cloudbank. Momentarily mesmerized by the fiery spectacle, they soon went scrambling toward the blaze. Misty heard them shouting orders, and watched as brave rescuers charged forward, prepared to risk their lives to save hundreds of trapped inhabitants.

Misty stared upward at the magnificent, beautiful, display of glittering light. Refocusing her gaze back on Conn's face, she saw a look of pride there—*pride of workmanship.* "You did that? You made all that happen at just the perfect moment?"

"We need to go. That spectacle won't last too much longer." Smiling, he held out his hands. "Shall we?" Maggie took one hand as Misty took the other. Together, laughing, they ran north into the darkness.

Now a mile away, the three slowed down, out of breath from running so far. Misty asked, between panting, huffed breaths, "So are you going to tell us? How you arranged all that? That was amazing!"

"Toag helped me. Took us most of the afternoon to set things up."

Maggie said, "That was chemistry in action. Conn loves chemistry."

"Among other sciences," Conn said. "But yeah, chemistry is pretty awesome."

"But the sparks! Why didn't it call down God's Rampage? You could have destroyed your home."

Conn shook his head. "They're not electrically-based. They're made from ChemBurn, which comes in part from the cloudbank itself. They don't incite the lightning."

"How would you even know how—"

"For almost ten years, Conn was Professor Dob's apprentice," Maggie told her.

"Dob called them rainmakers. Like sparkler cannons. In the past, we'd set them up for big outdoor summer celebrations, and such forth. Kind of like fireworks but not that complicated, if you know the recipe: a special mixture of ChemBurn and other combustible elements. Toag helped me set up fifty rainmakers as individual blast cannons. We placed them in various open windows, on both the northern and western-facing sides of the building, all the way to the top floor. Once he heard my whistle, Toag had to scramble to light the various sets of rainmakers on various floor levels."

Misty looked away from him. When she realized he was still holding her hand but not Maggie's, she freed her hand from his, shoving it into her pocket. She no longer felt exhilarated. Misty found it hard to fathom the level of education it took to do what Conn accomplished tonight. Her own education, little more than homeschooling, had mostly consisted of Purgeforth Scripture. Sure, she'd found many old books she wasn't supposed to read, but they didn't provide her with a real education. Not even close. *God, he must think I'm a cretin—a stupid peasant girl.* She wondered if the reason he was always so nice to her was just because he felt sorry for her. She hated the idea of him pitying her. *What could possibly be worse than that?*

Brig was waiting for them outside the 432 Park Avenue building—the Drummond Clan tower. Misty craned her head way back to better glimpse the top of the building. But it was so tall, so perfectly flat on each of its surfaces, it was difficult to even differentiate the building from the dark sky above it. Unlike the Empire State or Chrysler building, with their progressive, stepped architecture that felt more like art than a building, the Drummond tower possessed little if any real character. All its windows seemed to be tightly affixed in place. None could be opened to let in the fresh air.

"You got inside there?" Conn asked the boy.

Brig nodded hesitantly. "It took a while. There's a guard posted inside the lobby."

Misty could tell something was bothering Brig. Gesturing toward the facing side of the tower, she asked, "So where exactly are the Drummonds hiding in there?"

"Well, the entire building houses the Drummond Clan and its followers," Maggie said. "But the actual Drummond family members are situated on the top few floors. Remember, Adaira is my cousin. We used to visit them pretty often, up until I was about fourteen. Adaira would have been around fifteen."

"So what happened?" Conn asked.

Maggie said, "I told you. We were no longer invited over. They sort of just disappeared. Only my uncle, CloudMaster Gunther Drummond, is ever seen out and about anymore, though even that is still a rare event."

"What was his excuse for his family being so unsociable?" Misty asked.

"I don't really remember. I don't think he talked about them much. People just figured they were a bunch of shut-ins," Maggie said. "Too scared to venture out into the world. Anyway, I remember many other noble families live here, below theirs. And sept families too, down on the lower floors, as well as on floors within the cloudbank."

Conn turned his attention back to Brig. "So, what else? Did you go all the way up to the top? See the Drummonds?"

Brig nodded, looking uneasy.

"What's wrong with you? What's with the stupid moping?" Conn asked.

"I'm not moping. I just think we should leave them alone."

"What's really wrong?" Misty asked.

The boy shrugged. "I guess you should see for yourselves."

"Yeah, that's why we're here," Conn said. "How do we get past the guard?"

"He gets up to take a piss break every hour or so," Brig said, glancing over his shoulder. I've been keeping an eye on him, it's been well over an hour now."

"Okay, go on over there and watch him. Let us know when he leaves again."

Brig nodded and headed away.

"Do you have to be so mean to him?" Misty asked.

"Brig? I'm not mean to him."

"Sure you are. You talk down to him."

"He's half my height, I have to talk down to him."

"It's not funny! You're going to give him *issues*."

"Really?"

"Yes. You're going to make him feel unworthy, like he's inferior, or something."

"That's ridiculous! Brig's used to me; that's just how I treat him."

Maggie watched their back-and-forth bickering in silence.

"Hey!" came Brig's hushed voice from the building's entrance doors. "Guard's gone."

Once inside, they moved quickly through the lobby, past where the guard sat keeping his evening vigil, and began their vertical trek up the winding stairwell. It took them about forty minutes. As it was well past one o'clock in the morning, they passed no one else along the way.

Someone had freshly painted the words *Level 94* on the

wall, with the clan name, *Drummond*, in fancy cursive lettering beneath it. The four intruders, panting, stood still, trying to catch their breath. Misty noticed, unlike the other stairwell doors on the floors below, the original door up here had been replaced with a formidable, dark timber-planked door. The big, ironwork handle reminded Misty of a drawing she'd once seen of a castle keep.

Both Conn and Maggie said, "Wait!" but Brig was already reaching out and thumbing down the handle mechanism.

"Relax. Been here, done this, remember?" Brig needed to use both hands to get the door open wide enough for Maggie, Misty, and Conn to file through first. He followed, making sure the door didn't slam shut behind him. With dim lantern light flickering all around them, they stood within a large marble foyer. Another door, this one even larger than the stairwell door, rose high before them.

"How are we supposed to get inside without waking the household?" Conn asked, eyeing the door.

"Not through there," Brig said, spinning around. He pointed to a smaller door at the far end of the foyer. Small and painted white, it was probably intended to blend in with the surrounding white walls. Brig added, "Utility access."

Brig, hurrying over, pushed through it. The hinges squeaked. "Come on, I found a way inside through here."

Once they were all inside the utility space, Brig closed the door. Total darkness engulfed them. Misty heard Brig whisper, "Keep walking forward. The room is narrow and winds around to the left up ahead."

Doing as he asked, Misty walked right into Conn's back. "Oops, sorry."

Continuing on, she had to waive away errant spider webs hanging down from above. Reaching out with her hands, she found both side walls had metal, electrical breaker cabinets, plus an assortment of thick vertical pipes. It reminded her of home. Misty heard, then felt something scamper atop her left foot— probably just a mouse.

"There's a rung ladder coming up on our left," whispered Brig. "You can't see it, but trust me, it's right there. We're going to climb it, one at a time, with me going first. Trap door's up top; we go through that and we'll be on the 95th floor, right inside the residence."

Five minutes later, they found themselves standing within the confines of a spacious walk-in closet. Some light filtered in through the narrow space beneath the door.

Conn whispered, "You made it this far earlier?"

Brig nodded. Pointing toward the door, he whispered, "That's Adaira's room."

Slowly, Brig reached out a hand in preparation to open the door. It suddenly swung open on its own, and Adaira Drummond stood there before them.

Or what was left of her.

Chapter 48

S he held a wooden rolling pin up high in both hands. In the dim light, it was clear her bare arms resembled narrow tree branches—knobby and gray and skeletal. Her flesh hung loosely, like saggy drapes upon a window rod. "I'll scream. Help will come. Stay back; I swear, I'll scream!"

"Adaira?" Maggie inquired, staring intently at the young woman. Entranced by the very sight of her, she exclaimed, "Oh my God, it is you. What has happened to you, dear cousin?"

Adaira's fleeting recognition of Maggie soon turned to something else. Perhaps embarrassment. Perhaps shame. She lowered the rolling pin and turned her head away, her dull, auburn hair hanging lank over her face. "Why have you come here this night, Maggie? To mock me?"

"Mock you? I would never—"

"You must leave. Leave now." Her voice was but a whisper.

Conn's eyes went to the girl's bedroom window, which was massive in size compared to those within the Empire State. And this room, with its high ceiling, was far more spacious than any bedroom he knew of within the realm. *This high up, the view from the window must be spectacular during the day,* he thought. He tried to make out just what was he was seeing so far below.

Adaira followed his gaze and said, "It's Central Park. There are a thousand Ragoon trees below the cloudbank, tended by the Grounders. Their branches are just now starting to peek through it."

Sitting down on her bed, her body half-turned away, Adaira asked, "One of you was here earlier? I knew I heard someone skulking around."

Brig lowered his head. "Aye, that was me. I'm sorry, really, I am."

"So, I suppose this is some kind of shakedown? Is it money you seek? Or perhaps favor with my father? You all must know he is a powerful CloudMaster."

"We have no need for your money, or for your father's influence," Conn said.

Like she hadn't heard him, she added, "I don't know, maybe it's time for the Drummond secret to be exposed, and all of us marched to a nearby quickfall patch, as would befit the family's Fall From Grace—"

"Stop it, Adaira!" Maggie interrupted, carefully sitting beside her cousin. She raised her hands up, as if to embrace her, then stopped short. Adaira looked so frail, the boniness of each rib visible beneath her nightgown. Her hollowed cheeks were sunken, her face deathly pale beneath sallow, droopy skin. "Tell me, what on earth happened to you?"

Adaira slowly shook her head. "It is a secret we all pledged to keep, never to speak of to anyone outside of the family. Not that I ever go anywhere." Her voice was bitter. "I can never leave these quarters."

"I am family, cousin," said Maggie. "And I would trust Conn and Misty with my life."

Adaira glanced toward Brig. "And the boy?"

Maggie shrugged, a crooked grin on her face. "Two out of three ain't bad, aye?"

Adaira smiled. Conn realized the girl must have been pretty, perhaps even beautiful, once upon a time.

"It's a shameful, genetic disease that affects our Celtic aristocracy, called The Gaunt. It destroys muscle mass. None of us knew we had it until I got it, when I was fifteen. My mother got it late in life, a year later than me."

"Why shameful?" Misty asked. "You can't control it."

Adaira lowered her eyes. "Familial interbreeding," she said quietly. "We're paying for the crimes committed by my great-great-great grandmother on my mother's side. She was . . . with her brother. Similarly, it happened twice before that, going even farther back in history. With this disease, three-times is the charm. Shows up in offspring a century later."

No one said anything, but something about her story sounded familiar to Conn.

"It's not contagious or anything. But it's still a crime, ye ken, having The Gaunt," Adaira continued. "One that demands anyone infected, or even possibly infected, be executed via Fall From Grace. My father, fortunately, is not of the same bloodline. He married my mother unknowing of what lurked within her genetic disposition. That's at least something, I guess. He's safe, as long as the secret . . ." Her voice trailed off.

"Did she know? Your mother—my aunt? What was lurking in her bloodline?" Maggie asked.

Adaira shrugged. "Does it matter? Now?"

Conn looked at Maggie, concerned. She must have noticed his expression for she said, "I'm related to Adaira, but on her father's side."

Conn knelt down and looked at Adaira. "I remember something about this, though the Drummond name was never mentioned to me."

Adaira said, "That's impossible. As I said before, we were all forbidden to speak to anyone of our plight."

"Even to Professor Claremont Dob?" Conn asked.

She stared back at Conn close to a minute, then said, "He was looking for ways to help all of us. At the very least, he was trying to halt the disease's progression."

"I was his apprentice," explained Conn. "I too worked on that treatment. And yes, Dob kept his word. I never knew who was sick."

"Help all of you," Maggie repeated. "How many ill are there?"

Adaira, taking a deep breath in, let it out slowly. She closed her eyes, then quickly opened them, as if she had come to some kind of decision. "Come with me."

She rose to her feet and led them out through her bedroom door. Her nightgown billowed about her, floating weightlessly on the air like a ghost, her waif-thin body practically nonexistent beneath it. She padded forward to the next door within the wide, marble-clad hallway. Extending out her boney toes, she used her foot to push the door open a little wider, providing enough of a gap for them to peer within.

Conn saw three beds. Upon each one rested a small boy, each clearly wasting away in the same manner as Adaira. Bathed in the flickering light of the hallway lanterns, he could see them sleeping. Their small faces appeared skull-like. The middle boy's eyes suddenly popped open, brown and huge compared to the rest of his drawn, small face. Like the face of a cartoon caricature.

"Adaira?" came his small, weak voice.

"It's just me, Peanut. Go back to sleep." She closed the door and padded over to the next door. Already opened wide enough to see inside, Conn could clearly see the room held another three beds with three small bodies lying upon them. Young girls, all fast asleep. Adaira whispered, "They too have the early stages of The Gaunt. I won't show you my mother. Too horrible." She led them back to her bedroom and, retaking a seat on the bed, said, "So now you know." Eventually she looked over at Maggie, tears in her eyes.

"We're not here to make life any worse for you, I promise," Maggie said.

Adaira shrugged, as if resigned to the fact her life would only get worse. "Our days are already numbered," she said. "My father's aides have told him about the oncoming war. I'm a Cloudwalker, and know I'll be expected to report. What will my family do then?"

"I may be able to help you with that," Maggie said.

Adaira glanced up, her interest piqued.

Maggie said, "This is Misty Casper." Misty, smiling, nodded to her. "A few days back we helped her escape from a life she no longer wanted to live. She's a Grounder."

"That's a serious crime," Adaira said, not looking the least bit sympathetic.

Misty raised a hand up to stop Maggie from speaking further. "A week ago, my father hung himself. I'm not sure why; perhaps due to shame. Or maybe from the loss of his wife."

Adaira asked, "So your mother died too?"

Misty shook her head. "She ran off with Deacon Terrence Lasher to become his third wife."

"I know of him. A miserable man."

"One of the last things my mother told me was that I didn't belong with her. That she didn't love me, not like a real mother should."

Now Adaira stared at Misty with genuine sorrow in her eyes. "I'm sorry."

Misty nodded.

"So what is it you want from me?" Adaira asked, sounding tired.

"I want to be you," Misty said.

The skeletal girl stared up at her, her brows knitted. Then a wide smile broadened out her thin lips. "Ah, I think I understand now."

"As I said," Maggie interjected, "I'm embarrassed to ask, cousin. Misty cannot return below the bank. The deacon would make her another of his wives."

Adaira offered a disgusted grimace.

"But if she's found up here, posing as a Skylander . . ." Conn and Maggie exchanged a quick glance.

Adaira said, "She will be imprisoned; or even worse, executed." She stood and stepped closer to Misty. Slowly raising her skeletal arms, she placed them around Misty's neck, drawing her in close. Misty wrapped her own arms carefully about Adaira. The Drummond girl began to weep, then sobbed; quietly at first, then louder.

Conn watched Misty's concerned expression change to empathy, and understood why Adaira was crying, why this evoked such heartfelt emotions in the ill-stricken girl. Misty wasn't here to do her any harm or expose her family's terrible secret. No—she was here to *save* her, and her entire family, from everlasting shame. Through Misty, Adaira could, in a way, live a full life.

"Promise me," Adaira said.

"Anything," Misty responded.

"That you'll tell me every little thing about your new life out there." Pulling away from Misty, she gazed at length into her eyes then placed her hand over Misty's heart. "I want to know this too: your secrets. Also your hopes and heartaches. We are sisters now, in a fashion, and I want to know you." She glanced over at Conn and smiled. "Be kind to her. To us."

Up until that moment Conn had maintained an emotional distance from the girls' close interaction. But her words pierced his outer shell just as easily as arrows pierced through flesh. His own eyes welled-up with tears that he needed to blink away. "I will. I promise."

Adaira walked over to a polished wooden chest and knelt down before it. She ran the palm of her hand over its intricately engraved lid. "This was to be my hope chest—" She glanced up at Maggie. "—for when I got married." She swallowed hard, then swung the lid open. She rifled around inside the chest for several moments before bringing forth a folded piece of tartan fabric. She held it up for Misty to take.

Misty, doing so, unfolded the fabric. It was a kilt, with thick lines of green and burgundy on a field of bright red.

"My Cloudwalker's kilt," Adaira said.

After rifling more through the chest, another kilt was held up for Misty to take, in the same tartan colors. "My dress kilt." By the time Adaira finished, she'd produced several white blouses and buckled shoes—the kind worn by *cicerones*—and an ancient-looking, collapsed rackstaff. "That belonged to my great grandfather. On my father's side," she said, humor glinting in her eyes.

Adaira closed the chest and stood, kissing Maggie first, then Misty, on the cheek. Then her gaze focused on Conn, her expression as serious as any he'd ever seen.

"I ask you a favor, but not for me, or for my mother, who is well past saving at this point."

Conn, listening intently, wasn't completely sure to what she was referring.

"Continue to do Dob's work." Adaira's eyes turned to the bedroom door that opened out into the hallway, where two bedrooms and six small children lay sound asleep in their beds. "Please help them, Conn."

Chapter 49

Conn waited upon the bank, some thirty yards from the Chrysler Building's entrance. He'd stepped away from directing his own company's early morning training exercises, leaving a subordinate temporarily in charge. Already close to an hour had passed, and he needed to get back, but he wanted to be there when Misty exited the building to be sure that she'd checked in okay, and was confirmed to actually be Cloudwalker Adaira Drummond. He wanted to be the first one to congratulate her, but was experiencing second thoughts. More than putting himself at risk, he was putting the realm at risk too, and for what? For a lone Grounder girl he'd known little more than a week? "I should get going, and attend to my responsibilities," he argued aloud to himself.

Conn looked out across the open cloudbank, first facing west, then east. Cloudwalker officers were barking out orders and giving directives to subordinates. Multiple companies—beneath flags flying the colors of their respective clans—contained hundreds of sept soldiers, all engaged in the rigors of various kinds of combat training, including archery practice, charging drills, hand-to-hand combat, and a variety of edged-weapons training. Tomorrow, war games would begin, clan versus clan: CloudMaster strategies versus CloudMaster strategies, and all under the watchful eye of the new CloudKing, Lidia O'Cain.

Conn looked across to the southwest, the direction from whence the Jersey City forces would surely come. There, in the distance, he could see the opposing city's skyline. It did not look too different from Midtown Manhattan, and it was populated by people not too different from those here. Celtic brethren all, but with one fundamental difference: Jersey City's populace had turned desperate. The ever-encroaching quickfall put the masses living over there at great risk. Jersey City Skylanders endured now the loss of community life and fellowship, and even worse, the possible loss of Skylander living. Conn focused his attention back on the tall towers of Midtown. Would the Manhattan populace respond any differently if the threat of quickfall were reversed?

He heard the sound of the Chrysler building's front entrance doors opening and watched as Misty exited out into the morning sunshine. She'd dressed in Adaira's Cloudwalker tartan kilt and her white button-down shirt. Hanging from a peccary leather thong at her hip was Adaira's collapsed rackstaff.

Misty, swiping strands of her auburn, windblown hair from her eyes, gazed out at the cloudbank's vista. Spotting Conn, she neither smiled nor waved at him. The doors behind her opened again and a large bear of a man strode forth. Conn recognized him at once: CloudMaster Gunther Drummond, Adaira's father. He too noticed Conn. He said something to Misty and together they headed his way. Neither one spoke, nor looked particularly pleased.

Conn met them halfway. "A good morning to you, sir," Conn said to Gunther, before giving Misty a nod of acknowledgement. They walked together until they stood in the shadow of the building, where they could not be as easily seen.

Gunther Drummond easily weighed three hundred-and-fifty pounds. But he evoked vitality and strength, everything his ill, secluded family members did not. His beard was well-manicured and his hair worn short. Both were a dark brown shade, though there were invasions of gray splotches sprinkled here and there. His eyes, also a dark brown, bore directly into Conn's own, making him nervous.

"Boy," he said, his voice a deep rumble. "I want to convey my condolences. Your father was a good man. A true friend. What the Folais Clan did to him, was, well, best I just leave it at that. A price will be paid, which is all I will say on the matter." As he glanced down at Misty, his expression turned more solemn. Anger, brewing deep within the man, was as obvious as the broad nose on his face. It occurred to Conn that quite possibly Gunther was here to escort Misty to the Dorcha Poileas headquarters in the Onyx Building. The elaborate plan for Misty to impersonate Adaira was not only insulting to the big CloudMaster, but also illegal. Misty was a trespassing Grounder, after all. Anyone assisting her would be guilty of a number of crimes. The penalty was imprisonment, possibly even death.

"I'm sorry, sir," said Conn. "Our scheme was probably ill-conceived. Put you in an awful position. It was my idea and I take full—"

"Oh, for God's sake, get over yourself, boy. You misread my dilemma, my disposition. Look, I woke up this morn to find a daughter I almost did not recognize. I had forgotten what my Adaira's smile looked like, what playfulness she was capable of. For that, I will always be in your debt. Yours, Maggie's, and Misty here beside me."

Conn was tempted to mention Brig's key assistance as well, but decided it was best to keep quiet on that.

"It is a good plan. One I am willing to endorse, albeit at great risk." Gunther glanced over at Misty, rubbing his beard with thick fingers. "But there is a problem. Too many within my clan will know this young lass is not my Adaira. Such close proximity to the other Drummond Cloudwalkers would not be prudent."

"But, sir, if she is to take on the role of Cloudwalker, she needs training. And she is required to train amongst her own clan. It is law."

"I am well aware of Skylander law," Gunther responded, sending Conn a cold stare. "There is an exception. One that would allow her to change allegiance and do so in a perfectly legal manner."

Conn noticed Misty was purposely looking away, anywhere but at him.

"Marriage," Gunther said. "As the bride of someone from a different clan entirely, she would be bound to change her allegiance to that of her husband."

Misty finally looked up at Conn.

Gunther paused momentarily, as if only now he was figuring out more of the details. "The same rules apply to one who is betrothed. She would immediately take on the colors of her fiancé. Adaira—Misty—would be wearing the Brataich Clan tartan, and training with Brataich Cloudwalkers who would stand no chance of recognizing her."

Conn had to force himself not to smile; not to appear overly excited. This was, after all, a business proposition, was it not? He turned to face Misty. *Why does she look so sad? Am I that distasteful to her?*

"I have already spoken to young Toag Munna. He already

knows young Misty's true identity, and he is accepting of this plan. A win all the way around, aye?" Gunther asked.

"Toag?" was all Conn managed to say.

For the first time Misty spoke. Her voice's inflection was soft, not that of a Skylander lass, but more like the Grounder girl he met on the streets below the cloudbank. "Yes, sir, that would be best. Toag is available. And he is a fine person . . . a good friend."

"But why Toag?" Conn asked.

"Who else?" asked Misty. "Your brother is CloudMaster, which would draw far too much attention, and while Maggie's proclivities are not forbidden in your culture, I'm told that marriage between two female Skylanders is still out of the question. And you . . ." Misty paused, averting her eyes from his gaze. "You are betrothed to another, Conn. To Lili Folais. CloudMaster Drummond tells me that Skylander law recognizes a betrothal as a legal commitment. One that remains in effect, even with the current situation, for both you and her, until you both formally agree to call it off."

Gunther's penetrating stare moved from Misty to Conn, then back to Misty again. "Oh for shit's sake. You didnae tell me this!"

Conn looked to Gunther. "I'm sorry, sir? Tell you . . . ?"

"Knock it off! I may be old but I'm not totally daft. It's clear both of you would never want to be married to anyone but each other."

Conn shook his head, his face revealing just how preposterous an idea that was. "Sir, I assure you, that's . . ." His words trailed off.

Misty, vehemently shaking her head as well, wore a similarly contorted expression. How absurd the CloudMaster's declaration was. Suddenly, she covered her mouth with her palm. Conn stared at her and could see she was clearly hiding a broad grin. Although she was doing her best to hide the smile, her eyes told a whole different story.

Gunther laughed, a deep and hearty fat man's laugh that carried far across the cloudbank. "No one will force you, Misty, to marry Toag. Not if you have your sights set on another fellow. But for now, it makes good sense." He shook his head and laughed again. "I must return to my duties, and you must as well, Conn. I'm sure you'll work it out." He started to walk away then turned back to face them. "Careful with her," he warned. "One who does not have the Sight should not be tromping around the cloudbank unescorted."

Conn nodded, but his eyes were locked upon Misty's—and hers upon his. He listened as the big man's footfalls became distant. She lowered her palm—attempting to look serious again.

"So, Toag is the lucky man?" he asked.

She raised her brow, raising her chin just slightly upward, as if in defiance. She said, "I suspect he would make a fine fiancé, and a fine husband, too, for that matter. Do you not agree? He is your best friend. Who knows him better than you?"

"I know he'd be a far better fiancé—or husband—if he was the one you were actually in love with."

"Well, don't get too fat a head there, Cloudwalker. I can see it in your eyes. I know perfectly well you're in love with me." Her eyes were bright and alive, her smile mischievous.

A kettle drum pounding in his chest, Conn at that moment only wanted to rush to her, to pull her into his arms and kiss her. He wanted to tell her that he did in fact love her like he had never loved another. But that would be dangerous, and stupid.

Then, throwing all caution to the Skylander winds, he strode forth, grabbing her by the waist, and pulled her to him, her face now inches from his own. Her eyes went wide and for a moment she looked hesitant. Then her eyes went to his mouth.

She whispered, "I've never . . ."

He kissed her and the world around them fell away. The kiss was slow and soft, intoxicating in ways he could never explain in words. His hand came to rest cradling her neck, just behind her ear, as his thumb caressed her cheek. Their breaths mingled. He felt her soft touch on his spine, pulling him even closer yet, until there was no space between them and their two beating hearts beat as one.

Chapter 50

When they separated neither one spoke. Misty felt somewhat dizzy and strangely out of breath. And she felt other things too, strange and wonderful sensations within her body.

"Best we go," Conn said. "Brataich Clan exercises are held off to the west of the Empire State Building."

She continued to stare at Conn, wanting to tell him how immensely happy she was. How right then, at that very moment, she truly felt her life had begun anew. How she loved his thick unkempt hair, and those sky-blue eyes which seemed to look right through her and read her very thoughts. And those lips that kissed her and made her want more. "Should I be using this thing?" she asked, taking ahold of the collapsed rackstaff on her hip. "Would any real Cloudwalker wander around out there with one just hanging idle?"

"Good point. Go ahead and pull it free from the hook on your belt."

Misty, doing as told, clasped the staff by its wood paw.

Conn casually glanced about them, checking to see if anyone was watching, then said, "You've seen it done a number of times by now, I'm sure. You'll want to give it a double flick of your wrist, while spinning your hand in the process." He then demonstrated the proper motion she should use with his own hand. "Try it. Don't worry, you can't hurt it."

Now it was Misty's turn to look all about her. Mostly, she didn't want to appear publicly ridiculous. And yes, she had seen many a Cloudwalker casually ratchet their rackstaff into its extended position. She'd envied them, the way Cloudwalkers wielded their rackstaffs with such confidence. It differentiated them from others walking upon the cloudbank. Gave them authority. And something else, too: mastery over the dangerous expanse of whiteness under their feet, which they made seem so deceptively safe. And the sound the rackstaff made. The fine mechanism, with all its intricately-made parts, first sliding and clicking, then—once engaged—a definitive locking sound.

"Just try it," Conn urged, prompting her again.

Misty tried to remember exactly what he'd said to do. *Give the staff a downward flick of your wrist, spinning your wrist at the same time.* She tried it. The rackstaff immediately responded, and she heard those wonderful, mechanical sounds.

"Okay, good first try!" he said.

She thought it was down-right perfect until she noticed the staff had only extended half-way out.

"That's called 'bringing about' the lockwood. You can see a steel blade has unfurled. You are holding a Cloudwalker's primary weapon. Don't worry, we'll teach you how to use it. But do not touch the blade. Not only is it dangerous—incredibly sharp—the acid on your fingers will tarnish the blade if it's not well cared for. Also, it's thought to be bad luck. Now, try it again. Go ahead and retract the lockwood."

Misty guessed that would require the opposite motion of the one she had just made. Doing so, the blade withdrew and the rackstaff returned to its fully retracted position.

"Excellent! You're a quick study. Now flick it twice and twist your hand, only faster this time. And with more force, angle it away from you a bit more. Like that, that's right."

She did as he said and watched as the point of the rackstaff sprang outward, then locked into position, becoming six feet in length. Misty screamed in delight then quickly covered her mouth. They both laughed, and she immediately wanted to try it again—almost as much as she wanted him to kiss her again.

"Come, walk with me. Stab the bank every few strides. Use it to test how firm the bank is, and try to look confident. Act like you see the proper course set out before you."

Nodding, Misty fell into an aligned stride with Conn. Again, she did as he said but quickly fell into a mild depression of sorts. How she wished she too could see what he saw; she wished she could differentiate between the subtle hue variations of the cloudbank.

They walked in silence for a long time. Every so often she felt his shoulder pressing against hers, his mere touch electric. She figured a full mile had passed before he slowed and raised the point of his rackstaff. "My company is this way. I must get back to them. See over there?" He redirected his staff's point to the far left. "That's Maggie's company. See, they're doing charging drills. And there's Maggie, standing up on that crate barking out orders."

"I see her!" Misty smiled at the sight of her friend taking charge.

"Head on over there and get her attention. The path should be safe and clear, don't worry. When you get there, take her aside and explain everything CloudMaster Drummond said to you. Ask her if you can join her company."

Misty nodded, but couldn't keep a wounded expression from showing on her face. "You don't want me in your company?"

"You know I do. But it wouldn't be smart. I wouldn't be able to concentrate. I'd worry too much about you, and be a terrible instructor to the others."

"And Toag," said Misty slowly. "Would he not be a good instructor?"

Conn tilted his head sideways, giving her an impatient look. He was jealous, and the knowledge sent a thrill through Misty. "Can't you just head on over to Maggie's company? For me?"

"Gladly," she said, and began to walk away, then stopped. Conn was still standing just where she'd left him. "Thank you, Conn."

"You're welcome, Adaira."

"I won't fall into a quickfall patch?"

Conn peered past her. She watched his eyes squint as he stared ahead far along the cloudbank.

"You'll want to walk straight toward that low, abandoned building. See it, maybe a hundred yards out?"

"I see it."

"Once you reach it, head in the direction where Maggie is standing. Keep walking in a straight line and you'll be fine. Use your rackstaff."

They stood there a moment longer, gazing intently at one another.

"Well, bye for now," she said.

He stepped closer, holding out the paw of his rackstaff to her. "Tap it."

"Why?" she asked.

"Just tap it with the paw of your rackstaff."

They tapped paws.

"Then you say, *step wisely.*"

Misty smiled. "Step wisely, Cloudwalker."

Parting ways, she thought of little else but the sensation she still felt on her lips from their kiss. She sighed, remembering the touch of his hand cradling her neck when he'd pressed against her. She soon reached the small building, which wasn't much of a building. She'd never noticed it before since it barely crested above the cloudbank. There were no visible widows, at least not on the near side of the structure. Now standing within the cool shade, she looked across the cloudbank to where Maggie still stood on a wooden crate. *Walk in a straight line,* Conn said. She let out a long breath, prepared to head out.

In an instant, Misty's head was wrenched backward. Someone behind had grabbed a fistful of her hair. Then came another painful yank, and she found herself falling backwards, pulled closer into someone. A tall man, her back was now pressed hard against his chest. His mouth was close to her ear and she could feel the scruff of his chin.

"Scream out and I'll snap your neck like a twig." His clenched fist tugged harder on her hair, pulling her head back even more. Her neck extended, exposed and vulnerable.

"What do you want of me?" she asked.

"It took a bit of time. It was bothering me. Driving me crazy —I knew I'd seen you somewhere. Recently, too." His breath was foul and she could see the oily strands of his long black hair.

"You're that Grounder girl. The one on the stairs."

"Stairs?"

"In the damn Drake Building. Don't play dumb!" He yanked down hard again on her hair, enough to force her down to her knees. Her hand slid down to the midpoint of her rackstaff.

"I'm Adaira Drummond. You'll . . . you'll be punished for this." She tried to sound insolent but couldn't hide the fear in her quavering voice.

Releasing ahold of her hair, the man stepped around until he was standing before her. It was Bryant Peirce of the Dorcha

Poileas. Standing tall before her, his broad, fluttering cape blocked her view of the world beyond them.

"Do you know what happens up here to Grounders caught trespassing?"

"I'm not—"

The slap came fast and hard to her left cheek. Hard enough Misty momentarily saw stars and tasted blood in her mouth. She wanted to scream and cry out, or melt into the cloudbank and beg for his mercy.

Chapter 51

"Grounder scum like you don't deserve to see our sunshine. You don't deserve to breathe our fresh air," Bryant said.

Misty stared up at him, watching the twisted smirk on his face. "I'm . . . not . . . a Grounder!" she spat, with far more force than she thought she was capable of.

He slapped her again, then kicked her in the stomach with the tip of his boot. She doubled over and began to retch. He took a step backward.

"How dare you wear the clothes of a Cloudwalker. You think of yourself as having noble blood, do you? But I watched you. You possess no more of the Sight than I do."

Misty shook her head, glowering at him but unable to speak.

"There are two things I hate more than anything else: foreigners and Grounders. They disgust me. Literally make me sick. And you want to know something else?"

"No!" she croaked.

"Whenever possible, I don't waste valuable Dorcha Poileas resources on such scum. No trial; no elaborate Fall From Grace ceremony. That's all so tedious, and time-consuming. I do everyone a favor by simply dragging people like you, usually kicking and screaming, to the nearest quickfall patch. I know where most of them are. Then I toss them into the void. *Goodbye.* I like to stand still and just listen. They usually fall silent after a brief moment. Perhaps they're praying. Or perhaps they've prematurely died of fright." He shrugged, a sick smile growing on his face. "Then I hear it, ever so faintly. The sound of a body thudding down onto the pavement far below. It's a glorious sound. It excites me! You know what I mean? Excites me?"

"You're disgusting."

Bryant smiled. His eyes, lowering to her chest, lingered there.

Suddenly something else occurred to her. "You're the one who pushed that Folais boy. Janis Folais. You killed him. Shoved him into a quickfall patch, didn't you?"

"I told you, I hate foreigners. I caught him skulking about Midtown after hours. When questioned, he became mouthy."

"You started a war!"

"The war would have started with or without his death— that Jersey City scum has been looking for an excuse for years. Anyway, it was worth it to hear his body hit the ground."

Eyeing her again, he said, "You should not be wearing the colors of a true noble. You bring dishonor to the Drummond Clan. Strip."

"What? No!"

"Take . . . them . . . off! The shirt first, then the kilt." His hand grabbed the handle of the knife worn on his belt. "I can cut them off your body, if you'd prefer. Makes little difference to me."

Misty tried to see around him. She could still hear Maggie, yelling orders in the distance. *This can't be happening. Am I really going to die like this?* "I need to stand up. To get undressed."

Taking Bryant's silence as a sign of compliance, she used her rackstaff to help propel her body up onto her feet, and then wavered. Although the pain in her stomach was still there, it was tolerable. She just needed time to think.

At some point, Bryant, she realized, had freed his knife from its sheath when sunlight glinted off its reflective blade. It looked sharp and incredibly lethal. She nodded, "Okay . . . first the shirt."

"Move it along. I'm inclined to just cut your throat and be done with you."

She found the shirt's top button but her hand shook too much to unbutton it. "I'm sorry, I'm just . . . so scared." Her eyes lowered to the cloudbank, mainly cast in shadow near the ugly little building. Except for one area, she noticed, over there; also, another area, right over there. *Curious.* She glanced to her right —toward the sunny cloudbank beyond. *Why wasn't it white all over? Like it was before, a bit earlier?* Tears filled her eyes and a smile formed on her lips as she came to a realization.

Misty looked down to find the sharp tip of his blade upon her chest. Pricking her skin near her heart, she felt blood trickling down between her breasts. A red stain blossomed there, spreading outward like a scarlet flower upon her shirt. *No, not Adaira's shirt,* she thought.

She remembered Adaira, so frail and vulnerable, and the promise she'd given her only last night, and then Misty became angry. Angry she was being forced to break her promise. Angry her new life was being stripped away. Angry that for the first time in her life she really wanted to live. Now, because of this horrible man, everything was being taken from her.

In a flash, Bryant's knife began slicing upwards. One, two, three buttons catapulted up into the air, leaving her cleavage exposed. She looked up into his eyes and he saw her hatred. She was gripping the vertical length of her rackstaff so tightly, her knuckles were turning white. Without any cognitive thought, she jumped backwards. She then took a further step back, followed by another. Bryant looked at her with mild curiosity. "You cannot escape the inevitable."

She raised the tip of her rackstaff, pointing it at him.

Now he was smiling. He made an attempt to slap it away, but she moved back before he could make contact.

"Move. That way, into the sun," Misty ordered, gesturing with a quick jerk of her head toward the right.

"Like hell I will! I'm going to enjoy tossing your Grounder ass into the—" he stopped speaking as he noticed the new expression on her face.

Misty was doing something she didn't know she could do; something she didn't know *anyone* could do. Somehow she was bringing forth an inner strength. *No.* Not strength from the inner, but strength from below, from the very cloudbank itself. She felt the energy coursing up through her legs, causing her entire body to vibrate. And the pent-in anger she felt now joined that same energy, becoming an incredible well of heat that filled her to the very core. Suddenly a blast shot forth from the tip of her rackstaff, the recoil so jarring she almost lost her grip. She stared at her rackstaff.

Bryant's desperate screams pulled her back to the present situation. The Dorcha Poileas captain was nowhere in sight. *Oh my God. Did I somehow vaporize him?*

When he screamed again, Misty saw the top of his head and both arms above the lip of a quickfall patch. His hands were frantically reaching outward for something, anything, to grasp onto. Misty pictured his lower torso, deep within the cloudbank and weighing him down, his legs bicycling all about. "Help me!" he cried, his cruel voice pathetic from fear. "Don't just stand there, you stupid bitch, help me! I can't hold on much longer!"

Misty walked toward him, carefully avoiding areas where the solid cloudbank met a quickfall patch. Bryant was a good seven or eight feet away from her, and she'd put him there. *Somehow.*

"I don't know, Bryant. You're pretty far out there. Would be dangerous for me to come much closer."

"Use your staff. Reach it out to me so I can grab it. Hurry!"

Pursing her lips, Misty thought about his request. "You were going to kill me. Or have you forgotten that already?"

"I was wrong to suggest that . . . I'm sorry. Truly sorry!" His eyes went wide as he slipped deeper into the patch, the tops of his shoulders now barely visible. Panting, he was afraid to talk, make the slightest movement.

"You still think I'm a Grounder? Don't deserve to wear the colors of my clan?"

His eyes, wide in their sockets, answered for him.

She stared down at her ruined shirt. "I could let you fall. Maybe I could hear that same sound, you know, the thud you mentioned?"

"So what are you going to do?" Maggie queried from behind her. Misty jumped in surprise. Her friend was no longer barking orders from the wooden crate in front of her company. Now, she stood only ten feet away, near the ugly brown building. Misty wondered how long she'd been there. *How much did she see?* Maggie's lips were parted, clear astonishment on her face. She looked as though she were staring at a stranger.

"I guess I should help him," said Misty after a moment.

Maggie nodded.

Misty turned back to Bryant, still doing his best not to move, hardly breathing. Lowering into a crouch, she swung the rackstaff out horizontally. The tip fell a foot shy of his closest hand. "You need to reach out for it."

"No. I'll slip through. I can't."

"So you want me to risk my life for you, is that what you're saying?"

Bryant nodded, almost imperceptibly.

"You'll be in my debt then. Forever."

"Yes. I promise."

Misty studied the nearby cloudbank and found an area free of quickfall. Crawling over to it, she again stooped into a crouching position. She swung her rackstaff around, then across, close enough for him to reach. "I can't grab the staff for you. You either need to reach out for it, or die. Your choice."

Bryant, reaching out, got a solid, one-handed, grip on the rackstaff. Hauling his body somewhat farther up, higher from the void below, was enough for his other hand to grasp onto the staff.

"Don't let go," Misty ordered, as she began to pull. Whatever she'd done before, it had drained her; she was exhausted. The man was so heavy she didn't know if she had the strength to pull him free. Then Maggie appeared by her side. Putting all her weight into it, she too began hauling in the rackstaff. Once they freed Bryant's body from the quickfall zone, they dragged him further atop the cloudbank. Letting go of the rackstaff, he lay there for several moments. Misty, who had nothing more to say to him, instead looked at Maggie, and asked, "Can I borrow a clean shirt?"

Maggie nodded, "Aye. Maybe you can do some explaining along the way?"

"Not sure I can," Misty said. "But I'll try."

Maggie stood and helped Misty to her feet. "You're not a Grounder at all, are you?"

Misty shrugged. "I don't know what to think."

The two young women set off across the cloudbank, Misty clutching her ruined shirt to her chest.

"You know you've made an enemy with that one," Maggie said, turning back to see Bryant still lying on the cloudbank. "He'll never forget what you did to him."

"I know."

Chapter 52

Bruised and sore from today's relentless battle training, Conn inwardly debated whether he wanted to head on down to Ginny's Trap tonight. He'd promised his company he'd make an appearance, if only for one whiskey—maybe two. Then again, he was curious, too, to find out how Misty's first day participating as a Cloudwalker-in-training had ensued. Fortunately, he knew he had Maggie to keep a close eye on her as she learned their ways.

Now close to nine o'clock, the Empire State's narrow stairwell was far more crowded than usual. Conn stood to one side as a family of seven, all talking at once, clattered noisily upward, oblivious to his presence. It then occurred to him that Maggie and Misty might not even be there. They were probably still back in the Pavicon building, each nursing her own assortment of injuries.

On reaching the Empire State's lobby level, he was surprised how many Skylanders were out and about this night. *Don't they realize a war was coming?* That any free time would be best shared among family, or even spent alone, to gain some deep meaningful insight by reflecting on life itself? *Wake up! We are on the brink of war, people!*

Conn entered through the double doors of Ginny's Trap and found a throng of people too dense to see past. He stood on his tiptoes to better look about. His senses were accosted by music playing far too loudly, too many *bow bags* yelling at one another, and a layer of dense smoke that seemed to linger most around head level. He debated whether he should just turn around and go back home.

"Conn! Conn! Over here!"

Conn saw a hand waving at him over a group of heads to his right. When he caught a glimpse of dreadlocks he knew Toag was hailing him. He made his way through the inebriated crowd, receiving more than a few painful pats on the back and shoulders from friends, and from others in his company. By the time he wedged himself into a spot at the bar, he was feeling even more irritated and drained than he had before.

Smiling, Toad gave Conn an affectionate pat, which felt more like a smack, on his tender back. "Glad you made it!"

Conn winced and attempted a half-smile back, as a glass of whiskey appeared on the bar before him.

"That's on me. Looks like you need it," Toag offered, draining the last remnants in his own glass.

Conn gulped down the whiskey then signaled the barkeep for another. "Seen Maggie?"

"Sure, she's around. Along with my bonnie green-eyed fiancée," he said, giving Conn a smart-ass grin.

Conn waited for the strong temptation to punch him in the mouth to pass before asking. "Whereabouts?"

Toag said, "They're making their rounds in here. Maggie's introducing Misty—*Adaira*—to her friends. Hey, did Maggie mention to you anything about what happened today?"

"Happened? What happened?"

"To Misty. Something about your old friend accosting her."

"What old friend? What are you talking about?" Conn's head throbbed. Toag was beyond irritating.

"Peirce! I didnae get the whole story; it was too loud in here. But she's fine. Better than fine," he added, giving another toothy crocodile-like smile. "We'll get the whole story when we find them."

But Conn was already fuming. The mere mention of Peirce and Misty's names in the same sentence was enough to raise his blood level to the boiling point. He tried to reason out when that Dorcha Poileas sociopath found time alone to accost her. Conn replayed the moment he left Misty on the cloudbank earlier that day, telling her how to carefully traverse the cloudbank in order to safely reach Maggie, and her company. He thought of the nearby squat, ugly little building, which cast just enough of a shadow for someone to hide, lurking or lying in wait. That some-one, it seemed, was Bryant Peirce. Conn glanced over his shoulder toward the entrance. He'd go find Peirce and set things right. *Once and for all.*

"I'm telling you, she's fine," Toag said, no longer grinning. "Look, the place is beginning to clear out a bit. I'll get us a couple more drinks then meet you over by the fire, aye? I think that's where the girls were headed."

Conn, exhaling a pent-in breath, gave Toag a halfhearted smile, then turned and headed toward the seating area at the back of the pub. A fire burned brightly there beneath an iron hood. An overstuffed chair, not occupied, was situated next to the circular, stacked-stone surround. The chair had been Dob's favorite place to sit, where he'd rest his weary bones at the end of a long day, usually accompanied by several strong drinks. In that moment, Conn had no problem picturing him still sitting there.

He found it difficult to swallow. He pictured the professor

leaning over to tap-out old remnants of tobacco from his long-stemmed pipe. He'd be glad to see me, Conn imagined. He'd say, *Sit down, my boy . . . get warm by the fire.*

Since the day, not so long ago, when Dob—his friend, his mentor—had been taken from him, Conn had managed to stave off the memory of the accident. It had come at the cost of his ability to sleep at night, but he felt it a fair trade. But now, seeing Dob's empty chair, the memory of his friend so strong, he couldn't help but remember.

It rarely—almost never—snowed atop the cloudbank. Something to do with falling precipitation not reaching far enough down into the atmosphere to actually freeze. And the world-encircling cloudbank was the reason why. In all his seventeen years, Conn had never seen or experienced snow. But judging by Dob's forecast, this very day that strange climate anomaly would indeed take place.

The old professor's excitement was contagious. Conn rose early in order to help Dob lug the heavy test equipment in his Chrysler building lab down to the cloudbank. First thing, Dob set up both the aneroid barometer and the mercury barometer. Large, clumsily heavy, and very old, each was made of brass, with intricate internal workings. The devices were similar to clocks in appearance, with their circular bezels, large dials, and a crystal that was actually made of precision-blown glass. Depending upon the atmospheric pressure, calibrated to the elevation of the cloudbank, a singular clock-like hand would point toward STORMY, RAIN, CHANGE, FAIR, or VERY DRY. Each barometer, weighing approximately ninety pounds, sat upon a custom-built tripod; its long legs were fitted with dinner-plate-sized pads that would lie flat upon the cloudbank, instead of piercing through it like the tip of a rackstaff did. There were various other items, including three different thermometers—each one the length and width of Conn's arm—along with wind speed detectors, and directional equipment. As Conn got everything set up, Dob was preoccupied, making entries into a large, leather-bound book. Every so often, he would peer into the sky, then mumble something unintelligible.

"Why do you need two kinds of barometers? Don't they do the same thing?" Conn asked, tapping his fingernail on the one closest to him.

"Don't be tapping on that! It's very sensitive!" Dob thought a moment, then said, "There is an important difference . . . an aneroid barometer measures the atmospheric pressure using the expansion of metal, whereas a mercury barometer measures the atmospheric pressure by adjusting the height of liquid mercury held within a small tube. I enter both readings in my book, then calculate the variance in the measurements between the two later on."

The cold today was more extreme then Conn was used to; he had foregone his kilt for a pair of long pants he'd nicked from Michael's wardrobe, and was glad for the extra warmth even if the constricting fabric around his legs felt odd. He tried to keep busy by moving around. Every so often, he blew his warm breath into his cupped hands to keep his fingers from going numb.

"Doesn't seem like much is happening, Professor. Maybe your forecast is a little off."

Professor Dob glanced up from his book, a deep crevice between his eyes. "Patience, my boy, the snow is coming." A smile suddenly formed within the curls of his messy white beard. Raising-up his nose, he breathed-in deeply. "You can smell it!"

Conn too breathed in the frigid air and, much to his surprise, did smell something different.

Ding! Ding! Ding! Ding!

Conn glanced up to the heavens, then to the professor. "We have to get out of the weather. The warning bells . . . a rampage is coming."

"Well, of course it's a rampage! That's exactly what we're waiting for, young man. You think snow falls from sunny blue skies? You think a once-in-a-century climatic extravaganza comes forth with no risk attached?" The professor tossed his book onto the cloudbank, then spread his robed arms out wide. Staring up into the now-darkening heavens, he shouted, "Wackata-camocha!!" He laughed and yelled, "Wackatacamocha," four times, as he faced North, then East, then South, then West.

Ding! Ding! Ding! Ding!

Conn felt it too. Pure exhilaration. Aye, from Dob's melodramatic exaltations, but also from the now-charged atmosphere, as tiny white flurries began to fall and swirl around them.

"It's snowing, Conn! Isn't this magnificent? Have you ever seen anything this beautiful?"

Flurries quickly turned into snowflakes, big and fluffy, that drifted down, settling upon their heads and shoulders and all the equipment.

Ding! Ding! Ding! Ding!

The buildings all around them were fleeced in white. Conn had never witnessed anything so magical. Laughing now, he looked at his mentor and yelled, "It's a Skylander wonderland, Professor! Like nothing I've ever seen!"

Dob, still staring up toward the heavens, held his rackstaff higher into the air.

The first lighting bolt took out the aneroid barometer, a fantastic explosion of fire and sparks. The next lightning bolt rose up from the cloudbank, mere feet away. Great consecutive flashes of light branched out in every direction. Crack! Crack! Crack! The thunderclaps were now so loud that windows of the nearby Chrysler Building began to burst. More and more lighting bolts erupted—a continuous, self-feeding, electrical frenzy. When the other barometer blew apart, mere feet away, Conn dove onto the cloudbank, covering up his head with both arms. Terrified, Conn *stole a glance toward where he'd last seen the professor. Surely, he too dove low, making himself less of a target. But instead, Dob still stood there, his rackstaff held high up, almost defiantly, into the air.*

He yelled, "Get down!"

Conn saw an immeasurably bright lightening bolt strike; an ear-shattering thunderclap immediately followed. One moment the professor was there—the next moment gone. Vaporized in a millisecond.

"Conn?"

Pulled back to the present moment, Conn turned to see Misty standing beside him. There was concern in her eyes.

"What is it? What's wrong?" she asked. "Are you crying?"

Chapter 53

Misty inwardly chided herself. *Why did I embarrass him like that? I can see something is going on, something I know nothing about.*

"This dreadful haze," she said, swiping at the air. "I had no idea so many Skylanders liked to smoke."

Conn blinked away the tears, banishing whatever sorrowful thoughts he had, and gave her a lopsided smile. More than anything else, he looked relieved to see her.

"You look . . . ecstatic," Conn said, as Maggie approached them through the crowd. "I heard you had quite a day, Misty."

Maggie joined them, holding out a whiskey glass in each hand. Handing one to Misty, she said, "Sorry, Conn, didnae ken you were here. But here, you can have mine."

"Nah." Conn held up his now-empty glass. "I'm good."

Misty and Maggie looked at each other. "You tell him yet?" Maggie asked, a smile tugging at her mouth.

Misty shook her head, "Not yet." She pursed her lips, not knowing where to start. "First of all, I think I have it."

"Have it?" Conn repeated.

Misty glanced over at Maggie questioningly, trying to remember what *it* was called.

"She means the Sight," Maggie said.

Misty watched Conn's reaction. She'd been more than a little apprehensive about telling him. *Would it be an insult?* This know-nothing Grounder girl, claiming she too possessed this amazing ability, one all the nobles up here flaunted and took as such a source of pride.

But Maggie vigorously shook her head before Conn could respond. "Who cares about that!? Conn," she said, lowering her voice. "The girl's a conjurer!"

Misty shook her head. "I don't know anything about that . . ."

But Maggie continued, "I was there. I saw it. She used her rackstaff to propel that *bow bag* Bryant ten feet away. Into a quickfall patch!"

Conn looked both confused and intrigued at the same time.

Before he could offer them a response, young Brig burst through the crowd. Huffing and puffing, out of breath, he said, "You have to hide!"

"Hold on, boy!" Conn said. "Why don't you take a deep breath first, then tell us exactly what's happening?"

The boy was beyond rattled. His hair was damp with perspiration, as he struggled to catch his breath.

"The Dorcha Poileas! A gang of them, maybe six or seven, including Peirce. They're coming now."

"What do they want?" Misty asked.

"Not what, but who!" Brig stared up at Maggie, then Misty. "They're coming for the two of you. They're coming to take you both to lockup!"

"It's because of today," Maggie said. "What Misty did to Peirce."

"Well, he deserved it!" Misty exclaimed.

Conn glanced in the direction of the entrance. "I ken Peirce as well as anyone alive. He isn't right in the head. And one thing I'm totally sure of, getting revenge is one of his favorite pastimes."

Maggie said, "I didnae do anything wrong. I was just a bystander."

"Oh well, thanks a lot!" Misty barked back.

"I didnae mean it like that."

"You both were together at the time. That's the problem," Conn said.

Maggie raised her palms. "Hold on. We should find out what the charges are. Might be nothing."

Brig said, "No, you should hide. I heard them talking. I heard Peirce say something about a Fall From Grace. He was like a crazy person. Ranting!"

"That's ridiculous!" Conn said. "An execution? For doing what?"

"Okay, okay, Brig's right. We'll hide," Maggie said. "Then see what this is all about. Maybe let things settle down first. We can hide in my building, or maybe with the Drummonds. Adaira will take us in, I'm sure of it."

"No," Misty said. "We can't involve anyone else."

"Then what?" Conn asked, exasperated.

"We'll go below, beneath the cloudbank. I know where we can hide down there," Misty said.

"So, we'll be like, what, Grounders?" Maggie said unenthusiastically.

"Misty's right," Conn said. "That's the best idea for now. You should go. And hurry."

Misty looked up into his eyes. She didn't want to leave her new life here. She didn't want to leave Conn.

Conn placed a hand on her cheek. "I'll find out what's going on. Then I'll find you, I promise." He looked at Brig. "Go with them, but only as far as the street level, then come back. You hear me?"

"Aye! I hear you."

Together, Brig, Maggie, and Misty hurried toward the exit.

Chapter 54

They all knew the long and treacherous journey south to Manhattan was almost over. Oliver's bites were indeed severe enough to require stitches—sixty-five of them, to be exact. Hobbling along, needing his staff for support, he'd slowed their progress. The beast, which everyone now called a Smite, had survived its injuries, as well. Stabbed twice by Oliver's rackstaff, it nearly bled out on the cloudbank. Danu had insisted, to unanimous discord, that the animal, too, would be properly sutured and bandaged, at least to the best of her ability. She'd made a connection with the creature that she couldn't explain to the others traveling with her . . . nor to herself. What she did know, though, was that the fate of the strange, alien-looking creature was, somehow, bound with her own. For the same reason, she insisted the Smite be dragged along behind them on a makeshift sled. Its jaws were partially muzzled, allowing it to pant yet still take water and hopefully not bite. Hansen took it upon himself to do most of the pulling, although Jeremy did offer to take a turn every once in a while.

Danu was exhausted. They all were, after trudging

hundreds of miles. One exception seemed to be Julie, who talked nonstop.

Compulsive, Danu thought. She gave the girl a quick glance as they walked side-by-side together at the head of the contingent.

"Where will we live, High Priestess? It's not like we can, um, just show up and say, "Hey, here we are everybody. We're hungry and tired, oh and where are our accommodations?"

"Please, dinnae worry, Julie. I have made arrangements. They may not be ideal, but they are tolerable. Even for you."

"How? How did you make these arrangements?" Julie asked.

Danu blew a tired breath out through her puffed cheeks. "Dear God, girl, you are exhausting."

"Just tell me, and I'll shut up."

Danu didn't believe that was even possible. "Pigeons. They use pigeons to communicate here."

Julie slowed, then stopped. She stared at Danu, standing in the near-total darkness, and asked, "Here? You said here?"

"That's right, Julie. Here. We have arrived." Danu raised the point of her rackstaff and leveled it toward the distant horizon.

Julie gazed forward, her facial expression both serious and contemplative. "Oh my! I see it! I see lights! I see the city!" she shouted, spinning around. "Everybody! I see Manhattan!"

Cheers from the others erupted loudly. Hoots and hollers, as fists punched the air high overhead. "We did it!" Jeremy screamed.

Oliver was last to join the long row of onlookers. Like the others, he too was smiling, wearing a big toothy grin. He placed a hand upon Danu's back. "I never doubted that you would get us here."

Danu closed her eyes, simply allowing herself to enjoy this

singular moment of triumph. But when she opened them again, her sense of victory slipped away like it had been dropped through quickfall. Her heart began to beat in her chest as she took in the scene in front of her.

"Something is wrong," she said.

Chapter 55

Two thousand well-trained Skylander warriors, twenty-two companies in all, moved with both speed and stealth across the cloudbank, where the Hudson River separated the two estranged great cities. Now, a mile out, they were poised, ready for the night's invasion upon Manhattan. First came the archers, their bows already unslung from their shoulders. Behind them, long spear combatants fell into battle formation. Interspersed throughout the forces—leading their respective companies—were the surefooted Cloudwalkers. Young sept flag bearers held their flagstaffs up high. Unseen in the night's darkness were each flag's colorful clan coat of arms, now flapping wildly in the driving winds. The Jersey City army awaited the command to attack.

The late night was frigidly cold. His labored breath billowed eerily out from his gaping, open mouth in rhythmic puffs of white mist. CloudKing Gordon Folais tried keeping up with his twin sons, stride for stride, but soon recognized the futility in attempting to do so. Nearly half their size in height, he was well aware that they, more likely than not, were not the spawn of his own seed. He thought of his wife Margaret, and of the years of sporadic, at best, couplings they'd shared. He was a busy man, with great responsibilities. He also far preferred the warm beds and firm young bodies of any number of sept concubines, looking to better their own meager stead in life. He had little doubt that his wife, too, had found pleasure bedding with another man over the years, though the subject had never come up between them.

"Dearth.. Garret, hold up!"

Doing as ordered, both sons came to an abrupt halt upon the cloudbank and turned around in unison, peering down at their father with the same perplexed expression. As if only then did they recall his actual presence, several paces behind them.

"Stay close," Gordon said, catching his breath. "Dinnae go wandering off."

Neither of the ginger-haired boys bothered to respond back. Gordon honestly wondered if there were enough functioning brain cells between them for even one person, let alone two. But he still preferred them to be nearby this night. What they lacked in intelligence was made up for by raw, physical fortitude. Could they fully protect him from the new arrivals from North Carolina? He feared not. His sense of dread had only increased, seeing what magic these robed priests and priestesses were capable of. He knew there'd been a good reason to exile the lot of them those two decades past. But what else could he do now? This endangered, faltering city would not have endured without intervention.

Gordon watched them now, toiling away in joint enterprise. Most often working in groups of either twos or threes, they sometimes surrounded one of the tall Jersey City towers then worked outward from there. Their long staffs—held parallel to the cloudbank—looked like ancient, long-barreled rifles as they summoned the magical forces held deep within the cloudbank. Gordon had learned their names, even got to know them, to some degree: High Priest Finlay Bigham was a bald-headed man with a scarlet birthmark atop his hairless pate; High Priestess Freya Gemmill, the youngest of them all, had a tongue so vile Gordon found her frightening; High Priest Aaron Leckie, squat and droopy-eyed, was the least formidable of them all; High Priest Ethan Malles and High Priestess Zara MacTaggart were a handsome married couple that never strayed far from one another. Finally, there was High Priest Dwaine Kincaid, their leader. So dark a soul, even Gordon himself had been careful not to turn a blind eye, or his back, to that particular high priest.

Within the span of four days, their combined conjuring forces had indeed pushed and prodded much of the quickfall areas away from the city. *But at what price?* Gordon was well aware a reckoning would be forthcoming soon—a payment extracted for their services rendered. Beyond any doubt, they would be seeking changes in the power structure. Here first, then later across the river into Manhattan. Fortunately, he knew exactly where the *Sùilean Uamhasach*—the terrible eye—was hidden deep underground, an infallible safeguard which could once again, when the time was right, incapacitate this dangerous lot of priests and priestesses. Twice Kincaid had asked about the object's whereabouts. Gordon had been adamant in telling him he knew not—only that the thing had been stolen.

Gordon heard slow, crunching footfalls approaching in the darkness behind him. Not those of his third son, Spinter Row, or the footsteps of his light-footed daughter, Lili. Ah, he knew the owner of those steps.

"Their work here is coming along nicely," came the old man's voice.

Gordon said, "Aye. According to Kincaid—you can see him over there—he assures me, a fortnight. No more than that."

"Even so, you know it is but a temporary fix. It will last a year, maybe two. Then the quickfall will return to Jersey City," the old man said, stepping up beside the CloudKing and towering over him. "You cannae change the dynamics of science."

Gordon made a flabbergasted expression that went unseen in the dark. "I'd hoped my threats of an impending war would remain just that—mere bluster. That these wizards would make Jersey City sound and secure for a good many years to come."

"At one time, I may have been able to help. But not now."

Gordon waived away the comment. "No need. With Robert dead, there is a lack of any real leadership over there. Manhattan is mine for the taking,"

"Aye, I watched the forces heading out across the cloud-bank. I was quite surprised you were not amongst them. Are you not the CloudKing?"

"*Pfft*, my officers are well-trained; they have their orders. Clearly, I am not built for battle." Gordon turned, gazing up at the taller man. Even in near-total darkness, he still could make out the ragged scar tissue upon the man's jawline and upper neck. He knew the ear on that side of his head was nearly non-existent, though his messy white hair mostly covered up the injury. "And you . . . you've no compulsion to be standing instead on the other side of the Hudson this good night, Professor?"

Professor Claremont Dob stared wistfully toward the distant horizon as Gordon gave the order and the army began its descent on Manhattan. He didn't answer the CloudKing's question.

The End

*Thank you for reading **Cloudwalkers**. If you enjoyed this book, PLEASE leave a review on Amazon.com—it really helps!*
My Book

PLEASE NOTE: I, Mark Wayne McGinnis, have written over 40 science fiction novels; some are part of a series, while others are stand-alones—all for your reading enjoyment. Check them all out on Amazon. And to find out about future books, please join my mailing list - I hate spam and will never share your information. Jump to this link to join: http://eepurl.com/bs7M9r

Thank you, again, for joining me on these SciFi romps into space.

Acknowledgments

First and foremost, I am grateful to the fans of my writing and the ongoing support for all my books. I'd like to thank my wife, Kim, she's my rock and is a crucial, loving, component of my publishing business. I'd like to thank my mother, Lura Genz, for her tireless work as my first-phase creative editor and a staunch cheerleader of my writing. I'd also like to thank Emily Krempholtz for her superb editing, her amazing attention to story detail, and her ability to make my pros sound so much better. Thank you, Viatcheslav Vlassov, for your in depth technical guidance across multiple science disciplines.

Others who provided fantastic support include Lura and James Fischer, Stuart Church, and Eric Sundius.

Check out the other available titles by Mark Wayne McGinnis on the following page.

About the Author

Mark grew up on both coasts, first in Westchester County, New York, and then in Westlake Village, California. Mark and his wife, Kim, now live in Castle Rock, Colorado, with their two dogs, Sammi, and Lilly.

Mark started as a corporate marketing manager and then fell into indie-filmmaking—Producing/Directing the popular Gaia docudrama, 'Openings — The Search for Harry'.

For the last nine years, he's been writing full-time, and with over 40 top-selling novels under his belt, he has no plans on slowing down. Thanks for being part of his community!

About the Author

Mark grew up on both coasts, first in Westchester County, New York, and then in Westlake Village, California. Mark and his wife, Kim, now live in Castle Rock, Colorado, with their two dogs, Sammi, and Lilly.

Mark started as a corporate marketing manager and then fell into indie-filmmaking—Producing/Directing the popular Gaia docudrama, 'Openings — The Search for Harry'.

For the last nine years, he's been writing full-time, and with over 40 top-selling novels under his belt, he has no plans on slowing down. Thanks for being part of his community!

Also by
Mark Wayne McGinnis

Scrapyard Ship Series Series

Scrapyard Ship: (Book 1)

Scrapyard Ship: Hab 12 (Book 2)

Scrapyard Ship: Space Vengeance (Book 3)

Scrapyard Ship: Realms of Time (Book 4)

Scrapyard Ship: Craing Dominion (Book 5)

Scrapyard Ship: The Great Space (Book 6)

Scrapyard Ship: Call to Battle (Book 7)

Scrapyard Ship: Uprising

Mad Powers Series

Mad Powers (Book 1)

Mad Powers: Deadly Powers (Book 2)

Lone Star Renegades

The Star Watch Series Series

Star Watch (Book 1)

Star Watch: Ricket (Book 2)

Star Watch: Boomer (Book 3)

Star Watch: Glory for Sea and Space (Book 4)

Star Watch: Space Chase (Book 5)

Star Watch: Scrapyard LEGACY (Book 6)

The Simpleton Series

The Simpleton (Book 1)

The Simpleton Quest (Book 2)

Galaxy Man

The Ship Wrecked Series

Ship Wrecked (Book 1)

Ship Wrecked II (Book 2)

Ship Wrecked III (Book 3)

Boy Gone

(Expanded Anniversary Edition)

Cloudwalkers

The Hidden Ship

Guardian Ship

Gun Ship

HOVER

Heroes and Zombies

The Test Pilot's Wife

The Fallen Ship Series

The Fallen Ship: Rise of the Gia Rebellion (Book 1)

The Fallen Ship II (Book 2)

Junket: Untamed Alien Worlds

USS Hamilton Series

USS Hamilton: Ironhold Station (Book 1)

USS Hamilton: Miasma Burn (Book 2)

USS Hamilton: Broadsides (Book 3)

USS Hamilton: USS Jefferson - Charge of the Symbios (Book 4)

USS Hamilton: Starship Oblivion - Sanctuary Outpost (Book 5)

USS Hamilton: USS Adams - No Escape (Book 6)

USS Hamilton: USS Lincoln - Mercy Kill (Book 7)

USS Hamilton: USS Franklin - When Worlds Collide (Book 8)

USS Hamilton: USS Washington - The Black Ship (Book 9)

ChronoBot Chronicles